RAGE OF THE ANCIENTS

THE SANCTUARY SERIES, VOLUME TWELVE

ROBERT J. CRANE

OSTIAGARD PRESS

Rage of the Ancients

The Sanctuary Series, Volume 12

Robert J. Crane

copyright © 2022 Ostiagard Press

1st Edition.

PROLOGUE

One Thousand Years Ago

*T*hey stood together at the end of the world and knew that it was coming.

"I really thought we would have made a better show of it," Calene Raverle said into the quiet of sundown, flashes of blue dancing down the Blades of Fulmenar, the Claws of Lightning, which she had bound to her right hand. The Plains of Perdamun were near silent save for the roaring wind rushing around the edge of the crater. They were all on horseback, arrayed around the edge and beside the granite monument. The smell out of the north was death, and it was coming soon. "We killed the gods, after all. You'd think this, these scourge...I mean, what kind of an encore is that?"

"The kind that stopped us in our tracks," Terian Lepos said bitterly, his long black hair swirling around him in the wind, Noctus, the Battle Axe of Darkness, slung behind him. Everything was lit in a glow of orange from the setting sun, and his lips were twisted, sullen in his rage here at this end.

1

"We did all we could," Samwen Longwell said in a mournful tone, his blued armor catching the last rays of the sun, and Amnis, the Spear of Water, stowed in the saddle at his side. He was quietly downcast – like his voice. "Restored hope where we could. Drove every last soul we could over the Perda–"

"It wasn't enough," Aisling Nightwind said, her leather armor making a faint squeak as she nosed her horse around. Black ichor stained the brown leather around the bracers on her wrists, and hints of it were in her hair from a small force of scourge they'd run across five miles north. Only a dozen, they hadn't seen her coming with Epalette, the Point of Atonement, in her hand.

"Never enough," Zarnn said, his green skin given a yellowed glow by the sun, his savannah cat purring beneath him, and Rodanthar, the Saber of the Righteous, glowing faintly in his grasp. "Never be enough with this many dead."

"We were always at the disadvantage," came the quiet voice of Mendicant, the goblin. His scaly green skin seemed dark, and with Terrenus, the Hammer of Earth, hung at his side, he stared at the spectacle before them as though it were the end of all things – though that was behind them, and coming soon. "Every place we faced them, their numbers were so great they would flank us. Always they kept coming, always at our backs."

"I can't help but feel we let him down," Ryin Ayend said. In his hand he held Torris, the Scepter of Fire, its glow reflecting off the golden silk inlaid in his robes. "That if perhaps he'd been here...if we'd all been here together–"

"Cyrus is dead," Terian said grimly. "If he was alive, there's no way he would have missed this fight." He bowed his head, staring into the depths of the crater.

"Well, we had a few years of peace, didn't we?" Calene asked, her eyes catching on the granite monument. She could read the names, and her eyes caught on the one at the bottom: Vara Davidon.

"With the moat around Reikonos, the doors buried at Saekaj and Enterra, and every other living soul on the continent behind the river

Perda," Aisling said, "perhaps we'll be back to peace for some time more. Be hard to mount an invasion when we're trapped underground and there's an ocean of scourge between us and anyone we might fight."

"Hard to bring a proper army in using just the portals, yeah," Longwell said. "But it's going to be hard to keep Reikonos and Saekaj and Enterra fed using just them, too, though."

"We weren't able to get a portal in before we had to shut the gates," Mendicant said quietly. He held up a small, clawed hand. "But long have my people subsisted beneath the earth, and I will lead them properly so that they continue to."

Calene felt a faint rumble in her stomach at the tone and tenor of that; probably nothing. "Still and all...we're not likely to see each other often after this, are we?"

"This was the Sanctuary ten-year reunion," Terian said bitterly. "What would you see us do for the twenty? Or the centennial?"

"Has it really been ten years?" Ryin mused quietly. He pushed back his now-long hair off his forehead. "Ten years since–"

"The end," Zarnn said quietly. "Or what we thought was end."

"Now we think this is the end," Aisling said. "Yet still we stand."

"Not all of us," Terian said, sweeping a hand over the crater where Sanctuary had once stood. Here at the end of the world they'd known – at the place where their world had nearly ended a decade before. "Not nearly enough." He looked over them once. "And Scuddar?"

Ryin shifted uncomfortably on his horse. "The scourge veered west around the Inculta Desert and the oasis where his people make their home in their mad rush to get to us on the lines before Reikonos, the southern confederation, and Saekaj. He's taking his people south into the swamps of the bandit lands, he said."

"That's suicide," Longwell said. "He should bring them to Reikonos. Or across the Perda."

Terian shook his head slowly. "The desert people are a different breed. They don't play well with the other humans. And besides...those swamps in the southeast are thick." A bitter smile graced the face of the Sovereign of Saekaj, the first that had crossed his face in some time. "I give them a fair chance."

Aisling stiffened upon the back of her horse, and her eyes tracked to the north. "They're coming."

And so they were. Calene turned her horse halfway around to see them, emerging at last over the hill that hid Sanctuary from view of the portal to the north. A shadowy, writhing wave, undulating in the rays of last light, swarming across the empty fields like a living mass in the dim resolution of sunset.

"I would fight for this place until I ran out of arrows and they ran out of scourge," Calene whispered, glancing back at the empty crater. A decade of weather had smoothed the edges; they looked less scorched and jagged, like the mighty haven that had once extended into the depths had been gone a hundred years or a thousand instead of a bare ten.

"This is not the last farewell," Ryin said quietly. "It simply feels like it."

"It's been a thousand partings since that day in the Realm of War," Calene said. "I've not seen some of you since. And I doubt that'll be changed by some of you being buried in the ground and the rest spreading to the four winds."

"Face it, Calene," Terian said, baring his teeth in a grimace, "they were the ones who brought us together, held us together – Alaric, Cyrus, Curatio, Vaste – hell, even Vara. And without them...we're all stumbling in the dark on our own trying to figure out where the chamber pot is."

"That is a worrying thing to hear your nation's leader say," Aisling muttered.

"It happens to the best of us," Mendicant offered.

"Zarnn not agree," the big troll said. He was three heads higher than any of the rest of them, mounted as he was on his savannah cat. "What we do here – save people, try and restore hope? Is what they would have done. We do it as well as we could. Not the same as them. Best we able. It not enough because...it never enough. But we did all we could. Now...now we go." And he looked once more at the coming wave of scourge. "This fight over...for now."

"This fight is over," Terian said. "On that we agree."

"Goodbye, all," Mendicant said. "Though this is not how I would have chosen to say goodbye, it is the way that has been given us. My people need a time of consolidation, of introspection...we need to find new ways."

"And you're going to do that for them?" Terian asked. His voice held a cynical quality.

"I am," Mendicant said, his pointed teeth showing in the rising darkness. "And they need my full attention." With a wave of his hand and a sparkle of light, he vanished into a return spell.

Terian watched him go, then shook his head. With a glance at Aisling, then the rest of them, he added, "Any of you come calling at Saekaj, you'll be welcomed as the heroes you are." With a glance back at the crater and another shake of his head, he added, "But I can't stay here any longer. You'll see her safely home?" Now he was looking at Ryin, though his intent was clear: Aisling.

"I'll make the rounds of drop-offs," Ryin said.

"I might be gone a few days," Aisling said, stroking the back of her horse's neck. "I'm not ready to go back under the ground just yet."

"See you when I see you, then – and that goes for all of you," Terian said, and with a flash of light from his own hand, he, too, was gone. Then there were but five of them.

"I just can't believe it ends this way," Calene said sadly, watching the scourge thunder across the plains toward them, toward this place. Defiled before by gods, and now this.

"Not the end," Zarnn said.

"It just feels like it," Ryin whispered. They all heard it, though.

And as they vanished moments later in the light of Ryin's spell, whisking them far from this place that had once been home, Calene could not help but feel that...

...yes, it truly was the end of the world, and that all those who survived were merely limping away, as if all the magic had gone out of their lives.

As if something very important – maybe the most important thing they'd done with their lives – was now over. And nothing would ever be the same again.

CHAPTER 1

VARA

One Thousand Years Later

"*I* find you human men absolutely insufferable," Vara declared as she was marched at spearpoint through a grove of trees, her sister Isabelle beside her and Longwell with his wild beard and his blued armor limping along behind. She'd not been stripped of her armor, but that was of little comfort. She was responding to a muttering about her being an elf, about all of them being elves, really, because Longwell's helmet was covering his ears and this lot were surely too stupid to realize that he was one of them. The bearded wild man was hardly making his own case; he'd only jumped into their spell at the last moment, after all, and only after receiving a well-deserved thumping at her hands for trying to confine them all in the Realm of Life forever, where they could be putatively safe.

A spear clinking against her back armor she had to admit, clearly, he'd not been entirely wrong. Though Vara was loathe to voice that sentiment to him now. Because of the insufferable arrogance of human men, naturally.

"You would know, you married one," Isabelle said softly, but with an appropriate leavening of sarcasm. They were not clinking their spears against her, Vara could not help but notice, though that might have had some small measure to do with her being clad in dirty, ash-stained, once-white robes rather than armor.

Vara felt the clink again as she held up a moment. "I am seeking my husband, Cyrus Davidon," she said, looking sidelong at the nearest human, one with a flintlock pistol in his hand. He stared evenly back at her over the sights.

"Aren't we all," the man muttered after a pause, then beckoned with his pistol for her to keep moving. "Come on, then, elves."

They passed under leafy green canopies shadowed by the light leaking from between the iron-colored clouds overhead, boughs of the trees hanging above like shadowed bones. Vara was not blessed with an overabundance of confidence that should these men decide to kill them, she would survive.

"Where are we?" Longwell croaked. His armor clinked quietly, and he was led easily along, somewhat surprising her. He'd surrendered Amnis as easily as she'd given up Ferocis. Now both weapons were in the control of some human in green attire reminiscent of a ranger of old. "I thought this was Pharesia, but you're men of the south?"

"Quiet, elf," the man with the pistol said.

Longwell did not respond to this, even to argue with him. He merely shuffled along meekly, looking around.

There was light ahead, Vara realized, and they moved along this rutted, dirty trail in silence. A mighty tent rose ahead out of the glade, a pointed top with flags decorating it, flapping in the wind against the gray clouds.

A siege tent, Vara realized. For their generals to parlay in, as they tightened their noose upon the elven capital.

Damn. Then the hour was later than Vara realized. The humans were moving upon the elves in the south, Reikonos had been destroyed, Malpravus was extending his hand across the land – everything had pointed itself directly to hell and was proceeding there at breakneck speed. "Who are you taking us to see?" she asked.

"And why were you guarding the portal when it hasn't been in use for hundreds of years?" Isabelle asked when no answer was forthcoming.

"Silence," the man with the pistol said, but lackadaisically.

Sound came from within the tent's blue and white-striped walls – voices, though she couldn't quite understand them through the muffling effect of the rough-spun canvas.

"Fawsett, what are you doing here?" asked a man in vestigial armor, the seal of Emerald upon his cloth tabard. Green peeked out between his joints, and he wore a scowl on his face.

"Well," the man with the pistol declared, lowering his weapon as they came to a flap of the tent, "we were in camp when this triad of elves appeared in light."

"What?" The tent guard stared. "Magic, you think?" He scratched a stubbly chin beneath a pointed helm, then glanced at the tent. "Better take 'em in, let the Administrator decide." And he lifted the tent flap.

"Oh, no," Isabelle said with obvious consternation.

Vara looked at her. "What?"

"He means the Administrator of Emerald Fields," Isabelle said, quietly enough that only Vara could hear her. "You know–"

"Yes, I know the position you speak of," Vara said. "I don't suppose I could hope it's still Cattrine Tiernan in that seat?"

Isabelle shook her head. "Tiernan's been dead almost a thousand years, sad to say. The current administrator was, I thought, a rather level-headed woman, but if she's in camp around Pharesia mere weeks after I left Termina–"

"It means she's sieging Pharesia, yes," Vara whispered back as they were led in under the flaps. The sprawling tent was the size of a large house, with tables laid out in a rough circle around the center. She was shoved roughly forward the moment she entered, and thus the world around her blurred as her balance was lost and she struggled to find it again.

"Administrator," the man named Fawsett announced, "these elves appeared in our camp out of light, like magic." Someone shoved Vara forward again, and she had a time catching herself before landing on the table.

A fire burned at the center, the air filled with a rich wood smoke. Vara lifted her eyes to see a woman standing behind a table before them. Hazel hair and bright, slitted eyes, this was a woman in charge.

"Yes, we appeared as if by magic," Vara said, brushing herself off as she drew back to standing in the middle of the circle of tables, but her attention was fixed on the only point that mattered – the Administrator who held Vara's fate in her hands. "Because it was, indeed, by magic. Not that this lackwit would have understood that."

"Elves," Fawsett muttered behind her.

Vara did not dare look back at him, even though his voice fairly dripped with condescension. He probably imagined no one could hear him. He was, naturally, quite wrong. "Humans," she fired back, in exactly the same tone.

"Trolls," came a familiar voice to her right, and she snapped her head around to look. There at the table, looking very self-satisfied was–

"Vaste?" Longwell muttered, taking a clinking step to look closer at him.

"Vagrant," Vaste replied. He was flanked on one side by that immense, yellow-skinned battle troll from Reikonos, who had a generally pleasant look on his face, and on the other by the tallest human woman Vara had ever seen. To either side of them, though were–

"Merrish?" Vara asked, staring at the once-lord of Traegon. Time had scarcely faded his good looks, though he had scars that he'd not had before. On the other end of their table was a slightly chubby-looking elf that had the appearance of one who'd once been in fine condition and now had gone slightly to seed. "And I don't know you."

"But I know you, Shelas'akur," the man said, bowing his head. "I am called Glaven."

"He's my manservant," Vaste said, dipping Letum toward the man. "Oh, and this is Aemma." He nodded at the tall woman. "She's..." He glanced at her, she glanced back at him. "...uh. Uhm?"

"So you know each other?" The Administrator drew their attention back to her commanding presence. Her eyes were flaring.

"Alixa?" Longwell was caught staring at her now. "Alixa Weltan?"

"Yes?" She stared back at him for a moment in mild curiosity, then her mouth fell open. "Longwell? Samwen?"

"Yes, it is I," Longwell said, brushing a clanking gauntlet against his breastplate.

"It is a time of many reunions, it would seem," came another familiar voice, this one to her left. Vara's gaze swept the nearest table to the Administrator – Alixa's – right and swiftly took in Shirri Gadden, her mother Pamyra, and Hiressam, along with a faintly green, exceptionally tall man in armor who appeared vaguely elven in appearance and by his ears, and another who was more familiar, though he wore an absurd bowler hat. Beyond him–

"Alaric," Vara said, weak in the knees, for there was the old knight at the table beside theirs, his battered armor and lone eye looking at her. Beside him stood that fool Guy, as well as a new man, and, beside Alaric in her knee-length brown coat, Captain Mazirin of the Yuutshee. "You're alive, then." She looked back at Vaste. "Both of you." Then, to Shirri, almost apologetically. "All of you."

"Almost," Alaric said, and here a vague sense of worry came over her as he bowed his head.

"Cyrus," she said, striking out in the direction of Alaric, no longer worried about the men with spears, or Fawsett with his pistol. "Have you seen him? Did he make it out of Reikonos before–?"

A faint squeak of metal behind her made her turn; the guard must be upon her, had not relinquished his charge, was surely driving his spear at her even now, and she would be struck down here, so close, so close to–

And he was close, right there behind her, his face practically upon hers–

But he was not the guard.

"You're alive," Cyrus said, as he swept her up in his arms, lifting her from the ground of the tent and she – heedless, lightheaded, in the arms of her husband again at last, tittered wildly with glee, and wrapped her arms around him–

And gladly let him sweep her off her feet.

CHAPTER 2

CYRUS

"Captain Beniye told us he'd let you off in the middle of Reikonos," Cyrus said once the kisses were done, and now Vara was before him again, her hands in his as she looked up, her blue eyes sparkling with – if his did not much deceive him – hints of tears. Her golden hair shimmered in the candles that circled the tent. With a glance past her at Isabelle and a nod, he added, "But the city was burned to ash almost a month ago, and he found no sign of you after he lost you in the streets."

"When we lost the airship, we made our way to the catacombs," Vara said, looking quite flushed. "And into the Realm of Life, where we found–" And here she turned to point at Longwell, who now had the Administrator of the Emerald Fields standing beside him, her hand upon his gauntlet, looking into his eyes with concern, but before the sweep of her gaze quite made it there it went over the table beside Vaste, where a Cyrus-sized hole remained between–

"Hell and damnation," Vara breathed. Cyrus cringed, felt the stab of hard worry hit him in the belly.

"You found hell and damnation in the catacombs?" came the voice of the wrinkled, elderly dark elven woman standing beside her son.

Baynvyn looked slightly abashed, but his mother did not. "And how did you escape Malpravus, I wonder?"

"You're the hell and damnation, and I encounter you here," Vara said, narrowing her gaze. With a flicked glance to Cyrus that made his stomach writhe, she added, "I trust you've made peace with these two, then?"

"And Terian, thankfully," Cyrus added. "Look, I'm not going to apologize again for–"

"You need not," she said, and her face fell. Was this...chagrin? "I was wrong to leave you." She looked around the swelling circle and cocked her head at the sight of yet another familiar face. "Calene?"

Calene Raverle waved a noncommittal hand. "Yeah, I'm here. Just...didn't want to yoke myself into the drama."

"Yet drama we have," came another familiar voice, one in so many. Vara turned, this time back to Cyrus's table, where, just slightly to the right of Baynvyn stood–

"Ryin Ayend," Vara said, struck dumb after a long moment of staring at the druid.

"We sought him out after leaving Saekaj," Cyrus said, putting a hand on Vara's shoulder. "And then we put together this...well, this conference."

"Some of us had a greater hand in it than others," Vaste said. "Brought more to the table, as it were."

"You brought your considerable belly to the table," Aisling said. "I take it there was pie in the ether?"

"Curatio didn't make it," Cyrus said, lowering his voice to a whisper as the noise kicked up around them, the conference dissolving into a dozen individual conversations. "Malpravus killed him, drained his life and Sanctuary, and–"

"Yes," she said quietly, "I felt that. And saw the spell consume Reikonos, obviously." She looked around the tent, caught sight of the Pharesian delegation, a spread of five elder elves, all of whom nodded at her in deepest respect. "But what is this?"

"We're trying to unite everyone to fight Malpravus," Alaric said, moving over to them rather smoothly. Vara looked for a moment as though she might embrace the old knight, but decorum caught her. That made Cyrus smile for some reason.

"How goes it, then?" She cast a withering look back at Aisling and Baynvyn that made Cyrus's blood curdle. "I see the slattern and bastard contingents are present."

Cyrus felt the throb of a vein in his head. "Vara..."

"Yes, I will let it go...eventually," she said rather hastily, looking up at Cyrus. "I am sorry, you know. Truly. That I left–"

"Don't start apologizing now," Cyrus said stiffly.

She favored him with a rather wan smile. "Because you'll get emotional?"

"Because I'll like it a little too much," he said, feeling the twist of a grin start to tug at his lips. "And you wouldn't want me to become accustomed to you saying you're sorry."

"I doubt very much that will become a common experience." Vaste shouldered his way past Longwell, who was still talking in hushed tones to Administrator Weltan, to join the three of them. "And unlike Alaric, I have no reserve to keep me from doing this." And he grabbed up Vara before she could protest in a hug that was surprisingly delicate considering he lifted her off the ground with it.

While she was spun ("Leave me my dignity, you green abomination!" "You forfeited that when you apologized to your husband!"), Cyrus turned to Longwell and Administrator Weltan. "I'm sorry," he said, causing them both to look up, "How do you know each other?" He didn't feel he knew Administrator Weltan at all, really, though Calene had introduced them before the opening session of the conference.

Weltan stared at him with those frightening eyes. "We shared an adventure a very long time ago...almost a thousand years now. Samwen helped set me upon the path that led me here."

Cyrus started to ask, then noticed Fulmenar, the Claws of Lightning, flashing on Weltan's belt, hidden just beneath her green cloak. "Ah," he said, as she caught him looking.

ROBERT J. CRANE

"Alixa is the last true Luukessian," Longwell said, brow furrowing as he saw a gray figure on all fours trotting over to him. "And is this...?" He knelt, joints of his armor clinking as the Niamh-scourge made her way over to him.

"It's–" Cyrus started to answer, feeling the tension in his muscles as the dragoon locked his gaze on the scourge; this was the part that never went well, and he tried to spit it out before the Luukessian could strike–

"Niamh," Longwell said, rubbing her head. "It's been so long."

Cyrus raised an eyebrow. "Okay. Usually when I bring her 'round new people they scream or ready an attack – they don't know it's Niamh." He glanced at Alixa, who had knelt and was gazing benignly down at the former druid, her own hands working the gray flesh around the scourge's neck. "I get the feeling there's history here."

"Did you bear him home?" Alixa asked; she'd taken no notice of the scourge before, huddled as Niamh had been behind his table during the opening procession. Cyrus had asked her to remain there, close at hand with him, and she'd done so.

The Niamh scourge lifted her head to look Alixa in the eyes, and – if Cyrus's eyes didn't deceive him – they looked a hint misty in the deep ebon of the wide pupils. But Niamh nodded, unmistakably, and then it was Alixa's eyes that were suddenly teary – and Longwell's, too.

"Samwen, I can't believe you've come back to us," Alixa said, putting a hand on the dragoon's shoulder. "I knew the Lord Protector was a fraud, but I had no idea who he was until–"

"Until a great ruddy red light burned through the lives of several million people?" Vara shouldered her way in next to Cyrus, the conversations around them like the dull roar of a cataphract. His wife was looking pointedly at Administrator Weltan.

"Even then I didn't," Weltan said, drawing back up to her full height. "I had little exposure to the stories of Malpravus, save for what tales I heard from Calene, Longwell, or on infrequent occasions, Ryin." She sort of half-shrugged. "I had no idea where you were, or

16

that you were still alive, Samwen. I would have sent people after you. Hell, I would have come myself."

"It would have done you little good." Baynvyn squeezed his way into the outer edge of their circle, lifting his spectacles upon the peak of his forehead. He seemed to only require them in brightest light and at all other times his pale blue irises were visible for anyone to behold. And Cyrus beheld them now, uncomfortably, as if looking in a mirror. "Malpravus had set himself a throne before the portal underneath the Citadel. I expect he spent quite a bit of time down there, with his guards, milking those realms he could reach dry. Only after he left – after the spell – would you have been able to pass below and into the place where Longwell was. Did I hear you say 'Realm of Life?'"

"Yes," Vara said a bit stiffly, though – if Cyrus was not mistaken – with an attempt at an accommodating tone. "Though why Malpravus might not have found it if he were diligently ransacking the magic from the upper realms, I do not know."

"The spell of Realm of Life was not widely known," Isabelle said, squeezing in next to her sister. She had aged greatly, lines carved into her face at the corners of her eyes and along her cheeks. She glanced at Cyrus briefly, gave him a nod, though she looked tired. "It was not raided by the guilds of old – that I recall."

"Fortunate for our friend Longwell, then," Alaric said, easing in next to Cyrus. He looked at the dragoon–

–And Longwell looked away.

"This is becoming a bit of a quorum of apes," came a loud, supercilious voice from behind Cyrus that made his eyes war between a roll and a flutter. Half a day he'd known the speaker and already he was immensely tired of the man.

"Is that the Head Arcanist?" Vara said after turning to look at the elder elf. The man's hair was platinum, his robes of finest red, and his lips made him look as though he'd taken a deep draught of the sourest pickle juice. "Dioro?" Her brow puckered. "How are you not dead? You were ancient a thousand years ago."

Dioro's thin lips pursed; the man could not have been any more

17

piquant if he'd been suckling on lemons. "I see death has not stolen your impudence, Shelas'akur."

"We killed death," Vara said, staring the man down icily. Cyrus doubted she knew that he was one of a council of five that ran Pharesia, for he had not been in that position when she had died, nor even when he'd departed Arkaria a year later with Sanctuary. Still, he'd discovered, this was what Pharesia was now, a strange, stultified society of the old. "Malpravus is but a pale shadow and want-to-be imitator, trying to grasp for apotheosis."

"And we're trying to stop him," Cyrus said, putting a hand on her shoulder. "With the help of all gathered here." He gave Dioro and his party a sidelong glance; they all wore their finest robes, every one the head of what had once been the Pharesian leagues, back when they'd had such things.

"It's been a month, you said?" Vara turned to look him in the eyes. "A month since you saw me?"

"Near," he said, brushing a few blades of grass out of her hair, where they'd turned the blond green. "A lot's happened since you left. Reikonos – obviously. But also–"

"Malpravus has the scourge under his control," Vaste said. "Entirely. And they've disappeared from the banks of the river Perda, a place they've remained for nigh on a thousand years."

"What does that mean?" Vara asked, her forehead prickled like elephant skin. "What is his plan?"

"We don't know," Cyrus said, feeling a great void within, a worry he had carried almost since last he'd seen her, "we only know that he's not done...and that he wants to devour every single soul in Arkaria."

CHAPTER 3

"*W*hat is our plan, then?" Vara asked, looking at the blurred assemblage around her, the familiar faces mingled in with the strangers. "Sanctuary destroyed, Malpravus ascendant, and you lot have had a month to prepare – what do we do?"

"Here we come to the glue pot," Dioro said, and moved into the center of the tent with aged grace, an intricately rune-carved staff in his hand. "My people attended this assemblage of our enemies because of the call of Lord Davidon, hero of our age." His gray, bushy eyebrows lifted and fell. "But we are aware that we are the hen amidst the foxes."

"No one means you ill here," came the voice of Gareth, the elf in the bowler hat that had been seated with Shirri and Pamyra. Vara peered at him, and Cyrus wondered if she recalled him. She seemed to, after a moment, though the ranger certainly did not look as he once did. Gone was his green cloak and bow in favor of a finely-tailored suit and that ridiculous headpiece.

"You cannot be serious," Dioro said, looking pointedly at Administrator Weltan. Bad blood lingered between the elves and the Luukessians; Cyrus hadn't been here long and already he could discern that. "Emerald was days from marching on our border when this all broke loose. And war was already well declared between the men of the north and Termina. You couldn't even prevail on them to put aside their grievances to show their faces here."

"Perhaps because the Terminans slaughtered their brethren," said Aemma, the excessively tall woman who stood behind Vaste. Her cheeks burned, as did her eyes, and Merrish was looking pointedly away as she spoke.

Vara looked sharply at Cyrus. "Is this really happening now? Arkaria falls to discord as Malpravus prepares to destroy us?"

That uncomfortable, writhing sensation worked its way through Cyrus's guts. "Unfortunately." He felt his lips purse in distaste, as though channeling the spirit of Dioro. "Somehow they live on less than one quarter of the land we had before the scourge and yet possess five times the grievances with each other."

"Lord Davidon, I know you've been gone for some time," Dioro said with such thick condescension that Cyrus's stomach nearly rebelled at the dosage, "but for nearing a thousand years Pharesia has given way on our southern border." His bushy eyebrows knitted together in a dark thunderhead. "Well, no more. Enough elves have been driven off their lands."

"They sold their lands, you doddering fool," Administrator Weltan said. "Sold them because they grow old, sold them to humans because no one in your own kingdom wants to go into farming at the ripe age of three thousand. Sold them because tilling the land is hardly a high-status occupation around Pharesia."

"Yet eating remains quite the high-status occupation," Vaste chipped in, perfectly timed as ever, and drawing a rancorous glare from Dioro.

"The elves of Pharesia will not concede one more inch," Dioro said.

"The people of Emerald are little concerned with your piddly inches," Administrator Weltan said with great humor, "and would prefer you keep them to yourselves."

"Malpravus has no concern for your small squabbles," Alaric said, drawing not an eye but those of the long-standing Sanctuary members, "and he will make you all equal in death."

"I think even in death I'm still better than all of you," Vaste said, and now everyone did look, "especially in terms of qualities like beauteousness of arse."

Cyrus glanced at the Amti table, where Shirri sat unspeaking, stricken almost, but watching everything. Her face stood out to him in a sea of them all blending together, the new and longstanding members of Sanctuary prominent but hardly the only attendees in this tent nearly filled. There had to be over a hundred people in here, after all.

"This is getting us nowhere," Cyrus said, and everyone looked to him; Alixa Weltan's anger seemed to subside a whit, and even crusty Dioro appeared to withdraw. "The hour grows late. Dioro – is there no worry in your heart at the approach of Malpravus?"

"I fear any man who could command the scourge," Dioro said, drawing himself up to his inconsiderable height (for he was several heads shorter than Cyrus). "But what good does it do me to save us from this dire threat and then lose all we have left to the insatiable appetite of Emerald?"

"You might still have your life and your soul," Vaste's voice rang out, naturally. "Trifling things, it's true, and of small consideration next to having land and a city and walls and whatnot, but you'd probably miss them if Malpravus got his hands on them."

Cyrus fought back a cringe. "Perhaps we should adjourn for tonight and start anew on the morrow." He could feel the weariness creep in; close to a month of flying around western Arkaria trying to bring together these various factions only to have it culminate in this. Other than Vara's sudden appearance, it was wearying.

"As the hero of Arkaria wishes," Dioro said with a slight bow, and Cyrus could not tell whether he was being sarcastic or not. When the remainder of the Pharesian delegation bowed as well, he was left to conclude...perhaps not. They filed out in a procession, taking with them nearly a quarter of the tent's population.

Other groups started to clear as well; Alixa Weltan waved her hand and the Emerald delegation began to make their way out, though she remained firmly by Longwell's side. The rasp of silken robes and cloth could be heard over the mutters and whispers of delegates finding their way through the open flaps of the tent, a refreshing night breeze making its way in and washing away some of the scent of bodies gathered in the stifling space.

"I knew you were alive," Vara said, her fingers rattling as she touched her gauntlet to the small of his back, clinking against the armor there.

"Of course. Like I told you before–" He drew her close, pulling her tight to him as he looked into her eyes. "Legends never die."

CHAPTER 4

ALARIC

"It was as though I were not even here," Alaric said, stepping out of the tent into the brisk, cool air, Mazirin matching his pace a few steps behind. Guy and Edouard had gone on before them, sharing a tent hastily allocated them somewhere in the Emerald legation. The evenly ordered rows of tents spread before him for what seemed like miles, the scent of wood smoke from the fires and night watches sweet in the air.

"A strange and yet fitting position for a ghost to occupy," Mazirin said, hands clasped behind her back, the train of her long, brown coat flapping just below her knees. She wore the trace of a smile. "You have been gone a thousand years, and are hardly as well known in these lands as your man Cyrus. What did you expect?"

Stepping clear of the tent flap to allow the humans of Emerald to pass, and watching them take no notice as they did, Alaric sighed. "Something more than being ignored."

"Your friends listen to you," Mazirin said, keeping her hands by her side. "And everyone listens to Cyrus. It seems to me, if you wish to have influence, you have a clear flight path – use him to deliver your message."

"I have fought for this land for eleven thousand years," Alaric said, the bite of frustration creeping out in his pinched tone. "You would think that would offer me some small amount of influence in the current events."

Mazirin's dark eyes glittered in the procession of lamps being lit as the Emerald delegation continued to pour from the tent. "A ghost is insubstantial, Alaric; they have little or no influence save for adding a dollop of fear to life." She shrugged lightly, as if to apologize for what she was saying. "I am sorry it is not as you wish it. You have offered nothing but wise counsel in my view."

Alaric stood there for a moment, then nodded. "You are, of course, wise yourself. Come – let us give Vara and Cyrus their moment, and then, on the morrow, before the sessions begin, perhaps we can all come to some accord about what needs be done next."

"Then this is where I leave you, I suppose," Mazirin said with a short bow of her head.

"What? Oh, yes," Alaric said, returning her bow of the head. She'd been given a tent all her own some distance away on the northern edge of the Emerald legation while he'd received one closer to where their airship – the *Raifa* – was moored. He paused for a moment, searching for the appropriate salutation. "Good eve, Mazirin."

There was a moment's hesitation, a hint of reluctance, but Mazirin finally nodded. "Good night to you as well, Alaric." And slowly, she made her way down the torch-lit trail toward her tent.

CHAPTER 5

SHIRRI

"That was the truest circus I've ever seen," Pamyra said, pushing past the tent flap as they left in the company of the Amti delegation, Shirri feeling quite uncomfortable in the company of all these pureblood elves. She should have become accustomed to it by now, really, given she'd been in Amti for nearing three weeks when Cyrus's call for this conference had reached her there. "That didn't involve a dancing bear, in any case."

Shirri glanced around; they'd lost Hiressam. Or, more accurately, perhaps, he'd chosen to remain to give his regards to Vara. Shirri had been torn on that, too, ultimately coming to the conclusion that she barely knew the woman, and surrounded as she was by truer friends, it would be best if Shirri just moved on. So she had, with Gareth at one side and Birstis the trelf at the other, her mother trailing behind and muttering all the while.

"Little progress is being made," Gareth said, fiddling with his bowler hat, rolling it between his fingers. He mopped perspiration from his upper lip as they strode along the boulevard made between the pitched tents of the Amti delegation's quarter of the camp. "Dioro and the elders of Pharesia have nothing but fear for Emerald, while you cannot even get the men of the north to show up in the same place as Termina." He glanced at Shirri. "Still, isn't it curious that so many of you from Sanctuary are in attendance, and representing so many different factions?"

Shirri waited a moment to be sure he was talking to her. He was, and was watching her for reaction.

"I was 'with' Sanctuary for less than a week before Reikonos fell," Shirri said, stirring herself to speak as she trod along the dusty path. "I doubt they'd consider me one of them." *I doubt anybody would, under less pressing circumstances.*

"I am still not convinced the better course would not be to flee to Bithrindel or Azwill," Pamyra muttered, though there seemed no real fire in it. "Listening to this lot bicker–"

"It is a poor time for our divisions to come out," Birstis said, the pale green tinge of his skin almost lost in the light of the torches that lined the makeshift avenue. "Elf at the throat of human in the north and south, while to the east a dark power rises."

Shirri frowned. That was another thing – it had been nearly a month since the destruction of Reikonos, and almost as long since Malpravus had made his attempt on Saekaj, according to Cyrus.

Where was he now? Why did the axe not fall upon them, and swiftly?

"You said hardly a word in there, Shirri," Gareth said, still playing with his bowler hat.

"I...didn't feel I had much to contribute," Shirri said. "Not in that company."

Birstis nodded. "It is an august bunch." He drew a slow yet sharp breath. "Cyrus Davidon has returned. I had not thought I would live to see the day."

Gareth frowned at the trelf. "I wouldn't have thought you a Davidon worshipper."

"I am not," Birstis said. "But my order, the Brotherhood of the Savannah Cat, traces its origins back to Cyrus Davidon bringing my ancestor trolls into his fold under the aegis of the Grand Knight of Sanctuary. After the fall they made their way to Amti, offering their service." Gareth seemed mildly annoyed at having this explained to him, which made a certain amount of sense, Shirri realized, for he had been there for it all. "Without Cyrus Davidon, I would not be here."

"Nor would Shirri or I," Pamyra said, a bit archly, "for he was my father's closest friend, and his loss bit keenly, causing me to look deeply into his disappearance from these shores. Still – I might not have looked as hard as I did, nor draw my daughter into it, had I known all that would result from my search for the bones of Cyrus Davidon."

"Well, we've found more than his bones now," Shirri said in barely a whisper, taking a last glance over her shoulder. The tent flap was still open, and within she could see Cyrus and Vara in a tight embrace.

"It might have been better if that's all we'd found," Pamyra said, nearly to herself, but it did not seem she had anyone agree with her.

"Tomorrow," Gareth said, his voice changing as he seemed to decide on something – that things would be different on the morrow, Shirri thought. "Perhaps a good rest will change the fermented attitudes around this place, allow everyone to see clearly what needs to be done to stave off these twin dangers of Malpravus and the scourge."

"Perhaps," Shirri said, keeping her true thoughts to herself, for in reality she was near certain that it would not, in fact, be enough to move this company. That certainly nothing she said or did – and perhaps nothing anyone could say or do – would be enough to make the entrenched powers of this land give up their old grudges and unite against the common enemy poised to smite them all.

CHAPTER 6

VASTE

"*P*erhaps it was the wrong thing to say," Aemma offered, trailing after Vaste, Glaven, Qualleron, and Merrish coming too in his wake. All it had taken was a few words of innuendo from Vara and he'd gone, willingly and swiftly, the Termina delegation coming behind him in all their guilty glory.

"I have a history of doing that," Vaste said, filing out down the Termina path, into the tents set up for their delegation. In a way it bothered him that he was separated from Cyrus, from Alaric, from the others putatively of Sanctuary, like Shirri and her group. Not enough to draw him their way, for he was certain they would talk later, as they had before this conclave. "It's sort of my thing."

"It's not representing Termina in the way I might have hoped when I pushed for you to receive this accommodation," Merrish said, ruddy cheeks flushed in the lamp light. Vaste turned to better look at him; he did not seem angry, exactly, but perhaps displeased.

"Did our discussions of these last weeks give you the impression that I am thrilled with the way your people have conducted themselves?" Vaste asked, resisting the temptation to bonk the elf on the head with Letum. "In our discussions with your ruling council, did I seem restrained and straitlaced, willing to sit back and allow idiocy to be spoken without challenge, without mocking?"

"No," Merrish said, "I merely hoped that here, among your own, spearheading our reply to this threat, you might be a bit more...serious."

"Listen, Merrish, if I can't be unserious when certain death is coming for all of us, I just don't know where I would fit in," Vaste said. "This is my role. I bring to light by absurdity what others dare not say."

"So you're a jester?" Aemma asked. "The fool?"

Vaste started to answer that, and saw a very slight trace of a smile on her lips. "I have been quite the fool, yes. But the point remains – yes, a jester. Can I represent Termina's interest in not being dead while also making mockery of the hidebound nimrods in Pharesia? Yes, yes I think so."

"Don't you think it might be a touch counterproductive?" Qualleron rumbled. The big troll had said little during the discussions, but seemed to be taking everything in, his eyes moving to watch every speaker and none of the eye glaze or drool evident that Vaste had fought so hard against. Especially during the windy speeches of the Pharesian elves.

"Listen, troll, I don't tell you how to swing that meat cleaver of yours around," Vaste said, "so you don't tell me how to represent the murdering elves of Termina." That elicited another wince from Merrish, but he said nothing about it.

It was true, after all. The accounting had been done, in the light of day and with cold regret in full effect, and as near as could be determined the Termina elves had killed roughly a quarter of the human population in their city. Stragglers were still fleeing north even now, across the green fields toward haven in the northern holdfasts of men.

But in the city, it was done, and a delicate peace had settled, with a lack of exultation. The streets of Termina were dead as if all had gone into that night, and the gossamer spirits of the dead had already started to move on from Vaste's sight.

"I can see this is not a useful conversation," Merrish said with a sigh. "I will see you again on the morrow, where – hopefully – something of note may be accomplished."

"Do you think something of note might have been accomplished if I'd kept my mouth shut?" Vaste asked, and for a moment he truly wondered.

"Perhaps not," Merrish said, face ashen in the torchlight, a gentle wind stirring his long hair. "Perhaps the entrenchments are already too deep, and our factions are doomed to stand behind our own separate ramparts as death comes for us." He looked into the dark sky. "Or perhaps death will spare us, seeing as it's been some weeks and he's yet to come."

"He's still coming, be assured of that," Vaste said. "Whatever he has his bony nose into now, I guarantee it won't keep him away forever. He'll be back, and sooner than we would wish. I only hope we're ready when he does come."

With a nod, Merrish moved off, slipping between rows of tents to the side. A pair of Terminan soldiers watched Vaste with mild interest, stirring a stew pot between them.

"I feel in the mood for a constitutional after all that sitting," Qualleron announced, setting his hands on his hips as though ready to break into a round of calisthenics, or perhaps give a speech. "Would anyone care to join me?"

"Listen, after having my delicate arse planted in a chair for that meeting, there's only one remedy – to pack myself off immediately to a comfortable, tender bed to allow it time to recover," Vaste said. "Enjoy your walk."

"Will you be requiring my assistance, sir?" Glaven asked with a deferential bow of the head.

"No, Glaven, you can walk if you wish, I'm not planning anything dramatic this eve other than falling into bed and hoping it catches me without surrendering," Vaste said, giving him a little wave of the hand.

"Very well, sir," Glaven said, and off he went, walking in the shadow of Qualleron and leaving Vaste alone with Aemma.

He was only silent for a moment, and it was a pregnant pause filled with his own insecurity. "I've only ever been a clown, really. The jester role...it's all I know how to fill. It's what I do."

Aemma stared up at him with dark eyes glinting in the firelight. "On that bridge in Termina, when the elves were coming for me without reason in their eyes or mercy in their souls...I saw more from you than idle jests."

"An aberration, I assure you," Vaste said, lowering his head. "Though, really, wasn't it hilarious how I rolled them all, vomiting and terrified, down the bridge? Because it seemed like high comedy to me, and thus very much in my realm of expertise."

"I am not saying that you are not funny," Aemma said, and with a gentle hand she reached up, stroking his cheek. "I am only saying...you are more than just that." And with a slight inclination of her head in deference, she, too, turned and strolled off, leaving Vaste to brush his hand against his cheek and ponder what exactly she might have meant by that.

CHAPTER 7

CYRUS

*I*t took a while to get everyone soothed, organized, and settled, all the necessary hands shook and well wishes received. Vara, Isabelle, and Longwell arriving in the midst of the conference had thrown a mighty handful of water into the gunpowder of the conference, though Cyrus was the first to admit that things had hardly been progressing at propitious speed before they'd been thrust in among the delegations.

"...after we managed to locate Ryin," Cyrus said, Vara sitting on the cot in his tent almost an hour later as he wound his story of all that had happened since their parting to a close, "news of Alaric came in shortly thereafter, once he'd returned to Termina after his adventures with Chaarlandian pirates."

Vara's brow puckered slightly. "Char-what-ian what?"

"Never mind," Cyrus said with a grin. Two small lamps shed enough light for him to stare comfortably at her, trying to recommit to his memory every detail of her face, of the curves of her armor. "Point is, he's got an airship now."

"Alaric does?" Vara's voice came high and skeptical. "The man who denounced our use of firearms as 'dishonorable?'"

"That very fellow," Cyrus said, feeling amusement glitter in his eyes. "I've seen it – and guess what? It has cannons."

"I imagine it was all he could do to keep himself from pushing them overboard somewhere over the sea," Vara said, reclining before him on the cot. She seemed so very statuesque save for the dirt smudging her hair, face, and shining silver breastplate. "That's quite the tale. I imagine the others have eventful ones of their own, given where they've ended up. Shirri, the mouse, in charge of the Amti delegation? Vaste, a troll who never met a wisecrack he could restrain himself from delivering, representing – unless I'm much mistaken – the elves of Termina?"

Cyrus nodded slowly. "Almost entirely elves in Termina now, though their outlying areas are still somewhat mixed. And there's a whole alliance of men inhabiting the lands north of Elintany to the edge of the swamp and your old holdings."

"They gave the humans who fled the scourge Nalikh'akur?" Vara asked, with barely a raised eyebrow. "Fair play, I guess. Even in the short time I was the lady of that territory the population was diving precipitously."

"I don't think 'gave' is the right word, exactly," Cyrus said, grimacing slightly as he shed his bracers, placing them on one of the wooden dummies the elves had left for him. Of course, there'd only been one when he'd left the tent before the meeting. Now there were two; the elves had been nothing if not hospitable. "There's been tension all along, a slow push as they drove the elves steadily south. A similar effect has come from Emerald toward Pharesia, a creeping invasion now boiling over."

"Of course," Vara said, a frown puckering her own brow. "Because this is the perfect time for us to be at each other's throats. And here I thought the God of Evil was dead, yet still I see his hand at work in these events."

Now shucking off his boots, Cyrus couldn't help but offer an impish smile. "And here I thought you were a lapsed Vidaran."

"I am a firm believer in our luck being composed of absolute horseshit," Vara said, lifting herself off the cot. "What have we accomplished in the interregnum since we parted?" Raising her fingers, she counted off events one by one. "Curatio murdered, Sanctuary destroyed, Reikonos annihilated, the scourge bent to the service of Malpravus – and all the while, our remaining peoples are in the midst of hating one another so fiercely they seem to want to compete with that damnable necromancer for the honor of killing us all first."

"But we've taken steps to try and unite the remainder of Arkaria," Cyrus said, leaving behind his greaves, chainmail rattling lightly even as it glinted in the lamplight. "No convocation of this sort has been held in centuries, but we drew together five of the six major city-states remaining in less than a month. And while there are some difficulties, they are talking, and the slaughter in Termina has stopped." Cyrus unfastened his breastplate. "Hell, according to Vaste, the elves of Termina seem to be evincing remorse and public outrage for what their leaders did. That's better than you get in most pogroms."

"Oh, wonderful," Vara said, eyeing him suspiciously. "The murderers have remorse. That will surely make everything right. And what do you think you're doing, exactly?"

"I am getting out of this uncomfortable armor in preparation to rinse off from that basin over there," Cyrus said after confirming that yes, there were now two basins, both filled with clean water. "And after that, I'm planning to lie down on that cot there," and here he pointed to the one beside her, which had, in fact, been there earlier. "Why?"

She shucked off her own bracers, watching him carefully all the while. "I have been married to you for some time, you know. Counting the ether, well over a thousand years."

"If you want to count the ether, sure. Otherwise, more like one. Speaking of, I feel we've missed some anniversary presents–"

"My point is that we may have been absent each other's company for the last month," Vara said, now unfastening her own breast plate, as if hurrying to catch up to him, "but I still know your mind, husband."

Cyrus suppressed a grin, but only barely. "Why, whatever do you mean, wife?" He hung his chainmail over the dummy carefully, so it would not slip off in the middle of the night and awake him in a great, frightful clatter.

"You know damned well what I mean," Vara said, now out of her own greaves and boots and down to but chainmail.

Cyrus made his way to the basin, splashing his face with water to keep him from having to reply. When he raised his head, he saw her beside him in her own underclothes, face glistening with moisture from her own basin. "Do I?" he asked, pulling back his long hair as he picked up a cloth and began to dab at himself, wiping away the sweat and grime of the day. "Because it seems to me I'm preparing for bed."

"You're preparing for bed in wartime," Vara said, dabbing with her own cloth. "When you would be best served wearing your armor. In case of attack in the darkness."

"Maybe I'll put it back on after I rinse off," Cyrus said, just a touch impish.

"The hell you will," she said, catching his hand and tossing aside his towel. She pulled his head down to her, kissing his lips, and for a little while he forgot all about Malpravus and what was coming.

CHAPTER 8

"*A*hem."

A loud clearing of the throat jarred Cyrus out of a deep slumber, Vara sleeping warm and soft against his side. She, too, stirred, blond hair puddling around her angelic face in the morning light that seeped in through the gaps at the tent's edges.

Cyrus feared to wake her, especially as she turned her face into his shoulder, eyes barely fluttering at the sound of the throat-clearing from outside the tent. It came again a moment later, and this time she groaned, eyes coming open and gazing into his own with her cool blues. "What the ruddy hell is that?" she asked, nearly croaking her question.

"Someone seeking a meeting with your august personages," came the high, prim voice of Dioro. "Would you kindly make yourself presentable so that I may present myself – and my request?"

Cyrus looked intently at Vara, who stared back at him. "Underclothes or full armor?"

She only stared at him for a moment before answering. "If time is of the essence, perhaps Dioro would not mind seeing us clad only in our cloth rather than our steel."

"Yes, yes, that's fine, I suppose," Dioro sniffed from outside. "Kindly hurry – I don't wish to be seen lurking out here."

Cyrus shrugged, but did as requested, dressing himself while watching Vara. Doing so gave him ideas, ideas he'd already pursued the night before but wished to again, and she smiled at him, slightly and mischievously as she pulled her shirt over her head. Later, her smirk told him, and he resisted.

"Come in," Vara announced once they were clad in their gray and weathered cloth garments. Years of sweat colored the soft cotton, and it was loose enough that it did not cling to her curves, leaving him only last night's memories to play with.

Dioro pushed his way through the tent flap with his ornate staff in hand, a look on his face that matched perfectly his usual sense of disdain for anything and everything he encountered. "Thank you for seeing me on such short notice."

"Glad we could accommodate you," Cyrus said, placing a hand on Vara's shoulder since Dioro made no move to undertake that most human of greetings, the handshake. "What brings you to our tent so early?"

Dioro used his staff to lift the flap again; sunlight flooded in, and visible beyond was a camp in full motion. "It's nearly mid-morning, and we have a session at noon." He glanced to his feet, where an envelope sat in the dirt. He kicked it toward them without disturbing the dust. Graceful, really, especially for an elf beyond the turn. "A session I see no point in attending unless we are able to come to a private agreement beforehand."

Cyrus shared the barest glance with Vara, who had the same reaction as him: What could the Pharesians possibly want from him? Or from them, really. "Do tell – what is your demand, Dioro?"

"It's not a demand, exactly," Dioro said, fiddling with the head of his staff, rubbing nervous fingers over the smooth decoration there. "More of a hope that you see the wisdom in what I am about to say. Malpravus – he desires to steal the substance of life to empower himself, yes? To drain it from a populace in order to feed his own power in these days when magic runs short?"

"Yes," Cyrus said.

"And he remains thwarted with Saekaj," Dioro said. "Every airship that crosses the interregnum between Coricuanthi and here confirms it – the scourge are no longer at the wreck of the old tower. A morning flight from Muratam reports again the same, clear lands and empty fields."

"Yes," Cyrus said cautiously. Every airship that had come through for a month confirmed that much; the scourge had seemingly disappeared from eastern Arkaria, though Cyrus believed it more likely they were gathered somewhere far from the trade routes where airships commonly flew.

"Does this give you some false hope that perhaps Malpravus has given up?" Vara asked. "Because I can assure you–"

Dioro waved her objection away. "You need not reassure me." He seemed guarded for a moment, then perhaps a hint...ashamed? "I believe he is bent on destroying all life. No, I come now to reason with you about the course of his plans. If he has failed at Saekaj Sovar, the most bounteous, tightly packed, easily-harvested population remaining in Arkaria, I propose to you that his next, ripest target is obvious."

Cyrus felt himself stiffen slightly, goosepimples running up his spine. "You think you know his next target? Kindly share."

The elder elf sighed as though disappointed that a pupil was not catching the drift of his teaching. "Pharesia, naturally. It is the most sensible choice."

"I'm going to need you to explain that one to me," Cyrus said, feeling Vara stiffen at his side, now. By the widening of her eyes which he could see in profile, he suspected she might agree with the aged elf.

"Certainly," Dioro said, thudding his staff's tip against the earth. "Pharesia's population, while not nearly as many as, say, Emerald, or Termina, even, is still considerable, in the range of a million...and tightly compacted behind our walls with very little expansion beyond.

Many from our outlying areas have found refuge within the city proper these last years, in fact, as the invaders from Emerald have slowly encroached northward to us."

"A million people is not that many," Cyrus said with a shrug, "though your argument about the compaction of your populace is compelling, I suppose. Still, with Emerald being at four million–"

"But they are greatly spread out, you see," Dioro said, and his eyes glittered though his lips twisted almost in pain. "We are confined – and we offer an additional advantage not found in Emerald." His eye twitched.

"They're all elves," Vara whispered.

"Quite right," Dioro said sadly. "And thus worth, even with a median age of three thousand, some thirty or more times what a human life is." He coughed when he saw Cyrus scowling at him. "In magical terms only, I mean – not in moral ones."

"Shit," Cyrus said, because now he saw it as well. "And Termina, it's–"

"More populous, but spread far beyond the bounds you remember," Dioro said, "and positively laced with half-elves. Certainly I could see Malpravus deciding upon it first, perhaps on his way to us, but it will be a more difficult plum to pick."

"He's right," Vara said quietly, eyes pointed into the middle distance, staring at the fabric wall of the tent. "There is no richer target in Arkaria than Pharesia. Why, he could stand on the deck of an airship and cast his spell, putting the whole city to death in mere minutes like Reikonos instead of having to chase his way around sprawling suburbs that go for many miles. I saw Termina with my own eyes – it is five times the size it was when I grew up there."

"Fine, I accept your premise," Cyrus said, balling his hand into a fist. "What private agreement do you seek from me?"

"None of us would countenance Malpravus to win," Dioro said, and here it seemed as though he might be squirming with discomfort, his eyes on the ground. "I hope that is apparent. But in order to mobilize the sort of assistance you are asking for...it leaves us in an uncomfortable predicament."

"Because you feel you are the greatest target," Vara said, her eyes narrowing once more. He had a sneaking suspicion the word 'coward' lurked somewhere upon her tongue, ready to leap out.

"Because we will not defeat him alone, none of us," Dioro said, and his withered hands worked the staff. "Anyone who can cast the spell that consumed Reikonos is beyond any of us, even the elders. And we are diminished, obviously – perhaps not as much, magically, as the others, but considerably, still, from even five centuries ago when this hobbling of magic began." He shook his head slowly. "Coupled with our population woes, our shrinking borders..." He licked his parched lips.

"I am neither wise or long-lived as you," Cyrus said, "nor am I subtle in my ways. Say plain what you want from me; dance around the topic and I may miss your meaning, and you will not get what you want."

Dioro hesitated, looking quite stricken. "I want you to defend Pharesia."

"There are five city-states at this conference," Vara said, outraged on all their behalves. "You would have us forsake the rest in order to–"

"No," Dioro hissed, looking around the tent as if someone had snuck in behind them. He lowered his voice, composed himself, and spoke again. "You misunderstand. I would give you...everything. Anything. All you ask, even." He cleared his throat, and looked remarkably pale. "All our soldiers. All our mages. Our airships, our motorcars, our gold – all at your disposal."

"To defend Pharesia?" Cyrus asked, squinting at the elf. "You want me to–"

"No." Dioro shook his gray head furiously. "To do with as you like. To allocate where you feel they must go, from Termina to Amti to...Emerald, if you feel it best," and here he shuddered, looking quite pained. "What I ask is that you...you yourself, with none of your other people...you come to Pharesia and pledge yourself to defend it."

"How does it help you to have one warrior defend the city if we take all your other forces elsewhere?" Vara asked. "He's barely even a mage at this point, what do you expect him to do against Malpravus by his lonesome?"

"Little," Dioro said, looking a bit gray around the gills. "But that's hardly the point. We'll all be dead if Malpravus has his way, it's just Pharesia will go first. But I don't want you there because I think you can beat him yourself." The elf swallowed deeply, obviously, almost painfully. "It's because...if you're going to take all our troops, all our mages, all our resources elsewhere...you can't leave our people hopeless. That's what I want you for. Not any staunch defense you might put up with sword and pistol..."

"But the hope that comes from having Cyrus Davidon at your walls when the cataclysm comes," Vara said, glancing at Cyrus, who felt a strange rumbling deep in his gut. "So they will feel as though they are not being thrown to the wolves while we take their troops elsewhere for the real fight."

"Exactly," Dioro said, and his voice rattled in his chest, and again he swallowed, and looked so...small. "I will give you everything I have, even down to my fellow council members to put wherever on this board you would like for the defense of Arkaria. But I ask this from you, I *need* this from you...hope, for my people, who have long lacked it. And the hope you would not sacrifice yourself if you intend to sacrifice us," the elder elf said, and, his message delivered, he looked ready to collapse in on himself, "the few of my dying people who still remain in these lands."

CHAPTER 9

*A*fter Dioro had left, after a few minutes of contemplation of
his offer, Cyrus remembered the envelope that had come in
with the elf and opened it. A short missive waited within, but it sent
both he and Vara scrambling for their armor.

MEET IN THE TENT BEFORE THE MORNING SESSION – WE NEED
TO COUNCIL.
-ALARIC

Hurrying through the camp, they found the sun shining down on
the evenly ordered tents, and drew stares of reverence and whispers
of interest as they walked. Cyrus tried to nod and acknowledge
everyone he passed who watched him or said hello, but their haste
was obvious enough to make every person in their path steer wide of
them; when he thrust open the flap of the great tent at the center of
the conference grounds, he found to his surprise–

"You're late," Vaste said, at the center of a knot composed of the
same quartet he'd surrounded himself with since arriving: Qualleron,
that immense, armored troll with the pleasant countenance, the
woman, Aemma, who was only a head shorter than Cyrus, which was

a rare thing in his experience, Merrish – whose appearance and nod at Vara made him tense – and that servant Glaven who trailed Vaste everywhere now. Somehow less obsequious than the steward of his own mansion on Ilanar Hill, Greenan, he couldn't help but feel Vaste had, by far, gotten the better end of that deal. "That means you owe each of us a kiss. I'll take mine–"

"If you say 'on the plump yet succulent arse,' I will kick you squarely in it," Vara said, brushing some dust off her shoulder as she stepped into the shadowy dark of the tent.

"Does he ever not talk about his arse?" This from Pamyra, who stood clotted with Shirri and Hiressam, along with Calene. Strange that they were all starting to divide along the lines they'd used when separated in the fall of Reikonos.

"Seldom," Alaric said, and he was grouped with Mazirin, Guy in his grubby clothing, and that other fellow whom Cyrus had met only briefly, Edouard. He had a shy look about him, and scarcely made eye contact.

"He always said it was his most valuable attribute," said Longwell in a scratchy voice. He stood, a bit sunken-eyed, beside Alixa Weltan and Isabelle, who stood slightly away from them beside Ryin, who was clad in his runed robes. A most curious grouping.

"It beats the hell out of the little he carries in his purse." Cyrus turned to find Aisling and Baynvyn sitting in the shadows, the Niamh scourge lying flat on the ground beside them, her head perked up at Cyrus's entry. He acknowledged her with a nod, and she put her head down again, but kept a watchful eye upon them. He made a mental note to thank her later for not following him back to his tent.

"I see that the purpose of this meeting is to make sport of me and my glorious arse," Vaste huffed. "Very well. We can endure your jealousy-spurred calumnies and stand ready to take all attacks, physical or verbal."

"That is not why I summoned you all here," Alaric said, stepping into the center of the circled tables.

"Though it would be a much easier fight than the one you mean to direct," Ryin said, shuffling his way forward. "Can I just say..." He glanced around, and a faint smile appeared on his thin lips, "...it is a pleasure to see those of you again who have long been missing. Regardless of the circumstances." He looked right at Vaste. "Even your green and disagreeable arse."

"I must ask," Merrish said, glancing around the (rather large) circle, "why are we meeting now, in advance of the meeting?"

"This was supposed to be more of an 'officers and members of Sanctuary' meeting," Alaric said, sounding a bit grumbly to Cyrus's ears. "But you are welcome, since Vaste invited you. And the purpose should be plain – to devise an end to the threat Malpravus represents to all our peoples."

Cyrus felt himself sag a bit. "I must admit...I struggle more than a little with how to defeat Malpravus."

"Are you jesting?" Vaste asked. "You killed the God of War, remember?"

"I recall it well," Cyrus said with some irony, feeling Vara's hand upon his forearm, "looking into his red eyes as they faded for the last time." He drew himself to his full height, as though that summoned some additional authority. "But that fight is not this one, and to treat it the same would be folly."

"But are not the problems the same?" Aisling asked, rising from her place in the shadows. "Malpravus is becoming a god like the old ones, is he not?"

"Yes and no, I think," Cyrus said. "He has an army of scourge, first of all, and should he do something like, oh, I don't know – conjure a bridge to complete the one that stretches halfway across the Perda in Termina, his godly self will become only one of a host of problems we cannot solve."

Calene shuddered visibly and made a slight groaning sound. "I was there at the last evacuation, when we said our farewells at the crater of old Sanctuary and let the scourge have the east. The thought of that ravening horde coming across..." She shuddered again, and it lacked theatricality.

"So he has a dead army," Vaste said. "That's bad, sure. But you know what's worse? Him being godly. Kill him, his army is released, and we're back to status quo ante, with the scourge over there and the people over here. Problem solved."

"Maybe," Cyrus said, letting go of Vara's hand. "But if he manages to bring them across the Perda, even if we kill him...the game is over. Arkaria is finished."

"So we take the fight to him," Vara said. "Pull out all the tricks you used on Bellarum and the other gods – black lace, cessation spells–"

"A bounty of godly weapons that we cram up his bony non-magnificent arse," Vaste said.

"You have airships now," Mazirin said, speaking up at last from her position behind Alaric, her accent strong. "You can bombard him at a distance, turn him into a puddle of blood."

Cyrus shook his head slowly. "I don't know the exact details, but last time we fought Malpravus, he had a hardened exterior, like an exoskeleton."

"It was his godly magic," Alaric said, a bit hoarsely. "Something that is not stopped by a cessation spell, and a blade coated in black lace will do nothing to it save perhaps chip away, because you will not be able to put the poison into his bloodstream, where it would dilute his power."

"The old bag of bones studied us well," Vaste said. "He's aware of what happened to Bellarum. In fact, I think we could easily argue he gave us a harder fight on an individual level than Bellarum did once we broke past his army."

"Because Bellarum was trying to use the God of Evil's magic against me," Cyrus said, pulling the medallion out from under his armor, "but it was stopped by Sanctuary. Had he focused on more conventional magics or a physical offense he might have given a better accounting of himself."

"But Malpravus has gotta be bloody swimming in the magic of Sanctuary, don't he?" Guy spoke up at last, nosing his way forward into the conversation. He looked like a changed man since Cyrus had first laid eyes upon him, and even Vara seemed surprised at his appearance. He looked thinner and less weaselly, the light of the torches giving his face a healthy glow and his chin possessing a determined set that had been absent before.

"Not that it matters anymore," Vaste said, "what with Sanctuary being dead and all."

"I think it very likely he is filled with Sanctuary's – and by extension, the God of Good's – magic, however that works," Alaric said, nodding slowly. "But...I must dispel one notion you seem to have, my friends." And, lifting his hand, Alaric slowly moved his wrist in a wave—

—and it disappeared into a cloud of mist, along with the rest of him, reforming seconds later after drawing a gasp from Shirri.

"Sanctuary is not dead," Alaric said, his smile resolving back out of the etherial mist that had given the Ghost his name. "It is simply back in the ether again, waiting until we find a way for it to be withdrawn."

CHAPTER 10

SHIRRI

She couldn't help but gasp, not once she saw what Alaric had done. The air felt thick and heavy around her, and her eyes fixated on Alaric's arm as it passed back into ethereal mist and his eyes locked onto hers – just for a moment after he made his pronouncement.

"How, Alaric?" Cyrus asked, the tall warrior's eyes narrow as he stared into the dark of the tent. Shirri watched him, but said nothing. "If Malpravus drained Sanctuary–"

"Much like Bellarum's attack on Sanctuary, I do not believe the thing was completed," Alaric said. "Sanctuary has some element of sentience, after all–"

"We heard its voice when we were rousted to help Shirri," Vara said, looking right at her and making Shirri's cheeks burn. "'Save her,' it said."

"About me?" Shirri's cheeks burned even hotter, like someone had cast a fire spell before her. "Sanctuary said that?"

"When you invoked the Plea of the Dying," Pamyra said, her brow puckered in concentration. "But then...can we not just attempt to summon it back now, here?"

Alaric shook his head slowly. "It is, unfortunately, not that simple."

"Naturally," Vaste said. "A powerful weapon against our enemy exists, so of course there's a quest or something complicated required to bring it back to us. And surely not something joyful, like us all dancing around in a circle or some such."

"Sanctuary has life energy, just as the rest of us do," Alaric said. "Malpravus sapped nearly all of it in his quest to ascend, leaving Sanctuary barely alive, trapped in the ether, unable to physically manifest while it tries to recover. If left to its own devices, this is a process that could take...well, I don't even know how long." He looked around the tent. "Without some sort of effort at interceding on Sanctuary's behalf...it will remain in the ether, locked away from our use...possibly forever."

CHAPTER 11

VASTE

A silence hung over them all for a few moments, and when it was broken, to Vaste's own surprise, it was him, and it was not with a joke. "There's something that's been bothering me," he said, and every eye swiveled to him.

"The continued existence of squirrels?" Vara asked, blue eyes glittering with amusement. She had a slightly sweaty look about her, and Vaste felt a quiver of distaste. That'd be Cyrus's doing, naturally. Damn them both, having joy in one another.

"That too, but it's a lower-order worry – for now," Vaste said. "Once we get rid of Malpravus it's back to worrying about squirrels full time. Did I tell you what I saw when the Machine thugs die in Reikonos?"

"Blood," Guy offered. "Blood and perhaps a bit o' unseemly cryin'?" He glanced around. "What? I'm just guessin.'"

"Yes, also that, I suppose," Vaste said. "But I mean after they died – their souls were dragged from their place of death, a place they normally would have inhabited for minutes, hours or even years postmortem – to the Citadel." A variety of reactions greeted this news; clear disgust from Vara to wincing distaste from Alaric. "He was pulling a Mortus, I'm afraid, at least in that place. Feeding his magic with purloined dead before he finally got hasty and decided to make everyone dead immediately, the better to enjoy the benefits of their magical energy now."

"Well, as you pointed out," Cyrus said, slowly, into the quiet that followed that proclamation, "he's now killed them all, and surely the ones he took in the great spell outweigh the gradually dying he absorbed before so...what does that matter?"

"All that magic he stole has to pool somewhere," Vaste said. "Somewhere in him. It sits there until he's ready to use it, like a magical bladder...I think." He did a little wincing of his own.

"This seems important," Alaric said. "If there is some reservoir within him that holds his power—"

"Then if we're going to kill him, it would be extremely helpful if we drained it first, yes," Vaste said. "And furthermore, cut him off from being able to absorb the life of any of our own that die during the battle."

"Yes, I would like to not be soul-eaten during the battle," Shirri said.

"What you're talking about are long-dead magics," Isabelle said, gliding forward into the conversation for the first time. "Necromancy was always a frowned-upon branch of spellcraft, barely taught in Arkaria when the leagues were in control. After they were destroyed by...someone," and here she politely coughed in the direction of Cyrus, who frowned, "that entire area of study didn't exactly flourish. This was before the fall of magic, obviously."

"The leagues tried desperately to control such inquiry," Alaric said. "It was a fond wish of the gods that no one follow in their footsteps. I recall them working particularly hard to squeeze the number of necromancers trained down to a very low number, something on the order of two or three a year, and only in Saekaj by the time Sanctuary came along. I think we all now wish they had stopped much earlier."

"Necromantic studies ended in elvendom much earlier than that," Ryin said, with a swish of his robes as he stepped forth. Something about him itched Vaste; he seemed less likely to argue for the sake of it, he was calmer somehow. "They never really took to it, being life-worshippers, but the practice was banned about three or four thousand years ago. That said..." he had a bit of a smile, "...after the fall of the leagues, I promise you some of these old elven mages like Dioro...they dabbled."

"In necromancy?" Pamyra asked, sounding a little shocked.

"I could see that," Isabelle said, looking thoughtful, the lines on her face seeming much deeper than when Vaste had seen her last, a thousand years before. "When the leagues were destroyed, there was a bit of a renaissance in magic across elvendom. A great deal of exploration, of inward searching, crossover, if you will. Necromancy could certainly have been a sudden area of interest, especially after Vidara betrayed us in the Realm of War."

"We need to speak with someone who knows more of these things," Vaste said. "Dioro, his council–"

"They are the foremost remaining mages in all the world," Pamyra said confidently.

"That is not entirely true," Mazirin said, stepping into the circle of conversation from where she'd been hanging back. "There is still a branch of mysticism alive in Azwill across the sea that endures to this day. Their religion has a strong focus on the dead and lingering spirits. They have mystic shamans that specialize in what you speak of."

"Yes, but Azwill is many thousands of miles to the west," Pamyra said, "so they're not in easy reach, even by airship."

Mazirin nodded. "It is seven days' flight to their eastern shores. To their western coast would be another three or four."

"A journey of weeks, then," Alaric said, calculating all this. "Weeks we do not have, especially when Dioro or perhaps one of the other mages here might be able to answer Vaste's inquiries. This strikes me as a most crucial question – how do we pry that magical reservoir away from Malpravus's bony grasp? For without it, he would be much more vulnerable."

"Without magic to swell his body, strengthen his blows, or burn us to ash," Cyrus said ruefully, "I might be able to kill him myself." Vara clanked a gauntlet against his side, looking daggers at him. "Or you can. Whoever. I want the bastard dead, I'm not particular about how it happens."

"So long as it doesn't unleash the scourge upon the surviving fraction of Arkaria," Alaric warned darkly.

"Yes, please don't do that," Alixa Weltan said. "I have a question – about all of this, really. The dead, the living, how it all interacts...I once knew someone who could see the dead as you say you can." She looked to Vaste, curiosity smoldering in her eyes. "Has this Malpravus been absorbing everyone who has been dying? Everyone the world over?"

"No," Vaste said, feeling curiously grateful for the question. "His reach only extended as far as Reikonos, thankfully."

"Is there a way," and now Baynvyn – Blue Cyrus Jr., as Vaste had taken to thinking of him – said, "to stab Malpravus perhaps, put a tap into him the way syrup makers might do to a tree, to drain that magic out of him?"

"I would really like to know," Vaste said. "Thus...I bring it up to all of you." He looked around the circle; gosh, there were a lot of them, and a great many shrugs. Not one person seemed to have an answer. "Fine. I'll ask Dioro, then. He seems the forthcoming sort, doesn't he? I'm sure he'll answer in no time, and with zero reluctance."

"He will," Cyrus said, nodding. "Because this morning Dioro came to us," and here he nodded at Vara, "and committed everything Pharesia has to offer to our cause."

This produced a great moment of quiet. "Truly?" Alaric asked, his eyebrows creeping up his forehead. "That is wonderful news, brother, and unexpected–"

"There's a catch," Alixa breathed. "Trust me – with these elves, there's always a catch."

"He will give us everything," Cyrus said, nodding slowly, "provided I – and only I – remain in Pharesia to act as their defense. And their propaganda tool to keep the masses confident and pliant. Every soldier, every mage, every airship, every piece of equipment they have is at our disposal provided I stay here to defend Pharesia."

"This is going to sound strange coming from me," Pamyra said, her lips pursing between sentences, "but I'm not sure that's a fair bargain."

"Nor am I," Vara said, "for if he stays, I will be remaining with Cyrus as well." And she shot him a look before landing a hand – annoyingly gently – on Cyrus's side, and the two exchanged a look of love that made Vaste want to heave up the succulent porridge he'd had for breakfast.

"Why would you stay here, Cyrus?" Alaric asked, frowning. "You need to be mobile to counter Malpravus. We have no idea where he might strike next; is not the more likely point of impact at Termina?"

"I'm not sure that's true," Cyrus said. "Dioro makes a compelling point – that the life-years here in Pharesia are very tightly centered on a smaller city footprint, and each elf within its walls has thousands of years of life ahead of them."

"He makes sense," Merrish spoke up at last from just behind Vaste's shoulder. He had his arms folded, but was nodding along. "If you were to pick a target ripe for the plucking, Pharesia does outweigh Termina."

"But won't he be bringing across the scourge?" Calene asked, weighing in at last. She had been so silent, Vaste had nearly forgotten she was there. Gone was the thin, cringing slip of a ranger she'd been. Now she bore scars on the face that gave her a rough look, and her voice was cool and strong in its questioning nature, hints of iron behind it. "Isn't that his plan, to unleash them upon us like he did on Saekaj?"

"We don't know his plans," Alaric said, folding his own arms across his breastplate. "He waits, for example. Why has he not attacked yet? Where does he lurk with his scourge, why are they out of sight of the airships crisscrossing eastern Arkaria coming in from Coricuanthi and Amatgarosa?"

"He would not simply sit idle," Cyrus said. "He's planning something, doing something to add to his own strength." He glanced with some concern toward Aisling. "Hopefully it doesn't involve tunneling into Saekaj Sovar so he can drain them, because there's more life there than in Pharesia."

"If I know Terian," Aisling said, her voice a little papery, scratchy, age having settled hard upon her face, "he'll be doing everything he can to make sure there's lots of stone between Malpravus and the people of Saekaj Sovar. He'll be ordering tunnels dug in inconvenient places, possibly even over to this side of the Perda."

"Can...can he do that?" Vaste asked. "The Perda is many hundreds of miles from Saekaj or Sovar."

"We had a lot of time underground with nothing to do but tunnel," Aisling said dryly. "We've actually reached the Perda on several occasions. Unfortunately the tunnels were never quite deep enough, and the river came flooding in. We managed to blow them closed before significant drainage occurred. We never had cause to try again," and here she nodded at Ryin, "after building the tower."

"I want to know about this tower," Vara said, looking from Aisling to Ryin. "As I understand it, it held the scourge at bay–"

"It held the mindless scourge at bay," Cyrus amended. "Like the Perda. It couldn't hold back a concerted effort by the scourge under Malpravus's command, and neither can the Perda, again begging the question – why isn't he here already?"

"He must have some more succulent target at hand," Alaric said, and now he looked to Ryin. "Brother...you are a man of great power, as I understand it."

Ryin raised an eyebrow slightly. "I am a man who has power in certain arenas. Holding off an army of 'mindless scourge' as Cyrus put it...this I can do." He nodded at the warrior. "As to the sapping of magic...I have no more insight than the rest of you. Magic is not what it once was. It has become weak, and it takes much power to produce a middling result."

"Hold on a minute," Merrish said, looking at Vaste rather accusingly, "you made a flame the size of a building and nearly dropped it on my platoon only weeks ago – and that was after force blasting us down the ruin of the Grand Span." He looked to Ryin. "How does that jibe with your talk of the hobbling of magic?"

"It doesn't." Ryin's eyebrows rose rather precipitously as he looked to Vaste. "Is this true?"

"It is," Vaste said, a dim sense of awkward recognition coming over him, "I was able to do that, and surprisingly easily. But when in Reikonos, I could barely cast a healing spell."

"So...there's a distance effect?" Shirri asked. "Distance from Reikonos?"

"Perhaps a bit," Ryin said, folding his arms in front of him. "I haven't been close to Reikonos in years. My magic is still greatly diminished, though, so even if there is a distance factor, the overall hobbling remains."

"Does this mean someone constrained magic specifically around Reikonos?" Alaric asked. "Or more heavily around Reikonos? And if so...does this mean we have an ally in the fight against Malpravus that we do not yet know? Someone keeping him from achieving his full magical potential?"

"Wouldn't that be nice?" Vaste asked. "I remember what it was like having friends. Oh, right," he added, looking at Alaric, Vara, and Cyrus all in turn. "I missed you so very much."

"You're still thinking we owe you gold for that Malpravus wager, don't you?" Cyrus asked.

"Hah!" Vaste said, pointing Letum at him. "So you admit it!"

"Shhh," Vara said, holding up a single finger. Her head was cocked, her pointed ear prominent in the tent's semi-darkness. "Someone's coming."

A moment later the flap swung open at the push of a staff, and in strode Dioro, taking assessment of the crowd in the tent swiftly. "It would appear you've decided to have a meeting before the meeting" he said, a bit archly, "and left the rest of us out."

CHAPTER 12

VASTE

"This isn't what it looks like," Cyrus said, trying to get ahead of Dioro's umbrage. It was true, they were meeting here, in advance, not so much as a delegate in sight and yet the representatives of Saekaj, Termina, Emerald, and Amti were all present.

"Oh, don't patronize him," Vaste said, standing tall and nearly brushing his head against the slope of the tent ceiling. "Of course it's what it looks like – the old officers of Sanctuary discussing what's to be done in comfortable company, including what do with his offer."

Dioro raised a bushy gray eyebrow to that. "The representatives of Pharesia might take insult at being excluded from such discussion."

"That was not our intent," Alaric said, also on his feet, and sounding eminently cautious. Reasonable, even, like he was addressing a very angry dog and trying to soothe him.

"Really, the man is nearing six thousand years old," Vaste said. "Let's just cut the bullroar, shall we? Merrish – is Termina in on this fight against Malpravus?"

Merrish, who had been listening quietly up until now, face half-shrouded in shadow, looked as though Vaste had slapped him, singling him out in this manner. "Wha – well, yes."

"All your armies?" Vaste asked. "All your materiel of war?"

"Yes," Merrish said, nodding, his arms still folded in front of him, looking just a bit confused.

"Great," Vaste said, then turned to Alixa, who stood next to Long-well, resplendent in shining, silken green blouse and pants. "Is Emerald committed to this fight in the same way?"

"Whatever it takes," Alixa said.

"Is Saekaj willing to pledge to the fight?" Vaste asked, looking at Aisling now.

"Of course," Aisling said, rasping a touch. Baynvyn, beside her, wrinkled his forehead slightly but nodded along.

"And Amti?" Now Vaste turned to Gareth, who had been cradling his bowler hat, standing beside the trelf Birstis.

"We are in this fight," Gareth said, his voice sounding a bit small. "With you."

"Wonderful," Vaste said, and now turned back to Dioro, who was frowning, very near scowling. "Now, if we give you Cyrus to parade about in your city like the old war horse, you're willing to give us all your support? Every drop of it?"

"Yes," Dioro said, face relaxing a touch.

"Sold," Vaste said, and reached out with Letum to clank Cyrus on the back plate, which sent a touch of a sting rattling through his armor, making Cyrus frown at the troll. "Now – perhaps we can talk about something truly important–"

"That's it, then?" Alixa spoke up. "Four hours of discussion yesterday, all the tricks of diplomacy, all the efforts this past month, and a troll hammers out an agreement in less than a minute?"

"I'm a very gifted troll," Vaste said. "Which you would know if you'd ever looked at–"

"Vaste," Alaric said, shaking his head.

"Fine," Vaste said, and refocused his attention upon Dioro, who had left the tent flap slightly ajar. Light streamed in behind the man. "I need to ask you about necromancy. Specifically, how does Malpravus's magic work? How does magic get stored in us? And how might we pry away the magic of the dead which is fueling him?"

Dioro seemed to squirm a bit. "That is not...a...a proper area of study. I wouldn't even know where to begin with that, the necromancy, life-stealing bit."

"We don't have time for squeamishness, man," Vaste said. "He's planning on using that unseemly business to drink us all dry of our own magic and our lives. We need to cure him of it, if possible, and part of that comes down to depriving him of the ability to rip souls out of bodies with spells. Have any of your people experimented with that branch of magic? And if not, why are you lying to us?"

"We experimented plenty when the strictures around magic fell," Dioro said, exasperation breaking loose from his voice, "but there was not an abundance of expertise at hand. So, yes, we studied old volumes, we did things, looked into things – but only a few hundred years, and made little progress. More promising avenues opened, though, and then magic began to diminish, and so any experimentation into that branch became less than useless. It simply isn't done in Pharesia, I'm sorry." He huffed, and seemed to try and draw himself up. "Now, the magical reservoir question – well, that I know a bit more about, but I'm afraid I don't have good answers for you; the only way I know of to drain a person's magical energy is for them to cast a spell or for you to kill them. That is it."

"Damn," Vaste said. "That was a comprehensive no."

"'Ang on a minute," Guy said, pushing his way forward. "Do you know any Azwill mystics? Those death studiers from the west?"

"I know what an Azwill mystic is," Dioro said. His gaze softened and his face became thoughtful behind the wrinkles. "And yes, I've met one or two personally who have traveled through on the way to Firoba, or who just came on a pilgrimage of their own. They are quite versed in magics, probably some of the few remaining on the planet who are." He nodded slowly. "Yes...yes, they might have answers to your necromantic questions, I could see that."

"Wonderful," Vaste said. "Unfortunately, they're quite a distance away–"

"Are you sure about that?" This came from Birstis, the trelf, and he was easing his way past Merrish. "Because I've heard rumors that Azwill mystics are visiting the old troll lands."

Dioro's face wrinkled in concentration. "Oh."

That seemed to suck all the air out of the tent. "'Oh?'" Vaste asked. "'Oh' what?!"

"It could be true," Dioro said, smoothing his vestments, that archaic piece of clothing dating back to the leagues. "See, there was a troll shaman who lived there some thousand years ago–"

"Yes, I know," Vaste said, snippily, "he was my mentor, Oroguuk, and he taught me all I know about seeing death – and saved my life."

"Well, when the humans decided to remove the trolls," Dioro said, "Oroguuk and a few survivors managed to get out by boat. They sailed down the coast and made landfall at the port of Darnassis – Pharesia's port. They requested haven–"

"Tell me you gave it to them," Vaste said.

"It wasn't mine to grant," Dioro said. "And so they sailed west, toward the then-rumored land past the sunset. They must have made it, for when I talked with the Azwill mystics one of them mentioned Oroguuk. He remained with them for some time, I suppose, training some of them, training with them – I don't know. There was some kind of bargain. Perhaps he still lives in the swamp ruins, I wouldn't know. Perhaps with some Azwillian mystics. I have heard rumor of them coming out to trade with the men of the north."

"I've heard those rumors, too," Aemma said. "They dwell in peace there. But the mystics are human, only, and Azwillian. No trolls, only men, and I don't think they've been seen in some time. They exist beyond the habitable spaces, in the misty, uninhabitable bogs."

"If they had a troll among them, they'd be wise not to bring him to town," Vaste said, and his face wavered. "I could see him surviving, that one. Oroguuk was...clever. And wise. And likely feeding on the dead a bit himself, if he lived until the trolls were wiped out." He clapped his massive hands together. "That seals it – I have to go north and seek these mystics."

"What do you hope to learn from them, brother?" Alaric asked.

"I hope to learn from them some way of prising the cold, dead souls out of Malpravus's cold, dead hands," Vaste said, filling a new determination. "Because unless I do, we're going into a fight with the most powerful sorcerer in the world with our magical hands tied behind our backs."

CHAPTER 13

CYRUS

"Wait, you can't leave," Cyrus said, his mouth suddenly feeling very dry. "Vaste – Malpravus is coming." He felt the weight of his armor upon his back, the draw of his brows knitting together in worry.

The troll turned to him, brushing away tent fabric that sagged down to his forehead. "Cyrus – surely you must realize that if we fight Malpravus now, without even the benefit of Curatio's spellcraft...we will die."

"He's right," Vara said. Her hand was gently upon the bracer covering his wrist, and she tugged it, as if stirring him out of his shock. "We could all stand together outside Pharesia right now, armies behind us, and if Malpravus came–"

"We'd all fall down," Alaric said. "We need strategies, things to use against him."

"We have armies," Merrish said.

"Our armies will not be enough," Aisling said in her raspy voice. "They might work to hold back the scourge for a time, but that is all, and it will be a meatgrinder of death if we're forced to use them in that way." She glanced at the Ghost, then Vaste. "We need tricks. We need cleverness. We need–"

61

"A new way forward," Vara said, nodding at the dark elf. "But those armies may still be needed, if the scourge cross the Perda."

"Well, you have our army," Dioro said, looking at Cyrus. "If we have your assistance."

Cyrus felt the weight within him. "If we receive word that Termina or Emerald are attacked...will you hold me in place here, at Pharesia? When the battle is clearly going to fall elsewhere?"

Dioro shook his head. "No. In fact we would give you use of our fastest airship and speed you to the fight." His eyes danced. "This is not a death pact, Lord Davidon. My people are older and wiser than your short-lived ones, and many remember a thousand years ago when we left ourselves unguarded to the dark elves and the only thing that saved us from calamity was Cyrus Davidon."

"Like Sir Vaste the Wry or Lady Aisling the Crafty weren't even there," Vaste groused.

"I'll stay," Cyrus said, causing Vara to intake a sharp breath. "If those are your conditions...I will make my preparations to fight from here, and leap upon your fast airship at the first sound of trouble from elsewhere." He looked around the dim tent, and saw Alaric nod his approval. "Someone will need to cover Termina, Emerald, Amti..."

"The north," Aemma said, looking at Vaste. "If you mean to go up there, to the swamps, you'll be passing through the north. Can I prevail upon you to let me speak to the men of those lands, try to involve them in this?"

"I don't...actually know how I'm going to get there," Vaste said, looking at Alaric. "Uh...can I borrow your airship?"

"Actually," Qualleron spoke up, that rumbling mountain of a yellow troll, "I was hoping to borrow an airship myself. But my destination is in the opposite direction – south, and toward a cause that will, I hope, help us all."

CHAPTER 14

ALARIC

The tent became terribly quiet all at once. A strong undercurrent of whispers had been going throughout all the talks, but now they were stilled in favor of Qualleron's request. "What need did you have of an airship, Qualleron?" Alaric asked. "Are you leaving us?"

"No," Qualleron's big head swung wide, "I seek to reinforce your...forces." The troll's big brow furrowed. "Your language is strange. Anyhow," and he seemed troubled no more, "I have been trying for some weeks now to send a telegraph message to Firoba, but have been informed the lines are down somewhere in the southern mountains."

"A tele...what?" Cyrus asked.

"Telegraph," Calene piped up. "It's a message sent through these metal wires draped high on poles throughout the land. You can write out a message here in Pharesia, for instance, and they can read it in Termina in less than an hour."

"Well, that's...handy," Cyrus said. "Did anyone try that with those men up north?"

"They ignored our messages," Alixa said.

"I wish to inform the brothers of my order – an ancient and august company of knights – that honor and battle is still to be found in this world," Qualleron said, his massive chest swelling with pride or excitement, "and that they should come immediately for a great and final campaign against the Grand Archon of Deceit, Malpravus. That here we will nobly save the soul of this world."

"I should attempt to get a message to my people in Firoba as well," Mazirin said. "I have not heard from Dugras though I sent him to Xiaoshani to deliver my report. Whether they ignored him or are debating, I should weigh in as well."

"Why not just send an airship message?" Cyrus asked, squinting at them both. "Airships are going out daily to Coricuanthi, to Amatgarosa. If these lines are down, I mean."

Mazirin bristled. "I would not trust a freighter airship crew with this message, nor am I likely to receive a reply in a timely manner. And the lines are apparently down somewhere in the valleys south of Amti, but before the city of Balaar, that last outpost at the tip of the continent where the strait divides your land from Firoba."

"It's true," Gareth said, sighing, twirling his odd bowler hat with true dexterity between his fingers. "The lines are down. I'd hoped they have been fixed by now, but sometimes this happens. It's a long line, after all. Lots of ground to cover."

"If you want my order's help – and there are hundreds of us," Qualleron said, "I need to get a message at least as far south as Balaar. If it can get to Firoba, the message will make its way from there."

"The same with mine," Mazirin said when Alaric looked at her. "There are embassies of Amatgarosa there that will spread the word as appropriate, and perhaps we might get some Imperial assistance as well."

"Imperial assistance would be lovely," Hiressam muttered; he'd been in the shadows, silent, all this time. "Even Malpravus would surely shudder at facing down an Amatgarosan air squadron."

"Then we've got two different airship needs, and going in two different directions," Vaste said, his big brow furrowed.

"And you've got two airships," Aisling said, slipping her way into the conversation. "Well, more if you want to count the Pharesian ones." She looked up at the big troll. "Why don't I give you a ride, big fellow?"

"As long as it's not the kind you gave Cyrus," Vara muttered. "Because that kind tends to produce great troubles a thousand years hence." Aisling just rolled her eyes.

"Hey, I've come around," Baynvyn said, his spectacles pushed up on his forehead.

"It would seem I'm captaining the southbound ship to Balaar, then," Mazirin said, after Vaste had nodded assent to Aisling's proposal.

"And I'll be going north," Vaste said, nodding to Aisling. Aemma slipped in beside him, a hard thing for a woman so tall, yet she did it with admirable grace. The group was dividing already, becoming their own formations as Qualleron and Mazirin stood together, Cyrus and Vara in their own small party.

Alaric looked to the blinking Shirri, and spoke. "There is another task that needs to be done, and I think it is you who must spearhead it."

Shirri was suddenly wide-eyed. "Me? What? And why?"

"Because someone needs to make an effort to bring Sanctuary back out of the ether..." Alaric said with great certainty, "...and you are the only one here who has done that in recent memory."

CHAPTER 15

SHIRRI

"I don't understand," Shirri said, every eye in the tent looking uncomfortably upon her, "what do you expect me to do?"

"Have to admit, I don't get it, either, Alaric," Cyrus said, the light streaming in through the tent's side on the warrior in black. "Shirri summoned Sanctuary once, when it was healthy and ready to be summoned. What do you expect her to do now, with it wounded and hiding in the ether like an injured dog?"

The old knight let a slow smile creep across his face. "I expect her to undertake a journey. A quest, if you will."

"But why me?" Shirri asked, the question just bubbling up out of her nervous stomach. "Why not you, Alaric?"

"Yeah, you're gonna leave the important work of trying to bring Sanctuary back to this lil' waif?" Guy Harysan spoke in the voice of Shirri's own heart, disbelief bordering on shock.

"Certainly not, Guy," Alaric said, with a smile that, on anyone else, might have appeared mischievous. "At least, not to Shirri alone. You, for example, should go with her."

"I – whut now?" Guy did a double take.

"You will need to return to the ashes of Reikonos," Alaric said. "Where I believe you left behind your medallion."

"Hid it," Shirri said, squinting at Alaric, then shaking her head. "But yes. Why do I need the medallion, though?" She pointed a small finger at Cyrus. "He already has one."

"I do," Cyrus said, reaching under his breastplate to bring up the medallion. He offered it to Alaric, and the knight took it.

"We have already tried this, Cyrus," Alaric said. "In its wounded form, more needs to be done to conjure Sanctuary than simply mouthing the prayer at this point. Consider how it is summoned."

"The Plea of the Dying?" Pamyra asked. "What does that have to do with going back to Reikonos?"

"It's a quest for Sanctuary, then?" Hiressam asked, his hand on the hilt of his long sword.

"Precisely," Alaric said. "My own attempts to resummon Sanctuary have yielded no result, for I am not about to die, nor is anyone here." He glanced about. "There is urgency, but not desperation, hence it continues to protect itself by remaining in the ether. Yet it watches. Sanctuary waits."

"I'm feeling a bit desperate at the moment, mate," Guy said.

"As am I, but I don't want this responsibility," Shirri said, feeling her voice crack at the weight of all the eyes that swiveled to her when she spoke. "This sounds far too important for someone who has just come to the company of late."

Alaric locked his lone eye upon her. "It is in the proper hands, and I think it best to leave it there."

She tried to speak again, against this foolishness, but Shirri could not find her voice. The eyes traveled away, on to the next speaker and next topic, but Shirri remained quietly in their midst, wishing she could scream at this terrible task that had, somehow, been handed to her, sure she would fail them all.

CHAPTER 16

CYRUS

"Is that it, then?" Cyrus asked quietly. They'd divided amongst themselves, a strange drift as members of their company felt pulled as if by gravity to one of the four distinct groups that had formed in their midst. "We finally make it back together after a month apart, a month sundered by the destruction of Reikonos, and after a day we part again?"

"We are united in purpose," Alaric said, voice cutting through the quiet of the tent. "Divided in body, because much must be done before we clash again with Malpravus. We cannot remain camped around Pharesia, hoping he comes with conventional armies you can maneuver against and destroy on the field. We already know he won't, for his pool of magic and his limitless supply of scourge wait to be unleashed upon us, to overwhelm like breaking waves upon the shore."

"I can't think of any party of people anywhere I'd trust as much as this lot," Calene said, sweeping the burnt remain of her cloak off her shoulder. "If there's to be a chance to defeat this world-ending threat, well..." She looked quietly, piercingly, at Cyrus. "...I believe in Sanctuary to do it where no one else could. Because in the days of old, before the fall, we did it all when others couldn't."

Alaric looked Cyrus in the eye. "You are sure you are willing to stay behind and direct the defense of Pharesia?"

Cyrus felt slightly called out, unsure of his footing as if attacked on rough ground, unbalanced. "Yes," he finally answered. "I have to beat him. I have to protect the people, and I think Dioro is right – Pharesia is the natural target. Pharesia or Termina first, all else after."

Alaric nodded, then turned to Vaste. "And you? You are certain of your course as well?"

Vaste exchanged an uncomfortable look with Aemma – one that, to Cyrus's eyes, held a bare hint of something deeper between them, or the possibility of it, at least – and said, "Yes. I need to find these mystics if they're in the north, and perhaps bring the men of that land around to our cause." He looked right at Cyrus. "After all, I'd rather not leave them to be scooped up by Malpravus if left alone and isolated."

Alaric did not now look at Shirri, and Cyrus thought that wise as he spoke, "Then we are decided – Pharesia, Reikonos, the south and the north – these are our courses, and to our individual tasks we will go." He looked over the company assembled, and Cyrus felt a swell in his belly; everyone was listening to him here, even Dioro: "Decide quickly who you wish to go with, what quest you wish to pursue." The skin around Alaric's surviving eye crinkled in a deep crow's foot, though, and he added in a hushed, near-whisper. "For we must be ready when the hour comes around that Malpravus returns, because if not...he will tear us apart separately, if we are not at that hour reunited and standing strong, waiting for his attack."

CHAPTER 17

SHIRRI

"*A*laric – Alaric!" Shirri scrambled out the tent flap, batting the heavy canvas aside and flinching against the bright sun of midday as she chased after the old knight's retreating form. He did not slow his measured pace, but his legs were considerably longer than Shirri's, so she was forced to practically run the dirt trail into the bustling camp to catch him, braving the dust and the smell of stew already cooking in a thousand pots for luncheon.

"Walk with me, lass," Alaric said as he plunged forward into the busy avenues between the tents.

"I don't want to walk," Shirri said, finally falling in line with him at a hurried jog, her robes absorbing the dust kicked up by his passage and that of a thousand others down this road in the last hour. "I don't want to run – I don't want to go, Alaric!"

At this he halted and turned that surveying eye to her. "I know."

"Then why are you trying to get me to do this?" Shirri asked, feeling as though she exploded within. She pointed back at the tall tent. "You have in there the greatest assemblage of Sanctuary members that has been together in over a thousand years. Trustworthy souls. The finest fighters. Mages of greatest renown, even in these days of waning magic. What good could I possibly do in this,

Alaric?" Her voice strained. "I am *no one*. I am not good enough to be in that tent, let alone near enough to have this asked of me." Some of the hysteria faded, and she was left cold. "You cannot put this in my hands, Alaric."

"I can," he said simply, and he thrust the chain and medallion, warm and metallic, into the palm of her hand. "I have. Now you must decide for yourself, Shirri, whether you want to try and take up this great responsibility and rise to the mighty destiny you have ahead of you – or if you simply want to fold like wet parchment...and fall apart."

"But someone else could surely do this better!" Shirri cried, because Alaric had turned from her in her stunned silence, and already started walking away again. "Someone nobler, stronger, wiser–"

"You seem to labor under the illusion that because you might not be best at those things," Alaric said, pausing and looking back, "that you do not possess them at all." He looked in her eyes with his own, and there was real fire behind the cool blue, some belief that made Shirri's knees feel strong where a moment before they had felt weak. "But though our acquaintance has been brief, Shirri, I see in you great possibility." He smiled, then shrugged. "Also, there is no other who can do this, so if you do not, it will not be done. So decide whether we can afford your inaction on this matter, and act accordingly."

She watched him recede into the stream of passing soldiers. "Did you impart this task to me because there is no one else?"

"No," Alaric said, but this time he did not look back. "I gave it to you because you can do it – and you need to, in order to become what you are meant to become."

"How – how do you know that?" she called back; her voice was flimsy, though, weak, really – like her.

But Alaric did not answer, for he had already disappeared into the crowd.

CHAPTER 18

VASTE

*H*e was left standing with his doubts yet afraid to give voice to them after Alaric swept out of the tent. Vaste watched the man known as the Ghost disappear into the sunlight outside, and he swallowed hard on a mouth of dust, grains of sand having taken up residence on his tongue in the darkness of the tent, and he wished there was somewhere he could collapse – like a chair or a bed – without breaking his tailbone or a flimsy chair meant for less glorious arses than his.

"Will you take me north with you?" Aemma's soft breath breezed into his ear, projected from where she stood just below his shoulder. He glanced down at her uncommon height, unused to looking a woman...well, not quite in the eye, but near enough for anyone who wasn't Birissa. That name alone caused a pang in his gut, adding to the other pangs rattling around in there.

"Certainly," Vaste said, though it came out a bit hiccupped.

Aemma definitely noticed, her youthful face making slight lines as she frowned at him. "What is it?"

"It's..." He glanced around the tent; a few of their number seemed to be drifting about, and the Niamh scourge was at his ankles, looking up at him plaintively with those odd, black eyes. "What do you want?"

The scourge made a hacking noise, then bumped her head against his tree-like leg. "Fine, you can come, too." With that, she settled down at his feet, laying her head on his boot.

"Vaste, what?" Aemma tugged at his arm. There was a sadness in her eyes since Termina, but it had seemed to lighten a bit of late, with every day that passed. She stared up, her hand slightly rough upon his wrist. "What is it?"

"Perhaps..." Vaste said, his voice catching slightly, "...perhaps this is foolish." He caught her brow furrowing further, and hastened to explain. "Not your part in this, your quest for aid from the northerners. That's smart." He shook his head slowly. "I mean my part, this harebrained idea of seeking mystics of Azwill in the swamps while Malpravus could land his blow here at any time."

Aemma nodded slowly. "Can you defeat him? If you stay, I mean?"

Vaste sighed. "No. Most assuredly...no. I would be barely a pebble in his path. A shapely one, to be certain, but...gone swiftly, and as worthy of ignoring as ever I was to Malpravus."

"Then it seems to me," Aemma licked her lips, "grasping at even the most desperate straw seems a better use of your time than swiftly becoming a corpse at the side of your friends." Here she glanced at Cyrus, who stood, imposing and implacable, talking to Vara and his boy, Baynvyn.

Vaste sighed. "I suppose. Besides, if this is foolish...I am just the man to do it. Being a fool and all."

"Who is the bigger fool?" Merrish's strident tone came over his own as the elf stepped up and landed a hand on his arm. The faint twitch at the corner of Aemma's eye heralded his arrival, and the former lord spoke again: "The fool or the one who follows? Because I feel called to come with you, Vaste." His eyes glimmered while Aemma's face became stony. "To the north and to the swamps – I will accompany you, and see what good I can do there."

CHAPTER 19

CYRUS

"*B*ut I'm your son," Baynvyn said, staring blankly at Cyrus. The flap of the tent continued to be thrown open at regular intervals, flashing blinding light into the dimness for a few seconds before it died away again as some soul entered or left, the company breaking. "I should stay with you."

"I've enjoyed getting to know you these last few weeks without the constant trading of blades in each other's directions," Cyrus said, clapping a hand on Baynvyn's shoulder. He didn't wear plate armor, instead favoring the mobility that came from a durable leather jerkin. "But I am going to be pinned in place guarding Pharesia – and you need not be."

"Let's not talk of need," Baynvyn said, frowning as he dropped his darkened spectacles over his eyes, another opening of the tent flap causing him to squint half-blind in the direction of the bright sunlight streaming in. "Malpravus is coming. Do you not want my help here?"

Vara, blessedly, stayed silent, though she too was offering a vaguely perplexed look to Cyrus as well. "Want has little to do with it," Cyrus said. "Though if you want my honest opinion – I want you to go with Alaric."

"The old man who wears Terian's armor?" Baynvyn looked in the direction Alaric had gone when he'd left, and couldn't help but guffaw, clearly, for one escaped him. "Why?"

"You may be my son," Cyrus said, keeping the weight of his hand steady on Baynvyn's shoulder, "but you were raised by Terian – and both he and I were raised in our own ways by Alaric." Cyrus stared into the cool, shaded blue eyes of his long-lost son. "I think you might benefit from some time spent with the source of our leadership abilities."

Baynvyn looked pointedly at Vara. "And this is not your doing?"

"I would have you remain here," Vara said tensely, "where we could keep a closer watch on you." Now she, in turn, glanced at Cyrus. "I have no idea why he would send you with Alaric, save for the reason he enumerated."

"Which is *the* reason," Cyrus said. "You're a capable assassin, son, but you could do with a little honor in your life to balance out the desire you have to resolve so swiftly and viciously any trouble that crosses your nose. There's no one better than Alaric to give you that instruction." He felt his cheeks burn briefly, but warmly. "Certainly not me."

"Are you certain?" Baynvyn asked, and here he sounded a bit strangled. "You don't want me here?"

"When hell comes calling?" Cyrus asked, with a faint smile. "If it were up to me, I'd send you all away." He received a clank of her gauntlet against his arm for that from his bride. "Go with Alaric, son. Learn from him. Help the man. And return...well, hopefully a touch better than you were before."

Baynvyn seemed ready to argue, his jaw clenched, but Cyrus watched it slowly relax, and he gave an abrupt bow. "I will do as you have asked, and for the reasons you have asked it. I will take it on faith that you are being true with me."

Cyrus smiled. "That's good. Because a month ago you wouldn't have taken me as being true if I'd told you airships sailed the sky and grass grew in the earth. It's progress."

With a last bow of his head, this time at Vara, Baynvyn added, "Step-mother." It almost sounded respectful. Almost.

"Step-son," Vara replied, in much the same manner. And with that, he was gone.

CHAPTER 20

ALARIC

*T*he Ghost grabbed his minimal things from the tent and headed straight for the *Raifa*, the bulky Chaarlandian airship moored at the far eastern edge of the camp in a temporary dock hauled out by elven soldiers. It rested with the turning blades still atop the tall masts, sticking out in all directions like off-centered compass points.

The gangplank squeaked with his every step, and Alaric hauled up his small, purloined bag of leather whose provenance he did not dare question. The Chaarlandians were vicious, cannibalistic, and he had not been sorry to kill the last of the crew of this ship over Luukessia weeks before.

Mazirin called out to him as he crested the top and found Edouard already waiting, his sunken eyes catching shade from the overhead sun, that pained wince on the former executioner's face a strange contrast to his Chaarlandian garb, which had replaced his black rags and gave him the aura of a savage.

Alaric turned to find Mazirin stepping over the gangplank onto the deck, her own bag slung over her shoulder. Hers was tasteful, though, well made, and lacked the uncomfortable likelihood of being made from human flesh. Behind her, moving this way from the distance, Qualleron stood out on the tent avenue. "Yes?" he asked, taking all this in with a swift look.

"Why are you coming with us, Alaric?" Mazirin asked, dropping her voice so that Edouard could not hear. She slipped closer as Qualleron's heavy footsteps lightly shook the gangplank and the ship, and now she was practically breathing in his face, warm and somehow pleasant. "Surely you're more needed elsewhere than a simple run to the strait of Balaar."

"Perhaps," Alaric said with a quicksilver smile, "But I have a sense I may be needed in this direction."

"Is it because you believe the dragons are involved in the telegraph line going down?" Mazirin asked, and there was a halting, a hesitation in her voice.

He did not answer quickly enough, and the ship shifted slightly in the makeshift dock as Qualleron stepped aboard. "Alaric," the mighty troll said, "it is good to fight by your side. I had feared after Reikonos..."

"I feared the same, my friend," Alaric said, "for many of us, indeed." He offered his hand, then watched his gauntlet be swallowed up in the massive yellow palm of the troll's hand. Qualleron had gauntlets, but they hung upon his belt. "Still, nearly all of us escaped death's cold teeth then, and now we must make way for the rest of the world to do the same."

"Is that what we're doing?" A calm yet seeking voice came from the shadow of Qualleron, hidden entirely behind him. The big troll turned sideways, and beyond him Alaric caught a glimpse of the pale dark elf with the tinted spectacles on his eyes, the dagger Epalette and a boxy pistol on his belt, and the rifle slung on his back. He looked uncertain, in spite of his tallness, as though he felt perhaps he were on the wrong ship. "A simple messenger run to the far south and yet it will enable us to win, somehow?"

"Not on its own, I think," Alaric said to Baynvyn, giving him a cool nod of respect and greeting, "but then, the component pieces of Sanctuary's membership never seemed particularly daunting when compared to the armies of the world. Still, somehow," and here Alaric smiled, for even in the time when he was bound by Bellarum and tortured madly, he found pride in Sanctuary's accomplishments, "we were always a force to be reckoned with even among armies of a hundred thousand or more. They feared us, and were right to, not because we were many, but because we few working together had power they could not conceive of."

"Is that so?" Baynvyn glanced around the ship with an appraising eye. "My father asked me to come with you."

Alaric cocked his head. "Truly?"

"He said I could learn from you," Baynvyn said, though there seemed a quiver of doubt in his voice, "the way I've learned from him, briefly, and Terian, mostly." He shrugged almost dismissively. "Or perhaps he just wants me away from him for a time so he can be with his bride alone." A trace of resentment was there, and Alaric noted it, reminding him for some reason of the time in his youth when Chavoron sent him away from Sennshann.

"I very much doubt it's that," Alaric said. "If Cyrus Davidon tells you he wants you to learn something from me, well...I take him at his word and am entirely flattered." Stepping – wide – around Qualleron, he offered his hand to the roguish dark elf. "And I am quite pleased to welcome a man of your provenance aboard, Baynvyn, for the two men who most taught you are two I would consider as near to me as my own sons." That Terian was, in fact, descended from him, Alaric did not feel compelled to mention at present.

"I will need assistance making the *Raifa* ready to sail," Mazirin said, looking hard at Baynvyn, appraisingly. "Do you have experience aboard airships?"

Baynvyn's dark eyebrows rose slightly, then he surveyed the wide deck, apparently just realizing that the only crew aboard was the five of them. Edouard slouched near the forecastle, while Qualleron stared blankly at Mazirin. "I...yes, I do, actually," Baynvyn said. "I have experience in all aspects of airship operation, though I make a poor engineer if that's where you mean to stick me."

"You are the best we have available," Mazirin said, and snapped her fingers imperiously at Edouard. "You – he's going to teach you all he knows," she said, nodding at Baynvyn. "That way we will have two inadequate engineers aboard instead of just one." She said something dark under her breath that Alaric took for a swear. "Perhaps we can stop at Emerald and hire an experienced engineer so as to free these two up for other duties – for we are unlikely to find someone with experience who's free here in elf country."

"Are you sure?" Edouard asked, his gaunt face pale in the midday sun – or perhaps at the thought of his new responsibility.

"I have made inquiries for the last several days and had no luck," Mazirin said. "Yes, I am sure. Now get to work."

"Come along," Baynvyn said, surprisingly gently, to Edouard. "Let's get stowed away and then we'll take a look at the engine room together. Perhaps given its Chaarlandian origin, it'll be easier to operate than a Firoban or Coricuanthi airship..."

"I don't know how to do anything but tie the rope lines," Edouard said plaintively, letting himself be led belowdecks. "I'm good with ropes...similar to nooses, you know..."

"I would assist them," Qualleron said, looking right at Mazirin, who met his gaze evenly, "but am I wrong in assuming this vessel is not made for someone of my size?"

"You assume correctly," Mazirin said. "You likely will not even fit belowdecks."

"Then I will make myself as unobtrusive as possible sleeping on the deck," Qualleron said with surprising magnanimity. "Where would you prefer I make my quarters? The forecastle?"

Mazirin seemed to bite back her first response. "That will be fine," she said after a moment's pause. "Please square your things away so they do not go rolling around – or overboard. Thank you." And with that, she seemed to dismiss him, turning away to look at Alaric.

Qualleron took the hint, bowing to Mazirin and then humming

lightly as he made his way toward the fore of the ship. A thrum from belowdecks gave the vessel a quick rattle, then the sound of the dread engines starting below infused the boards, sending a thrum from Alaric's boots into his armor.

"I would have an answer from you on that other matter," Mazirin said, seemingly torn, giving a swift glance to the wheel waiting on the quarterdeck. "Before we leave."

Alaric nodded, then sighed. "I suppose you deserve one, and I can hardly deny it to you, given all the troubles my secrets have caused over the years. Very well – I send Shirri because I sense she must become more in order to be of maximum aid to us – and because I find myself wishing to go with you."

Mazirin shuffled a step back, seemingly startled by this admission. "Me?"

Alaric nodded. "With you, yes." He reached out and touched her elbow, gently. "Mazirin...in my long life, I have been a ghost for entirely too long, always fading away, never staying. I am unremembered by the people of this land, barely remarked upon in this camp," and swept a hand around to indicate the city of tents, "ignored in my counsel save for by those who have known me longest and best."

"But those who know you," Mazirin said softly, as the hum of the machinery cranked to life, and the central masts began to turn, the big blades above starting to spin, "they respect you, Alaric. You're more than a ghost to them."

"Indeed," Alaric said with a nod. "But I must be more than a ghost to the others, too – and so we go, to inform Amatgarosa, the largest force on this world, and Qualleron's order, troops of immense strength from beyond our borders. Let Vaste use his skill to learn how to disempower Malpravus, and Shirri find hers trying to summon Sanctuary back from the void." His hand on her elbow, he tightened his grip, pulling her near and holding her there, against him, where she did not resist. "But as for me...I must become more than a ghost who fades away...and perhaps the start of that, other than trying to gather the most powerful reinforcements we can, no matter how unlikely, is to listen to my instinct as a man for the first time in...so very long..." And with delicate fingers he brushed her chin, raised it up, and kissed her lips right there on the deck.

It was, he thought, not a bad kiss...for a man who'd spent entirely too much of his long life insubstantial.

CHAPTER 21

VASTE

"This is a nice airship," Vaste said, nosing around the dark elven vessel with Aisling before him and Merrish, Aemma, and the scourge Niamh trailing behind. The crew was all dark elves, all serious, and had the aroma of men in a hard job about them, earthy and tangy and – well, rank. But the vessel seemed well-maintained, though it had clearly seen some hard use. Dirt still stained the hull where it had kissed the ground at some point, that much he saw walking up the gangplank.

"I always stole the nicest things," Aisling said breezily, her voice having acquired a rasp in her older age. Vaste always remembered her in the early days as being so freewheeling. It was only later, after the truth had come out, that he'd seen the real weight behind her eyes, that which she'd hid so expertly. It was still there, he thought, though he doubted it was quite as heavy as it had been before, in the olden days.

Or perhaps she'd simply gotten better at carrying it.

"When can we leave?" Aemma asked, still stealing little poisonous glances at Merrish. Vaste had thought the fight between them had ended at Termina, but the resentful glances from her, from him, when they were in proximity told him otherwise. Perfectly timed, of course, their enmity. Excising poison from a wound was never a simple matter, even in the best of times, and these were hardly those.

"Immediately, if Lord Vaste the Wry so wishes," Aisling said.

"Lord Vaste so orders," Vaste said. He'd seldom had power in his life, and he wasn't near drunk enough on it to pass up a taste when it was offered him. "Also – what kind of food do you have on this vessel?"

"Nothing you're going to care for," Aisling said. She turned away and barked a command in dark elven. "I'm afraid your arse is not going to benefit much from what we have in provisions, but think of all the good it'll do for your soul."

"To hell with my soul," Vaste muttered, standing by the gangplank and leaning on Letum. "What about my belly?"

"Master?" the soft voice of Glaven overcame the hum of the starting rotors, and Vaste turned to find the elf waiting, his arms tucked behind him, that fancy rifle of his slung over his shoulder.

"Ah, Glaven, good," Vaste said. "We're about to set off, and–"

"I think it best I don't come with you," Glaven said, giving him a gentle sketch of a salute. "I will – if you wish." A glance around the deck traced his intent. "But quarters will be tight, and if you don't mind me saying...I don't think you'll find much use for a manservant here."

"What about an armed bodyguard?" Vaste asked.

Glaven smiled. "I can, if you wish. But I'd like to remain with Lord Davidon." He lowered his voice. "Maybe it's because I've been under their command before, but I don't trust these Pharesians, and that Dioro..." he shook his head slowly, jaw settling hard, "...there's lies coming out of his mouth. I'd stake my reputation on it."

Vaste felt his brow creep up his forehead. "How do you know?"

Glaven's lips twitched. "Because his lips are moving, and there's words coming out."

Vaste pondered that for a moment. "I find your argument compelling, possibly because I've been cast out of the best establishments in Pharesia, and by exactly the sorts this Dioro represents. Very well – you have my permission to remain with Cyrus. Do you want to play manservant to him?"

It was Glaven's turn for his brow to rise, and a twist of an amused smile curled his lips. "Do you really think he'd let me? Because I expect I'd have enough of a fight asking to be his bodyguard."

"Hm," Vaste said, and rummaged in his knapsack for a piece of parchment and an inkwell – which he'd shamelessly stolen from the Termina council. Once found, he quickly scrawled a letter to Cyrus using the ship's boards as his desk:

Dear Cyrus,

I send to you my manservant, Glaven. He and I both suspect foulest, goat-buggering treachery from the Pharesians, and since we both know I am right all the time, Glaven is to act as your bodyguard and manservant at my behest. He will protect your overlong arse until such time as I return to help do so myself. Please treat him with all the kindness you should treat my arse with, knowing that if you do I will consider all that gold you owe me to be a debt fulfilled.

Your friend,
Vaste (the troll)

Quickly he rose, capping his inkwell and blowing on the parchment to speed the ink to dry. "This will work, I think," he said, offering it to Glaven. "Serve him as you would serve me, and keep him safe – both of them."

"I will see it done or die trying, my lord," Glaven said with a bow of his head. With a smile, he added, "Time to play the soldier again, I suppose."

"Knowing where you've fought, I'm sure you were a fine one," Vaste said. The whip of the blades began above him. "You should be off. We'll be leaving shortly."

With a brief salute, Glaven gathered the parchment and went over the gangplank, the boards squeaking as he shuffled down, his rifle slung over his shoulder.

Once he was gone, Vaste found Aemma standing there beside him. "No Glaven for this trip?" she asked.

"I think he's more needed here," Vaste said tautly, then looked behind him, at the stairs. "Besides, if this airship is like the others I've been on of late, I won't be going belowdecks if I can avoid it." He brushed the top of his head. "My skull is far too delicate and supple to be constantly knocked upon the beams every two feet below."

"Yes," Aemma said, her lips briefly puckered as she paused, then curling at the sides into a smile, "that is something I've noted about you. That you're not at all thick-headed."

"Well, you don't have to be sarcastic about it," Vaste said. "That is my job, after all, and if you do it, then what am I to do?"

Aemma smiled gently. "I believe, in this instance, you're to be the leader – and the hero leads us to victory."

"That's a terrible deal," Vaste said. "I'm the jester, dammit. The cutup. I'm not to be serious like Cyrus. I don't have it in me to become Mopey Vaste – again, I mean." He shook his head. "No. I don't like this at all. I'm going to have to take up the role of jester, where I'm good and comfortable, and someone else has to be leader."

"The person who has the ability to say that and make it happen?" Aemma's eyes danced with amusement. "That'd be the leader."

"Bloody hell," Vaste said with great irony. "Well, dammit – I don't have to like it. And I will still make jests."

"You could hardly be stopped from doing so," she said, standing gently upon one foot and pressing the other back as if pawing the deck boards. It was a curious thing. "Given you're the leader."

He did like the sound of that...for some reason. "Well, as long as I don't have to give up the sarcasm." And he stared out over the camp and watched the dust begin to rise along with the airship, slowly, over a few minutes, and then very quickly indeed, until they turned north and began to cut through the wind toward their next destination.

CHAPTER 22

SHIRRI

"This is it, then?" Shirri asked, looking about nervously. Was there any other way to look, though, standing at the rail of an elven airship whose blades were already spinning, her robes stirred by the gusts coming off them? Forlorn, that was how she imagined she looked. Scared shitless, also.

"I think so," Hiressam said, standing beside her, his calm hands still upon the surface of the wooden rail. He was a tall, immovable oak, incredibly reserved, a monument to stillness and patience.

But Shirri fidgeted. She kneaded the oak rail with her fingers, felt the smoothness and varnish there, looked over the elven crew – who were studiously ignoring her, all save for one – and doing about their business.

That one, though...he sidled over to her, under his bushy beard and with his twinkling eyes. "Anything I can do for you, Ms. Gadden?"

"No, Houk, thank you," she said with a bit of a sigh – though in her heart she wanted to say, "Be a dear and take responsibility for this whole endeavor."

She could not, though, and if Houk read it in her eyes, he did not say anything, instead nodding and retreating away to stand beneath the rotating mast. Houk was neither crew nor captain; he had found her in the camp and introduced himself, given his name and told her he had orders to get her on an elven ship that would strike out for Reikonos, "As soon as you're ready, m'lady," he'd said with a swooping, exaggerated bow that smacked of old manners of the Pharesian kind.

"Who's that?" Hiressam said, giving Houk a vague glance. He didn't look like the other crew, after all, clad in his black suit with long-tailed coat and white undershirt. He appeared as if dressed for a fancy dinner party.

"He's the one Cyrus or Alaric chose as envoy for us with the elven crew," Shirri said. She worked her fingers over the unyielding rail. "Tell me, Hiressam – did you see my mother before you came here?"

Hiressam nodded slowly. "I did." He winced, ever so slightly. Practically a scream of exclamation from him, he was so generally even keeled.

"And," Shirri chewed her lip, "she is not coming?"

Hiressam slowly shook his head. "I'm afraid not."

"Did she say why?" Shirri stopped working the rail for a moment.

"I got the sense she did not wish to go back to Reikonos," Hiressam said. "Though there did appear to be other thoughts on her mind. She was sidling up to Lord Davidon when I saw her last. She meant to speak to him, about what, I couldn't say."

"Well, damn," Shirri whispered. Behind her, she saw Guy Harysan emerge from the dark belowdecks, stretching now that he'd shed the bag that had weighed down his small frame. He still wore that sword on his belt, though, the one that Cyrus had when first she'd met him. Her heart sank a bit at the thought that this was what she was going to be forced to make do with – and do. "I guess we're on our own."

The clunk of heavy metal boots on the gangplank rattled through the rail clutched in her hands, and Shirri looked up to see the armored, bearded figure of Lord Longwell – the real one, not the faux Lord Protector, making his way up the plank with his spear in hand. When he reached the top he locked eyes with her, and Shirri felt her breath stick in her throat as he made his way toward her unerringly, like an arrow aimed at her heart.

"Lord Longwell," Hiressam said with some surprise.

"You're in charge of this expedition, yes?" Longwell's voice was raspy, like it hadn't seen much use in the intervening years, and he ignored Hiressam in favor of speaking directly to her.

"I...uhm...yes," Shirri managed to finally stutter out. Her heart was fluttering in her chest; this was, after all, the real Lord Protector, the one who'd saved Reikonos from the scourge and governed it with fairness and wisdom for fifty years or so before disappearing into legend.

"I wish to come with you," Longwell said, glancing about, his eyes darting, yet somehow fixed in a thousand-yard stare when they landed on something – or someone.

"Oh – of course," Shirri said, trying very hard not to trip on her words. She stroked the rail, patted it, tried to draw strength from it. "You are – are most welcome. We could use your help, in fact–"

"Marvelous," Longwell said, and, with a nod, headed for the staircase belowdecks. It was clearly not his first time on a vessel of some sort, if not an airship. He did not stop for Guy, who tried to thrust his hand out for an introduction but was ultimately forced to almost throw himself out of the way to avoid being run down by the armored man. Once Longwell was past, Guy looked around with some embarrassment, red glow highlighting his scruffy cheeks. Shirri looked away so as not to contribute to his embarrassment at the snub.

"Well, there you go," Hiressam said with some enthusiasm. "Now you've got one of the old legends of Sanctuary aboard." He nudged her with an elbow. "It's not all on your shoulders anymore."

"You're right," Shirri said, putting aside the thoughts about her mother leaving her to this, about Alaric throwing her here into the deepness of this ocean. She caught a look from Houk, and he offered her a solicitous bow. Again. But this did put a bit of confidence into her heart, this late addition. After all, if the Lord Protector was coming along on her journey, she wasn't entirely on her own, was she?

CHAPTER 23

CYRUS

"What the hells?" Cyrus muttered, reading the parchment that had just been presented to him by the well-dressed elf who had been introduced to him as Vaste's manservant. He frowned as he reached its end. "He signed it, 'Vaste, parentheses, the troll.'" Glancing up, Cyrus frowned at Vara. "Did he think I know other Vastes that aren't trolls? What is the point of that?"

Vara's narrow shoulders were quaking with silent laughter. "That's a very Vaste thing to write, isn't it?"

He stood in the dusty tent, reading the letter with the fractional Eagle Eye spell he was able to cast, though it seemed to last about five minutes before he needed to recast it for even this minor benefit. The word must have gotten out, for the delegates had stopped coming, the tent flap stopped opening, and mostly the Sanctuary army was gone. Now he was left with Dioro, Pamyra, Gareth, and that troll-elf from Amti.

Oh, and his sister-in-law, who lurked just slightly behind him, cutting a more ominous presence than he'd ever seen from the usually affable Isabelle.

"I believe Lord Vaste was simply being himself," Glaven said, with a solicitous bow of the head. "He wanted to offer you my services as bodyguard, but could not, of course, do so in the truly formal way such a request might normally require."

"That sounds like Vaste all right," Cyrus said, balling up the parchment and tossing it away. Dioro glared at him for that, but Cyrus little cared. Someone was going to clean up this tent; surely they could deal with it then, there was no shortage of other litter lying about. "Well, I'm fine with that if you are, dear?" He got the nod of assent from Vara, and turned back to Glaven. "Just knock before you come into our tent or bedroom or whatever."

"Bedroom, I would imagine, Lord Davidon," Glaven said, casting a sidelong look at Dioro. "I expect you'll be staying in the palace at Pharesia, yes?"

"Naturally," Dioro said.

"Great," Cyrus said, letting the sarcasm truly drip. "I've never yet stayed in that place without someone dying, and I reckon that winning tradition won't end at this late hour, given what we're to be facing." He looked Glaven square in the eye. "Precede us there and make sure our quarters are set and safe?"

"It will be as you say, m'Lord," Glaven said, and gave him a sharp bow of the head. The rifle strapped to his shoulder came down, too, and Cyrus caught a glimpse of it. It was a bit smoother than the flintlocks he'd become accustomed to in Reikonos, and had a boxy magazine like Baynvyn's rifle.

"What kind of rifle is that?" Cyrus asked, catching the manservant just before he fled. "And can I get one?"

"They are a bit rare in these parts," Glaven said, "but it's not out of the question. It's a Muceainean Auto-rifle." He unslung it and offered it to Cyrus.

Cyrus stared at it covetously for a moment, then waved him off. "You need that more than I do, but make some inquiries into the elven armories, see if you can get me a pistol or auto-rifle or, failing that, a series of flintlocks. Damned handy in a fight, those things."

"As you wish, sir," Glaven said and, with another bow of the head, this time retreated out of the tent, letting in the blinding light for a long moment.

"Now," Dioro said, striding forth to take advantage of the opening like Cyrus would have on an opponent dropping their guard, "are you ready?"

Cyrus stared at him blankly. "...For what?"

Dioro just stared back. "The parade, of course. To inform the people you are with us, that you are here."

"Oh," Cyrus said, and he looked sideways at Vara. "I...well, I need to make arrangements for the defense of Termina—"

"Then make them," Dioro said, clicking his staff against an old, dried root of some long-dead tree that ran across the earthen floor. "You'll need to send a general to conduct your affairs there, you know."

"Too true," Cyrus said, and glanced around. Ryin was present, as was Birstis the trelf, watching Cyrus expectantly from beside Gareth. He winced; either would do in a pinch, though his experience with Gareth was a thousand years past and he didn't know the trelf at all. Pamyra lingered in the background, still waiting to speak to him by the look in her eyes; her experience with combat was minimal. The answer, then, was obvious. "Ryin?"

Ryin shook his head, smiling enigmatically. "I would be better staying here, and you would be wiser sending another in your stead. My generalship is of the earth, not of people and airships. I would not be of much use to you in this."

"Damn," Cyrus breathed, for in his heart he knew it was true. "I find I lack a good right hand, a Castellan of some worth." He turned again, settling his gaze on Vara.

"No," she said. "I remain with you – and I have never been much of a general in battle, not even when I was with Amarath's Raiders. A strategist, certainly, and an adviser, but not the ablest commander."

A faint cough behind them made Cyrus turn and, again, he saw Isabelle in the shadows, which made him break into a grin. "Well, well, if it isn't my dear sister-in-law – and a capable general in her own right."

Isabelle's lined eyes settled on him, unamused. "I will do this thing for you – for Termina, really – but need I warn you to take utmost care of my sister?"

"I have always endeavored to do so," Cyrus said.

"In all the ways," Vara said.

"Very well," Isabelle said, and turned to Dioro. "You will transfer your command to me, and I will need a list of everything you have to offer – spellcasters of worth, soldiers, and materiel."

Dioro nodded. "And where would you have it, my dear? All moved to Termina? Or would you split the difference and spread your forces?"

"Concentrated, I think," Isabelle said, looking to Cyrus for approval. "In Termina. If we have sufficient air freightage, we can move an army into position in less than an hour, and I don't know that I want to commit everything here when the scourge entry point to western Arkaria is clearly at Termina or points south."

Cyrus nodded. "If trouble comes, we'll be about an hour away."

"If Malpravus comes," Isabelle said, "I expect we'll be dead in minutes, or else broken as a fighting force." She drew herself up, her white robes stained with dust and dirt. "But I will see the defense done, regardless."

"We will go with you, then," Gareth said, taking the bowler off his head as he looked to Isabelle for approval. Birstis nodded along; clearly the Amti contingent would be going to the border, then – and Cyrus approved that, too. "And prepare to hold the line at the Perda."

"Good," Isabelle said. "Then we leave within the–"

She was interrupted by a great hubbub as someone pushed through the tent flap in a terrible huff. Cyrus was blinded at first by the shadow of a woman – long hair, thin figure, but tall, or at least commandingly posed. As the light faded with the flap falling, his spell-aided eyes cleared, and he saw Alixa Weltan striding toward him, her eyes ablaze, the claws on her belt spitting lighting. "Where is he?" And she was spitting lightning, too, it seemed to Cyrus.

"Where is who?" Vara beat him to the answer, her hand subtly resting on Ferocis, for Weltan's approach lacked subtlety, restraint, and peaceful intent.

"Longwell," she barked, coming to a hard stop inches from Cyrus and Vara, like a ship run aground to the draft. "Did you hear where he went? Because I heard he boarded an airship."

Cyrus and Vara exchanged a look, and in his wife's eyes he could not help but note a hint of panic. "I have been here since the meeting ended," Cyrus said, "and Samwen did not deign to speak to me before leaving. Hell, I didn't even notice he went. Not that he's been much of a conversationalist since he arrived anyway." He frowned. "He went with one of ours, then? One of the ships we sent out?" When Weltan nodded, Cyrus pushed further. "Which one, then?"

"The one to Reikonos," Weltan said, her fury faded, and replaced by a clear worry he saw reflected in Vara's eyes. She lowered her voice, and in a hushed whisper, added the near unthinkable: "I believe he's going to try and return to the Realm of Life – this time to stay."

CHAPTER 24

ALARIC

"*A*laric."

The voice echoed down the gangway and into his room, dark outside the pined planks that made up the wall of his quarters, stirring him out of his bunk. He sat up, still in his armor, just out of a deep slumber, the thrum of the *Raifa's* engines around him and rattling gently through his metal encasement.

"What is it?" he asked, thinking he recognized the voice as Mazirin's. He got out of his bunk – one he shared with no one, for though he'd given over the captain's suite with its heavy fur covers and broad bed to Mazirin, he had kept a closet-sized secondary cabin for himself. Opening the door, he found her staring in at him, and another figure lurking behind her, scarred, half-cloaked, clad in green– "Calene? Calene Raverle?" he asked, her name coming to him just in time.

"Aye," Calene said, casting a subtle, surly look at Mazirin. "I told her I knew you."

"We're in flight," Alaric said, still fighting through the ponderous feeling of sleep hanging around his head like a cottony blanket. "Where did you come from?"

Calene laughed, a short, sharp bark that made Mazirin twist to look worriedly at her. "I was here before the rest of you," Calene said. "Grabbed a bunk below deck and caught a snooze. Your man Baynvyn just discovered me and tattled before I woke up and came to tell you myself. Didn't mean to cause a ruckus, but I figured I'd come with you."

"Why?" Alaric asked, now rubbing his eyes; his helm rested on the small table bolted to the deck beside the bunk. "Surely you would have been more comfortable with Cyrus or Vaste or even Shirri."

"Surely you'll be needing my help more than any of them," Calene said, "because I know the southern lands from Amti to Balaar better than any other living soul. My job has me hunting my way through them, killing dangerous animals down the settled paths to allow for Amti's expansion to the southern tip." She wasn't a short woman, but neither was she absurdly tall. "What use am I in Pharesia against Malpravus? Or in Reikonos, where I haven't been for nearing a thousand years?" She shook her head. "I know best who'd require my assistance, and it's you." She shot a sidelong look at Mazirin, one filled with irritation. "Just my bad luck I didn't say something before taking my nap. It just took forever for you lot to get here."

"I can sympathize with being tired," Alaric said, looking at the nearest porthole to find, yes, it was dark outside. Clouds bore reflections of a bright, white moon that hid somewhere beyond, but it left plenty of trace to tell it was out there. "Very well; I'd hardly turn away good help." He nodded to Calene, then Mazirin. "Onward."

"Go on, then," Mazirin said, tautly. "But keep in mind a captain likes to know who all is aboard their ship."

"Then maybe post a guard at your ship next time," Calene said, already disappearing into the shadows. "Keep those pesky intruders at bay."

"Calene," Alaric said, "could you kindly search the ship for any intruders we might have missed? Given your...expertise at these things."

She gave him a curt nod, her face cloaked in shadow, the scars now invisible. "I'll see it done. Think Baynvyn's already about the business, but I'll give it a second look." And then she was gone.

Mazirin remained tense, watching after her. "She's fine," Alaric said, trying to reassure her. "I knew her in the past, Cyrus and others knew her better but...she's a good ranger, a good person."

"Too sneaky," Mazirin said. With a nod of her own, and one that suggested she was not in the least mollified, she stalked off, boards squeaking as she headed toward the stairs topside. Alaric shut his door to retreat back into furtive sleep.

CHAPTER 25

VASTE

*H*e slept like the dead, and woke to the sound of those very much not. Vaste's head lolled at the edge of the hammock, the sun coming up and filling the sky with bright orange, blazing in from his right with the wind rushing past him on either side. They'd strung his hammock between two posts on the forecastle, the forward deck of the airship, and no dark elven crew had apparently disturbed him in the night, for he had been...well...undisturbed.

But now with the sun coming up, the sound of the winds rushing past was drowned out by raised voices, one male, soft, mellifluous, even, and the other female yet rough, scratchy, and he rolled against the cloth to find himself looking back over the ship's deck.

Merrish and Aemma stood in the midst of it all, she towering over him, him barking up at her. Her fists were clenched and one of his hands clutched at the knife on his belt, prompting Vaste to hurriedly eject himself onto the deck with a prodigious thud that shook the entire vessel and made the two of them look up, in surprise, their quarrel momentarily forgotten.

"What in the blazing loins is this?" Vaste descended the forecastle steps, his knee aching from his unkind landing. It was all he could do not to clutch at the bruise on his leg as he tried to get between these two before words were exchanged that could not be taken back. Or knives. Knives were notoriously hard to take back, especially after being buried in the ribcage.

"A discussion about the history of murder and usurpation," Merrish said, his even teeth bared like a snarling wolf as he looked Aemma right in the...well, chest, actually, because that was eye level for him.

"You would be the perfect one to lecture on murder," Aemma said, her eyes slitted thinly, "seeing as you have recently done so much of it."

"Why did you bring these two?" Aisling popped up at Vaste's elbow; he hadn't even noticed her, yet suddenly she was here, and quite interested. "Were there no rabid chipmunks available to spit and fight and make your passage more difficult?"

"Rabid chipmunks do not merely make one's passage difficult," Vaste said. "And aren't you supposed to be steering the ship?"

"Oh, yes, I forgot all about it in the drama," Aisling said. "Relax. I'm the Shipmaster, I only steer when I want to. We'll be arriving in New Idiarna in about fifteen minutes."

"Which one is New Idiarna?" Vaste asked. "Which old elven city, I mean? I looked at the map a few weeks ago, and everything that used to be elven is all 'New this' and 'New that,' named after human cities across the Perda in scourge land." At that, Vaste heard a whine and turned to see Niamh lying on a grate. "What? Not you, too."

"It used to be Traegon," Aisling said, glancing at Merrish and Aemma, who seemed to have paused their squabble in order to listen. A curious thing, a conflict so easily halted, he thought. "Now...if you could keep your people from disemboweling each other on my deck, I'd appreciate it. I don't do clean up, and neither does my crew, at least not when it comes to blood and guts, so if they make a mess, you're doing the mopping." And she turned, striding off in her leather armor, still such a spritely figure.

"I like her," Aemma said, watching her go.

"What's not to like?" Aisling called without looking back. She ascended the quarterdeck with careful steps, matching herself to the sway of the airship.

"Get your hand off your dagger, Merrish," Vaste said, stopping himself just shy of rapping the former lord's knuckles. "This isn't a bar fight or your dinner table."

"She threatened me," Merrish said haughtily – but he did take his tanned, rough-knuckled hand off his weapon.

"I have no weapon," Aemma said, ignoring the fact she looked down upon him the way Vaste looked at just about everyone, both physically and metaphorically.

"Yes, but you could easily bonk him on the head and cause catastrophic damage to both his brain and self-esteem," Vaste said, gently inserting Letum between them and pulling her back a step. She took it with grace, and he did it slowly, giving her plenty of time to take a step back of her own volition. "Have you forgotten why we came here?"

"I have not forgotten," Merrish said haughtily, turning his nose up. "It seemed likelier I could help you here than be of use charging down some battlefield in Termina."

"I can see why you would find no use there," Aemma said, "given there are no unarmed women and children upon that field waiting to be slaughtered, their necks wide open for you to put your knife to."

"I did not kill women and children," Merrish said, the veins in his throat standing out against a sudden redness, along with a prominent one on his forehead. "I killed armed insurrectionists in the northern woods – you know, your kind."

"If you truly want to help," Vaste said with a great dollop of irony, "not fighting each other would be a tremendous start."

Merrish stared up at her, gestured to her for a moment as if to say, "Look – just look at her." But he said nothing, and after a moment of waiting for some reaction from Vaste he shook his head, snorted, and stomped off.

"That goes for you as well," Vaste said as Aemma tried to slip down the rail, her head low as if chastened by his chiding. She did not look at him as he took a step to follow after her. "Did you start it or did he?"

She turned, and her eyes were red around the brown irises, though no tears were present or glistening in them. "I don't even recall anymore," she said hoarsely. "And I don't suppose it matters. A field of insults lies between us like shards of glass, and anytime we approach one another we are cut. Yet we remain bound by our hate, always dragging one another deeper into the field, always drawing more blood between ourselves."

"And what is the natural end of that, do you suppose?" Vaste asked. "Of such poisonous hatred?" He waited, and stared at her dull eyes, bereft of reaction, her tawny hair lank around her face. "That was rhetorical. We all know: murder."

"That's all that's ever been between us," Aemma said. "The human and the elves in the north. Blood and murder." She turned, placing a hand upon the rail to steady herself. "And I don't see how it could be anything but." She turned slightly, so he could see her profile. "You should leave Merrish aboard when we reach New Idiarna. He will win you no friends in that city." And she shuffled away, leaving him wondering what the hell he could possibly say that could compel the humans of the north to lay down those age-old hates in order to unite with the elves – for if Aemma and Merrish could not, how the hell could utter strangers with nothing in common do so?

CHAPTER 26

CYRUS

"They really are doing a parade for us," Cyrus said...in the midst of a damned parade.

He didn't quite believe it when Dioro had said it. But as he rolled down the main street under the immense, gray walls of Pharesia in the back of an open-topped self-propelled carriage with crowds of elves lining the streets and hurling flower petals at him by the millions, he was forced to more than believe it now.

"I had a sense that Dioro was not fibbing," Vara said, waving her silver-gauntleted hand in a manner that reminded Cyrus of a contestant in a beauty pageant he had seen in Reikonos Square long ago, in the days when he was the guildmaster of the Kings of Reikonos and had but Andren and Narstron with him. Seeing his wife imitate the action with a tight smile on her lips as they rolled into the city, packed crowds filling the sidewalks...

...Well, it made Cyrus's stomach rumble in a less-than-pleasant way.

"I am a man of my word," Dioro said from the passenger seat of the horseless carriage. He, too, was waving, though he was seated and thus less visible, and did not turn to favor them with his stern expression, though it was audible in his tone of voice. "In all ways, good and ill."

"I'm certainly feeling the 'ill' part of it," Cyrus muttered, sure that Dioro could hear him and equally certain that he did not care. He'd gotten what he wanted, after all, what was a little grumbling to him? Ignoring that queasy sensation writhing in his guts, Cyrus waved to the crowd as well, eyes sweeping over the faces of elves that varied from relatively mature-looking to the desperately old; there was not a child anywhere in sight and, indeed, as his gaze alighted on a woman who appeared – perhaps, at best – in her mid-thirties by human reckoning, Cyrus realized something jarring–

Pharesia was, indeed, a city where the youngest living here were well into their thousands.

He did not give voice to this thought, though, because even amidst the cries of his name and paroxysms of joy at his and Vara's arrival, he knew that every soul within a hundred meters could have heard him if he'd even whispered it to Vara here. So he buried the thought for later, but it, too, churned his guts with worry.

It had been a thousand years since he'd seen this city, and that millennia had not been kind to Pharesia, not at all. The white towers and green gardens which lined every street, the rich landscapes and gardens and waterfalls running between buildings to make it the most verdant city he'd ever seen had aged badly, like the city's populace. Nearly every other park was overgrown, weedy, the waterfalls and small ponds overtaken by blooms of green algae. Not a single building looked – or was – new, and this, too, seemed to fit with the impression he got of the populace crying out for him on these streets.

"Lord Davidon!"

"Lady Vara!"

Exultations of their names sounded like worship in temples, and it made Cyrus want to recoil. He'd met gods, hated them, and did not like hearing his name abased in this fashion. But he kept the smile frozen like cold Northlands ice had taken his face. Could these elder elves see through to the emotional turmoil beyond with their long experience? He hoped not, but there was little he could do about it, especially now.

Cyrus cast a look back at the carriages behind them. Ryin was there, watching, not waving, a placid smile upon his lips. Glaven, too, was with him, but they were not speaking to one another.

"The old war horse on parade," Cyrus said. Something about that made his nerves twitch, but he gathered within him the strength to wave on and even smile as he rolled through the streets of this dying, once-great city.

CHAPTER 27

SHIRRI

*T*he sun set and rose again, and Shirri slept as the airship churned through the air to cross the Perda and slip over the dead, gray land of eastern Arkaria. She slept in the bunk she was allocated in the ornately carved elven cabin, allowed the lull of the ship on the currents of wind to carry her off to sleep and back to wakefulness again. After washing her face in a splash of water from a newly filled cask, she found herself on deck, staring at the climbing sun and realizing it was nearing midday.

"Did you find a pleasant rest?" This from Houk, his black waistcoat with tails an odd stylistic statement for this endeavor. Perhaps that was a fashion in Pharesia; Shirri wouldn't have cared to hazard a guess, for she'd never felt she would be welcomed in that haven of pure-bloodism.

"I did," Shirri said, glancing around the sun-dappled deck. The elven airship had a deep mahogany tone to the wood, a freshly varnished appearance that was a far cry from the newly made and slapdash airship she'd ridden from Amti to Pharesia. That one had been rough angles and unpolished wood lacking the extra sheen of varnish. It was as if old elvendom had put her efforts into this new thing and it alone, like airships had a pride of place for them and received an outsized share of their attentions. "And you?"

"I rest well enough," Houk said, with a surprising amount of cheer beneath his thick mustache and cheek-beard. His chin was bare, his hair wild at the sides and top, and his age was tough to discern, even for her. His ears came to a perfect point, naturally – no half-elf could be allowed to give command to a Pharesian captain, surely – and he kept his hands inside his coat, denying her the chance to see how weathered or calloused they might be. If he worked on a ship like this regularly, they might be calloused indeed. If he was only here to be her emissary...well, they were probably soft as a courtier's. He flashed her a quicksilver grin beneath that mustache. "The peace of a clean conscience."

"Oh, what that must feel like," Shirri said, a bit darkly. She still had Reikonos on her conscience, at least a bit.

"What a day," Hiressam's steady voice reached her, and presently he was at the rail with them, his armor gleaming as though freshly oiled, and his hair much the same. He looked to Houk. "When will we reach Reikonos?"

"Soon enough," Houk said with a grin. "An hour, perhaps less, and you will see it upon the horizon."

Hiressam nodded, then turned to Shirri. "Where did you leave the medallion?"

Shirri pursed her lips, considering carefully what she should say. "Near where Sanctuary was before we moved it. Do you think it would be best if we had the captain drop us by ladder into Davidon Park? Or would we be better served trying to park at the dock and make our way through the city there?"

Hiressam's lips twisted and brow puckered as he considered. "If the fires were as bad as reported, the city streets may well be unnavigable. In that event, I imagine the closer we are able to get to our destination, the better."

"Quite right," Houk said. "Fire undoes stone edifice, given time with which to work its destructive charms, and even the residual trace of the wood buildings that made up the city shall leave behind their ashy bones obstructing street and block."

"We talking about wandering the city?" Guy's heavily accented voice made its way over them now, and Shirri turned to find him shuffling, looking half asleep, to the rail. His Machine coat of purest ebony was long gone, and now he was clad in a jerkin of gray and simple trousers to match, his scrubby face red and stubbled, hinting that a shave had come recently, but not this day. "Because I'm not in favor of doing that blindly."

"It's a dead city," Hiressam said with a hint of amusement. "Why would you fear it?"

Guy looked at him as though he were flatly dumb. "Because of carrion, you pointy-eared innocent. How old are you again? Because to my ears it sounds like you were born yesterday."

"Thieves, you think?" Shirri asked, her heart leaping at that thought. Of course she hadn't considered it, because though what they were doing was obviously robbing a tomb, of sorts, it wasn't for idle profit that they were doing it. But naturally others would, thieves and carrion eaters, and the thought of putting herself in the path of them...

...well, that prickled more than a little concern in her heart.

"I'm sure you'll rise brilliantly to this occasion and find your courage," Houk said under his breath, catching her eye with that knowing smile.

Shirri was not so sure, but she did not give voice to this thought. At least not before a lookout on the quarterdeck shouted something very loudly in elven: "Ship aft!"

She turned, leaning over the rail to see behind the bulk of the ship. Sure enough, a few hundred feet behind there was a smaller vessel, churning through the air quickly enough to overtake them. "Hm," she said. Just another ship traveling this transit lane.

Or perhaps not. "They're flagging us to stop, Captain," the rear lookout called, loud enough for everyone to hear it.

"With the flag of Emerald flying?" The captain's voice carried, too, incredulity dripping from his every word. "Who do they imagine they are, to think we would stop for them?"

The lookout practically gulped at that. "I don't know for sure, captain," he said, this reedy little man with a spyglass, "but I think on their quarter deck I see...and I'm not certain..."

"What, man?" the captain spat. He sounded like his patience had been tested to Shirri.

"I think it's the Administrator of Emerald herself," the lookout said, offering the captain his spyglass. "I'm pretty sure that's Alixa Weltan right there."

CHAPTER 28

ALARIC

The night passed and he slept sporadically, the smooth thrum of the *Raifa* carrying them through the moonlit dark, and on the morn he woke without realizing he'd slept again, into a dusky, ash-scented air that made him cough in his small closet of a room.

Alaric stirred to life swiftly enough and was on deck in minutes, the sun somehow closer to them in feel than it had been the day before. Ashy barrens waited below, the wastelands of old that Alaric knew were once the exclusive domain of the dragons.

"Hail, Alaric," came the watery voice of Edouard, who stood at the wheel with Baynvyn behind him, bleary-eyed even behind his dark spectacles. The two of them stood watch, though neither looked well-suited to it. At the far forecastle rail Alaric saw a burnt green half-cloak trailing in the wind, and brown hair turned away from him. Calene, huddled at the rail beside the massive yellow figure of Qualleron. All were awake and present save for Mazirin, who must surely have slept her way through part of the night if these two were at the helm.

"Edouard, Baynvyn," Alaric said, casting another eye over the side. A tall and lonely peak waited ahead, with at least two others in close attendance; he knew it at once as the dragon city of Hewat, and wondered what it must look like in these diminished days. "Mazirin rests, I take it?"

"She woke me in the late watches of the night," Baynvyn said with a yawn, "from my hammock in the engineering space. Said I needed to keep an eye on the greenhorn at the helm, that she would relieve me mid-morn." He peered at the sun, high in the sky. "It would seem I've been misled."

"I can relieve you if you wish to take some measure of rest," Alaric said, stepping over to the spoked wheel. "I trust I simply keep this pointed south," and he laid a gauntleted finger upon the compass mounted in a wooden pedestal beside the wheel, "and continue until the land comes to a point?"

"That's the long and short of it, yes," Baynvyn said with another pronounced yawn. "Balaar is at the very tip of this land, the triangular point jutting into the strait, and beyond the waters you can see the shores of Firoba in its emerald glory, beyond the cerulean waters and white beaches, its brown stone cliffs like desert sands in the far distance."

"Then I relieve you, for even I can carry out these simplest instructions," Alaric said, "provided the engines run and the wheel still steers."

"I would know immediately if the former ceases," Baynvyn said, already heading for the stairs down from the quarterdeck, "and there's little I can do about the latter, so try not to break it." With a last wave he disappeared below deck, into the darkness.

"This is easier than I imagined," Edouard said once he was gone, tentatively – and tensely – rolling the wheel slightly in his grip to adjust the heading a degree back to true south. "I watched you and Mazirin do it back from Luukessia, of course, but I never imagined I would be doing this."

"Where did you imagine life would take you, Edouard?" Alaric asked, keeping a wary eye on the horizon line. The careful breaks in the mountains, the sharp valleys down to ashen floors between those peaks ahead made it look like some sort of geometric arrangement; time had been that each mountain had its own element pooling within the peaks, from ice to poison to water and fire at the center, each maintained by their own elemental kind.

Now they were all still, no hint of smoke from the central, tallest mountain, Monneusig Monscul. The field of mountains was dead, the mounds like tombstones around a center peak. A fitting epitaph for the dragons, perhaps, though Alaric did not care to count them entirely out yet.

"I don't know that I ever thought about it," Edouard said. "At least not after the city guard grabbed me and my sword and ran me through the gates of the shipyard the day I met you." His lip quivered. "I'm not sure I had much of a conception of my life before that, either. Just...show up to work, take heads at the block, stretch necks at the gallows, torment those souls in chains in the dungeons." He looked pained, his pale face twisted in discomfort. "I feel as though I've just been gliding through the air since, much like the airship, with someone else at the helm." He lifted his face to the wind.

"But you believe in our cause?" Alaric asked. "In beating Malpravus?"

"Surely," Edouard said, and that much was sure, though he then evinced a touch of discomfort. "But...I'm not like you, Alaric. Not like the others, either. I took that Chaarlandian captain's head, but not in a fight." He stared into the distance, perhaps, too, watching the dead peaks. "I just don't know what use I am to you, other than doing things like this. Things anyone could do, really." He shrugged, brushing a hand against his hip. "I don't even have a sword anymore, and you're all fighters." His scabrous cheek blushed. "What good am I to you?"

"Whatever good you can do," Alaric said. "For it is not just the grand things that make the difference, Edouard. Not the swung sword every time, though you saved my life by your strength at that; if you can but steer an airship through the night while others are sleeping, do you not think that is of service? For it is." He smiled. "We fighters cannot be vigilant at all hours, cannot steer the ship through the night and fight through the day, at least not for long. Do not discount the help you give by doing so simple a thing as this, or learning how to run the engines. For defeating Malpravus is not a battle of one against one; none of us can take him thusly, as Curatio sadly proved." Alaric felt a twist in his belly at the thought of his old friend. "It will, I think, come down to all of us throwing every bit of weight we have to give onto the scale of effort, in hopes that when measured fairly, all our contributions somehow outmatch his own."

"But will they, though?" Edouard asked, voice scratchy, brittle. "I feel I do so little, whereas he is so...powerful."

"We have to hope so," Alaric said, staring at the once-deadly mountains in the distance. "For times change and things change with them. Once, if you had dared to cross in close proximity to these mountains, your death would have been nearly assured. Drakes and wyrmkin slithered the peaks, and full dragons crossed the skies like birds at the shore. Now..." He waved a hand toward those same distant peaks. "All power can be overthrown given enough time, and steady effort. We have the effort...now we just need to see if we have the time." He smiled.

"I hope you're right," Edouard said. "I just hope you're right."

CHAPTER 29

VASTE

*G*reen forests and bright fields swirled past on either side as the ship came closer to the ground. Ahead, a once-white city looked faded, mud-daubed human buildings and ones made of hasty wood in among the classic minarets and white walls of the unmistakably elven bones of what was now New Idiarna, and the seat of the Northern Confederation, humanity's redoubt here across the Perda.

"Make ready for landing!" Aisling called across the deck, and Vaste seized the rail, clinging tight to it. Aemma was just down from him and did the same, perhaps even a bit more aggressively with her statuesque figure.

They swept wide around the towered city toward a set of airship docks that were smaller by far than those of Reikonos, situated outside the aging white line of the city walls. When at last they settled into the dock less than five minutes later, Vaste breathed a sigh of relief because his stomach had at least, for the moment, settled. Air travel did not agree with him.

"Delegation coming up," Aisling called from the side, where she was supervising the lowering of the wooden gangplank against the ship. Vaste made his way over and she muttered, "I guess someone sent a telegraph letting them know we were coming, because they look official."

Vaste caught sight of them, a formal party of men with flintlock rifles and that weird, vestigial armor with breastplates that covered about half what those a thousand years ago had, just the center of the chest. At their head, a man in silken clothing with a stern look and gray hair that was long and hung around his shoulders as limply as the leaves of a thirsty shrub.

Once the gangplank was extended to bridge the gap, and Aisling's crew had unclipped the chains stretched over the gap in the rail, the silken man came immediately onboard without so much as a "How do you do." "Are you the shipmaster?" he asked with a preening sort of haughtiness.

"Yes," Aisling said, then jerked a thumb at him. "But he's the man in charge of this diplomatic mission."

The silken dandy looked to Vaste – then up, and up some more, his jaw falling an inch or so. "Uh – very well," he said once he'd gotten ahold of himself. He cleared his throat. "You of the dark elves and you of the...uhm, wherever...are welcome to trade and wander about the town." He cast a look past Vaste to Aemma and gave her a nod. "Humans as well. However..." And here he caught sight of Merrish, and his slightly wrinkled visage darkened. "No elves are permitted in New Idiarna."

"I wasn't planning on going ashore anyway," Merrish announced with a lightness of tone that was not quite reflected in his tight lips.

"Good," the silken dandy said, turning back to Vaste. "Additionally, your diplomatic mission is not to be received at this time."

"What...what does that even mean?" Vaste asked.

"Means they don't want to see your beautiful arse and admire it in their hallowed halls," Aisling said.

"What an insult," Vaste said, puffing his chest up. "Do you have any idea who I am?"

"I don't even know *what* you are," the silken dandy sniffed. "I only know that we are in a state of war with the Termina elves and, likely, the Pharesians as well, and possibly Amti. We have little time for representatives from any conference that include them." He sniffed again. "So...enjoy our hospitality, but do not expect anything else, for we have nothing else to give but our custom."

"You really haven't heard anything about the man who controls the scourge?" Vaste asked as the dandy turned. "The one who wiped out Reikonos with a spell?"

The dandy turned back, tossing his gray hair slightly. "No man can cast a spell that can wipe out a city, that's ridiculous. Now, if you please...I have things to do today."

"Do you indeed?" Vaste asked. "Well, I hope they include 'not dying.' Because death is coming your way."

"He's right," Aemma called after the dandy. "Trouble comes from across that river, more trouble than the elves."

This time, the dandy did not deign to turn back and address them. "Then we will deal with that...but only after first dealing with the elves. Good day." And he swept his silks about him and retreated down the gangplank.

"Well," Aisling said, sidling up to him, "what do you want to do now? Yell? Chase after him? Bean him with a coconut?"

"Maybe the last one," Vaste said, then sighed. "No. No, scratch that. I want to go on. You can lead a horse to water, after all, but if you try and make him drink, he'll drown, and this fellow? He has the look of a drowned horse. And not just because of that horse blanket he wears, either."

"They're on a war footing," Aemma said, standing mountainously tall next to Aisling. "They will not listen to outsiders now."

"Adding whatever puny army they have is hardly going to win us this war in any case," Vaste said with another commanding sigh. He shook his head, and waved at the gangplank. "Might as well pull it up, we'll get no further here and even if we did, it's a waste of time. Take us on, to the swamps, and perhaps we can get the real answers we came for. Because without them," and here his stomach grumbled a bit, "we're just adding more kindling to Malpravus's fire."

CHAPTER 30

SHIRRI

*T*he elven airship came to a shuddering halt above the gray, dead land with no writhing scourge below as a chain and plank bridge was thrown across the gap between them and the Emerald airship. Shirri watched the operation with rising concern, then watched the green-clad figure of the Administrator of Emerald cross the rickety, swaying bridge and step onto the deck before her, face red, a towering temper clearly ready to be unleashed. But all she said was, "Longwell. Is he here?"

"Belowdecks, yes," Shirri said, for Weltan had addressed the question to her. "Would you like me to get him?"

"If you please," Weltan said, her face dropping a few notches in clear relief.

"I'll fetch 'im." Guy was standing behind her. "Haven't had a chance to properly talk to the Lord Protector, might be a nice opportunity to get a moment wiv' 'im." He scampered toward the stairs, and Shirri had no desire to pursue.

"I don't remember your name," Weltan said after a few awkward seconds.

"Shirri." Shirri felt a hot blush under her collar. "Shirri Gadden. I'm from...Reikonos."

"Yes, well, it's been a real flurry of introductions the last few days," Weltan said, clasping her hands in front of her. "I'm usually more mannerly than this."

"It's fine," Shirri said, "no one ever remembers me. For good reason." She almost giggled, but it died in her throat. Had she truly just self-deprecated to zero in front of the Administrator of Emerald? That was like the queen to them.

"Just a peasant girl from Reikonos?" Weltan asked with a steely calm that belied her youthful appearance. "I was just a villager on the abandoned coast of Luukessia until destiny caught me in its sweep. That was a thousand years ago, almost."

"At the rate we're going, I'm not sure I have another week in me," Shirri said, again choking off a giggle. That wasn't good, was it?

"No one can say for sure how much time they have," Weltan said, her face suddenly gray, peaceful, as she stared off the bow of the ship and into the distance. "I knew a young man barely past his boyhood that was taken by fate, but not before he helped save me – save us all, really. He did much with his small count of years, and I have tried to do the same with my many." She turned back to look at Shirri. "You may have more time than you think, Shirri Gadden, or less – but you would do best to use it as wisely as you can."

It was hard to argue with that, especially with the lightheaded sensation Shirri was feeling. She'd spoken to queens and councilors, and told the great Davidon to his face that she thought him a fraud. A month ago she'd been a debtor to the criminal syndicate that ran Reikonos, and now...this. Sure, death was still hanging over her head in the form of Malpravus, but hadn't things taken a dramatic turn? She giggled again, helplessly. "Sorry," she said, cutting that off immediately.

"...right there between the docks and the bars, you know?" Guy's voice drifted up through the open hatch, the tread of his feet overcome by the whirring blades above and the strong footsteps of metal boots against the deck. "Not the nicest area."

Longwell's blued helm came up in Guy's wake, and the bearded man's face was screwed up in concentration, nodding at whatever Guy had been telling him. "It was not a nice area in my day, either. I had guards constantly patrolling there to stop the cutpurses and cutthroats that washed in across the Placid Sea. You know the worst of them came from Firoba."

"Not anymore," Guy said, shaking his furry head. "Now the worst come from Chaarland."

"Chaarland?" Longwell's eyes narrowed. "Why, I've been to Chaarland. It was a pleasant enough place, a thousand years ago. I spent time in Aiger Cliffs–"

"Aiger Cliffs?" Shirri blurted out. "How did you survive?"

"It was a near thing," Longwell said, looking past her at Alixa.

"Aiger Cliffs has changed a bit since our day, Samwen," Alixa said. "A bad element moved in – and remains to this day. Chaarland is no peaceful haven anymore, either. It's more advanced yet more savage than Arkaria, if you can believe it."

"I cannot fathom it," Longwell said, "but then when last I saw it, Reikonos was a city teeming with life, so..." he shook his head. "...Things change." He leveled a steady gaze at her. "What are you doing here? I thought you were in Pharesia."

"I followed you," she said, gesturing to the ship hovering behind her. "I have a question." And here her eyes lit bright with anger. "What do you think you're doing?"

"Whatever I damned well please," he said, without any milk of kindness. "I have been on my own for nearing a thousand years, Alixa, and I don't find I have any call to explain my decisions to you – or anyone else."

"These are extraordinary times," Weltan said, steely calm, replying with none of his heat, "and you have come back to us at an urgent moment. Do you not think–"

"What I think," Longwell said with considerable, searing anger, his nostrils flaring, "is that who I give my aid to in this crisis is none of your affair, and coming galloping after me because you want to know is the province of petty tyrants and children." He made a show of looking her over. "But you're not the child I met all those many years ago, no, you're long-grown, Alixa. So why do you follow me? Have you nothing better to do? Have you not the Emerald Fields to save?"

She remained calm, and, if possible, became calmer still. "I was worried about you. You disappeared without a word."

"I disappeared with nary a word before, too," he said, cackling in a way that made Shirri cringe. "No one came looking for me then, and I spent a great many years imprisoned because of it."

"Perhaps I don't wish to see the same mistake repeated," Weltan said gently.

"It's a bit late for that," Longwell said.

Weltan turned to Shirri, who dimly realized that she should have left when the two of them started arguing, yet could neither make her feet move nor find polite words to extricate herself from what had been, nominally, a conversation with the Administrator of Emerald. Her manners failed her, as did her wits. "Where do you plan to make landing in Reikonos?"

"Ahm," Shirri said, caught a bit off guard, "somewhere near Davidon Park. As close to our, uhm, target, as possible."

"We have not received a ship from Reikonos or its vicinity in many weeks," Weltan said, seemingly musing out loud. "We know not what to expect." She started to nod along with...herself? Shirri was hard-pressed to know, but it seemed she was reasoning her way through something. "I think it best if we accompany you in case of danger."

Longwell, who'd fallen silent but watched her suspiciously, burst out laughing now. "You are transparently false; you do not do this thing out of worry for her mission," and he nodded at Shirri. "You do it to follow me still. I have told you—"

"I worry," Weltan said, her strong voice now quiet, barely audible over the whip of the blades high above. "You have just come back to us, Samwen. I don't wish to see you lost again. I erred last time; I should have come looking for you, looked harder, deeper, but I allowed Malpravus to push me away, to hide himself, and it was nearing five hundred years before I discovered the truth – that he was not you." She laughed joylessly. "I thought you had shunned me because of some thing I'd done wrong, only to find no – it was never you." The lines of her face became hard. "There was nothing I could do against him, so far from my base of power and so fortified as Reikonos was. I will not let you disappear in there again."

Longwell stared at her for a long moment. "I can hardly stop you from trailing us or giving us aid." He looked down at the deck. "Nor would I."

"Good," Weltan said. "Then that's settled." And she shuffled toward the gangplank. "I really did miss you, Samwen."

Longwell lowered his gaze. "Yes," he mumbled. And he did not watch her as she returned to her airship, the lines were cast off, and they started forward against the wind, toward Reikonos once more.

CHAPTER 31

ALARIC

They were running out of ground. South of the abandoned mountains of the dragon city Hewat, the abundant land that had filled the horizon to either side of them began to taper swiftly together, blue seas appearing at the lines to east and west. By the hour it diminished, pulling closer and closer with rocky shores until finally Alaric, over the bow, could see the end of it.

And it was beautiful.

"I...I suppose that's Balaar," Edouard said, still uncertain at the wheel, if at least a bit more steady-handed now. He was squinting against the high sun overhead, shining down on his pockmarked face and sunken cheeks.

"So it would seem," Alaric said. Calene remained at the bow, but Qualleron had risen from his hammock and now joined her in quiet, companionable conversation. Neither Baynvyn nor Mazirin had been seen nor heard from this day, or, at least in the case of the former, since Alaric had relieved him in the morning. Edouard seemed to show little sign of flagging, which Alaric had been watching for. Still, he doubted the former executioner had it in him to bring the airship in for a careful landing. "It would appear we'll be there in five or so minutes. If I'm not back in three, decrease the speed."

"I...I can do that," Edouard said, a slow, creaking smile breaking across his face. "I know how to do that."

"You are fast becoming a master, my friend," Alaric said, clasping him on the shoulder for reassurance. He sensed that this man, in particular, needed it. That done, he descended the quarterdeck and made swiftly for the hatch and stairs to carry him below, where he would – hopefully – find his way to Mazirin.

The rush of wind faded as Alaric descended the rattling stairs and into the dark belowdecks. To either side were the cannons, lined up like black marble statues in the shadowed dark, the gun ports battened closed with ropes tied tight.

He thought he caught a flash of movement out of the corner of his eye as he rounded a bend. There was a brief flash of a man with a thin face and pointed nose, and Alaric turned to look–

But he was gone, if ever he had actually been there. Alaric stared into the darkness for a moment more. Why, it had almost looked like–

"No," he decided, though he stayed still and turned his head a few more times, taking in the full sweep of the tight corridor. "No, it couldn't have been." As if trying to talk himself out of it.

He found Mazirin's cabin moments later and landed his metal-clad palm against her door roughly, the sound ringing out down the hall, echoing in the confined space. "Come in," she said in a plaintive voice, muffled by the door.

Alaric hesitated, then turned the knob, swinging the door wide to find–

"Oh," he said.

Mazirin was still in her hammock. Wide windows sat at the back of the cabin, wider than any he'd seen anywhere else on the ship, so large he could have crawled through them in his armor. They cast the room – larger than any other aboard, but still remarkably small – with bright sunlight. Barely seeing him through those half-closed eyes, Mazirin, bare-footed but otherwise completely clad loosed a small, continuous moan as if the very prospect of either him or the day was too painful to contemplate. "Unnnnnhhhhh..."

"You are not a morning person, then?" Alaric asked, feeling the hints of a smile tug at the corners of his weathered cheeks.

"I was up until the small hours manning the watch myself," Mazirin said, closing her eyes tightly. "I curse that I sent my crew back to Amatgarosa."

"You should have kept them with you," Alaric said.

"Could you pay them?" she asked, lifting an eyelid to stare at him reproachfully. "Because I could not."

"I could not at the time," Alaric said, inching closer to her. She did not seem well-disposed to rising. "I imagine the funding could be found to pay them now, plus whatever they lost in the waiting, given how eagerly Pharesia gave us all else they had. I came to tell you – Balaar is in sight."

"Are you certain?" Here she moaned in pain again.

"It's a city at the end of a peninsula past the dragon mountains, with a sea beyond." Alaric folded his arms in front of him. "If it is not Balaar, we have taken a terribly wrong turn."

"One of us certainly did, somewhere along the way," Mazirin moaned, but she sat upright. Slipping her dainty feet into silken foot-covers slowly, she asked, "How far out are we?"

"Likely only a minute or two away at our present speed," Alaric said. Then he felt a subtle shudder through the bones of the *Raifa*. "Ah. Edouard decreased speed as I asked. Perhaps a few more minutes away, now."

"You left that fool Edouard at the helm?" Mazirin vaulted out of the hammock. "Without help?"

"I relieved Baynvyn in the early hours of the morning," Alaric said as Mazirin hurried over to the door and bolted out of it. "There was no one else."

Mazirin thundered down the short corridor and as Alaric passed the point before where he thought he'd seen...well, it didn't matter...he looked again. Just to be sure. Then he followed Mazirin up into the sunlit day.

"Do you see it?" Calene shouted over the entire deck as Alaric stood blinded in the bright sunlight. He listened to Mazirin's hurried footsteps run up to the quarterdeck and unleash a torrent of her own language upon Edouard ("Huh?") before she shouldered him out of the way and took the wheel. "Come and see!" Calene called.

Alaric did as he was bid, curious more than a little on his own account. He took the three easy steps up to find himself beside Qualleron on the forecastle, and approached the rail at the tapering front of the *Raifa*. Looking down, he could see–

It took his breath away.

Not just the long strait, but the water that became the horizon, that encompassed the horizon. But there, just beyond, a tip of land, a distant shore, green and promising, with cliffs of orange and hills behind. And there, closer, almost beneath them now–

Balaar was a thing of its own beauty, backed to the edge of the promontory, a creation of orange-sand walls and bright ochre stone, with intricate towers and squares with monuments in their center the like of arches, all hewn from that same orange stone that gave the city such color. It was as though the town were bathed in perpetual sunset, and Alaric's breath caught in his throat.

"There's the end of Arkaria," Calene said with some glow in her chest like pride. "And beyond, Suijnara."

"I thought Firoba was across the strait," Alaric said, entranced by the beauty of Balaar, by the teasing possibility beyond the water. A new land that was neither familiar Arkaria or dead Luukessia, it seemed to hint at possibilities that he considered, but not truly reckoned with. Not in his heart, not in his gut.

"It is Firoba," Calene said with a patient laugh. "Firoba is the land's name, like Arkaria. Suijnara is the nation, though it's bigger than all western Arkaria combined together. We're a bickering collection of city-states; Suijnara is a nation of united peoples, a land unto itself. There are three other countries almost as large in Firoba, and all at the off-compass points. Suijnara to the northwest; Vanreis, more temperate and green, to the northeast; Binngart, wintry and forbidding and mountainous in the southeast; and then Muceain, the flat, cold high desert and plains in the southwest. Between them, and squeezed around their borders, are a host of other duchies and commonwealths and minor kingdoms all living in their shadow like us Sanctuary survivors in that cast by Cyrus."

Alaric chuckled. "I believe you have explained that in a way perhaps only a few of us could have understood it – but understand it I do, now."

Calene smiled, and beneath the scars there was a lightness in her like he was looking back a thousand years at the ranger she'd been. She adjusted the bow on her shoulder and it caught his eye; it was Caraleen's, of course, and he knew it by sight. She followed his gaze to it and said, "That's my godly weapon–"

"Vita, the Bow of Life, yes," Alaric said, brushing a hand along the smooth woodwork. "I helped carve it out of a bough that Caraleen – Vidara, I suppose, though I never got used to calling her that – pulled out of the old Waking Woods."

Calene blinked a couple times. "Wow. I knew you were around for a lot of the old days, but I never figured you had that much of a role in the affairs of the old gods." She pulled it off her shoulder. "You want to hold it?"

He shook his head. "The echoes of her are within it, for those who know how to listen, and I would not care to hear her voice in my head again, given how she ended."

"And who she ended before hers, I suppose," Calene said, and when Alaric stared blankly at her, she added, "I mean Quinneria. You were close with her, weren't you?"

"Quite," Alaric said as the *Raifa* shuddered. "She was the reason Sanctuary came out of the ether in those days. I had been in for many years before she summoned us out, right there in the Plains of Perdamun where you first encountered it."

"And where last I saw a great muddy crater," Calene said. "It's still there to this day, did you know? The old monument and the hole in the earth, weathered with a thousand years of rain and mud slid down its slopes, but still present, if not as deep. You can see it if you fly over the southern plains, a dimple in the earth or a great rut, depending on how high you are when you cross over it."

"We leave our marks on this world, still," Alaric mused as the ship came to a graceful curve. They'd lost altitude, a few hundred feet by his reckoning, and were coming in on the walled city from the south, over the water. He couldn't see an airship dock, now that he looked, but there were a plethora of them in the water.

The look on his face must have been obvious, for Calene said, "Yes, we're landing in the water, for why not?" Her lips were puckishly twisted. "Airships fly over water so much of the time, that's why their hulls are still shaped like those of the water ships of old. Though I have seen some of a more blocky variety, meant to land flat on the earth, this is more common, with prettier lines, so that if needed it can splash easily into the ocean or lakes and sail upon them without difficulty."

"And so we dock in the sea," Qualleron rumbled behind him, drawing Alaric's eye for a moment as the honorable troll broke his silence at last. "It feels long since last I saw Firoba. A year or more – more, for certain, since I last laid eyes on Suijnara and its sun-kissed coast."

"Would that I could see it for myself other than at a distance," Alaric said, but already it had dipped below the horizon with their descent.

"We could run," Calene said with quicksilver smile, but he knew in his heart she did not mean it.

"I have not been in Arkaria for these momentous events for too long," Alaric said, the ship drifting closer and closer to its meeting with the waters below. A harbor with high walls and gates thrown open waited in Balaar, he could see it now, and soon they would be within them. "I cannot fade away from this fight." He tightened his grip before the moment of landing, and it shuddered, a splash below heralding their arrival. "Not again."

"It is not honorable to run from such things," Qualleron said. "Though the impulse is natural, when the threat is so great. Still, though – I cannot imagine letting this stream of abuses Malpravus has unleashed pass unchecked, even though my homeland calls, and I have not seen my living children in many years." He squinted his eyes against the bright sun. "No, honor calls me more powerfully, and duty – as it calls you, and you answer it above the call of your own heart."

Alaric turned, slowly, as the ship landed in a splash of water that rose outward from the bows, a surprisingly delicate and barely jarring ending to their flight. "Indeed," he said, though his eyes were on Mazirin at the wheel, in her raven-haired glory, and flushed with faint triumph as she steered the wheel and the ship moved upon the still waves as it had upon the air, toward the open sea-gates of Balaar's harbor.

CHAPTER 32

VASTE

A few hours flight and they were soon over New...whatever, it was still Nalikh'akur to him – and then they went beyond, not even bothering to stop for the airship docks were occupied and Aisling grunted, "It's the swamps, let's circle and see if there's anyone up there before we waste time landing," and no one argued with her because no one wanted to bother with the damnable humans of the north, anyway.

The coast came in sight within an hour or three, and Vaste spent his time at the rail with Niamh at his feet, looking out over the sweeping vistas afforded him by this commanding height. It was like having your own mountain with you everywhere you went, and the solitude wasn't bad, either. Merrish kept his distance and that was no imposition, sulking on the opposite rail. Aemma kept hers, and that, strangely, was. She stood brooding back at her own rail, staring into the distance to the west. Thinking about her people? Wondering at her place in all this since they'd been soundly rebuffed at New Idiarna? Vaste did not know, and though he cared, he did not pull himself away from his place at the bow, facing into the onrushing wind as they crossed over the dark and green swamps below.

Their vessel squeaked beneath them as it started to tack to the west. Vaste leaned to counter it, and the coastline began to bend away from them. It was blue ocean and quite placid now that the gods no longer roiled it to keep outsiders at bay.

Peering into the sea of green boughs beneath them, Vaste could see the ruin of what had once been Gren far ahead, at the split of two fingers of the coast. Great peninsulas stretched out to either side, and there in the overgrown mess between, squarely at the opening of that natural bay, were the last vestiges of the ancient Protanian settlement that the trolls had claimed for their own.

"Is that where we're going?" Aemma's quiet voice reached him, and he turned to find her at a respectful distance, as if hesitant to approach.

"Yes," he said, trying to discern any movement. It was pointless at this distance, though it did not appear as though anything sentient were living down there. No fresh buildings jutted out of the canopy, no new streets had been cleared, no fresh fields were plowed in the overgrowth. "That's my hometown. Or it was, anyway, a thousand years ago."

"It was destroyed, I take it?" Aemma asked, peering at it in the distance as she brushed tawny hair back behind her ear.

"In a similar manner to what happened to the humans of Termina." Vaste stole a look over his shoulder at Merrish. "Though it's hard to be sure at this distance, with so few willing to talk about it. Either way, they're gone now, driven from these lands to the last, probably almost entirely wiped out save for Oroguuk and whoever went with him into the west."

"Was this a great city once?" Aemma asked.

"Gren was never a great city," Vaste said. "All the best cities have indoor plumbing in my estimation." He sighed, though. "We had no great architecture of our own, all the greatness was the ruins of the past. The only thing the trolls added was wood dwellings with thatched roofs. No tile to hold out the rain in the manner of the elves, no stone walls to keep out the winds like the humans figured, and no glass panes in the windows of the sort that...well, everyone pretty much figured that one out. The trolls were the worst-developed people in Arkaria, as backward in our day as Arkaria is now. But it was home." He sighed. "Even though I didn't belong...it was still home."

She patted him on the arm; he hadn't even realized she had gotten close enough to do so. There was something reassuring about that, something that reminded him of a friend long gone. Like Niamh, he realized, though she lay at his feet, staring up at him with those big, black eyes, as if trying to say something.

"You see anything?" Aisling called out from the mid-deck. She was moving toward them, gliding up the steps onto the forecastle with greatest ease, and Vaste pulled his arm away from Aemma sharply, some instinct telling him to do so—

"I didn't do anything," Vaste said, then thought about what he said. "'See.' I haven't seen anything." Aisling was staring at him in the most peculiar manner; Aemma had a thinly amused smile. And Niamh...

...Well, she made a noise like a groan deep in her throat and rolled over.

"How are we supposed to find Azwillian mystics in this?" Aisling asked, finding her way to lean on the bow rail. Swamp waters waited below, and the broad patches of fields held a harvest that was all weeds, weeds as far as the eye could see, and sparkles of the sun on the sea.

A soft pop in the distance made Vaste turn his head. There, some six hundred meters off the bow to the right, was a brightly coruscating flash of red.

"Are those fireworks?" Aemma asked, squinting at them.

Another popped, sending green sparks out in a star pattern, not bright in the daylight but certainly visible.

"Ah," Aisling said, her hands on her thin hips. "That's probably the sign we're looking for, isn't it?"

"While we seek the mystics," Vaste said as she shouted orders to the quarterdeck to begin the landing, "the mystic seeks us in return."

Then he frowned. "I only hope they're kinder disposed than the last people who lived in this place."

"I thought this was your hometown?" Aemma asked.

"Oh, it was. But that doesn't mean they were welcoming," he said, then traced the line of scars on his forehead. "They gave me this the last time I visited without an army at my back. Let us hope our welcome today is more charitable."

CHAPTER 33

SHIRRI

"So strange to not see any scourge down there," Hiressam said, leaning against the rail. Reikonos was barely upon the horizon as the sun began to get lower in the sky. The plains beneath were bare and dull, gray, without a hint of green or grass or trees. "I remember when forests girdled this land, great copses like in the west."

"The scourge ate the greenery, huh?" Shirri stared dully down at them. She didn't know that for sure, but it seemed a not-totally-illogical assumption.

"They did," Hiressam said. "I suppose they got tired of waiting for meat after the first fifty years or so. We could see it, of course, back then, because you could still use Falcon's Essence to lift a caravan above the earth and traverse from here to the west. Back before we got the ships running regularly up the Perda and along the coast. And yes – after a time, sure enough, they turned on the grass like cows, on the trees like goats, and within another hundred years..." He waved a hand. "...Now there's not so much as a sapling down there. The scourge are the most effective mechanism I've ever seen for wiping out life – other than Malpravus's spell. No other army comes close."

"And where are they now?" Shirri asked. She felt strange inside, heady in a way. There was a lightness in her from having Longwell aboard, though he'd disappeared back below decks after Administrator Weltan had returned to her ship. Now the Emerald vessel was pacing alongside them, a smaller, faster ship than this elven hulk.

"Out there wherever their master is." This came from Houk, with his funny beard and mustache, and odd smile. "Champing at the same bit, chasing after the same enemies."

Hiressam frowned at Houk. "You may have a point. Also – have we met, sir? You seem quite familiar."

"I expect we've both been around a good long while, friend," Houk said with a toothy smile and an extended hand. "Surely we've run across each other some time before now, even if memory doesn't permit us to recall."

"Too true," Hiressam said, shaking his hand. "Are you from Pharesia originally?"

"No," Houk shook his head. "I'm from all around, really. Here, there, everywhere. Spent more time on the move in my life than anchored in the same place, you know."

"It was much the same for me," Hiressam said, "which I suppose increases the odds we've run across each other in the past."

"So long as we continue to do so in the future, eh?" Houk grinned. If he'd had a glass in hand, it'd have been perfect toast.

"Hark," the captain said, loud enough to be heard all across the middeck. "A ship above Reikonos." He was squinting into a spyglass, then slowly pulled his face away. "Chaarlandian dreadnought."

"Seventeen hells," Hiressam whispered, peering into the distance. Shirri looked, too, but the dreadnought was but a speck above the pea that was Reikonos to her. Elven vision was exceptional, but her half elven sight was barely half as good. If anyone on board needed the spyglass, it was surely her.

"Turn about," the captain ordered. "Take us back."

"Hold on a minute," Shirri said, and felt a strange, clutching sensation in her belly. She found herself running, the most curious thing, sandals clapping against the forecastle steps as she came down. "You mean to take us back?" She stared down the captain in his colored coat with gold piping on the sleeves and collar. "Back to where? Pharesia?"

The captain shrugged his broad shoulders. "It's a Chaarlandian dreadnought, ma'am. We are outclassed."

"It's the fate of the world here," Shirri said, the words springing, outrageous, from her lips – until she realized they were true. "Can we not defeat the dreadnought?"

The captain's eyes seemed to spin up and back in his head like one of those machines they used in casinos with the lever to pull. "By ourselves? Surely not. It is a dreadnought." He pointed again in the distance. "They are immense, ninety-two guns, while we are but a ship of seventy-four."

She stared blankly at him for a moment. "Is that how you measure these things? Who has the most cannon?" When he nodded, she took two steps to the right and pointed at the Emerald vessel abeam of them. "How many do they have?"

The captain winced. "Seventy, I would say."

"Then we have a hundred and forty-four guns to their ninety-two," Shirri said, holding her chin strangely high. Her heart hammered within her chest, yet outwardly she felt calm, clammy almost, as though the wind had chilled her down. "I give you this choice, captain – we fight this dreadnought in order to get what we came here for, and possibly die, or we retreat now and definitely die when Malpravus comes for us, because we will lack the means to destroy him." Her lip threatened to quiver, but she kept it stiff. She had said not a single thing false, and that gave her some strength in spite of the desire to pull her robe over her head and hide within it. A strong urge, but she resisted.

"We don't know if the ship from Emerald will follow us into that fight," the captain said, his eyes still wide. "They may decide to leave us to our fate."

"Signal them, then, if you worry," Shirri said, inspiration coming right to her. "Ask what they're willing to do. They may surprise you."

The captain hesitated, then nodded to the junior man beside him. "Signal them."

There was a strange dance of flags that Shirri watched over the next minutes, Hiressam coming up to her side. "That was well and boldly said."

"It really was," said Guy, who had appeared beside her. "My first temptation when hearing about the dreadnought? Run. And we just faced one of those, well, me and Alaric, anyway. Big ships. Lots of guns, very mean."

"Didn't you end up capturing that ship, though?" Shirri asked. "Didn't you arrive in it to the conference?"

"Yeah, but it was a bit hairy there for a while," Guy said. "Alaric got in there and did his thing, you know. As a ghost. Really saved the day." He brushed his hand against the hilt of his sword, then anchored his grip solidly on it. "Reckon he's not here this time, though." He brightened. "But we got Lord Longwell, don't we?"

"Indeed you do," Houk said, slipping up to their waiting circle, watching with them as the crew moved the flags up and down, signaling. Shirri could not tell what any of it meant, but she trusted it meant something. "But of more import will be the disposition of the ship from Emerald, called – quite propitiously, the *Lady Quinneria*. Coupled with this vessel they will be of much more use to us in breaking through this blockade than Lord Longwell and his lance." He smiled, almost apologetically.

"*Lady Quinneria* signals back their willingness," the captain announced, looking down on them. "Beat to quarters." He set his jaw. "Make ready for battle."

CHAPTER 34

ALARIC

The screech of the sea birds was a strange sound to Alaric's ears. There were unfamiliar ones mixed in with the bog-standard seagulls that frequented the port of Reikonos, brightly colored compared to the white gulls.

He found himself walking down unfamiliar streets in the sun-dappled town, shadows already growing long beneath the tall towers. They were nothing like the minarets of elvendom, nor the trees of Amti, or even the old wood structures of Reikonos. Nothing in his experience looked like this, these mud-daubed buildings that looked like they had been cast in the light of a dragon's breath, stone and orange tile roofs, with easy streets and open squares where elves and men of Arkaria and with a slightly foreign cast walked and talked and sold and shopped.

"You need to stop gawking," Mazirin said beside him, drawing a chortle from Qualleron, who lingered back a few steps. When Alaric looked to her, he found the thin hint of a smile on her lips. "You draw enough attention as it is with your peculiar garb."

"I am a knight of old," Alaric said, for yes, the people they passed were looking at him quite strangely. Or at least the humans were, and the occasional dark elf that was scattered among them; the elves seemed to take him in stride, as though it were not unusual to find a man in full armor walking their streets. But then for them, such things probably seemed like a relatively recent fashion.

"You could have had him leave his armor in the airship, with the others," Qualleron said in his low rumble. "If you were that concerned about it."

Did Alaric's eyes deceive him, or did a faint hint of redness appear upon Mazirin's cheeks? "I would not wish him to be undefended should we be attacked."

"Truly?" Alaric asked, for he felt perhaps he was missing something. He had little time to reflect on it, though; a man in a brightly-colored tunic caught his eye. Leaning against an orange wall, it was not his own brilliant attire that caught Alaric's eye, but rather the black spot of an armband that stood out amidst it all. "Damnation."

"Hm?" Mazirin looked to him, then beyond, where he was looking. "Is that...?"

"Why, he wears the garb of the Machine," Qualleron said in mild surprise as the man slipped off the wall, more casual in his movement than the three of them watching.

"I thought we'd seen their end," Alaric said, "along with the city."

"They had tendrils all over this land," Mazirin said. "Making inroads elsewhere, like a sea monster with its...tendrils," she finished lamely. "I don't know another way to say it in your language."

"I don't wish to leave this particular task unfinished," Alaric said, surging forward into motion again, after the thug, who'd disappeared into the alleyway. "Not least because the way he looked at us suggested, at least to me, recognition. Who knows if Malpravus still pulls those strings?"

"It would be a little funny if he had killed them all save for these, and yet they serve him," Qualleron said, pacing behind at a jog that thudded the cobblestones.

"I suspect that is what happened," Alaric said, slipping into the alley. It widened ahead, but the man was gone, and they could see entry onto another of the town's avenues. Alaric followed after, but as the alley widened on either side leaving blind corners, he heard a click and turned–

There waiting in the lee of the building, was not only the Machine thug he'd followed into this alley, but more. Through an open door they filed out, a dozen, more, making a circle around Alaric, Mazirin, and Qualleron, pistols and daggers drawn and pointed, ill intent clear–

They were surrounded.

CHAPTER 35

VASTE

*T*here was no landing, for there was nowhere to land, per se. The fields around Gren that had appeared to be weedy and overgrown were indeed, and not flat, no sign of airship docks that could be used or repurposed. After one pass over the harbor Aisling had written that off, too, as too silty and in desperate need of dredging. "We try and harbor here, we'll be stuck in the mud," she said, shaking her head. "Nothing for it but to leave her at a hover and use the rope ladder."

And so they had, and Vaste cared for that not one whit.

His beautiful arse swayed in the breeze, the rope ladder swinging as though a madman had hold of one end – the bottom end, of course – and was trying to drop him the last thirty feet from ship to ground, the better to damage his beautiful arse on the endless briars and brambles that waited in the so-called field beneath.

"Are you quite all right?" This from Merrish, who waited above for him to finish his downward transit. Aemma waited with him, and Niamh the scourge, too, their three heads poking out all in a line watching as he swayed wildly back and forth on this damnable ladder.

"I am desperately trying to be all right," Vaste said, keeping Letum gripped carefully in his hand, sandwiched between it and the rope on his right side, for the increase in grip strength and speed to assess the sway and movement of the rope ladder was the only reason he had not yet taken a dramatic fall, "but the wind and ladder are doing their best to be sure I am not."

"Just take your time," Aemma called, the voice of encouragement.

"I could spend all day on this thing and it would only make things worse," Vaste grumbled. The swing of the ladder, like a pendulum, only grew more pronounced the lower he climbed.

"You're doing...fine," Merrish said, and there was no honesty there. He sounded as though he were cringing.

"You're over halfway there," Aemma said, more honestly. But then, a cardsharp was more honest than Merrish had been.

"What is the hold up?" Aisling's voice came over the side, and then her face appeared. "Did I need to send one of my men first, to show you how it's done, Vaste?"

"You can send all the men you want, they're not half the man I am, and that is the problem," Vaste called back, taking another uneasy step down. "It's an issue of weight, of swing – or possibly just the deliciousness–"

"This has nothing to do with your arse," Aisling said.

"When you have an arse as gorgeous as mine, everything has something to do with it."

"What's all this about his arse?" Merrish asked quietly, barely audible over the chop of the blades. "I've never met anyone who talked about their arse so much, and I once encountered a woman from Binngart who made quite the living off hers."

"It's his thing," Aisling said. "He has so little in his life to be proud of, we just sort of let him run with it. It makes him more bearable to believe it's of special value."

"How dare you insult me so," Vaste said, making another step, carefully, as the ladder swayed what felt like perfectly sideways. He hung on. "You have no room to talk, you once clung to Cyrus's long arse. Who are you to judge?"

"I'm sure your arse is perfectly fine," Aemma called down to him. "Focus on climbing down safely."

"You people don't know good arses," Vaste said, taking another step. Only a few to go, now. "It's that you don't have trolls anymore, you see. Your frame of reference is the tiny arses of your people. Small is not good. Small is not a proper frame for excellence. Why, imagine a painting of the great masters that's on a canvas of two inches. That's your people's arses. Narrow. Bony. Starved, practically. Not enough room for the brush strokes of excellence. You need wide hips. You need perfect proportions. You need–"

"To shut up and take the last step," Aisling said.

"–you need space to make perfection," Vaste said, taking the last step and feeling his feet sink into the loamy ground all the way up to his claw-like toenails. "There. Now my perfect arse is home at last."

"I don't know, *gisomari,*" came a voice from beside him, "I got a good, long look at your arse on the way down and...I just don't see what the fuss is about."

It was all Vaste could do not to emit a girlish shriek and leap his arse away from the unexpected speaker. Instead he raised Letum high and took a step back, moving swiftly with its aid but as though he'd seen a mouse.

A pair of eyes was looking at him from a thicket, and facial features could be discerned in the gray dirt peeking out from beneath a cap with grass sprouting from beneath it. White teeth grinned at him. "'Lo, *gisomari.* How you do?"

It was a man, though his bottom half was hidden in the shrubs he blended seamlessly into, his skin coated in soil to disguise him. He rose as Vaste took another step back, but there were no weapons in his hand, which were open, and a more natural shade of human skin, a sort of bronzed color. He rose, his grass hat swaying in the wash coming off the airship, and a slight thump next to him made Vaste turn–

Aisling had descended the rope ladder mere seconds, a pistol in her hand and pointed at the man, who had his hands up, but did not look particularly like he was surrendering. "Who are you and what are you doing here?"

"My name is Asa-tee," he said, still grinning, keeping his hands raised, "and I was waiting for you. So..." And he brushed a clod of dirt off his back where it had hidden him from the airship, "...now that you're here...I can take you to meet Huaviri."

CHAPTER 36

CYRUS

"I hate this part," Cyrus said, grimacing, for truly, he did. This was the second day in the palace, and the routine was already well-set. Much of his time was his own, but this – this was part of the requirements of the job, and non-negotiable.

"It's only fifteen minutes," Vara said, a sigh under her breath the only sign that she, too, found this unbearable – or at least unpalatable.

"Per day," Cyrus said. "Every day." He rested a hand on the pommel of Rodanthar and took a deep breath of the citrus-infused air. The palace had a dusty aroma; it had seen little use, at least this wing, in the last thousand years. It had changed greatly, in Cyrus's estimation. Not only decaying, in disrepair, they had also...changed things. Not all for the better.

This was, in his estimation, much for the worse.

"Remember when this was all palace grounds, practically all the way to the horizon?" Vara, as if harmonizing with his thoughts – or perhaps merely trying to assuage him – brushed a comforting hand on his arm. He barely felt it, though, because of the armor, and somehow this annoyed him still more.

"Yes," Cyrus said, staring out through white shears into the noonday sun. Beyond lay a great balcony above the portico where all the visitors had come and gone in his day. But now, instead of miles of palace grounds–

There was a crowd of thousands, and the city intruded almost all the way up into this space.

The door to the antechamber behind clicked as someone stepped inside. Cyrus could already tell who it was going to be, because the hour was at hand. Dioro, of course – and a dozen attendants came along behind.

"I see you're ready for today's viewing," Dioro said with much enthusiasm.

"It does feel much like a viewing," Cyrus said dourly. "Of the funerary variety."

"Come now," Dioro said. "You're hardly dead."

"Yet."

"Dead is the death of hope," Dioro said, leaning on his staff as the attendants crawled all over them. Plucking cheeks to add rosiness, brushing armors, giving it a sheen (which failed in Cyrus's case, always). "This is about giving hope." He rustled in his robes and brought out a piece of paper with a yellowed hue. "Look at these handbills making their way 'round the city. Tell me there's no good in what you do."

He offered it to Cyrus and it was grudgingly accepted over the polish brush of one of the attendants moving over his arm at the time. Cyrus stared at the handbill, with a crude drawing of his face printed on it, his helm distinctive in this time of little armor and funny hats. A second picture was much more interesting and detailed. It appeared to be him riding in the back of the motorcoach with Vara when they'd arrived. He peered at it, the reproduction of the moment white paper and black ink, but with a surprising amount of grayness as subtle shading. It looked more real than any painting he'd seen, and he said so, lifting it up so Vara could see it as well.

"It's a photograph," Dioro said. "A sort of mechanical painting, if you will, using a machine. It's all the rage elsewhere on the globe but such things are still rare here. Anyhow, they took it when you came into town."

"I don't look like that, do I?" Vara asked, practically ripping the thing out of Cyrus's hand. She probed self-consciously at her cheeks.

"Every bit as lovely, my dear," Cyrus said. "They made more than one of these?"

Dioro chuckled. "Many thousands, probably. They're circulating all around the city."

Cyrus tried to read the elvish in bold lettering at the top, but he couldn't put it together. A variation of 'return' seemed to be one of the words, but the rest made no sense to him. "What's the purpose of this?"

"Communication," Dioro said, preparing to pluck the handbill from Cyrus. Vara beat him to it, frowning deeply as she stared at the picture as though it carried the very secrets of life within it. "You can keep it," he said hastily. "As I said, there are countless more."

"But I'm not exactly looking my best in this, am I?" Vara waved the flyer.

Cyrus turned his head slowly to look at his wife. "I'm sure that will be of great concern to Malpravus when he comes to kill us. 'Vara is not looking her best. Perhaps I'll kill them twice as hard now. No – thrice!'"

"It's easy for you to not care how you look," Vara said, flushing a bit as she lowered the handbill. "You're not from elvendom, you don't know the people. The voice of your mother is not in your head presently, telling you to appear presentable when in public – especially when attending a parade given in one's own honor." She grimaced. "I should have kept my helm on, my hair is simply atrocious."

Cyrus blinked, then looked to Dioro, who nodded sympathetically. "Many people are having this experience now. Mirrors are clearer and lack the blurriness that came from imprecise glasswork; photographs show us in unforgiving detail."

"I had a smudge of dirt on my face," Vara said, apparently realizing

145

for the first time. "It must have come from when Isabelle and I battled Longwell." She reached up to her cheek and rubbed at it urgently.

"It's gone now," Cyrus said. "You got it in the bath last night."

Her eyes became inflamed. "You knew?"

Cyrus stared at her. "Of course I knew. We were together the night before, did you think I would miss it?"

"And you did nothing?" There was a fiery lethality, a warning in her eyes. "You did not even warn me?"

"Who are you?" Cyrus asked, "and what have you done with my wife, who was once more concerned with lopping the heads off our enemies than with whether she had acquired a smudge of dirt on her cheek? Honestly, who cares."

She flushed a bright red, then thrust the handbill back at him, thumping it against his breastplate. "Unlike you, I have the capacity to worry about more than one thing at a time. And looking presentable when out in public was one of Mother's great worries when I was a child. I had a reputation to maintain, after all, as Shelas'akur. Had I seen what I looked like – flat hair, dirty face, I could have washed my face more thoroughly and worn my helm." She pointed a finger at him rather violently as if for emphasis. "Tell me next time."

"I assure you," Dioro said, gesturing to the retinue of elven servants that waited behind Vara and, as her anger subsided, swarmed her once more to fret about her hair and cheeks and all else, "your husband need not worry, for we will be much more careful in the future. Your image is of paramount importance, and we have people that will concern themselves entirely with that."

"Great," Cyrus said, watching two elves with polishing cloths work on his armor. It didn't seem to do much good; the quartal had always been incredibly black, not a natural shade for the metal. "One less thing for me to worry about." He caught a glare from his wife and it made his stomach rumble in a way that peril in a thousand battles had not.

"Come, heroes," Dioro said grandly, waving them over to the balcony and the roaring crowds that waited beyond the curtain. Cyrus

146

blanched, teetering up to the curtain, Vara at his side, the elven servants finally finished with their primping, one of them muttering about her hair, and some grand plan for it on the morrow. "Come and see the hope you bring."

Cyrus did not feel much hope as he stepped out onto the balcony, but the roar of the crowd was unlike anything he could recall. It surged to life and for a moment he felt desperately alone, as if standing before a commandingly terrifying foe; Malpravus times a thousand, cold and evil, and lacking even the familiarity of that damnable necromancer.

But he felt the clink of gauntleted fingers against his own, and looked to find his wife's hand on his. She smiled shyly at him, all trace of her anger gone. He felt braver with her by his side again, and raised his hand to the crowd in the manner of some fool waving to an old friend. He set his face against the task and did it, Vara at his side, bringing hope to these roaring masses in the only way he presently could.

CHAPTER 37

SHIRRI

The Chaarlandian dreadnought did not waste time; as they approached, it tacked swiftly toward them, gliding across the darkening land toward them. Its bow was cutting through the early evening like it was upon smooth seas.

"If that dreadnought's captain is worth his salt," the captain opined, "he will sail squarely between us, unleashing a broadside on both our ships." His chin was set, face grim. "And if we are lucky, he will strike our decks and sides but miss the engines and blades." He favored Shirri with a taut look. "This will become bloody. There is no avoiding it."

"Oh." Shirri had, dimly, realized that was to be the case. It wasn't as though she'd sought blood in this, or any other decision she'd made since this mess had begun. It was just a natural outgrowth of the path she'd found herself on since taking the Machine's "loan." Hard to believe a simple inquiry into history had led her from loan sharks to an airship battle with the fate of Arkaria and the world somehow in the balance...yet here she was.

"Increase to three quarters," the captain ordered. "Let's make it a swift pass; run out the guns!"

The order echoed beneath, and the flaps of wood that covered the gun ports on the deck beneath flapped and clacked, opening as the clunk of heavy iron cannon straining against wood wheels issued forth. Shirri leaned against the rail and could see the black barrels appear below as the cannons were secured, sticking out of the sides like porcupine spines.

"Enemy ahead!" the spotter on the quarterdeck called. "Four hundred meters!"

"Make ready!" the captain shouted, with other voices relaying his command below. Shirri braced herself against the rail, keenly aware that metal would be soon flying. "Bow chasers – fire as you come to bear!"

Two small cannons at the forecastle blasted just then. Shirri watched the immense dreadnought – a beefy ship, positively bursting with additional width and length compared to hers.

"I don't even know this ship's name." Longwell was suddenly beside her, spear in hand, eyes focused off in the distance. He chuckled, and it sounded dry and dark. "I might die on this ship and I don't know its name."

"It's called the *Grace*," Guy said. He'd appeared, too, footsteps covered in the running out of the guns.

"That's not quite right," Shirri said, her eyes focused on the dreadnought, which had registered no impact from the forecastle cannons save for slight puffs of dust along the bow, signifying nearly nothing. "It's called the *Grace of the Shelas'akur*."

There was a moment of silence punctuated by the bow chasers firing again. "What was Alixa's ship called?" Longwell asked.

"The *Lady Quinneria*," Shirri said. There were a lot of cannons bristling out of the dreadnought's sides. And they were drawing ever nearer.

"I've come so far," Longwell said after a long moment, "yet I still cannot escape these infernal Davidon women."

A wild chuckle escaped Shirri. "I hadn't thought of it that way." When she noticed Longwell's head tilted, broad, bearded face holding an expression of incredulity, she added, "Well, they're both very common names these days. Every fleet in Arkaria has a *Vara* or *Lady Vara* or the flowery elven version we're on now. And every human fleet has a *Quinneria*."

"Consider yourself lucky you got ships from the women of Davidon collection," Hiressam added. The dreadnought was now a hundred meters away and steering to pass close, the *Lady Quinneria* running almost parallel to them. As the captain had noted, it would pass between them, probably hammering them on both sides with its immense cannons. "The only more common names are some variant of Cyrus Davidon. It would not be inconceivable for you to take a ride every day of the month on a ship named for him."

"I hate what this world has become," Longwell muttered. It was nearly drowned out by cannon fire.

"Bank and dive!" the captain shouted as the dreadnought began to pass between them. With a lurch, the *Grace* tilted sideways, away from the Chaarlandian vessel, and also dropped some twenty feet in a sudden plunge that forced Shirri to cling to the rail.

"The *Lady Quinneria* is mirroring us," Hiressam said. "Look!"

Through the bulk of the Chaarlandian destroyer he could see the Lady Quinneria moving opposite them, rising while they fell, rolling left as they did, as though the two ships were matched on an invisible swell, the broad sides still pointed at the Chaarlandian vessel, which was caught between them, unable to tilt swiftly enough to match them both.

"FIRE!" The captain shouted, and the last part of the word was drowned out.

The cannons beneath them exploded into fire and fury all as one, the dreadnought matching their volley and beyond it, the *Lady Quinneria* doing the same though Shirri could barely see it. The *Grace* shuddered, then shook, something exploding above them, shards of metal raining down and striking the deck.

"Blade hit!" someone shouted over the din.

Shirri held fast to the rail as a shining piece of metal glinted, hurtling overboard as if flung from a sling. One of the Chaarlandian cannons had struck a turning prop, breaking it free and launching it. She raised her eyes to the underside of the dreadnought, watching the *Grace's* cannons strike true; armored flashings of metal were breaking free, and dozens of holes had appeared in the underbelly of the vessel. Half a body was sticking out of one, a rain of red drizzling out like a leaking pipe. Black smoke was coursing out of the top deck, and Shirri stared blankly at one of the big holes looming above as the dreadnought smoothly passed her by, and she lifted her hand, breathed a whisper of magic–

And sent a ball of fire into the hole with unerring accuracy.

It seemed to explode within, a muffled WHUMP! barely audible over the straining engines of the *Grace* and the brutally loud ones of the Chaarlandian dreadnought.

"Take us low and around!" the captain shouted. Below, she could hear screaming for the gun crews to reload.

"*Lady Q* is going high!" the watcher called.

"And we'll go low," the captain said.

"This is a bit more dramatic than I hoped this trip would be," Guy said, clutching the railing, his cheek red where he'd rubbed it against the wood during the volley.

"Same," Longwell said, similarly anchored. If the rail took a hit...they'd all be in real trouble.

"Dreadnought is remaining on course – she's speeding up!" the watcher shouted.

"Level the ship, come down on the port, and fire as your guns come to bear!" the captain shouted.

Near as she could tell, the ship had flattened out slightly and now was leaning left again, raising the guns to point at the retreating dreadnought. Almost directly above them – perhaps fifty meters out from Shirri's head – was the *Lady Quinneria*, crossing above as the *Grace* crossed below. Both had a perfect angle on the dreadnought, its tail retreating as it started to turn to double back to its right–

A rolling staccato broadside bloomed from the front of the *Grace* to the rear, cannonballs launching forth like black spots in Shirri's vision as she clung to the rail. They impacted the rear of the dreadnought with ferocity, sending panels of armor falling to the gray earth, opening holes in the exposed planks, spots of darkness within the vessel opened to the waning daylight.

As their rolling broadside reached its end, the *Lady Quinneria* began to open up – with slightly less ferocity but perhaps more accuracy. There had been a series of windows at the back of the Chaarlandian vessel; they were gone now, blasted out as though an explosion had opened the rear of the ship. Twin spinning blades had been there a moment before. Now, after an eyeblink she didn't realize she dared take, neither remained, and a sparkling metal shot from the rear of the dreadnought and planted itself in the gray earth.

A mighty cheer rose from the deck of the *Grace*. "Her props are destroyed, Captain," the lookout called, eye fixed to his spyglass. "She's dead in the air."

But that did not seem entirely true to Shirri. The dreadnought was in a slow turn – painfully slow, like it was gradually listing to its right, only a quarter of the vessel's side visible, and none of her cannons in position for a shot. "Signal *Lady Quinneria* to break off," the captain ordered. "We'll ride her tail and finish this with–"

"They're firing stern chasers," the lookout shouted.

"Too little, too late," the captain said with a grim smile. "Ready the broadside, and elevate us to fi–"

There was a distant pop of the Chaarlandian ship's rear cannons, and the soft whistle as the cannonballs passed overhead, crashing into one of the propellers with a sound like thunder, and something struck Hiressam, sending him to the deck under a spray of blood that spattered the boards. Shirri cried out as well, for something sharp punched her in the side where she clung to the rail, and the *Grace* lurched.

"Direct hit to the center prop," the lookout said with unerring calm.

"Fire broadside!" the captain shouted as the ship lurched again – then again, as the broadside was fired.

Shirri lifted her head as the *Grace* shook under the release of the broadside, flames leaping out from beneath her in a wild staccato. The back of the Chaarlandian ship disintegrated under the withering fire of the cannons–

The Chaarlandian dreadnought exploded with a roar of fire and force that sent the *Grace* tumbling sideways. Something jarred loose above and went overboard; a shadow passed like a great raptor out of the corner of her eye, and such was the force that she could feel its passage like a leaden weight moving at great speed mere inches past her head.

Then the *Grace* dipped, nose first, toward the ground...and began to pick up speed.

Shirri knew the feeling, knew it in the pit of her stomach as the ship lurched, the burnt and blackened city of Reikonos laid before them with its forbidding walls and endless ash contained within. The feeling of falling, of racing forward toward the ground without hope that the machinery of the airship – the damaged, broken machinery – would arrest that fall.

They were going to crash.

And they might not make it to the ruined city before they did.

CHAPTER 38

ALARIC

They were all around, troublesome mites. Black-banded thugs, the residual traces of the Machine in all its ugliness, strewn about the alley – and now behind them, too, Alaric realized, dropping off the short rooftops.

"How exciting," Qualleron rumbled. The sight of a full-blooded warrior troll among them did not seem to concern the dozen or so Machine thugs who encircled Alaric's small party. The orange stucco walls fenced them in on two sides, and the black-coated thugs took the other two, forming a box. Daggers were plentiful, and a few pistols were in evidence as well.

"Doesn't need to be," the lead thug said, a man with a peculiar and thick mustache across his upper lip – and no other hair anywhere on his head. His face suggested middle age, and his scars spoke of a man who'd been in this life for perhaps all of his. The checkerboard pattern told of knife fights that this man had survived, perhaps regular fights as well. His nose had a quality that hinted at repeated brokenness. "It can be quiet and painless – if you let it."

"I am not all about the silence," Mazirin said, and Alaric noticed she'd drawn her shorter, curved blade that rested at the small of her back, as well as her pistol. She drew a bead on the leader, pointing at him straight from the hip. "I am a citizen of Amatgarosa; you tempt the roar of my people with your act here today."

"You may leave if you like," the scarred thug said. "Our quarrel is not with you...nor the troll." He nodded at Qualleron. He focused his attention back on Alaric. "It's the old man we've got orders for. So...walk away, and nothing more need be said."

"You both should go," Alaric said, keeping his hands at his sides. "There's no reason for either of you to become involved in this."

"Honor demands that I stay," Qualleron said, his own hand resting upon his blade.

"Self-preservation suggests you leave," Alaric said, placing a hand gently upon Qualleron's arm. "My friend – you cannot dodge bullets, and it seems to me they will be flying in this alley shortly." He held his head high, and tried to wink at the troll, though he was not sure that it was received, for Qualleron squinted oddly at him, as if trying to perceive something.

"Fine," Mazirin said, catching his drift – and his intent. "Qualleron – we should go."

Scar raised a mangled eyebrow at that. "Wisest thing I've heard all day." He stepped aside, keeping his pistol pointed at Alaric. "No tricks, no coming back after you leave the field of battle, unnerstan'? You break the truce, it's all out, all the time til you're dead, you hear me?"

"In spite of your atrocious accent, you are understood," Mazirin said, taking up Qualleron's arm from Alaric. "Come."

Qualleron stared down at Alaric. "We will see you there, yes?"

"You'll see him in the next life, you jaundiced bastard," one of the Machine thugs guffawed. Others followed.

"Soon," Alaric said, nodding to Qualleron.

Qualleron nodded, and let Mazirin steer him down the alley. "Don't look back, my sweets," Scar called after them, leveling his pistol at Alaric. "You wouldn't want to be tempted to stay for this."

Alaric took a very slight step to the left, positioning himself in front of one of the Machine thugs who'd cut off his retreat. By his reckoning now...yes. He was perfectly lined up with Scar.

"You don't have very good friends, do you?" Scar asked, catching the nod from one of his black-coated associates as Qualleron and Mazirin rounded the alley mouth. "To leave you in the lurch like this."

"Part of friendship is trusting one another," Alaric said. "They left because they knew that I was in no true danger here, and they trust me to dispense with you. Which I am prepared to do peaceably, if you'd prefer." He stretched his fingers by templing them, then pushing; his knuckles cracked. "If you choose violence, however, I am prepared for that as well."

"I'm going to go with option A," Scar said, grinning as he raised the pistol in a perfect line with Alaric's head. He fingered the trigger, the blast rang out in the alleyway—

And behind him, Alaric heard the bullet hit home in a Machine thug's brain, splattering it all over the ochre wall.

To his left, Alaric saw another Machine thug with a pistol raise his own weapon. Two swift steps back and Alaric lined himself up perfectly again—

Thunder again cracked down the alley and a sharp grunt of pain was followed by a thud as another thug hit his knees. A quick glance confirmed he was bleeding from a chest wound, crimson fountaining between his clutching fingers.

"I think I heard Mazirin refer to this as a 'circular firing squad,'" Alaric mused aloud, catching movement behind him as the remaining two thugs lifted their pistols. He shifted slightly, spinning to face them with a grin—

The explosion of noise was, this time, followed by screams and gurgling. One bullet had struck a Machine thug in the throat, the second hit another fellow in the stomach and he was flat on his arse, mouth wide, screaming to the heavens.

"Recall that you chose this," Alaric said, at last drawing Aterum. Scar was fumbling with his pistol, trying to hurriedly reload it with powder horn and wadding, while watching Alaric with one eye and keeping the other on what he was doing. The men around him stood uncertainly at what they'd just witnessed; four were down, and nine stood around, torn between reloading and hesitating, their daggers glinting in Balaar's warm sunlight. "I tried to warn you away, and you are suffering consequences." His blade in hand, Alaric steadied himself. "Now you will suffer more."

"What are you waiting for?" Scar asked, pausing his reloading action. "A telegraphed invitation? Get the geezer!"

They did not all swarm him, but enough did that as Alaric faded insubstantial four daggers crossed through him at the same time, resulting in three of them being stabbed by their fellows. The screams were considerable, louder somehow than even the fellow who'd been shot in the gut.

Leaving all that behind, Alaric stepped sideways from the mass of arms and daggers and blood, swinging his sword behind him and striking true into the throat of the one man who hadn't been struck. He gurgled, blade slashing through his neck, and he dropped, blood spattering the dusty cobblestones.

Another came at him, then another, and he slashed through them methodically. It was not a challenge; these back alley brawlers had little craft and all strength, and when one would lunge toward him, he would go insubstantial, letting them pass through while bringing up his blade and slashing through them with Aterum. Between the augmented speed and dexterity of his sword and his ability to go etherial, there was little they could do to him.

Yet still they tried their best to kill him.

Thus he felt little compunction about killing them to the last – and the last was Scar, who was sweating as he thumbed back the hammer on his flintlock pistol and pointed it at Alaric. Great beads of moisture were coursing down the ridges of his face, and he swallowed visibly as he drew a bead on the old knight's head once more.

"Do you truly believe that you can stop me with that?" Alaric asked, staying his hand, Aterum in a high guard above his head. "When all your fellows have already fallen?"

"No," Scar said, voice hoarse, and the hints of tears in the big man's eyes, "but they'll kill me if I don't at least try. Their last directive was clear: 'End the old knight.'"

"Reikonos is ash," Alaric said, and for the first time, the scarred man evinced a hint of worry. "It was destroyed a month ago." He did not lower his blade. "Your Machine is gone, along with the city. The Lord Protector made it an ash heap, a pyre of sacrifice for his own grandiosity. You did not hear of this?"

"Whispers, only," he said, still sweating in the moist air. "Rumors, really." With his free hand, he mopped his brow; he was sweating completely out of proportion to the warmth of the day, though to Alaric it was like summer in the plains – or perhaps worse, like the weather out of the swamps south of the Inculta desert. "They're all dead?"

"Save for any that might be lingering in the other cities of Arkaria," Alaric said. "Or elsewhere." He cocked his head at Scar. "Are there other branches elsewhere?"

The man shook his bald head slowly. "Balaar is a free port. Just outside the easy reach of Amti, but not allowing the influence of the Firoban states to come across. This is the only place we were given space to grow." He looked slowly over the corpses in the alley and tensed. "I'm the last one left, now."

Alaric slowly lowered his sword. "Lay down your arms and walk away, then. Begin anew somewhere else – or you will die in this alley. This I vow."

Scar looked down at the pistol clutched in his hand. "I've never done anything but this." He chuckled weakly. "I don't know how to do anything else."

"And you never will," Alaric said, "unless you put down the pistol and walk away."

After a long moment of staring, the man uncocked the pistol and let it fall from his fingers. That done, he shed his dagger and it rang out like a bell as it fell to the cobblestones. He shucked out of his black coat and armband, leaving them crumpled in blazing sun.

"Now go," Alaric said, watching his eyes. He was defeated; there was little fight in the man now. "Go find a purpose for your life. Something grander than petty robbery and carving out a criminal fiefdom. Make it something worthy of your second chance. Something that helps people. Something that blots out that exquisite delight you got from hurting others all these years. Try to forget that – or better still, think about it every day – and do your best to atone for all the wrong you have done."

"Yeah," the scarred man said, pausing up the alley. "Maybe." His head was down, and he shuffled off down the sun-dappled alley.

Alaric watched him go, and pondered his second chance. The man was filled with regrets, that much was plain to see.

But Alaric? He had none, and as soon as the man shuffled around the corner, he started onward, in the direction Mazirin and Qualleron had gone, hoping to catch them before they got too far.

"Alaric..."

The whisper caught him before he'd made it to the end of the alleyway, and he turned back. He could have sworn it came from that direction, and yet there was no one moving behind him; no hint that the dead bodies were anything other than dead. Certainly wide, shocked eyes were looking at him, but there was no hint of movement, no suggestion–

"Alaric."

One of their mouths moved, and Alaric started. He clenched his hand on Aterum's hilt, his lone eye narrowing, for this time he recognized the voice...

...of the damned – and damnable – speaker.

"Hello, my old friend," the thug's corpse said, grinning in a wide rictus that deeply resembled the speaker, Malpravus calling out to him from however far away he was, "it's so surprising to see you again."

CHAPTER 39

VASTE

*A*sa-tee turned out to be quite the chatty fellow. His skin was a deep bronze, with almost a red tinge to it, and though he waited for Aisling, Merrish, and Aemma to descend the ladder – the Niamh scourge jumped on her own and Vaste caught her as the airship edged closest to the ground – he was soon enough off into the swamp, relying on the troll and his party to follow with only a steady patter to keep him on the trail.

"...really tough to keep quiet knowing you're about to land on me," Asa-tee said, dodging soundlessly behind a thicket of long sawgrass. "A couple feet to the right and you'd have plowed one of those feet into my belly." He paused long enough to pat his bare stomach, which was...well, not ample exactly, not like Vaste's, but neither was it the rigid wall of unappealing muscles found on, say, Cyrus.

"That would have been regrettable," Vaste said, hustling to keep up. He'd switched to his boots, thankfully, because in the swamp sandals just did not work particularly well. Asa-tee seemed to be barefoot, and damned surefooted as well, following a path Vaste couldn't see. "Who are you again?"

Asa-tee poked his head around the thicket, the sawgrass blades from his hat swaying in the light breeze. "Asa-tee. Need me to spell it out in your language to remember it?"

"No," Vaste said, stopping on a mound of dry grass. "My question is less about the spelling and phonetics of your name and more about who the hell you are." He tapped his chest with Letum. "For example, my name is Vaste, but who I am is more than my name."

Asa-tee looked at him blankly for a moment. "Name's supposed to be the essence of you. Of course, I know that's not exactly how things work over here for the other folk, but I thought things were different with *you*."

"What would give you that idea?" Vaste asked. How had they anticipated him? Because there were not really any dead to speak of, at least not in Vaste's sight, and it was hard to imagine that the spirits of the trolls were still lingering around Gren some three quarters of a thousand years after they'd been slaughtered.

"Because *you're* supposed to be different," Asa-tee said, as though this were most obvious thing in the world. "You came here to meet Huaviri, didn't you?"

"If Huaviri is a great teacher who can tell me how to beat the necromancer threatening this land, then yes," Vaste said. Aisling was somehow now behind him, ahead of both Aemma and Merrish. Hopefully the two of them weren't trying to kill each other out of his sight.

Asa-tee threw his arms wide and grinned. "You're in luck. Not only is Huaviri a great spirit teacher, but he has a phenomenal arse – compared to yours, anyway. Since you seem to care very deeply about that sort of thing. Now come." And he disappeared back behind the sawgrass patch.

"Hear that? A phenomenal arse." Aisling nudged him. "Isn't that exciting for you?"

Vaste frowned. "I'm more interested in the part about him being a shaman. I don't really give a rip about other men's arses." He glanced over her and saw – at last – Aemma and Merrish coming up from behind a patch of trees, looking quite warily at each other, the Niamh scourge pacing between them as though she were some small barrier between them killing each other. "That's not looking promising."

"Should have left one of them on the airship," Aisling said, looking back. The vessel was there, a few hundred feet back, hanging there and creeping along behind them. "Any of this area look familiar?"

"What? I never wandered outside Gren, especially as a child," Vaste said, glancing around. "That's a quick way to get yourself dead. Do you have any idea how many leeches there are in these swamps? How many alligators? How many outcasts there were who were trying to breed goats with alligators to create pet armies of complete domination?"

Aisling stared at him. "I imagine that last one didn't work out too well."

"Not for the goats, no. Though I imagine it was still better than being kept in Gren." He paused. "Because of–"

"The buggery, yes. I have heard."

"What a rousing hike," Merrish said with a dollop of faux-cheeriness as he came to a stop, Aemma trailing a dozen paces behind him, looking quite a bit more sour. A little of his cheer receded. "Do we have any idea how long we're going to be walking in...this?" His smile drained away slowly, as though he simply could not maintain his ebullience.

"Why?" Aemma asked. "Are you feeling weary, elf? Perhaps you should go back to the airship."

"No, I'm quite fine," Merrish said.

"Wonderful," Asa-tee called, peeking out from behind the sawgrass patch. "If you're coming, get moving. I'm hungry, and there's venison waiting on the fire back at the camp. If we hurry, we can be there in a couple-three days." And he was gone again, rustling the grass so they could easily follow.

Merrish's face fell. "I...he is joking, isn't he?"

"Who would joke so devilishly with a newly-met stranger?" Vaste asked. It would be worth the pain for the look on Merrish's face.

Perhaps. "Off we go," he added with extra cheer, and plunged off after Asa-tee, the others following behind.

CHAPTER 40

SHIRRI

"Signal the *Lady Quinneria* that we are in an uncontrolled descent," the captain said with a strange calm. His voice reached Shirri's ears over the rising wind as the *Grace of the Shelas'akur* picked up speed; she could not tell whether that was intentional on the part of the captain, trying to race to the walls of Reikonos before the inevitable crash. It seemed wiser than smashing into the ground outside, where some remnant scourge might make a feast of them.

But down they were headed, this much was certain, and swiftly, at that. The big question for Shirri, clutching at the rail, was whether they were destined to crash into the gray earth before the moat, splash into the moat itself, or perhaps shatter against the wall. The downward pitch of the *Grace* suggested perhaps some combination of all three; maybe it would strike the last inches of land, slide sideways into the moat, the prow shattering into the immense stone wall that ringed the city.

Shirri's stomach dropped with the ship, and she lost her footing, hugging tight to the rail. The *Grace* slewed sideways, the captain screaming something about controlling the descent. Someone flew overboard, screaming as they passed. The cannons rattled below, threatening to smash their way out the sides with the breakaway momentum.

The last gray of the earth below vanished from sight, the moat swallowing it up as the ship passed over. A moment later, Shirri heard – and felt – the distinct sound of shattering wood and a sound like a tailor ripping a seam. The *Grace* came to a good, hard stop and a great many things went forward, including Shirri's legs.

She, herself, did not join them, though she tried.

The world lurched madly, but Shirri's grip on the rails held. The ship seemed to stop for a moment, then another shattering noise filled the air–

Behind her, a great rent opened in the deck and the back half of the ship, quarterdeck and all, disappeared. One moment, Shirri was staring at Longwell's wide eyes as the ship broke and he held fast to the rail segment some ten feet back, and the next–

He was gone, simply disappeared as her portion of the *Grace* lurched forward and his vanished back, teeth of wall crenellations appearing between as though they'd chewed their way through the ship. Which they apparently had.

The front of the ship dropped again, falling forward as though caught on a children's slide. The prop overhead flew forward, weight dragging the remainder of the ship with it, tilting it precipitously forward, then sideways to the right.

"Aw, hell!" Guy's voice sounded somewhere in the clangor ahead and she watched as he slid briefly down the deck, his sword drawn in one hand. He caught hold of one of the metal grips in the deck, swung sideways and leapt overboard, cresting the rail without difficulty he moved so fast. "See you on the other side, lads!"

Other side of what? Shirri barely had time to wonder before the momentary stasis ended, and the reckless, uncontrolled slide of the front portion of the ship began again in earnest. The forward prop wrenched loose from whatever machinery belowdecks held it stable, and it fell hopelessly forward, ripping a trail through the deck like a great metal knife. Shirri blinked, watching it work, then realized–

It was tearing the remainder of the *Grace* neatly in two. And if it did, indeed, break cleanly as the back had from the front–

She looked down swiftly at Hiressam, who clutched the rail just below her. "We have to get off, Hiressam!" she shouted as the enormous metal shaft continued its tearing path through the finished lumber of the ship's fore. "When it finishes, it's not just going to carry us over the bloody edge, it's going to go in two pieces down over the wall!"

Hiressam nodded, seeming to get it. He hauled himself up to stand unsteadily on the deck, using the rail for support. Shirri was attempting to do the same but having little luck. She was in danger constantly of falling again; the deck pitched sideways once more. She felt as though at any moment a final jarring would send her knee through her face.

But even from her knees she could see the drop ahead...and it was considerable.

"Falcon's Essence!" Hiressam shouted, pointing down. He had wide, worried eyes, and she was not surprised. Reikonos's city walls were, after all, a hundred feet high or better.

She breathed the words and flung a hand at him, as if daring him to catch the spell. It must have worked, for he lifted up and leapt, the railing sliding past him, his hand out to catch her, now. He was passing at great speed, the ruin of the *Grace* picking up velocity as it slid from its balancing point atop the wall to over, to down, to death–

Shirri shouted the words this time to a near-empty deck, no one close enough to her to matter. She felt the sensation of solid ground beneath her feet and vaulted over the rail, grabbing Hiressam's hand as he pulled her clear of the sliding, falling ship–

But something caught him as it slipped past, seizing him as it slid past. It was a line of rope, attached to something heavy, and snagged him, dragging him–

"Hiressam!" Shirri called out, her hand firmly anchored to his.

But he let her go, and the rope kept hold of him, dragging him down with it as the ruin of the ship slid sideways, his eyes wide as he disappeared into a cloud of debris and dust with the falling ruin of the airship.

CHAPTER 41

CYRUS

*V*ara lay curled against his side that night in the opulent palace room, the silken sheets entwined around their naked bodies. Cyrus's breath had returned to normal and hers had faded into the slow rise and fall that told him sleep had claimed her. She lay across his chest, using him as her pillow, and he felt the subtle pressure of her head on his pectoral, her head rising and falling with his own breath. It did not seem to disturb her peaceful slumber, the motion, and he wondered if, in her dreams, she was sailing the sea or sky, with the rise and fall of his chest like the swells of the ocean to her.

There was a certain serenity in it, and he hesitated to disturb her. She'd been out for a while, though – surprisingly easily, given all that was arrayed against them – while he felt tired, weary, ragged, even, and yet sleep seemed not to want to visit him at all this night.

A prodigious need to empty his bladder was rising within him, and he was holding it off only with greatest effort. That damned pitcher of water the elven servants had left by his bedside table. He'd foolishly drained it coming in after the viewing, and now he was about to suffer the consequences. Or Vara was, rather, because he'd have to roll her over to free his arm and himself from her snuggling grasp in order to relieve himself.

"Dammit," Cyrus whispered, preparing himself for this complex maneuver. It seemed simple enough, on the surface. Roll himself, and Vara along with him, to the side, putting her on her back with his arm still trapped beneath her. Then, as she adjusted herself in deepest slumber, he needed to snake his arm free before she could come back to rest upon it. She seemed to sleep deepest roughly an hour after drifting off, and he counted on this to make his job easier, for he did not wish to wake her – out of consideration, only, for in truth he would have liked to have her awake to share his mind, though there was nothing new there, just the same stale worries running 'round in circles.

When he rolled to the side, she mumbled in her sleep, fingers brushing against his chest, trying to cling to him as he moved her onto her back. She jerked slightly, moaning lightly, eyes squinting tightly shut. It almost sounded as though she said something, but it was unintelligible. Now that he had her on her back he quickly withdrew his arm from beneath her head before she was settled, rolling off the edge of the bed and padding on bare feet over to the privy room.

It wasn't a large privy, certainly not as large as the one he'd had in the Sanctuary tower, but the walls were of plaster, not stone, and paint had been applied to nearly every surface. He stood over the toilet and relieved himself, listening to the patter of the urine hitting the water. The palace had indoor plumbing, blessedly; that had been little available in Reikonos, and the facilities tended to consist of holes in the ground whose stink inflamed the senses in the worst ways.

While he drained his bladder, Cyrus stared straight ahead, into the eyes of a wall-hanging stag that looked as though it had been here since the olden days of the palace. It wasn't dusty by any means – the palace staff had seen to its cleaning – but it looked aged, the fur matted and worn, the glass eyes dull in spite of the sheen put on them by someone very recently. Cyrus felt the last drops spatter into the water below and shook a few times, looking into the deer's faux eyes.

"Are you quite done now, dear boy?"

Cyrus spasmed, punching the deer mount so hard it flew off the wall, the wood within shattering under the force of his blow. It crashed down onto the porcelain water tank beneath the privy, shattering it as it tipped sideways, coming to rest on the floor as Cyrus leapt back. He stared at the head and blinked, wondering if he'd actually heard what he thought he'd–

"That was unnecessarily dramatic," Malpravus's voice came from the deer's mouth. "Destroy the wooden bones of this thing, shatter the eyes, it matters little to me. For my domain is death, Cyrus, and the dead part of this animal is the skin."

"What the hell are you doing, your skeleton bastard?" Cyrus asked, feeling the urge to run for his sword but simultaneously afraid to turn his back on this new horror. "And why would you assume I can't just turn this thing into a blazing pyre and be done with you, at least for now?"

"Because the important part of that question is 'for now,'" Malpravus said through the stag's oddly-moving lips. "You know that we must meet again at a point when you have a metal sword in your hand rather than your fleshly one – and that you will lose that battle. You know it. I know it. All know it, for I can hear them speak in the voice of worry and doubt all through this land you so love."

Cyrus felt naked before this raw display of power – for he was. Yet there was no visible threat save a chattering mount, and this felt like another of Malpravus's endless chances to taunt and goad him, so he did not scurry to his armor and begin strapping it on. "What's holding you back? It's been a month since Reikonos, since you tried to destroy Saekaj. I figured you'd have taken every city on the continent by now, or at least made a play for them." He folded his arms, not bothering to cover himself in any way, not feeling a hint of shame. Let the skeleton look up on him. Let him see Cyrus's supreme lack of worry – or at least the facade of it. "What's holding you back, necromancer?"

"I am not a necromancer anymore, dear boy," Malpravus said. "Like you, I have become more than what my humble beginnings should have suggested. That power I sought has led me to greatness, and as you can probably guess...I am on the cusp of acquiring more. Much more. Enough to give me license to drain your pitiful cities or simply let them exist without worrying about the paltry amount they will add unto me."

That was worrying. "And where does one find this much power?" Cyrus asked.

Malpravus chuckled, a raspy, dry sound. "I will gladly tell you – if you will come and join me."

"I've heard this song before, and the chorus tires me." Cyrus shook his head. "Don't you grow weary of asking me to betray all that I know and love to join you in a quest for power I have no interest in? Aren't you tired of constantly running into me as a block to your ambitions? I always beat you, eventually."

"Before we met on more or less even footing," Malpravus said, almost sadly. "I'm afraid after Reikonos, that will never be the case again, no matter how many allies you stir to your cause, no matter how many cities you enlist to your aid. I have...ascended. Become more than you could imagine, perhaps even more than I could have believed when I began this journey. Much as you might frustrate me with your acts of wanton disobedience, the time when you can deliver a firm slap to my cheek is well over, Cyrus. You are as an insect to me now, and irritation is all you are capable of when it comes to thwarting my plans."

"That's funny," Cyrus said, "because I don't devote any time talking to insects trying to sting me. I simply smash them."

"If you were the last man on earth, you might feel differently," Malpravus said. "Small as you are to me now, you are still the closest thing I have to an equal in this pitiful world. In the thousand years you have been gone, there have been no challenges to my rule from any quarter, any contender, that approached what you have been able to do in mere days. That marks you, don't you see? You remain a rather impressive figure for that reason alone–"

"I think you just said the important word right there," Cyrus said, staring into the glassy eyes of the hart, though he knew they were not, in fact, watching him. Perhaps Malpravus had no eyes in the room at all. "'Alone.' Have you come to me again because you've spent the last thousand years with all your grandiose power and no one of consequence to talk to?"

Malpravus hesitated. "Not 'no one.' But vanishingly few, to be certain. Surely you must have noticed that when you ascended to become the leader of Sanctuary, your conversational circle of acquaintance, those who would understand you grew small, for you have no equals. When I embarked upon a quest for power – magical power – I was similarly...constrained, for after the fall of the gods, only a few souls remained in Arkaria that had any conception of what I sought. Now...I am about to rule this world, dear boy. There is nothing you can do to stop me that I will even notice, save for perhaps kill everyone in every city yourself before my arrival."

"Since that would make me like you," Cyrus said, eyes narrowing in the darkened privy, "I'm probably not going to be doing that."

"Just as well," Malpravus said with a seeming flush of amusement. "You would not do it for moral reasons, but were you capable of it I would see you as much more of a threat. Instead we stand opposed as we always have; you constrained by your silly morality, me about to sweep power into my glorious palms."

"I don't think your bony hands have the tensile strength to handle that."

"I am perfectly capable of taking up the mantle of god," Malpravus said without a scintilla of humility. "Indeed, it is everything I have been working toward for a thousand years and more now. This is my destiny, Cyrus. The world will be mine, all will be beneath me, the way Reikonos was for so long. My desire for power is nearly fulfilled. Yet I come to you now to offer you one last chance. As I have every time, it seems – and been always rebuffed."

"Because every time you've just lost a major battle to me beforehand," Cyrus said. "Because every time you feel the need to hedge your bet, hoping that I'll join you so as to eliminate the risk I'll defeat you."

"The risk is already well gone," Malpravus said quietly. "And soon it will be a distant and forgotten memory. Gather your armies if you must. Unite all Arkaria – nay, all the world – against me. Rally them, choose your preferred field of battle, ride out to meet me. None of it will do you a drop of good. Perhaps I will be benevolent on that day, and merely use you as an example of what happens to those who thwart my beneficence. Or perhaps I'll finally beat some good sense into you that will let you see me as I am, as I have become–"

"I see you just fine," Cyrus said, reaching out and grasping the stuffed hart with both hands. "But I think I've heard about all I can stomach from you."

"Consider carefully, Cyrus," Malpravus's voice came from the animal's mouth. "This could well be your last chance. When I finish my business in the north...I will be coming for you again. All of you."

"What the hell is this?" Vara's sleepy voice reached Cyrus as he stalked across the floor of their quarters toward the closed balcony doors. He fumbled with them one-handed, trying to find the locking mechanism to throw it open. "Are you having a midnight chat with the wall decorations?"

"Consider your wife," Malpravus said, causing Vara to jerk and seize the covers, pulling them up to cover her entirely. "Consider those you care for, Cyrus. You talk about hope, and I would give it to you like a comforting blanket. Their safety could be guaranteed, if you but take your place at last at my side. All these lives you care so much for – I would place them in your hands. You could be the hero of the land, responsible for all their lives, for all governance. If you don't trust my benevolence, trust your own."

With a grunt of triumph, Cyrus found the lock and clicked the bolt, throwing the door open wide onto the moonlit night, the white glow drenching the balcony. He strode out and stopped when he reached the balustrade. "I not only do not trust your benevolence, I don't believe such a thing exists or ever has. As for your destiny – it's to die. It's always been to die, which is why you chose the path of the necromancer when you set out on your journey. Death is what you've always sought, Malpravus, and when you come back to me again – I'm going to give you your fondest wish."

"Think it over, will you?" Malpravus said. "I realize your temper runs a bit high under normal circumstances. Perhaps with a little time you'll come to realize–"

Cyrus sent a flame from both palms and ignited the stag, hurling it over the balcony with all his strength. It flew in a low arc, crashing to the ground below. The clank of boots was followed by the rush of musket-holding guards rushing onto the scene; they stood over the burning bust and stared up at Cyrus, naked upon the balcony.

"I decided to do a little redecorating," he said, because there was little point in running now, and even less in being ashamed.

"You hold the fate of the world in your hands, Cyrus Davidon," the hart said, the fires consuming its flesh, the glass eyes still sparkling in the depths of the fire. "Take care you don't sacrifice it for your own vanity."

He felt the touch of Vara on his shoulder, sheet clinging tightly to her body as she stepped beside him, looking down at the burning mount. The deer's face seemed to take on a grinning quality as the flames consumed the dead flesh, and Cyrus was forced to suppress a shudder as he watched it burn.

CHAPTER 42

ALARIC

"*M*alpravus, you damnable vulture," Alaric said, staring down at the corpse. He raised a hand, whispered a spell, and fire flew from his hand, carried along with a blast of force–

It struck the body and the corpse flew apart, consumed in the burning flames of Alaric's rage. He hadn't even realized how angry he was, but the necromancer's voice from a freshly-dead carcass seemed to give it new life. The body burned in seconds, so intense was the flame of his anger, and Alaric watched it go, surprised that he could produce such spellcraft. *The distance to Reikonos may indeed be a factor in spell strength...*

"I have so many options in this alleyway," Malpravus's voice came from another corpse. "Thanks to you. Do you really want to burn and sunder them all? Is your anger at me such that you cannot find it in yourself to speak civilly with an old friend for even a few moments?"

Alaric adjusted his aim and delivered another flaming blast that sent the speaking corpse against the orange wall. It, too, shattered into pieces at the force of the blast, and the fragments burned in the heat of his flames. Even the bone was consumed within moments...as dead things tended to be under a holy, cleansing fire.

"I have been watching you, Alaric," Malpravus said, speaking from yet another mouth. "Watching your efforts. You sail the skies like a hero of this age, taking lives everywhere you go, making more fodder for me with your every act. Even here, in this faraway place, where perhaps you might imagine you could be free of my grasp, you see...nothing is free of my grasp anymore, old friend. Nothing is outside my reach."

Another corpse. Alaric filled his palm with force and holy fire, and exorcised the demon. Then another, then another, all burning away like kindling into swift ash.

"I know what you come to Balaar to do," Malpravus said. "And I would not stop you. Have your trollish friend call all his order. Bring them all unto me; it matters not. Have your captain summon the Amatgarosan navy. Let them come from all points of the compass, the mightiest airships, enough to blot out the sun and moon. I am unworried. Do you not wonder why?"

Alaric was breathing heavy now; even with the loosening of magic's restrictions here he could feel the reserve of his magical energy waning with all this effort. Still, he burned another with the holy flame, and loosed still more upon the blade of his sword so that he could strike down these necromantic puppets if he had to. "I merely assume that, as usual, you believe you hold the whip hand, and that we pitifully small people are beneath your notice."

"Beneath my notice you may believe yourself," Malpravus said, "but you do not escape it, for my capacity is such that I cannot help but see you. I have changed, Alaric, from the days of old. Where once I had to scramble for all the power I wanted, now it is here, delivered unto me."

"Then what need do you have of me, necromancer?" Alaric asked. "Surely, if all you want is within your grasp, negotiating with me, wasting your time talking to me is...well, a waste."

"I have abundant time at the moment," Malpravus said airily. "Some...obstacles...take longer than others to surmount, as surely you must know. But all will fall before me, and I reach out to you now to tell you...I see you. And no matter how many you bring into this battle you seek, surely you, of all people, Alaric, must realize...this is a fool's errand."

"I, of all people?'" Alaric asked, setting another corpse aflame. The life-thieving bastard was running short of them now. "Why me?"

"You have watched these lands for ten thousand years," Malpravus said. "You have scope. You have seen the flaws in the gods of old and the nothingness that replaces them. You saw the folk in the streets of Reikonos when your lad Cyrus reappeared – they need purpose, just as you've always said. They're hapless creatures otherwise, empty and devoid of life's meaning without a god to steer them. And I say this to you because you have always known when to fight, Alaric – and when to vanish, when to accede to the demands of those stronger than you."

Alaric felt a tight grimace and a flush rise in his face. "You speak of my surrender to the old gods?"

"I speak of your bearing an unfathomable burden in the torture chambers of the gods, yes," Malpravus said. "What was that creature's name that tormented you for those years? Borean?"

"Boreagann," Alaric said. It was not a name he was likely to forget, ever.

"You knew what would happen when you gave yourself over to them," Malpravus said smoothly, the jaw of the corpse clacking slightly, broken where Alaric had struck him down. "But you did it anyway. Sacrificed yourself for a vision of the greater good that you carry. You know, for you have never truly been a warrior of great power; that's not to insult you, merely to point out...you are a ghost, Alaric. The course of events has gone on without you, often, because you know when you are outmatched." The corpse smiled sickeningly. "Surely you see it now, as well."

"You cannot expect me to surrender myself to you expecting mercy," Alaric said.

"I don't expect you to surrender at all," Malpravus said. "I am on the edge of receiving all the power I can handle. Draining your cities afterward would be like taking a sip after drinking the river; pointless. But neither can I turn away and simply let this world proceed without my hand at least gently upon it. There could be room in my vision for you, for the others, if you but chose your wise course again...and acknowledged me as the god I am becoming."

"I would sooner worship the rotting fish in the sea," Alaric said with disgust.

"You won't find them nearly as powerful – or useful," Malpravus said. "I come to you now because I need nothing from you, I want you to merely be what you have always been – a ghost, Alaric. A ghost here in my world, in my service. If you wish to see your ideals propagated upon these lands, I see no issue with that. Take them around this pebble in space, if you so desire, remake it in the peaceful image you wish. I could help, if you like–"

"In exchange for what?" Alaric asked, driving his blade into another corpse. It burned easily; Malpravus was inhabiting all of them, even if he only spoke from one. "My utter subservience? My knee, bent to you, my head bowed in your name? My sword, driven through the hearts of your enemies at your very command?"

"I could use a Hand," Malpravus said. "Much like the gods of old had in your old friend, Stepan."

"I would not kill in your name," Alaric bristled, smiting another corpse with a thrust, Aterum clanking as it hit cobblestones beneath. A rush of flame ran through the body, dissolving it entire. "I would not even scold in your name, Malpravus."

"This is why you're a fool, Alaric," Malpravus said with a sigh. "I offer you a compromise that requires you to do nothing save for nod to me, that demands you violate neither your principles nor your conscience, and still you cannot accept it. What is it about me you find so unpalatable?"

"I think it's...everything," Alaric said, exorcising yet another. "That you steal the dead for your purposes. That you seek power at the cost of all humanity. That you would kill, wheedle, or damn us all happily if it meant more for you."

"I suppose we'll find out on that last one," Malpravus said, "thanks to your refusal this day. Fine, though – oppose me with all you have.

See how that works out for your many. My army is one your forces have never defeated. My will is the thing you've never conquered, Alaric – not Sanctuary, not you. You've only ever been able to imprison me, not destroy me." He cackled through the broken jaw of the last corpse. "Stymie, not stop. And you are not more powerful in these days than you were then. I, on the other hand–"

With a blast of holy fire and the strike of his sword, Alaric burned the last corpse to ash. "I suppose we'll see," he said, and with a last nod at the piles of ash in the alley, Alaric sheathed Aterum and strode away. If he hurried, perhaps he could catch up with Mazirin and Qualleron.

CHAPTER 43

VASTE

*a*sa-tee cut a miserably quick pace through the swamp, especially considering he was so much shorter than Vaste. The smaller man wove in and out through hummocks and small washes, submerging his feet without hesitation, stalking through the dry paths with barely a whisper of noise. He lost his chattiness and became a shadow, visible only because Vaste kept him in sight, a dozen paces or so ahead in the tall grass and light washes of the swamps surrounding Gren. Beads of sweat traced courses down Vaste's face from his brow, down his back from his neck, and left him feeling seasoned like a rack of beef, except rather less pleasant smelling.

"He seems to be taking his time," Aisling said, only a few steps behind Vaste. She did not appear to be even breathing hard, and when he turned to remark on this, he found her utterly composed, and realized...he had not even known it was her behind him. Aemma and Merrish were not far behind her, and though Merrish looked mildly worn, it was Aemma's face that truly made him realize that he was the one holding up progress. Niamh, for her part, kept her gray head down, not even looking him in the eyes.

"Damn," Vaste said, pausing, bent over, his breath coming in great gasps. His eyes traced skyward; the airship was back there, trailing them, tilted slightly by a commanding wind, but following. "He's taking it easy on me, you say?"

"I didn't say it quite like that," Aisling said, "but I'm pleased to see you picked up the point nonetheless."

"Asa-tee," Vaste said, still huffing. "Please tell me you were not serious when you said this was a matter of days spent walking. Days of walking will see me dead, you see. Plainly."

There was a ruffling of the tall grass as the airship hovered behind, its turning rotors stirring them. Asa-tee slipped through them like a ghostly presence to stand before Vaste. He shook his head, his long, black braids shaking in the airship's wash. "I don't know if you'll make it, *gisomari*. Not in three days, anyhow. Not a one among us can carry you, either."

"The airship could," Aisling said, gesturing at the broad-hulled vessel looming over her shoulder. "But none of the rest of us could, or would want to."

"Such insults I have seldom weathered," Vaste said. "You abuse my heart."

"Not as much as you have," Aisling said. "Plainly."

Asa-tee shook his head again. "I don't make the distances, *gisomari*. Huaviri chose his camp with care, and the journey to reach him is key to your understanding of what you came here to know. And getting there, the suffering it takes? Is part of your journey. A key part."

"So I'm meant to suffer?" Vaste stared down at him, for he was still short enough in comparison to be stared down at. Like a bug. "Damn you all," he gasped, but began to trudge forward again.

"All will be revealed, *gisomari*," Asa-tee said, and he was off again, damn him, at speed, through the crunching tall grass and slurping wet ground.

"But will the revelation be worth it?" Vaste asked. That didn't elicit an answer, which he found almost as unsatisfying as the walk.

CHAPTER 44

SHIRRI

She touched down on the street below a few moments later, absorbing the shock of the airship crash and the ruin of the city she'd called home into her soul. It was a place of ash, a place where the blackened bones of houses and city buildings stood tall above the fields of black and gray. Where nary a thing lived, and the wind howled down the street.

And the only sounds seemed to come from the settling wreckage of what had once been the *Grace of the Shelas'akur.*

Shirri dispelled Falcon's Essence as she touched down, its power stuttering even for her. She'd descended gracefully enough from the top of the wall, but there was little hope it would have maintained itself much longer than that. Her shoes brushed the black soot-stained cobblestones, and she stared at all the ruin she'd unleashed.

The *Grace* was a wreck of shattered wood and metal, the tsk-ing sound of running machinery coming to its final stop echoing within. Blood and oil ran out into the gaps of the cobbles. The hundred-foot drop had put a firm end to anyone left alive within, and without...

Hiressam's body was shattered at the edge of the wall, staring blankly into the gray sky above, his own blood spattered wide around where he had fallen. His leg was at a terrible angle, still hooked where the rope had caught it, tethered at the other end to a black-barreled cannon that lay in a lump of iron upon the street. Shirri stopped some ten feet back from it and fell upon her wobbling legs, landing upon her duff, savoring the pain from that.

Didn't she deserve it? Hadn't she brought this on them all?

"Guy?" she called in a scratchy, rattling voice. "Guy?"

"I'm up here," Guy called back. She turned; he was down the wall some hundred or so paces, threading his way down a tower staircase. "You all right?"

"No," Shirri said, looking at Hiressam's body. No resurrection spell could fix this, not even if it worked here in Reikonos. Too much of him was splattered to be put back together.

Thousands of years of life and this was how he'd met his end. On this pointless quest to retrieve this silly thing...which would do them little good in their fight against Malpravus.

"Shirri?" Another scratchy voice commanded her attention, and she looked up. A helm peered over the parapet above, just past the place where the wall segments had been torn and destroyed by the crashing airship.

Longwell.

Longwell was alive.

She stared down at Hiressam rather than answer, and soon enough both Guy and Longwell found their way down the winding staircase to her. They all sat in silence for a time, the men talking among themselves and Shirri saying nothing until Guy finally spoke up to her.

"We should, uh...bury him, Shirri," Guy said. "We ought not leave him like this."

"Indeed," came a voice from nearby that made Shirri look up. "We should move, and soon."

"Houk?" Shirri stared at the mustached man in the perfect black jacket with tails. "Houk, how did you survive?"

He looked simply terrible, such that she wished she had not asked for the answer seemed obvious. His face was lined, eyes heavily lidded, but there was no hint of blood upon him. "I was the first to land, and managed to roll clear," Houk said. "The rest of the lads on the deck were much less fortunate, and as to those within..." He shook his head slowly. "...Well, you can guess how that turned out."

"How fortunate for you," Longwell said, staring piercingly at him.

"I suppose," Houk said. "Seems unlikely to make me feel good, though, seeing as the rest of the crew is quite dead...and quite a mess. I suspect I'll be seeing their faces for quite some time in my nightmares." He shuffled across the ashy ground.

"What the bloody hell are we supposed to do now?" Guy asked, looking skyward. The sky was gray, the ground outside the walls had been gray – and in here there was plenty of gray, too, with the tinge of all this ash being between gray and black. "Where's the *Lady Quinneria?* Did anyone see if it got blown up with the Chaarlandian ship?"

"I don't hear it," Longwell said with a calm that Shirri found shocking. Her stomach was quivering. Hiressam was dead, their airship had been destroyed, the second in their formation might have been blown up as well, and now they were trapped in the ruin of Reikonos with no way out. "That doesn't augur well." He thudded his spear's haft into the ashy ground. "We should go." He turned his eyes inward, toward the center of the city and the partially decapitated Citadel waiting above all the blackened ruin.

"But the dead?" Guy asked. "We just going to leave 'em?"

Longwell turned and stared hard at the ruined ship's front, then the body of Hiressam before shifting his gaze to Shirri. "You should make a pyre of them. Standing around here will do little but make us a target if any more scavenger vessels are lurking."

"He's right," Houk said, clutching at his side. His perfect suit was not so perfect any longer.

"Damn," Guy whispered. "I hate that you're right, but...you might just be." He shuddered. "I wouldn't care to run into any more Chaarlandian pirates up close. Not again. Not a third time."

Shirri felt drained, but clung to one certainty. "We...we can't just leave them–"

"We can," Longwell said, clunking his spear's haft into the ashen ground once more, vibrating the cobblestones beneath. "We should – and I shall. If you wish to come with me, then do so. For I shall be departing shortly."

"And where are you going?" Guy asked, frowning.

Longwell did not answer. He shuffled away, turning his back on them and showing them nothing but the blued backplate of his armor.

"Guy," Shirri pleaded, turning toward the only one of them she thought might pay her heed, "Hiressam was a longtime servant of Sanctuary. He carried the torch when no one else did. We cannot just–"

"In the days of old," Longwell said, his voice loud and clear, "when many of our number fell in the raid against the Dragonshrine, we set mementos of our fallen on boats and loosed them on the River Perda. As they retreated on the eddies of the currents, we sent flaming arrows out to light them, burning those last memories of our fallen comrades." Longwell turned his head, helm making him look hawk-like. "Sanctuary has never been a suicide pact for tradition, and if Cyrus, Vara, or Alaric were here, they would tell you the same. Hiressam has earned his name's place on the standing monument to Sanctuary; what happens to his earthly remains need not doom his comrades, nor would he wish it to." The dragoon shuffled closer to her. "If it was good enough for your grandfather...why is it not good enough for him?"

Shirri felt something subtle click within her, calming her to stillness where before she had quivered at all that had happened.

Guy stared at Longwell, then turned to her. "Bloke's got a point. You can make a pyre of them right quick, can't you?"

"Yes," Shirri said. She'd done this. Called for the battle, caused this, again–

"Night's going to fall in a few hours," Guy said, "and this place was killed by Malpravus. Our original plan was to land, to grab your gewgaw, and *git*." He rubbed his leather-gloved hands together. "That plan is toast, mate, and I don't want to be mucking about here in the streets after sundown if there's shelter to be found, because I don't know what the so-called Lord Protector might have left behind – or let come in behind, if you get my meaning."

"Where do we even go?" Shirri whispered, seeing the little hope she had in Guy die before her eyes. "With no airship–"

"I know places we can go," Longwell said. "But first – deal with your friend." He turned his back on them once more. "Do your last rites by him, and then we will go onward."

She looked to Houk and he nodded, to Guy and he did the same. With greatest reluctance, Shirri shuffled over to the ruin of the *Grace*, intending to light a pyre to grant passage on to Hiressam such that Reikonos had not seen since its own burning, in hopes that perhaps it might assuage her own guilt for getting him – all of them – killed.

CHAPTER 45

CYRUS

There was a thump behind him as Cyrus stood on the balcony, Vara nude in the sheets at his shoulder. He swung round to find Glaven storming in from the double doors to the parlor behind him in the suite, his auto-rifle raised now to the ceiling, expression serious.

"You're a bit tardy," Cyrus said, giving one last look to the burning hart's bust, now but glowing embers on the ground below. "Malpravus has come and gone."

"Were you in peril, my lord?" Glaven asked, shouldering his long, impressive rifle.

"Only of being talked to death," Cyrus said as Vara clutched her sheet tighter about her, squirming at Glaven's appearance in their quarters. "He wasn't here himself. He seized the carcass of a dead animal to jawbone me with."

"Ah." Glaven relaxed a whit. "Just a talk in the night, then, not a threat."

"The threat is persistent," Cyrus said, remembering at last that he, too, was nude, and that there was no convenient sheet at hand, for his wife was now thoroughly covered up in it, so he took two steps behind her to stand in her shadow, "now all that remains is for the hammer to fall."

"Aye, as you say, sir," Glaven said. "Do you wish me to remain?"

"I wish you would leave," Vara said under her breath. "For I have no nightclothes on, and all I wish at this moment is to return to my slumber."

Cyrus found himself grinning. "Excuse us a moment, would you, Glaven?"

"I'll see myself out, sir," Glaven said smoothly, making his way back to the open double doors where Cyrus could see the lushly appointed parlor of their suite. "I apologize for my tardiness; I was in a deep sleep in one of the guest rooms. I will draw up a chair outside your door for the remainder of the night."

"Whatever you wish, I am going back to bed," Vara said, shaking her head, wild blond locks stirring in the night breeze. She made her way over to the bed and collapsed upon it, headfirst into the pillows like a thrown spear, and without further word or ceremony.

Cyrus stared at her for a moment, as did Glaven, though he did so with some redness of cheek. "Call upon me if you need, sir," Glaven said, nodding once more.

"Are you all right?" a voice came from outside on the balcony, and Cyrus turned–

Ryin stepped in, green runed robes whipping in the night wind, stepping in off the air itself. He took Cyrus's appearance in with but a quick look, then anchored his eyes on Cyrus's own. "Ah. I see you were caught unprepared."

"I didn't think sleeping in my armor would be comfortable or prudent," Cyrus said, letting his hands drift down to cover himself. "Since we don't know when Malpravus is coming, and since my wife is here with me now–"

"Certainly, sir," Glaven said.

"You couldn't skip a few nights, huh?" Ryin just grinned at him.

Cyrus stared at him for a moment, then chuckled. "Try not to take this amiss since I'm nude, but – I have missed you, contrarian."

"I am flattered but entirely uninterested," Ryin said with great amusement. "Perhaps you should return to your wife and bed – in that order."

"His wife is similarly uninterested at the present time," Vara said, voice cloaked in tiredness.

"Perhaps it's that Malpravus just ambushed me while I was making water," Cyrus said, "but I don't think I'm going to be getting back to sleep anytime soon. I think I need the jitters to die down first."

"Perhaps a nightcap, sir?" Glaven asked, hesitating, looking as though he were ready to flee but unable to do so. "To calm the nerves? The council has provided you with quite the bar."

Cyrus paused, cocking his head in thought. "Perhaps I will avail myself, now that you say it." He looked to Ryin. "Care to join me?"

Ryin's amused smile did not dim. "Will you be putting on pants for this? Because your decision as related to your attire will determine whether I attend or not."

"Yes, I will put on pants for this. Or nightclothes, at least."

"Then I shall attend," Ryin said. He looked to Glaven. "Perhaps we should wait for Lord Davidon within...?"

"Right this way, sir," Glaven said, shepherding Ryin onward, toward the double doors.

Cyrus waited until they'd closed them, then said, "You don't mind, do you, dear?"

"Stop ruddy waking me with your questions," Vara said. "Or with your body. Drink all you like, provided you stop jarring me out of blissful sleep."

"As you wish," Cyrus muttered, and dressed in his underclothes quickly. They were new, and felt pleasant, modeled by elven seamstresses on the ratty and worn ones he'd had beneath his armor for a thousand years. Where had the old ones gone? Probably thrown out by those same maids and seamstresses, for now he had five sets hanging in his closet along with all manner of other clothes and smallclothes.

He carefully opened and closed the double doors to leave Vara in the bedroom, in the darkness, the balcony now shut tight. She was already snoring gently, back in her slumber without a trace of difficulty. Well, she hadn't looked his glassy avatar in the eye while taking a piss. Cyrus was actually thankful for that; heaven forfend if Malpravus had spoken to her while she'd been making water. He'd probably have had to talk her down from tracking the necromancer in the night in an attempt to murder him.

Glaven and Ryin waited in the parlor beyond, the gas lamps lit and burning to shed their light on the room. That had been a curious thing; you had to turn the valve to reduce them to nil, for if you blew them out like a normal lamp you could suffocate yourself in the night, or explode the room at but a spark. Such terrors and wonders this world held.

"We have a wondrous selection of spirits, my Lord," Glaven said, already standing behind the smoothly polished wooden bar, the cabinet of liquors open wide behind him. Upon its doors seemed to be some scene of great battle from elven history, though Cyrus couldn't quite place it. "Would you care for a Reikonosian whiskey, perhaps?"

"One of the last, I suppose?" Cyrus sidled over, the smooth, cool feeling of the elven-made smallclothes upon his skin like silk in the night. So much more comfortable than the cotton he'd been wearing all this time. The elves knew how to make things, and make them beautiful, comfortable, and pleasant. He glanced behind him at the drawn door to where his wife slept; well, mostly pleasant. "I'll take a glass."

"Pharesian brandy for me," Ryin said, emerald robes hanging loose on his tanned skin. Glaven took this in with a nod, already set to work opening a curious box with ice lumped in its depths. With a sharp spike of metal he chipped away at it, delivering it into the waiting glasses as Cyrus watched. He and Ryin both did, in fact. "You have practiced hands at this," Ryin said.

"In truth, I haven't done this in a thousand years," Glaven said, chipping away delicately at the seam between a lump the size of a

RAGE OF THE ANCIENTS

stone and the mass of the ice. "Tending to Lord Vaste's manse has been a task remarkably short of guests in the last millennium."

"I have some news for you: it's not going to get much better even if we win and he goes to live there full time," Ryin said with a smirk.

"Oh, I am well aware of the master's...ahem...shortcomings in the realm of socialization," Glaven said, popping the ice into one of the glasses with a well-aimed strike. It clinked in, swirling slowly until it came to a stop. "He did live there for several months after your last adventure, after all. Termina at the time was not a wildly social location for a troll, obviously – and I fear not much has changed, given recent events." He shook his head. "Coming out of this, should we win, I imagine the population of Termina to be quite elven and half-elven – and terribly insular."

"Cyrus," Ryin said as Glaven slid him a Pharesian brandy poured over that ice block, "tell me something – is it true you ended up in Termina before you went to Sanctuary? You know, a thousand years ago?"

Cyrus nodded, watching Ryin pull the glass slowly up. He had envy, eyeing it, even though he knew his was yet to come. "Yes. You were among the first I saw on my 'grand tour.' I wanted to retrace my steps through Arkaria, see some of the places I'd visited on that initial recruiting tour that I went on for Sanctuary, and after. I did end in Termina, yes."

It was Ryin's turn to nod. "And then after that, straight to Sanctuary? I only ask because after you disappeared – well, some time after, obviously, since you were wandering for quite some while – we tried to figure out where you'd gone, and when. We lost your trail after Termina. Isabelle saw you there, as did your steward, Greenan–"

"A singularly odd fellow," Cyrus said, watching Glaven chip the ice into his glass.

"That would be my brother," Glaven said with a smile.

"Odd can be good," Cyrus said hastily.

"You had the measure of him the first time," Glaven said, uncorking the bottle of whiskey, a peaty whiff wafting over to Cyrus as the servant worked. "He didn't become a soldier as I did, choosing instead the life of service as he began his career. His greatest aspiration was to be the capital mover in some great manse. Well," Glaven said with mirth, "he got his wish, after a fashion. A thousand years he's been in your service with no one to attend to, no social events to plan, no household power or influence to manage. Very sad for him, but...very fortunate, perhaps, for elvendom, if I may say. He needed a tour of duty to blunt his ambitions a touch before he sought power." He slid the whiskey across the bar's smooth surface to Cyrus with a flourish.

"Pour yourself something if you'd like, Glaven," Cyrus said, taking up his glass. It filled his nostrils with a rich aroma.

The elf hesitated. "I am the help, my Lord. I do not partake in the presence of–"

"I'm not an elf, I'm not a king, and I killed your last monarch and overthrew your people's caste system," Cyrus said, provoking raised eyebrows from Glaven. "You need not stand on such ceremony with me. I can respect a man for serving me a drink and consider him my equal at the same time."

"Then why aren't you the one serving the drink?" Ryin asked with a smirk partially occluded by the glass of brandy he held in front of his lip, giving his voice a slightly echoing quality.

"That's foolishness," Glaven snapped. "It's not his job. I am well paid for my service by the elven government."

"To serve Lord Vaste, not Lord Davidon, as I understood it," Ryin said.

"If it wasn't his job, and we were just three men having drinks on a social occasion, I imagine I would," Cyrus said, musing into his whiskey. "I certainly did serve others when I was guildmaster, pouring them drinks in my quarters on occasion. I'm hardly opposed to chipping ice and pouring from a bottle. It's much less degrading than the other work I've done. Besides," and here he raised his glass to Glaven, "you said you were in the service before this?"

Glaven nodded. "Elven army. For a few hundred years."

"I imagine you saw some action."

"Indeed," Glaven said. "I was on the Northbridge in Termina on the night of the defense against the dark elves."

Cyrus felt a sudden headiness that had little to do with the whiskey. "You men were damned brave that night."

"We had a damned fine leader that night," Glaven said, chipping the ice into his glass. "We were formed into ranks, you know – echelons. And the Northbridge was considerably narrower than the Grand Span where you were fighting; there was room for perhaps fifteen men abreast to bear shields and spears – or swords. And as well you know, those of us unblessed with godly weapons tire out a bit quicker..."

"Indeed," Cyrus said with a curt nod.

"The War Department has made great study of it, this sort of echelon fighting. Eight minutes is, I believe, what they determined a man could fight before wearying, even a warrior in top form," Glaven said. "After five minutes of fighting, our *Endrenshan* had the front rank fade back, the second rank move up – and shuffled us thusly, front rank to the back, and each to take their turn at the fore. Some would fall, of course, bringing up an earlier rank sooner. But thus it was through the whole night – Odellan would keep the count in his head, and every five minutes those at the fore would shuffle to the back, relieved to rest for an hour or more."

"That sounds a bit hellish, to be frank," Ryin said soberly, clutching his glass just before his jaw, as if he'd forgotten as he was about to take a drink. "You would stand there for more than an hour, awaiting your chance at death by the dark elves? Then fight for five minutes, then repeat it again?"

"It was, but also an honor and a privilege," Glaven said, at last pouring his own drink. It was the same whiskey as Cyrus had, and Glaven lifted it to his nose, sniffing it deeply before speaking again. "I'd been in other units, other battles, where the front rank fights until they fall, then the second, and so on." He shook his head slowly. "All night, our *Endrenshan* kept the time in his head – and all that night, he was at the fore." Glaven's face was deathly serious. "He never took a break."

Cyrus felt that one in his heart, and all he could do was lift his glass. "To Odellan – I never met a braver man."

"To Odellan," Ryin echoed.

"To the *Endrenshan*," Glaven said. "I left the kingdom's service after that and ended up only able to find work doing this. I almost didn't take it – considered striking out with Odellan, but he was long gone by then, off in that land beyond the sea, I heard, and momentum being what it was, I found it easier to just stay in Termina." He shook his head. "I suppose you could say I missed my chance at joining you a thousand years ago."

"Well, you're with us now, Glaven," Cyrus said, "as you were with us in Termina a thousand years back." He raised his glass. "To those who have fought alongside us, regardless of when."

"To them," Ryin said, raising his own glass.

"To all of us," Glaven said, clinking his glass with theirs before taking a drink. "And to the fights yet to come." He looked at Cyrus quite soberly. "This Malpravus...is he every bit the devil Lord Vaste makes him out to be?"

"And then some," Ryin said. "Why, he–"

There was a sudden, explosive knock at the door to the quarters. Cyrus and Ryin both turned away from the bar, Cyrus feeling for the weapon that was not at his side. He came up patting silken cloth, and damning himself for not at least grabbing his belt from the bedroom. "Who is it?"

"Dioro," came the voice back. Glaven had slipped from behind the bar and had his rifle in hand; at Dioro's words he seemed to relax a mite, then gestured at the door as if to open it. "I heard there was an incident? Something about fire and a dead animal."

"Yes, well, you know we savage humans and our disagreement with elves' vegetarian diets," Cyrus quipped. "If I'm not responsible for the death of at least one animal per day I start killing long-dead ones just to simulate the sacrifice required in my name."

There was a pause. "Do you intend to continue being ridiculous and having this conversation from behind that door, or may I come in so you can at least lie to my face?"

"Go away, Dioro," Cyrus said, raising his glass, "I would like to sleep."

"Then you should not be drinking whiskey at this late hour, it will upset your digestion and slumber. Still, though, since you are partaking, be kind to your host and let me in."

Cyrus nodded to Glaven, who threw the doors wide for Dioro. The older elf swept in, surveying them all appraisingly, then to Glaven said, "I will have a brandy as well."

"I don't recall asking you to have a drink with us, Dioro," Cyrus said. "I thought you just wanted to know I was safe."

"Of course not," Dioro said stiffly. "I could tell that through the door. Offer me a drink – it's the polite thing to do, and besides..." He stood stiffly, hand on his staff, "...we have matters to discuss."

CHAPTER 46

ALARIC

*A*t the corner of the alley Alaric almost walked into Qualleron and Mazirin. Citizens of Balaar had hurried away, apparently, at the first sound of gunshots. He frowned at them in the orange glow of Balaar's sunlit streets, for they seemed to be merely standing there, waiting, in silence. "What are you doing here?"

"Waiting to see if you needed help," Qualleron rumbled in that way he had. "So far, you did not."

"Ready to rush back in if needed," Mazirin added hastily. "But...unneeded, apparently." Her brow crinkled slightly. "Were you talking to the dead bodies as you burned them?"

"I was talking to Malpravus," Alaric said, adjusting his belt because he'd accidentally thrust Aterum back in his scabbard a bit too hard, "through the corpses. He decided to take possession of them to taunt me."

"A devilish one, that fellow," Qualleron said. "Using the bodies of the dead in such a way lacks any honor."

"He wasn't very honorable in his use of them in life, either," Alaric said, and nodded ahead. "We should go. I find it hard to believe this disturbance won't raise the local constabulary."

"There's not one," Mazirin said. "It's a relatively lawless place. Technically under control of Amti, but too far away for them to be greatly interested, and split under control of several different entities – companies, nations of Firoba and Coricuanthi – all have a presence here. Their foothold on your continent. It's probably why these Machine thugs could operate here without trouble. No one would challenge them, at least none of the big players here. Giving them room to operate with impunity against the smaller players. They'd just need to lie low for a few days if a Savannah Cat brother came through."

"Which clearly they are not," Alaric said, "at least not with any regularity. I find this state of affairs intolerable."

"Much of your southern part of the continent is like this," Mazirin said with amusement. "To say nothing of the other towns in the north as well. This is a land of city-states; they may control territory beyond the city borders, but they don't do much with it. Amti is just the worst, most obvious offender." She shook her head. "This would never be permitted in Amatgarosa."

"Let's move on anyway," Alaric said. "I don't wish to stand here and wait for gawkers to show up."

They moved on through the sun-washed streets, walking under the palms casting their dappling shade against the cobbles. The air held an aroma of citrus, that rarest of fruits in Arkaria.

"Here we are," Mazirin said far too quickly as they reached a worn shop. Alaric was forced to hurry forward in order to open a door for her before she could reach it. She raised an amused eyebrow and slipped inside. A wide glass window gave Alaric a view. Perfectly smooth and with none of the distortion so often present in the imperfect windows of the olden days, within he could see a short counter and three gnomes working behind it, tall enough that they appeared to be on some sort of shelf or catwalk.

"Thank you, honorable friend," Qualleron said, squeezing himself carefully through the door as Alaric held it for him. He tucked his head low, pulled his shoulders in, hunching his back, and bent nearly double, but he managed to get in.

Alaric followed him carefully, giving the immense troll space to move aside. His bulk practically blocked the window view to the street. He finally slipped inside after the troll, who was shuffling slowly forward, the gnomes eyeing him with something approaching worry.

Mazirin arrived at the counter first. "I need to send a cable to the nearest Amatgarosan station."

"That'd be in Ladrise, then," the gnome squeaked. She was only a foot and a half tall, very pink around the cheeks, with dark hair and large cheeks that reminded Alaric of a doll. "Are you authorized to send diplomatic?"

Mazirin reached into her brown coat and pulled out what looked like a leather-bound wallet. Alaric tried to get a look at it, but it was written in her own language, though it seemed to have a very accurate picture of Mazirin printed upon it, which was interesting. Alaric peered at it; how curious.

"I need to send a missive to the Order of–" Qualleron said, then followed it with unintelligible gibberish, at least to Alaric's ear. "I believe the nearest monastery is in Vanreis."

The gnome across the counter from Qualleron looked up – and up – and up. "Um...priority level?" he asked in a high, wavering voice.

"Utmost," Qualleron said, clinking his massive coinpurse as he untied it from his belt.

Alaric stood there, watching the two of them deal with the gnomes. Something was clicking in the back of the shop. One of the gnomes hopped down and disappeared behind the counter, and a set of doors flared open a moment later, revealing a machine clattering in the back.

That must have been the source of all the magic. For communicating between lands with such rapidity? That was most definitely a form of magic, much as teleportation spells had been to him. And the boy who grew up in Enrant Monge and went everywhere on horseback had never forgotten the wonder at seeing teleportation when he'd come to Arkaria.

"The southbound lines are open, yes," one of the gnomes squeaked to Mazirin. "We're only having trouble at the moment with the northbound lines."

"Any idea what the problem is?" Mazirin asked.

"No," the gnome said, writing something down in a hand that Alaric found too small to be legible, "our company has sent out two rounds of scouts, but so far they haven't patched the problem or returned." She looked up, and must have seen faint concern on Mazirin's face. "I wouldn't worry, though. This land is large, and largely untrammeled, so it can sometimes take a few weeks to locate the issue and patch the problem. I'm sure they're working on it. I'll get this out immediately."

"Amatgarosa thanks you," Mazirin said, turning away from the counter and sweeping her long brown coat closed as she did so. She shuffled over to stand by Alaric as Qualleron continued speak to the gnome, bent almost in half over the counter. It presented a very uncomfortable appearance, for his face – in spite of his efforts – hovered a mere couple feet from where the gnome stood boosted behind the counter. Qualleron looked slightly pained from maintaining such an uncomfortable, contorted position. Mazirin chuckled under her breath at the sight.

"When will your people get the message?" Alaric asked.

"Later today," Mazirin said. "It will reach the consulate in Ladrise – that's Suijnara's capital – first. From there, they'll send it onward. Where it goes from there..." She shrugged.

Alaric hesitated, deciding whether he should make mention of what Malpravus had said to him. Of course he should, though. "Malpravus knows what we came here to do."

Mazirin froze, turning her head slowly to look at him. "He knew we came to summon help?"

Alaric nodded. "It almost seemed he welcomed it. Welcomed us bringing more people for him to absorb."

Mazirin's forehead wrinkled. "So you don't think he's behind the lines going down?"

Alaric shook his head slowly. "No. He seems quite assured of his power. I thought perhaps he was behind the lines being down while he finished whatever business he was into, but now I don't believe he is. I think he feels quite ready to deal with whatever we can throw at him and that...that concerns me."

"He has never faced the might of Amatgarosa," Mazirin said stiffly. "We are the world's foremost military. Our airships rattle the earth, and nearly all fear to cross us."

"Save for those Chaarlandian pirates," Alaric said with a faint smile.

"Because they are tribal peoples," Mazirin said. "Not a nation. It's like being stung by a mosquito that flies off immediately. You kill the nearest of them, there are five million more, and none of them care that you're swatting their brethren. But for something like this...if Amatgarosa chooses to act, the power we could bring to bear should cow even Malpravus."

"Yet he doesn't seem cowed," Alaric said, "and he's been in your modern world a lot longer than I have. That is worrying."

"And it will go out immediately?" Qualleron seemed to be nearly done, though his face was awfully close to that poor gnome, who seemed to be sweating profusely just beneath him. Or was perhaps bathed in the drips of the troll's saliva. Either way...how very uncomfortable.

"Yes," the gnome said, not looking up, though his eyes were wide and he, too, was nearly bent double, as if to avoid the troll's breath on his neck.

"Excellent," Qualleron said, though his enthusiasm was muted. "Now, friend, excuse me...I must leave this tiny shop before I have an attack of anxiety...for it is entirely too cramped in here for a person of my stature." And he began to back up on slow, shuffling feet.

Alaric hurried to get the door for him, taking note that the gnome he'd been speaking to did not seem to breathe easier until Qualleron was halfway out. Alaric, though, wondered if he would find a way to breathe easier at all. After his encounter with Malpravus, it certainly seemed unlikely.

CHAPTER 47

VASTE

*T*he days were long and punishing, and Vaste bore the horror of each of them upon his very body.

"You're being dramatic," Aisling told him at the dawn of the second day. He lay flat on his back, the airship hovering nearby, but far enough not to disturb them with the sound of its incessant rotors.

The back he lay upon? It hurt. So did his feet, worn to nubs by the hiking of the first day. Bloody blisters covered the thick green pads, and he'd been wearing his boots, even, not the sandals he habitually wore around. He'd been as prepared for this hike as he could be, yet still his feet cried and mourned and moaned at their ill treatment. Crusted, dark green blood was dried in patches where his skin had given way. Yet on he'd walked.

"I am in pain," Vaste said, staring up at the sky, which had begun to blue. A terrible root was stabbing him in his arse, clearly aiming to touch beauty for itself. "I am hungry. I am weary. I am, I think, dead. No – not dead. Death would be the end of pain, and still I suffer–"

"And so do we all," Merrish said under his breath. He stood ready, as did Aemma and Asa-tee. Those two, at least, showed hints of pity; no such thing from Aisling nor Merrish.

"How many more days of this?" Vaste asked.

"Three," Asa-tee said.

"Three?" Vaste sat upright. "How can it be three? It's already been one!"

"We didn't make much progress yesterday," Asa-tee said, hesitant. "I thought we'd get farther..."

Vaste groaned, offering his pain to the heavens.

The heavens answered back with part of a wheel of cheese. Or perhaps Aisling did. He did not care to look a gift horse in the mouth, and took up the cheese in one good bite. "You think you can appease me with oblations?" He moved slowly to his feet. "Well, I suppose you can. Keep it coming, though."

Aisling just shook her head. "Trolls. So easy." She threw him another hunk of cheese.

"Don't get any ideas about how easy this troll is, missy," he said, shaking the chunk at her. "I'm not Cyrus. My virtue is harder to come by, and has all the more worth for it."

"His vice, on the other hand, is rather easy to get," Merrish said with great good humor, "but you shan't want it."

"I'll put you in a bloody vice," Vaste said, mouth filled with cheese. "And treat you like a goat."

"Come, *gisomari*," Asa-tee said, beckoning him.

"You keep calling me that," Vaste said, impelling himself into motion. "What is it? Please tell me it's not an insult."

"Just means easterner," Asa-tee said. "Our name for you savages over here." And he grinned, disappearing into a thicket.

"I'm following you into the bloody swamp, but somehow I'm the savage?" Vaste shook his head. But he went on. Not without complaint, of course, but he did follow.

CHAPTER 48

SHIRRI

*T*he fire was large, immense, really, but faded out in short order. They trudged through the blackened bones of Reikonos, through knee-deep ash and fallen beams turned to charcoal. The smell of burning lingered here even in spite of the weeks this place had surely been out – though perhaps that was guilt, or Shirri's scent of the fire still burning near the wall.

They'd poked through the forecastle of the airship one last good time – she, Guy, and Longwell together. They'd placed Hiressam's body within, confirmed all were dead, and scrounged a bit of food and half-cask of water from the wrecked ship.

When all that was done Shirri had touched a tiny flame spell to the trail of gunpowder Guy had left leading to a barrel inside, and when they were some distance away the explosion rocked them all, like the Chaarlandian vessel going up in the air before.

Shirri was thrown off balance by the distant explosion, and when she recovered she looked back. She couldn't quite see it from here under a film of thick, black smoke, but she could tell where on the wall it had happened.

"It was necessary," Guy said from beside her. She found the former Machine thug oddly comforting, which...she shouldn't have. Yet somehow they'd gotten into this mess together at roughly the same time, had gone through these remarkable changes – well, if not together, then at least somewhat simultaneously.

But Hiressam had been part of that, too, along with her mother...that new class of Sanctuary initiates. And what was left of them? Dugras was gone, Birissa hadn't been real, and Hiressam was dead.

Was this what her grandfather Andren had gone through when he'd been with Sanctuary? The tales she'd read had all been of distant legends; she hadn't considered the possibility that they'd been tales of sorrow even outside of Andren's fall.

But sorrow seemed to be all she had known since she had joined up with Sanctuary. Sorrow and failure.

"I've failed" felt like the thing written on Shirri's heart as she stumbled through the city of ash and char. It was like a distant drumbeat in her head, the thumps landing in time with her steps as she picked through the ruin. A city this large, this built-up, produced a great deal of ash when burned, and they made their way through streets that were utterly covered, like sands on a beach they were so deep.

The streets themselves were devoid of signage; only hints of what had been before, endless black wooden skeletons hinting at buildings now gone, and a partially decapitated Citadel in the distance that, though they labored toward it under the darkening sky, never seemed to get much closer.

"This was the cross-town train," Houk said, the only one of them not breathing heavily from the labors of wading through this mess. He pointed up at the skeletal remains of what it had once been, though the tracks were gone and all that was left was the timbers hanging in the sky, and residual hints of the wood supports above.

Shirri cocked her head, thinking, then turned back to the wall. "Then the main square is not far ahead."

Houk nodded, but Longwell paused, cocking his own head. "Is that so?" Longwell mused, and then looked around, his helm seeming like it was a particularly odd piece of machinery that swiveled atop his armored neck. He clambered effortlessly up a pile of burnt wood, gingerly taking care so it did not break beneath him, and stared out across the ruin. "Ah," he said. "This was the old slums."

"Indeed," Guy said. "Not far from the old Davidon barracks, then." When Longwell looked at him strangely, "You know, that old barn they replaced board by board every few years?"

"It was the old Kings of Reikonos guildhall," Shirri said, feeling a dull pricking in her soul. "That was the name of the guild Cyrus and my grandfather were in before they joined Sanctuary."

"I suppose the old barn didn't survive this," Longwell said, staring again into the distance. "Finally."

"It didn't survive before this," Guy said. "You catch what I said about them having to replace the boards every few years? Damned thing didn't have one original piece from a thousand years ago. They just kept rebuilding it."

"Had to keep the legend alive," Houk said.

"Come," Longwell said, hopping down from his perch. The wooden beam he'd been standing on disintegrated as he did so, and Shirri wondered how he'd kept it from happening beneath his feet as he'd stood upon it. "Let's make a slight detour."

"Thought we were heading for the Citadel?" Guy asked as Longwell led them west.

"I thought we were retrieving her item," Houk said.

Shirri didn't say anything. She didn't feel she had the right. Instead, she kept her mouth shut and tromped on through the dusty ash, which came alternately up to her calves, knees, and ankles depending on where she stood at any moment.

"There was a park right near here," Longwell said, cutting his path through the fallen ruin of what looked like a tall building. There was so little left of it now, just timbers that stretched far too high to be a small house or the like. "I dedicated it myself in the years after the fall, after the scourge."

"Yeah, it's the one that held that stupid barn they kept rebuilding," Guy said, and though he was only up to his knees when she glanced at him, somehow Shirri got the impression of a man almost over his head in the ash. "Swaddled it in green lawns and trees for half a mile around."

"That's the one," Longwell said absently, shuffling his way through a cobblestone street where the cobbles were actually visible in a few places; the wind had done its job here and cleared the accumulations of ash, and they piled around the burnt doorsteps. "Just a block or so – come on."

He led them onward, and soon Shirri could see it. She couldn't recall having visited this park, but it did feel familiar. There was little green now; only a fractional amount, and all at the center, beside a pond whose waters had turned black with the ash and runoff that had come since the fire. But hints of green grass stood beneath the accumulations of black and gray, and at the center of the park, behind the blackened boughs of surviving trees, with fresh buds already beginning, she could see–

"That flippin' barn survived," Guy said, almost in disgust. "Still."

"I'm more concerned about the statue," Longwell said, and he pointed.

Beyond the barn, a distorted, melted structure of copper stood. They threaded their way around the old barn – singed, but still in good repair, the margins of the park having protected it from the fire – and up to its stone base. The statue looked vaguely female, and stood some fifty feet high with a ten-foot stone plinth. The body appeared as though it had been covered in robes that were now partially slagged.

Still, it stood like a sentinel, as though it had stood between the barn and whatever harm had come its way during the fire.

"What...what was it supposed to be?" Shirri asked. It felt as though she were looking at it with teary, partially-closed eyes.

"It is the tomb of the sorceress Quinneria," Houk said, "though it's doubtful many remember that now."

"Cyrus had buried her elsewhere," Longwell said, staring at the ruined statue with his jaw set. "A quiet spot in a cemetery across town. But when I took over the city and we started to build, some workmen discovered her while they were digging the foundations of a new government center. I felt she deserved a bit more...recognition...for having saved us all." He seemed to blush ever-so-slightly. "And if you can't muster up a proper monument when you're the head of a city...well, what's the point? Come on." And he ushered them forward, heading for the stone base of the statuary.

"You just bring us here to pay respects, then?" Guy asked. "And to be honest – I didn't know that the Sorceress herself was in there. The mother of the Blessed Davidon? How did I miss that?"

"After a series of tomb robberies about seven hundred years ago," Houk said, shuffling forward in the wake of Longwell, yet moving gingerly enough to stir up no dust, "the markers mentioning that she'd been interred here were quietly removed. And so over the course of the years it was slowly forgotten. Thus, only those of us with a memory," and he brushed his elven ears, "recall that this is the final resting place of the Sorceress. Everyone else merely believes it a statue."

"It's so much more than that," Longwell said, making his way to the rear of the immense plinth. Now that she was back here, Shirri could see the outline of a door, ash blown into the crack to give it extra definition. Otherwise, it might have been hard to tell it was there. Longwell pressed it gingerly, his spear in hand, and it seemed to yield a little. "Guy, help me."

Guy brandished Praelior and obliged, and the two of them together gave it a very firm shove. Something moved within, and the door yielded, sliding back on a track that seemed to Shirri not to have been touched in decades, if not centuries. An aroma of old, dusty air came out, and Shirri resisted the urge to sneeze, for she'd been standing just behind the two men as they shoved it open.

"A little light, please," Longwell said, and Shirri generated a Nessalima's light ball, tossing it inside. It hovered just above the small room within, shedding light on a room a little larger than ten feet squared, centered around a stone pedestal in the middle the shape of a coffin.

Longwell stepped down into the recessed chamber and glanced

around. The only decoration other than the stone coffin at the center was a series of marble columns spaced every few feet along the walls.

"I would have expected a little better for the Blessed Mother of Davidon," Guy muttered as he stepped inside.

"It used to be better," Longwell said, a little sadly. "There was inlaid gold, vases, portraiture and paintings done by elven masters." He shook his head slowly. "We did the thing *right*. This was a tomb fit for a queen, with enough lucre to slake even the greediest treasure hunter's thirst for wealth." He brushed a hand against the marble columns, knocking his knuckles into the spaces between. "But, I hoped, not so much that they would keep looking forever."

"Wait," Shirri said, blinking, brow furrowed, "you knew the treasure hunters would get into it?"

"I thought I wasn't going to live forever," Longwell said, pausing between two of the columns, and knocking again. This time, they produced a different sound. "Or at least that I wouldn't be staying forever." He stared at the wall, and with resolve, waved his hand at Guy, who was only a pace or two behind him. "Get back."

"Uh, all righ,'" Guy said, and did so, keeping his own sword in hand, as though he anticipated being attacked by whatever Longwell was trying to do.

Longwell seemed unworried, though. He switched his spear to the other hand and held it there, setting his feet. Without giving a hint of what he intended to do, he brought his hand around in a punch–

It crashed through the wall and shattered stone; he buried his hand in up to the wrist. With a twisted smile he reached back and smashed it against the wall again, breaking open a section as wide as his mailed fist and a foot or better tall. With a wave of his hand, he cleared the area between the impacts of his punches, waving the shattered stone out of the way, brushing it clean along with a cloud of dust caught in the glow of the floating bulb of light hanging above.

Something was in the wall. Something...long. Something wrapped in aged cloth and dusty twine.

Longwell pulled it free carefully, the length some five or more feet.

He spun, clutching it, then his eyes alighted on Shirri and he tossed it to her.

She caught it out of the air, barely keeping from fumbling it. "What is it?" she asked, holding it carefully. The twine was disintegrating, and the cloth began to fall off, making her scramble again to keep it in her grasp. It was solid, and round, and as the cloth fell apart, her fingers touched wood, and something – very suddenly – changed.

"It's called Philos," Longwell said, and there was a rough, self-satisfied smile on the Luukessian's face. "The Burden of Knowledge." She held it up, and it caught the light streaming in from outside the tomb, all along the rough length of the weapon. "It was Quinneria's godly weapon," the dragoon said as she held it cradled in her hand, "...and now it's yours."

CHAPTER 49

CYRUS

"*W*ell, you invited yourself in, Dioro," Cyrus said once the elf was inside, "surely you must have something you wanted to talk about."

Dioro pursed his lips primly in the doorway, Glaven holding it open as Cyrus and Ryin lounged at the bar. "Yes, well," the elf said, striding in, spry for his age, "I wished to hear what happened directly from the horse's mouth, as it were."

"If you mean Cyrus, that's the wrong end of the horse," Ryin said before taking a sip of his drink, then giving Cyrus a smirk.

"Is the shelas'akur well?" Dioro asked, sauntering up to the bar to stand beside Cyrus. Glaven hurried back behind it, though Dioro took little notice of him.

"Well and tired," Cyrus said.

"And annoyed," came her sleepy voice from the next room. She did not sound terribly awake.

"Also, annoyed, apparently," Cyrus said. "Why must you annoy my wife, Dioro?"

"I doubt very much I'm the sole driver of that," Dioro said, brow puckering.

"Why?" Cyrus asked. "Has no one ever told you that you annoy them before? If not, why are people so terrified of you?"

"I imagine it's the nearly six thousand years of practiced wizardry," Dioro said. "Brandy," he added, to Glaven. "A proper one." Turning back to Cyrus, he said, "Not that you have any respect for such experience."

"I wouldn't say I have no respect for it," Cyrus said. "It's just that until recently I counted among my acquaintances those who've practiced for considerably longer."

"The old one, yes," Dioro said, looking down. "It is unfortunate that Malpravus killed the one spellcaster left in this world whose ability will be sorely missed in this upcoming battle."

"Hardly an accident, don't you think?" Ryin asked, sipping his own brandy. "If I were Malpravus, Curatio would be the first one of us I'd want dead."

"Followed, I think, by you," Cyrus said, rolling his glass between his fingers, the ice melting ever so slowly.

"Was that an insult or a compliment?" Ryin asked.

"Possibly both," Cyrus said with a smirk of his own.

"Oh, good," Ryin said, and raised his glass. "Keeping up old traditions."

Cyrus clinked his own against it, then looked back to Dioro, who'd just received his from Glaven. "What should we drink to?" Dioro asked. "Victory?"

"That feels like spitting in the face of fate," Cyrus said, brow puckering. "Tempting it to smite us. Why would you do that, Dioro? Have you not lived long enough to learn to avoid such curses on oneself?"

"I have lived long enough to lose my superstition of such foolishness," Dioro said. "What will happen shall happen regardless of what we speak of the subject, and if I'm to toast, I would rather drink to victory than defeat."

Cyrus looked at Ryin, who shrugged. Then to Glaven, who held his own glass. "To victory," Cyrus said, and they clinked glasses, though

Dioro looked almost scandalized when his glass touched Glaven's. He was old; the ways of caste died hard.

"I must give you some credit for your choice in friends, Davidon," Dioro said, a bit soberly, lowering his glass after the toast. "The Hierophant here...other than my own people – and few enough of them – he is without doubt the strongest spellcaster yet left in these lands."

"And I can do with ease things that even your mightiest druids cannot," Ryin said, his smile infused with an arrogance Cyrus might have found infuriating, had it been pointed at him and not Dioro. As it was, Cyrus enjoyed the satisfaction of it striking the elf, though there was little reaction. Glaven, too, had to hide a self-satisfied smile behind his glass.

"'Tis true," Dioro said, with a barely grudging nod of acknowledgment. "And don't think it doesn't pain our own to know it. I imagine Hierophant Bloom would love to be here at this moment, to ask how you do what you do."

"I wouldn't be willing to tell her, I don't think," Ryin said smugly.

"That's wise," Dioro said, almost sadly. "If she were in your shoes, I doubt she'd be willing to share her secrets. At least...not anymore."

Cyrus heard that, heard it and felt there was some deeper truth within. He feared the depths of it, for it struck a chord of worry in him that sounded deep into his gut. "'Anymore?'"

Dioro hesitated; yes, there it was, a rich seam of guilt. "Sharing with others of like skill, like ambition...it was our greatest joy once." Cradling his glass, slowly walking it around in his fingertips, Dioro regarded the glass and amber liquid within as though it were some magic orb with answers hidden in its depths. Then he swallowed the rest of it down. "No more."

Glaven hoisted the bottle. "No more liquor? Or no more do you share truths among yourselves and with others?"

"No more do we share truths," Dioro said, pushing his glass forward. "By gods, do not deny me my liquor, man. Not now." And he looked to Cyrus with...something. As if asking permission.

Cyrus nodded, and Glaven filled the old elf's glass. Now Cyrus's stomach was all aquiver, and in the worst way. "To the truths we once shared," Cyrus said, "may they do no harm to any but our enemies." And he raised his glass.

Dioro's fell, along with his face, and the old elf shut his eyes. Still, after a moment, he recovered, and lifted his half-heartedly with the rest. No clink of glass from him, though, it went straight down his gullet. "You know what I have to say."

"I suspect I know what is on your conscience," Cyrus said, not taking his own apportioned drink. "Still – out with it. Get it off your chest." Ryin shook his head sadly at the corner of Cyrus's eye; Glaven, for his part, watched with furrowed brow.

"He was the only one who understood," Dioro said, pushing his glass forward again. Glaven refilled it, again, after a subtle nod from Cyrus. Dioro's face was downcast, not daring to look up. "Do you know what that means? In this day and age? In a time when magic has declined so, and its teaching is near gone, here and elsewhere in this world of metal and steel and coke-fire and ambition?" Now he raised his eyes, and the fire of worry burned within.

"What did you teach him?" Cyrus asked quietly. Inside, he burned like a hearth with a fresh-tended fire beside it.

"Everything," Dioro said, drawing a quiet gasp from Glaven. "Everything we had, everything we knew. He was, after all, supposedly the great hero of Sanctuary, one of the ones who'd saved us all."

"And he had knowledge of his own," Cyrus said, quiet, in judgment.

"He had more knowledge than any human we'd ever met," Dioro said, slamming his glass down on the bar-top, though it did not break. "The library of Reikonos was at his command, and within were tomes he'd acquired, things the city had snatched up that even we had forgotten." He made a noise in his throat. "We didn't know what he was, not really."

"You had to realize at some point," Ryin said quietly.

"Of course we did – well, almost," Dioro said. "We knew, eventually, he wasn't what he said he was. After many visits on both sides.

But we could hardly know that he was the ancient enemy of Sanctuary. We simply believed he was, perhaps, a god that had survived the war. No trace of his real intention could be seen – not until...well..."

"Until he sacrificed Reikonos upon the pyre of his ambitions," Cyrus said. "And millions died for your error in judgment."

"We did not know!" Dioro said, fervent in his whisper. "We could not know. How could one see beneath such a perfect illusion? Even our greatest illusionist did not guess at what hid behind his facade of spellcraft."

"Cyrus?" Ryin's quiet voice poked into the silence that followed.

"Hm?" Cyrus stirred; it had been only a few moments since Dioro had spoken. All had lapsed into silence in that interim.

"Say something," Ryin said.

Cyrus glanced at Dioro; the elder elf appeared to be chewing on his lower lip quite heavily, hand upon not only his glass – which was now empty – but his staff as well. "I don't blame you, Dioro," Cyrus said, with an equanimity that seemed to well from deep within.

Ryin blinked a few times into the quiet that once more followed. "...Say what, now?"

"How can I blame this man for such an error?" Cyrus asked. "How long did we dance about with Malpravus? Hell, when I met him, we were allies. There is no more deceptive creature on this planet than that slimy sorcerer, and he's deceived us more than once. Look what he did to Curatio."

"You've mellowed in your old age," Ryin said, shaking his head. "I would have expected you to unleash a storm of thunder and rage at Dioro for what he's done."

"No," Cyrus said, looking down at his glass, still full. "No thunder, no rage."

"Thank you," Dioro said in a ghostly whisper. "It was foolishness on our part. On all our parts." He laughed nervously, and it became a hacking wheeze. "I was...afraid you might pull your protection."

"No. But neither can I absolve you, Dioro," Cyrus said, looking the elder elf square in the face. "The thing you have done...it may just doom your city."

Dioro looked stricken. "But you aren't leaving?"

"No, I'm not leaving," Cyrus said. "Merely pointing out that you might well have given Malpravus the tools with which to destroy you. You're too old for a lecture about being wary of what powers you tap, or I'd bat you over the head with it–"

"Oh, come now," Ryin said, with great amusement, "he's not too old for that. Hit him with that famed Davidon arrogance."

"Maybe I'm too old for it," Cyrus said, taking down the last of his drink, letting it clatter slightly on the bar. "And I'm certainly too tired. Unless there's anything else, gentlemen?" He waited a few moments, and when no one spoke. "Then I believe I'll be rejoining my wife. Good eve."

Once he was back in the shrouding darkness of their room, Cyrus stood for a moment with his back against the cool wood, staring across the darkened floor, blades of moonlight crawling across it. Vara's outline was barely visible in the bed, the slow sound of her breathing audible beneath the uncomfortable silence from the parlor.

"Damn," Cyrus whispered, closing his eyes. Why did it feel as though he were in a coffin, like a circus performer, with someone continuously thrusting swords through? With every stab, the available margin for error seemed to narrow, sharp death grew closer...and the chance for survival – not just for him, and for the survivors of Sanctuary, but Vara, sleeping quietly in the bed – became thinner and thinner.

CHAPTER 50

ALARIC

They got back in the air, back underway, beneath a sunlit blue sky. Heading north and leaving Balaar and its orange tones behind them, Alaric surveyed the ground ahead from his place by the wheel. Mazirin was at the helm as they lifted off from the water, trailing droplets behind them like an afternoon rain followed in their wake. The *Raifa* left the safe harbor of the bay behind and once more took to the sky, wobbling as it gained altitude and speed.

"You – take the helm," Mazirin snapped once they were airborne and their course was set.

"Me?" Edouard, who had been loitering by the rail, seemed perfectly speared by her request.

"Yes, you," she said, beckoning him over with an energetic wave.

"Didn't you say when last you took over for me that you'd not let me on the wheel again unless the world was on fire?" Edouard shuffled closer, but carefully, as if terrified she might unleash flame of her own upon him.

"And now my eyes are burning, for I want to sleep. Take the wheel." When he finally drifted close enough, she seized him by the arm and dragged him to the wheel, pushing him to take it up. "Keep it on this heading." She thumped a long, narrow finger against the compass. "Do not deviate."

Edouard nodded. "Yes, ma'am." His sunken chest seem to swell slightly.

"Wonderful," Mazirin said, and tromped toward the stairs, passing Alaric. "You should get some rest as well."

"I feel more or less awake," Alaric said.

"You should rest," she said, a bit more forcefully. There was something about the way she said it that set his mind to ringing some warning bell, telling him there was something he was not perceiving.

He received the message well enough to nod and say, "You're probably right." He cast a glance over the deck; Calene was at the forecastle, Edouard had the wheel, and Qualleron was splayed out, unconscious, in his double hammock. Surely the three of them would be adequate to the task of keeping the ship on course. Baynvyn was below, presumably at the engines.

Alaric followed Mazirin down, and at the corridor that split in twain to their respective cabins, he turned to say farewell...

...But she seized his hand.

He started to ask why, but found he had no need. There was something entirely right about it, and he found himself pressing against her, his armor against her coat, Mazirin wrapped now in his arms, and him looking down into her brown eyes. His lips found hers, and he lost himself in them for a time.

When they broke, it was brief, and Alaric's head swirled in the most pleasant way.

"So," Mazirin said, "are you tired?"

"Not remotely," Alaric said.

"Good," she said, and she led him to her quarters, where they closed the windows and spent the evening by themselves.

CHAPTER 51

VASTE

"*H*as it been three days yet?" Vaste asked, his lips dried and cracked. Not from lack of water, no, but from his licking of them incessantly at every break.

He lay face up on the sawgrass, staring into the blue heavens above, the airship, as always, hovering at the periphery of his vision. His feet were worn to nubs, he felt thirty – no, fifty – pounds lighter than when he'd begun this maddening journey, and his whole body ached.

"Almost there, *gisomari*," Asa-tee said. The Azwillian mopped his brow, disturbing the braids that hung loose around his chiseled face. "You have but to get upon your feet and walk the last distance."

It truly had been three days, then. Vaste wasn't sure. Didn't remember. Time had passed, a fleeting thing that seemed to slip through his fingers, through his mind. There was a cycle of day and night he had endured, a passing of the sun over the horizon and then back beneath it again, and through that he had slept, rested, and walked. Always walking.

"You should get up," Aemma said. She was beside him, her small fingers upon his hand, stirring him. They felt like a little butterfly fluttering along his wrist as she brushed them there, then upon his cheek.

"Yes," Merrish said, slightly out of his sight, "I'm starving, and the rations provided by the airship are feeble. As though dark elves have no thought for cuisine outside of mushrooms, suet, and spider meat."

"I ate horseflesh in the town where I met you," Vaste said. "Horse-flesh, and it was an extravagance to your people." He rolled to his side in an effort to stand. Well, it was a first step, at least. "Can you truly say that is a more worthy dish than anything the dark elves have offered?"

"We have wheels of cheese," Aisling said, sounding quite affronted. "What kind of effete snob doesn't like cheese?"

"It's the kinds of cheese," Merrish said.

"Yes, you should have offered a gruyere with a pinot noir," Vaste said, sitting upright. "Clearly you have committed a great flavor faux pas." Aemma's mouth twisted at the corners, amusement dying to get out. "What? You wish to take another stab as well, do you?"

"No," Aemma said, seemingly suppressing a laugh. "I just find it amusing that as soon as you bandy insults, you come back to life, aches forgotten."

Vaste stood, staring straight ahead for a moment. "I suppose I do. Well, it was worthily said, those insults."

"Come, come," Asa-tee said, "give your insults as you walk. I can smell Huaviri's campfire from here." He beckoned, and then once more disappeared into a patch of tall grass.

"I don't know how you smell anything over the swamp stink," Vaste said, falling in behind Asa-tee. His feet complained a bit less as his mouth complained more; how curious that was. "It's as if the trolls never died."

"Does this area seem familiar to you?" Aisling said, tromping along behind him, her delicate boots producing little noise, her steps near-silent next to even Merrish and Aemma's. Niamh was hardly silent, though; she nosed on through the brush with considerable noise, belly scraping the tall grasses as she tromped through.

"A great battle was fought here, once," Asa-tee said as Vaste came out the other side of the thicket he'd disappeared into. Now he was on level ground, hummocks ahead shaded in the light of the moon. "Many lives lost, many bodies left behind to fester. That leaves a mark on the world – spiritual as well as physical."

"This is the ground where the Battle of Dismal Swamp happened," Vaste said, realizing what Asa-tee meant all at once. A thousand years had removed all sign; no rusted helms remained, nor faded pieces of armor, or wagons. Time and weather had had their way with those artifacts of man, and the swamps had eaten the bones. "A lot of people died here, then."

Asa-tee grunted. "You can feel the spiritual rift from what was done here, if you know how to listen."

Vaste stared at him. "You feel it? Truly?"

Asa-tee nodded, braids bobbing. "Even now. Huaviri, though – he can more than feel it. He can *see* it."

"See it?" Merrish asked. "How?"

No answer was forthcoming, though; Asa-tee kept on, his silent motion leaving little sign, and Vaste following after.

Under the open sky in the distance, Vaste could see curls of smoke rising under the shade of a thicket. A hummock rose out of the low paths of the swamp, and some sort of triangular structure rose out of that, not native to the landscape. He peered at it, swaying side to side with each step, trying to discern what he was looking at in the distance.

"It's called a tipi," Asa-tee said, spying him looking. "A lodge, in your tongue. That's where Huaviri waits."

"Let's not keep him waiting any longer, then," Vaste said, picking up his pace. His legs had felt leaden before, but now they had new life in them; he walked with ease across the sloping, swampy ground with its peaty surface toward the lodge.

"I'll direct the ship to anchor...somewhere around here," Aisling said, halting in her march.

"I'm going to collapse here for a bit," Merrish said, and the bastard just tipped over, showing for the first time in the journey that he'd felt it as much as Vaste had. He must have, to just slump like that, right onto a fallen log.

"I knew you were exhausted, you right prick," Vaste said, hobbling on. Aemma remained behind him, though Niamh peeled off, splaying out beneath a cypress tree. Merrish appeared not to hear him.

"Yes, all exhausted," Asa-tee said, drawing to his own halt. "No one whined about it as much as you, though." He drew to a halt, too. "I wasn't tired." He sniffed, and ahead there was a fire burning, and beside it, long strips of meat hanging off metal racks. "I was envisioning this moment. Now – you to the lodge, me to the meat." And he waved Vaste toward the tipi.

Vaste made a slow slosh through a last channel of water that he was too knackered to avoid. The tipi loomed some twelve feet tall, above him and his leaden feet. He was suddenly grateful he'd switched to sandals on the last break, because now they ached, feeling quite too swollen for his boots.

Brushing aside the flap, he stepped into the tent.

And stopped.

...For standing there before him, waxy-pale as if shaded by moonlight...

...Was Cyrus Davidon.

CHAPTER 52

SHIRRI

"I don't understand why you would give me this," Shirri said. They were trudging through the ashen streets, though this time she was leading the way, as best she could, on a bearing that was easterly. Her old apartment was not terribly far, and the way was shockingly clear on the wider avenues. Here and there they now ran across piles of bricks that had survived, and even a few walls still stood more or less intact, though the bricks had a strange glaze to them in the fading daylight.

"When I put that thing in the wall," Longwell said, walking unhurriedly, "the world was a different place. We all thought Malpravus dead, the scourge at bay – and, hell, another godly weapon wouldn't have done a bit of good. We had many of them during the last defense and, well...it didn't do any good. One of our number even fell in the fields east of here," and he waved vaguely in the direction they were headed. "Don't think they ever did find Larning's body. Or Luminas. That was the Warhammer of Light."

"I suppose I just don't understand why you would give this to *me*," Shirri said. Nerves pinched at her stomach. Everything seemed to move slower now – or at least everything save for her, Guy, and

Longwell. "You could have reserved it for someone else." She chewed her lip. "Someone worthy–"

Longwell stopped short and stared into the distance. "I don't know what 'worthy' means anymore."

"It means someone who's worth a shite," Guy said helpfully.

Longwell paused, looking back at him. "Well...that rules us out, doesn't it?"

Guy's face fell, but he did not answer. Instead he kicked at the ash at his feet, stirring a dark pile to turn to cloud and drift.

"I mean to run, Shirri," Longwell said, and there was a curious lack of pretense as he said it, a refreshing boldness. "To go back under that tower there," and he waved his plated hand vaguely at the Citadel, "and find my way into the Realm of Life once more. If I can do that, and seal the entrance...yes, I'm going to do that, I am."

That caused a strange humming sound to fill Shirri's ears, like the ringing of distant bells. "You're...what? Why?"

"I've had my fill of war," Longwell said, shaking his head. "I couldn't take Malpravus myself almost a thousand years ago, and I don't reckon all you, banded together, stand much chance now, with magic almost gone and the necromancer having just fed himself to fatness on this city." He looked around. "Everywhere I turn, I see my failures. What I led this city to."

"This wasn't you," Shirri said, putting her head down. "This was me."

"I blame all of you lot," Guy said cheerily. "Not that you asked. Of course, my own conduct in all this is irreproachable. I was just draining the city's lifeblood a sip at a time as part of the ruthless syndicate that ran the place." He was grinning, shockingly. "Why, I didn't do a damned thing to cause any of this, not one little whit. Guiltless, blameless – that's me."

Shirri and Longwell both stared at him. "You...you had a little small part," she said.

For a moment, she expected him to argue; his grin suggested as much. "I had more than a small part, dove," Guy said, but he seemed unburdened by it. "I was trying to provide a counterpoint to you two sad sacks in your guilt-off about what happened here. Seems to me the two of you want all the blame when there's plenty enough to spread around." He ticked things off on his leather-gloved fingers. "Cyrus came back and stirred up all manner of trouble. Alaric decided to stick his nose in past the point when even Davidon wanted to quit, I heard. And Curatio opened up the bloody beehive and gave it a whack when he challenged Malpravus to a throw down, giving him enough juice to sap Sanctuary, which gave him enough to do the whole city." Guy cocked his head. "Shall I go on, and get to you two down the list? Or 'ave you heard enough to spare your tender feelings?"

"Your part in this was so little compared to mine," Longwell said. "I served this city up to him on a silver platter when I left to pursue vengeance on Baraghosa. And I couldn't prise it back when I finally returned. Exile was too good for me – but I took it. And I will again, rather than watch him tear my friends apart like a roast chicken." Longwell hung his head, his helm a shadow in the growing dimness. "I don't have it in me any longer to fight blame, to apportion it properly. There's plenty enough to damn us to go around. I only know what I need to do now."

"Sure, sure," Guy said, nodding. "Fidelity, loyalty, bravery – what's the point of those when you've done wrong? You can just run. Blame yourself and run, hide your face from shame." Shirri blinked; the former Machine thug was speaking with a surprising fire. "Or, alternatively...redemption's a bloody path we must walk every sodding day. Whether we want to or not. Rain, shine, ash–" He swung a hand around to indicate the city ruins. "–doesn't make one whit's difference. You want to go hide yourself forever..." Guy shook his head. "...Fine and dandy, I reckon. Wish you'd leave that spear with someone who could do something with it." He glanced at Houk, who'd been strangely quiet, watching the whole thing. "What about you? If he gave you that pig sticker, would you turn it on Malpravus?"

"I don't think I'd be of much use to you in a fight, my good man,"

Houk said softly, his face in shadow, but sober. "But I admire your spirit. Time was, when I was younger, perhaps I'd have taken it up anyway."

"I'm not giving up Amnis," Longwell said softly, menacingly.

"Well, forgive me for thinking so," Guy said. "You were giving up in general, thought maybe you'd go all the way on it and give the rest of us a bit more of a chance while you duck out."

"This does no good for us," Shirri said, shaking her own head. What Longwell had said...

It was like a strange dagger to her heart, his words. Yet she wasn't surprised by it. It felt a bit like a comfort, even, knowing that when he'd come aboard her ship, it hadn't been because he'd been asked to come, or been drawn to follow her...

...It had been because this was where he wanted to run. So that he could hide in the same place where he'd spent the last nearly-thousand years.

"They say don't meet your heroes," Guy said with disgust, "well now I see why. The once-vaunted Lord Protector, the real deal, people...and he's bloody craven."

"I fought battles across this land and others when your grandfather's grandfather wasn't yet born," Longwell said, surprisingly still at the casual slinging accusation of cowardice. Shirri certainly felt a desire to draw a deep breath. "If I've had my fill, perhaps it's because I've seen more of them, and more friends die, in hopeless causes than you ever will, even with that sword on your hip." Longwell shook his head slowly. "Come. Let us find your trifle – and then I'll help you build a signal fire atop the Citadel. After that...what you do with the rest of your lives, and that weapon...well, it's in your hands. I know what I mean to do." And Longwell plunged on ahead, seemingly unmoved by anything Guy had said.

Guy muttered to himself, but Shirri ignored it. "Come," she said gently, and hurried after Longwell, for he was, at least, heading in the right direction. "Maybe he'll change his mind."

"Maybe," Guy said. But he sounded far from convinced.

CHAPTER 53

ALARIC

"It's the strangest thing," Alaric said, tucked under the blanket in Mazirin's quarters, the hammock swaying gently around them with the movement of the *Raifa*. The tightly wound ropes prodded him through the blanket that covered them, but he could feel it – barely – through the wool. "There are times when I feel old – desperately old, old as the world itself." He stretched, her head resting against his chest. "And then other times, like this, when I feel...young again. As if I were back at the beginning once more, my whole life spread before me with all its hope and possibility."

"Whereas I just feel tired," Mazirin muttered sleepily, curling against his chest, her long hair tickling him. "Tired and ready for a rest, regardless of age."

Alaric smiled, looking over the side of the hammock. His armor was spread out on the deck, along with Aterum, and her long brown coat and clothing. Her pistols peeked out of the coat, and beneath the blanket he looked at her bare skin, the hints of gray lacing their way through her hair.

Yes, this was a strange contentment that curled through him. He felt from his chest all the way down to his toes, flexing them idly, lackadaisically, just for fun. Mazirin's weight against his side was little enough, a pleasing warmth against his ribs, her legs crossed up with his, a thigh draped over his own and her feet against his calf.

How long had it been? Since Raifa, surely. A very long time indeed, then.

He stared up at the wooden slats above, black pitch pasted between the boards to keep out the elements. He could not feel the wind through them save the slightest hints through the windows at the back of the captain's cabin, which squeaked in the hard wind.

There was a sense of peace within Alaric that it felt as though even Malpravus might not be able to touch. Not here, not now, not ever, if the fates be kind. For it had been so very long since Alaric had felt this way. Not with the innumerable maidens of his youth. Not with Jena, to his shame. Only with Raifa, truly, and for an entirely too short measure of time.

He dwelt in that silence, the peace, the quiet, the easy sway of the ship...

...until the bell began to toll above, heralding some trouble, and stirring his blood – and his lover – out of their contentment and back to life.

CHAPTER 54

VASTE

"What in the hell are you doing here?" Vaste asked, staring at Cyrus in his full armor, Rodanthar hanging from his belt. He was out of breath, tired, staring at the warrior in black, the man lit by the strange, pale glow in this swampiest of locales. "I thought you were going to Pharesia?"

"Do I know you, greenskin?" The voice was calm, almost unbelievably so. And deep.

"I should certainly hope so," Vaste said, staring at the pearly glow upon Cyrus's armor. His chin looked a bit odd. His nose too, come to see it now. "We've only known each other since – hey, wait a minute."

"I take it Rusyl here is not a friend of yours?" The voice from the shadows of the tipi was calm, accented in the same way as Asa-tee's. Vaste turned, and there, face lit by the red glow of a pipe, two eyes watched him with good humor under a mane of gray that tapered down to braids hanging over his shoulders. A pleasant, burning smell like incense drifted around him, and the fire in the center of the lodge raised the heat to a different, almost feverish level.

Vaste looked again; now it was more obvious. The haze in the tent from the fire and the pipe, the warm, smoky element had obscured the truth. That was no living man standing before him, not Cyrus Davidon...

...It was Rusyl Davidon. Cyrus's father. Or his shade, at least, given the man himself had departed the world before Vaste had even met Cyrus.

"You must be Huaviri," Vaste said, tearing his eyes from the shade of Rusyl Davidon to the man with the pipe.

"If not, I'm in the wrong tent," Huaviri said, taking another puff and exhaling it slowly. His face was deeply lined around the eyes, across the cheeks. "And the wrong continent, because this is no place for *the People*." He paused, thinking. "Or anyone, really. It's going to hell fast over here, I got to tell you."

"You don't need to tell me that, I'm here for that very reason," Vaste said. He brushed off some of the pollen coating his black robe. "I've come to learn from you to stop it, after all."

"Oh, is that why?" Huaviri asked. "Not my pleasant company? My spartan conditions – no, those wouldn't be of interest to a pampered *gisomari* like yourself." He seemed to take Vaste in with a long look from his toes all the way up to his head.

"If I'm pampered it's because people have recognized my true value and rewarded it accordingly," Vaste said, feeling a need to adjust his robes. They were riding up, which didn't seem possible given they were robes, and had very few points to cling to his body. Yet they were, and he discovered a dozen burrs situated around his arse that were causing them to bunch.

"Ah, yes, your true value," Huaviri said. He was sitting cross-legged, with a strange outfit made of leather, bones and beads, decorated with feathers. "Rusyl, what would you say the true value of a troll is?"

"Little to none," Rusyl Davidon said with a surprising lack of hate. It was as though he were stating rote facts. "Their blood doesn't even fertilize the ground well after you kill them."

"Well, what the hell does he know?" Vaste asked, barely giving the shade any consideration. "He's been dead a thousand years. Plus, he raised a son who barely knew any better than him. Why, I had to educate the boy myself on the value of trolls – and of not being a bigoted turd."

"You know my son?" Rusyl Davidon asked. Like most shades, he did not seem particularly aware. Hell, the fact that any of him remained after over a thousand years had passed was remarkable; most spirits departed the realm moments after their death.

Vaste's brow puckered. "How the hell did you escape being sucked into Mortus's spirit trap? You should be a scourge right now, clawing your way through the Mountains of Nartanis searching for shrubberies to uproot and eat or something."

"The thing about traps," Huaviri said, "is they have bounds. You can't rope the whole world in your snare."

"Ah," Vaste said. "So he couldn't quite reach this far."

"Couldn't," Huaviri said, "or didn't. Might not have seen value in these swamps." Here he grinned, displaying a full set of pearly teeth. "And can you blame him? A backwards-ass people inhabited here. I've talked to them. Walked with them. Their interests were war, wrestling gators, and goats." He shook his head slowly. "Terrible, terrible interest in goats."

"I just want to make clear that's not all of us," Vaste said.

"I wouldn't have assumed it of you...until you denied it."

"Denial is the only way to deal with such slander," Vaste said. "Just because my people had an interest doesn't mean I did."

"So as a young man here–" Huaviri said.

"As a young man I was hated here," Vaste said, opening the flap of the tipi. It was some sort of animal skin, thick and dried to leather. "Well, in the city, anyway. I mean, I never fit in, but it got worse after the war, after they killed all the smart trolls who'd been in charge of–"

"There's no such thing as a smart troll," Rusyl said in a pinched voice. Another rote, unthinking statement.

"My, you grow tiresome quick," Vaste said. "And no, there aren't any smart trolls anymore, because they were killed by their own people after the war with the humans. I left when I became old enough to realize the eye of suspicion was upon me. As did anyone else who had a hint of a brain."

"I knew one of them," Huaviri said. "The last of you – though I think you know."

"So I heard," Vaste said. "My mentor. Oroguuk."

"I knew him, and knew him well," Huaviri said. "He came before my own mentors and lived among us in the great Ojito desert of Azwill for innumerable years, finally passing into the great oblivion barely a century back." Huaviri brushed his gray, braided hair back over his bare, wrinkled shoulders, his beaded and boned vest barely covering them. "I knew him as a young man, but his spirit stayed with us for many more years after, holding a grip on this world and only gradually fading away, moving onward to the spirit realm."

"I need to know about this 'spirit realm,'" Vaste said. "The foe we face, Malpravus – he seems to have a grip on it, much like the spirit trap that swallowed people from this land when I roamed it a thousand years ago. I need to know–"

"You *need* water," Huaviri said, and smiled puckishly. "You *need* food. Though not immediately, in your case–"

Vaste felt his cheeks burn. "Excuse me, I did not come here to be insulted–"

"But you'll take it, in order to get what you want," Huaviri said with an easy grin. "*Want*, not *need*."

"No," Vaste said. "I *need* to stop Malpravus. It's not a want. The entire world rests upon it."

"No," Huaviri said, shaking his head. "The world lived before us and it will go on long after, even if only as a ball of barren rock. This Malpravus...he doesn't threaten the world. He threatens the people."

"The people are my world," Vaste said softly. "Without them, this lifeless rock, even were I to be on it...it would hold no life for me."

"Then that's what you *want*," Huaviri said. "Not need. Important distinction."

"Why?" Vaste asked. "What the hell does it matter? I'm going to fight like the dickens either way."

"Mmmm," Huaviri said. "Will you? You push a man's head underwater so he can't breathe...he will fight with everything he has, though not smartly. But if you starve him long enough, suffocate him, let him have no water...the fight goes right out of him. He needs those things. But he won't fight for them, because he cannot."

Huaviri pointed a wrinkled finger at Vaste. "You want to save these people, this land. You don't need to. You could run and hide in a distant cave. This Malpravus would never find you. Never get around to it. Not be able to sense you under the rock, the soil."

"I'm not a coward," Vaste bristled, and he accidentally looked at the shade of Rusyl Davidon.

"I never met a troll who was," Davidon said stiffly.

"This is very distracting," Vaste said, gesturing at the pale, armored figure. "Does he have to be here for this?"

"Where else would he go?" Huaviri asked. "We're sitting on his grave. He was here first. Doesn't seem right to make him move, especially since he's dead."

"This is his grave?" Vaste shuffled his feet; there was no sign of a grave, just rocky ground. But then, a thousand years in the soil of the swamp were unlikely to leave much sign of a tomb, let alone a body. "Well, that's uncomfortable."

"Every step you take in this world, you're treading on someone's grave," Huaviri said. "Some animal spirit. Some human, troll, some sentient – does it matter?"

"Well, it's a bit grim – but beside the point," Vaste said. "I'm more annoyed by him because he's the only one in a grave here that's speaking."

Huaviri chuckled. "We're all in our graves, *gisomari*. We walk from them, we speak from them, our words echoes traveling backward in time from that final resting place. Your fate is the same as his; we are all equal in death." He stood, slowly, his bones creaking as he rose. "Unless your bony friend Malpravus gets his way. Then we'll all be equal in death, still, but because we are slaves."

"Ah ha!" Vaste crowed. "So do you care what happens with Malpravus."

"Of course I care," Huaviri said.

"Then teach me what I need – want – to know," Vaste said, amending quickly.

"I can't teach you, *gisomari*," Huaviri said. "You have to *learn*."

"Fine," Vaste said, spreading his arms wide. "Help me learn. You know the secret to disarming Malpravus of his spiritual ammunition. So..." He waved his hand in a circling pattern. "...What is it?"

"If it were that easy, don't you think everyone would know? Azwillian and *gisomari*?" Huaviri took up a walking stick and shuffled toward the flap of the tipi.

"Where are you going?" Vaste asked.

"I've been waiting for your fat arse for three days," Huaviri said, mopping his brow. "In a sweaty lodge. I'm thirsty, my bones hurt, and I'm sick of talking to this joker." He waved a hand at Rusyl. "You talk to him for a while. You have a friend in common. See what you can learn from him. I'm getting some venison, some air, some sleep – I'll be back. And if you want to learn...you'll be here waiting."

"I'm hungry, I'm tired, I'm thirsty," Vaste said, turning to watch Huaviri as he opened the flap. A rush of pleasant, cool air washed in, and Vaste felt his lips swell like they'd become thin, thin and dry, like a worm in the sun sitting on a brick.

"No reason for both of us to be," Huaviri said cheerily. "For you – it's necessary. Fast. Pray. Visions are coming – if you let them." And he started to let the flap fall behind them.

"What the – what about you?" Vaste asked. "If this vision business is so important, shouldn't you join me?"

"I'm old and bony," Huaviri said, voice muffled as the tent flap fell behind him. "I might die waiting for you to get hungry enough to experience a vision. Just sit here. Talk. Feel the heat wash your bones, cleanse your spirit."

"What – but how long?" Vaste asked.

Huaviri's voice was fading as he retreated. "How long would you wait to save your world, Vaste?"

And Vaste sat, glaring irritably at the shade of Rusyl Davidon, who just watched him, glaring down with that glowing black armor. "Oh, shut up," Vaste said.

"I didn't say anything," the ghost said, sounding vaguely annoyed.

"You're a Davidon; it wouldn't have been long," Vaste said irritably. For he had a feeling he would be waiting quite some while.

CHAPTER 55

SHIRRI

The wind had changed and Shirri could feel it, a strange scent of dust, ash, and decay, cold and coming out of the north. Though the ash might have been from their efforts, it was hard to tell, for it blew all around, barely broken by the surviving bricks standing like tombstones over the place.

"You're sure this is where you lived?" Longwell asked, knee-deep into the ash, sifting through it with the end of Amnis, like a ferryman poling through the river.

She, too, was in the ash up to her waist, digging with Philos. "Yes," she said, looking at the brick stanchions that had – somehow – survived the horror of the fire. "It was here, in the basement of this building." She nodded into the distance, where a building stood just down the street, though barely, a metal clock face peering scorched, skeletal, out of a burnt tower. "That tells me so. It was just down the street. Two blocks from the park we passed on the way here."

"I don't know how you hid it from the Machine here," Guy said. "They would have tossed your place properly, turned it over right to make sure nothing got missed."

"It was hidden in the blocks beneath the floor," Shirri said, trying to find the spot where – beneath a rug – she had carved a place out of the basement floor. There she'd hidden it, the medallion of Sanctuary. Her prized – really only – possession.

"How do you have a block beneath a basement floor?" Guy's face was black from the ash; he was digging with his sword, making a real mess of it.

"These basements are quite old," Houk said. He did not deign to dig, nor did he look like he would be of much use at it in any case. Instead he paced above them, at street level, looking down. "In many places they intersect with the foundations of the old city, the Protanian one that stood here before the humans built Reikonos." He peered down, seeming interested if a bit distracted. "This seems to be one of those spots."

"That doesn't make any sense to me," Guy said. "You saying you stuck it somehow between the dirt floor and – what? An old city ruin from the ancients?"

"No," Shirri said, thumping Philos lightly upon the bottom of the basement, some three feet buried in ash, seeking for a ridge, a lip, any sign of a lump. "I mean to say–"

"I think I found it," Longwell said, thumping his own weapon into...well, something. It produced a dull thud as he moved it like a broom through the knee-deep black ash. "Yes," he shook his head. "Yes." Pushing down, he lifted – and an entire block came up, ash drifting over the sides.

Shirri waded through, peering into the space Longwell had cleared, Nessalima's light overhead shining down to see–

Nothing. There was nothing there.

"Well...damn." Guy said.

"It was here," Shirri said, kneeling, running her fingers through the ash that coated the small chamber. Yes, this was the spot where she'd left it, but it was gone as though it had never even been here. "Where...where could it have gone?"

Guy paused, cocked his head. "Better question. You hear something?"

"The quiet of a dead city," Longwell said bitterly, clinking the haft of his spear against the ground, muffled slightly by the ash. "The guilt of a thousand years. And the dying embers of hope fading. Other than that – no."

"No, it's not that," Guy said, still listening. "This is more like a..." He made a face. "...Clicking."

"What does a thousand years of guilt sound like?" Shirri asked. She paused, straightening her back. Her hands were black with ash, her staff covered with soot stains turning the wood almost gray. She stared at the empty space where she'd left the medallion; she didn't need to be told what the dying embers of hope fading sounded like. There was a rush in her ears.

Longwell froze in place, half stooped. "Like distant screams. Of all the people who died because of me."

"No, it's not that, either," Guy said, standing very still. "It's more like a...dull roar."

"That," said Houk, stepping off his beam very carefully, face ashen but without a sprinkle of the real stuff anywhere on him, "is the sound of scourge." He looked at each of them, his eyes slightly wide. "And they are coming this way – swiftly."

CHAPTER 56

CYRUS

"*Y*ou are pensive this morning," Vara said over the breakfast on the morrow. An array of fruits – melons, berries – lay spread on the table before them, along with a wide variety of breakfast meats – sausage, bacon, a plate of eggs vast enough that Cyrus could scarcely eat it alone.

"I'm a thinker," Cyrus said, clutching his fork. Overly ornate, it held a tinge of gold. Hell, Cyrus realized, adjusting it in his hand, it was gold. The elves were truly rolling out the red carpet.

"Indeed," Vara said, "but usually," and here she speared a segment of melon, "when you think, it's upon terrible things which you dwell." She still did not seem well rested, dark circles under her eyes. "So...you think of Malpravus this morning?"

"Of course."

"Of course," Vara said, a servant buzzing past almost unnoticed. By her, in any case. Cyrus was keenly aware of them, all of them, as they went by, forever bringing new plates of food, and at a clip considerably faster than he could have cleared them had he possessed his full appetite. Which he did not. His plate of eggs was barely picked at. "And what facet of the impending confrontation are you dwelling upon today?"

"Strategy," Cyrus said, letting the fork clatter unused to his crystal plate.

"Yes, I'm sure you need a good strategy to avoid eating the mound of eggs upon your plate. Then: ignore the bacon and finally – discard the sausage, uneaten."

"Well, I'm not as big a fan of sausage as you are."

She gave him a mildly amused glare. "I take it you are contemplating the destruction of Malpravus?"

"Or at least the failed attempts thus far," Cyrus said, pushing his plate away. How was he supposed to eat with this on his mind? "I don't know how to beat him, Vara. This task, it seems...insurmountable."

Her voice became soft, almost delicate, if such a thing were possible for her. "We've beaten him before."

"We've stymied him before. That's hardly the same. Imprisoned him–"

"We've beaten gods, Cyrus. Or at least you have. All of them, in fact."

"Don't think I haven't reviewed past victories trying to dream up a way to destroy him," Cyrus said darkly, rising, leaving his plate not nearly finished. An elven servant swept through and gathered it up without missing a step or slowing down. "I keep coming to the same conclusions–"

"Don't get defeatist on me now."

"I don't know how to beat him," Cyrus said, ambling toward the open doors to the balcony. No one was out there yet this morning. "Every idea I come up with, things that worked on Mortus, on Yartraak – they won't work on him."

"The cessation spell," Vara said.

"Doesn't function any longer," Cyrus said, shaking his head. "At least not as it should, not with the people we have to cast it. If Curatio were still alive..."

"If Curatio had cast it when he fought Malpravus..." Vara rose, coming alongside Cyrus. The sun shone down on them.

"He made a grave error," Cyrus said. "And I can hardly fault him for it. After all, the last time I actually tried to fight Malpravus, he–"

"Hit you so hard you went through a wall and enjoyed an airship-free flight halfway across Reikonos."

Cyrus felt his brow pinch. "No. He sent unending swarms of scourge over the parapets of Saekaj Sovar's airship port, nearly overwhelming us unto death. Keep up, woman."

Vara yawned and made a great show of trying to cover it with her bare hand. She wore a silken robe, and seemed to give little care or thought to the servants about. "I'm a bit tired this morning, I'm afraid. Almost as though someone disturbed my slumber repeatedly."

"Malpravus is going to disturb more than that if he gets his way," Cyrus said. "And I don't know what to do about it. Spell and sword won't work. I think back to when we fought him in the temple in the Waking Woods, how every attack was turned aside. He may have looked like a scrawny necromancer, but my mother was clear – he has powers beyond the physical now. Things that a properly functioning cessation spell can't even curb." He lay his hand upon the stone balustrade. "I'm at a loss." Cyrus felt a grimace break out across his face. "I cannot recall being herded into a battle feeling this helpless and unsure, not even the ones I lost."

"Yes," Vara said, laying her head on his arm. "But usually when you're defeated spectacularly, it's the time when you've run into it thinking victory is assured, so I don't worry about this quite so much as you do."

"I have to beat him," Cyrus said. The despair was settling, though he tried not to let it take root in his soul. "I promised Terian. I swore to the others – they look to me."

"They don't only look to you," Vara said. "This is not solely upon your shoulders, Cyrus. The others are out there." She swept a small hand across the blue horizon, the sun at such odds with Cyrus's mood. "They are working where we cannot. Finding ways to hurt Malpravus and bring aid to us in ways we can't." She lifted her head to look at him, her blue eyes glittering in the morning sun. "You'll figure it out. You always do."

He put on a brave face then, but he knew she could tell that his worry had hardly ceased. Still, they stood there together for a time as the servants behind them cleared breakfast, and the pit deep within Cyrus did not cease to yawn in that time, nor quiet even a little.

CHAPTER 57

ALARIC

*H*is armor came to him with but a thought, and Alaric disappeared and reappeared upon the deck above, fully clad and beside the bell. Calene was hammering it for all she had, Edouard upon the wheel and both of them looking into the sun. "What is it?" Alaric asked, sending Calene into a spin to draw her weapon and Edouard almost into the air, he was so jarred by the sudden appearance behind him.

"Forgot you could do that," Calene said, bow in hand. She clutched tightly along the green lower limb of Vita, as though intending to give him a good whack with it. His eyes skimmed off it; she'd offered it to him once, though he was hard pressed to know why. He could barely use one of those things. Pointing at the sun, Calene added, "See that?"

Alaric cupped a hand over his eyes and looked into the glaring brightness. "No."

"Look closer, it's there," Calene said, keeping that bow firmly in hand. "A great shadow, looks like–"

"Ah," Alaric said, squinting. He'd just about had to blind himself to see it, but yes, there it was. "You might want to keep ringing that bell. And also...send us in the opposite direction."

"Gotta be a bit careful about that," Calene said, nodding at

Edouard, who was back on the wheel and – gently – steering them slowly to the right, away from the sun and the shadow. "You run, they have a tendency to chase."

Mazirin skidded onto the main deck just then, almost colliding with Qualleron, who was lurking on the main deck, head at Alaric's knee-level, listening to this conference. Mazirin swore in her own language, that much was clear even absent his understanding. "What is this?" she asked, still putting on her long brown coat as she mounted the last few stairs. Her hair was wild and unkempt...and he could barely take his eyes off of her.

"Up there," Calene said, handing her a spyglass. Did it come with the wheel, Alaric wondered?

Mazirin swore again once she'd looked, then checked their course. "You did the right thing," she said, though it sounded quite grudging.

"You have experience with them?" Calene asked.

"Not much," Mazirin said, peering again through the spyglass. It looked tinted, almost black, at the wide end. Why hadn't Calene offered that to him, Alaric wondered. "I don't sail these winds. I prefer Amatgarosan routes. Too much uncertainty when you add multiple destinations in these savage...erm...lands." She looked vaguely embarrassed after she said it, but no apology was forthcoming. "This is the last place on the planet where you have these sorts of troubles, you know? Everywhere else they were hunted to extinction." She lowered the glass, then her voice. "As well they damned well should have been."

"We should avoid the dragon," Alaric said, for that was what it was, lurking in the shadow of the sun.

"We can try," Calene said. "But dragons, especially the young ones? They're not known for avoiding us. Hence," and here she inclined her head toward Mazirin, "why the airship captain advocates killin' em' off. They're a barrel of gunpowder with a lit fuse."

"I can't believe I'm dealing with a dragon," Edouard said, sounding very faint.

"Do we have a method of fighting it should it come for us?" Alaric asked. He'd had his own dealings with dragons, though obviously long ago. Plenty enough of them in fact to have been quite content never to lay eyes on the creatures ever again.

"If we were fully crewed, it would be a simple enough matter," Mazirin said, taking the spyglass off her eye. "Cannons can make quick work of them. But with our skeleton crew, and only – perhaps – three of us capable of even firing a cannon, and one of them slaved to the engines...I would say no."

"I don't know how to fire a cannon," Edouard croaked.

"I do," Qualleron rumbled. "But I cannot fit below your tiny decks."

Mazirin looked squarely at Alaric. "You cannot." Then Calene. "You?"

"I know how to fire a cannon," Calene said. "And you shouldn't sneer at Alaric, either – with Aterum in hand, he could probably have one launching pretty quick. You just need to show him how to roll it out and do it."

Mazirin gave her a curt nod. "If I have time. For now – keep us coursing away. Maybe the dragon won't follow."

"It's already following, I'm afraid," Calene said, turning her face again toward the sun. "Curving around like it means to attack."

Mazirin cursed once more. "Perhaps you should walk Alaric through loading and firing a cannon." She looked once again through the spyglass. "Just in case."

CHAPTER 58

VASTE

*T*he hours skated into days. Vaste's stomach rumbled, but he did not leave the sweat lodge.

"Why?" he asked through cracked lips. He could not quite conjure a reason that made sense.

The heat baked at him, trapped in the lodge, hemmed in as he was by whatever animal skins composed the tipi. The surface seemed to crawl with life, and he felt it upon his skin, sensations of *things* upon him, writhing.

"I wonder what my son is up to," Rusyl Davidon said.

"I am literally starving in front of you and you simply cannot get your mind off your stupid son and his overlong arse?" Vaste moaned into the dark of the shadowed tent.

The shade of Rusyl was quiet for a moment. "You know, I never really thought of it before, but now that you mention it...his arse was a bit long, I suppose, in proportion to the rest of his body."

"At last, common ground," Vaste muttered, giving in to the heat. The shade shut up again, though, blessedly, and he continued to stew in the sweltering air, trying to focus on...well, he didn't know what. But he focused anyway.

CHAPTER 59

SHIRRI

"To the Citadel!" Longwell shouted, scrambling before the rest of them. They ran through the ash and dust, and soon Shirri could hear it, sharp and terrible–

The click of claws on the ashy cobblestones paving the city streets. The dull roar of feral voices, growling in unison.

It was amazing to Shirri how quickly any thought of the missing medallion had faded. Before even one of the scourge had come in sight, she was prompted to run, and run she did. Guy, Longwell, Shirri – they all ran, and ran at great speed, their weapons giving them aid. She lost sight of Houk, and started to say something–

But he was there, suddenly, appearing out of a side alley, as though he'd taken a shortcut. His suit was unruffled and seemingly so was he, but he ran and ran furiously, the tall, partially destroyed tower looming above them on the ashen remains of the avenue.

"Scourge!" Guy shouted, and there one was, leaping out of a burnt window that lacked glass; a blackened wall with a square hole in its middle, really, and the gray thing was leaping out of it with flashing teeth and claws.

Longwell speared it and lifted it, hurling it over them. It crashed into a wall and the wall disintegrated, turning into a billow of ash.

The scourge made a strangled noise, writhing and thrashing and stirring up a black cloud.

None of them paused to see if it died.

"How did the bloody things get into the city?" Guy asked. More claws on cobblestones were audible now, all around Shirri in between gasps for breath.

"They're under the control of one man, now," Houk said, barely even winded as he surged into another side alley behind them. His voice reached them as he disappeared into shadows. "A single-minded focus could see them across in one spot."

"Can you teleport us out of here?" Longwell asked, huffing as they sprinted up the main avenue, the singed ruin of buildings on either side of them sticking out like blackened bones from dead earth. He was, Shirri realized, looking at her.

"I don't know the teleportation spells," she said, huffing. "By the time I came 'round, they were unsafe to use." Keeping Philos clutched in her hands was giving her aid in this run, but it was still thoroughly unpleasant.

"It's not the moment for discussion of the subject," Guy said, more winded than either of them, "but anyone else find it odd that elven fellow is keeping up with us, with our godly weapons?" Houk appeared out of an alley ahead, and this time Shirri had no explanation for how he'd managed the feat.

"Fullness – of – time!" Longwell said; the Citadel was looming ahead, it stood beyond the ruin of Reikonos Square, which they crossed at a dead sprint, leaping over the fountain in the middle, now blackened and drained from the intensity of the fire, all water within evaporated. Shirri then realized she was quite thirsty, and quite unable to do a thing about it.

The scourge was behind them in a ravening pack, but at a distance. Looks back provided Shirri a view of a streaming, surging ocean of gray flooding down the avenue, filling it from side to side. The scourge could not keep up with them, but still they came down the ashen street like an unstoppable torrent of death.

Now the tower grew close; no one spoke. They were all hurrying with all they had, though Shirri wondered at the reason for it. The light was waning, the sun well on its path beyond the horizon, the twilight settling in over the dead city.

Still, the Citadel grew closer, with its missing bulb of a head, abruptly chopped at the neck so it looked like a pillar in the sky. Shirri hadn't been there when that had happened, but she'd heard the tale later – Malpravus and Curatio had clashed, and the subsequent release of the energies pooling between them had torn asunder the entirety of the upper floors, leaving them a smoking ruin and the Citadel decapitated.

"Up or down?" Shirri asked, the thought suddenly occurring to her as they raced for the door.

"Whot?" Guy asked, his short legs blazing with speed.

"Which way do we go once inside?" Shirri asked. "Up or down?" Behind her, well back, the gap opening, but still quite fierce and dangerous, came the scourge.

"Down," Longwell said tightly, blue armor flashing in the last embers of daylight.

"What?" Guy asked. "That realm you're so in love with, it's a bloody trap, a permanent prison. We go in there, we're done, mate. You 'eard 'er – she's got no teleportation. We'll be stuck in there forever."

"And we'll live," Longwell said. "Which is more than I can say for the rest of them."

They came at last to the doors of the Citadel, thrown open to a public that no longer existed. Shirri could not recall a time when the doors had ever been open to this place, when the gates had been so easy to pass through as they'd just been, hanging off their hinges, half-melted.

"I'm going up," Guy said.

Almost at the same time as Shirri said, "I won't go down there."

They all stopped the moment they were inside. The interior was an immense chamber with a staircase corkscrewing its way up the inside of the cylindrical Citadel, narrowing above to allow space for rooms that hugged the exterior walls. As Shirri looked up, she couldn't see the top, but she could see shadows pooling in the center of the staircase, which disappeared into the ebony dark.

"I have been a coward my whole entire life," Guy said, taking a few deep breaths, and leaving a wary eye on the scourge coming; Houk managed to slip in just behind them, barely breathing hard. "I will not go down there and sit this out. I am done dodging the fight."

"What would you do?" Longwell asked, throwing a gauntleted hand in the direction of the scourge. "Stand up there and die in the dark?"

"The *Lady Quinneria*," Shirri said. "It may still be out there."

Longwell blew air between pale, thin lips visible beneath his bushy beard. "They are dead. Everyone else is dead. And so shall you be if you go up instead of down." He started toward a giant gap in the wall that had a faint blue glow to it; it seemed a passage, and beyond it a staircase that wended down.

"Come on, Shirri," Guy said, and without hesitation he moved for the upward spiral of the staircase, "let's go meet our end with dignity and courage, if that's what it's to be." The former Machine thug threw a look of disgust at the figure of the armored dragoon. "I'd rather die being pushed off that tower by the scourge, knowing I took at least a few more of 'em out of the fight for my comrades than live a thousand years more with these things in hand," he brandished Praelior, "remembering that I ducked out of the fight when the world finally found a proper use for me."

Longwell hesitated at the entry. "You'll die."

Guy was already gone; Houk had followed with him, the elf apparently making his choice just as cleanly, though Shirri could not quite understand why. The scourge were coming; only a few hundred feet away, the ravening hoard came surging toward the slagged and melted gates to the Citadel.

"We all die, Samwen Longwell," Shirri said. She felt strangely stiff, the weapon Philos clutched in her hand. "Delay it, run from it – your day of reckoning will still eventually arrive. And for my part, I would rather end it like Hiressam, earlier than anticipated, fighting in good cause than whiling away all the long days of my life by some brook's side, reliving forever the fears that drove me into the bosom of such safety. No, better to die swift, once, than live a coward for ten thousand years."

And she, too, ran for the staircase, a strange flutter of excitement in her heart. Not for death, which certainty seemed ever so much closer–

But for life as she was currently living it, with wild abandon, no longer in fear–

As a member of Sanctuary should.

CHAPTER 60

ALARIC

"The name of the game here," Calene said, as they stood in the cramped, dark deck below the main, "is to get the cannon wormed, sponged out, loaded, ramrodded, run back out, then fired – all as quickly as possible." She paused, hand on hip, eyes squinting now in the dark. "I suppose that's a bit obvious, though, isn't it?"

"Indeed," Alaric said, though he felt no need to drive the point home any harder. She'd shown him the rough sequence; if he felt a pistol was dishonorable, at least this had the virtue of being employed on a more dangerous foe. Fighting a dragon in the air with sword and spear was a fool's game. This, though – this evened the odds. And that meant it had honor to it. "Hopefully it won't come to this, but thank you for the instruction."

Calene squinted at him in the dark; perhaps she had something in her eye. "It's a dragon, Alaric. Why would you think it wouldn't come to that?"

"Perhaps we'll play a game of cat and mouse with it," Alaric said with a smile.

"More like dragon and goat," she said. "Or worse – troll and goat."

"Well, let's hope it doesn't come to that," Alaric said, sticking his face out the gun port. The wind was blowing hard against him, rattling his helm, so he brought his head back inside. A thoroughly unpleasant sensation, that.

"Make ready the guns!" Mazirin shouted above, her voice muffled by the boards between them.

If there were any doubt what she was saying, though, it was dispelled a moment later when Qualleron's voice bellowed into the belowdecks: "Make ready the guns! Battle approaches!"

"That's the vexing thing about hope," Calene said with a bitter smile. "It never does quite spring up where you want it to."

"Don't go losing heart just yet, lass," Alaric said, already loading his cannon as she'd taught him while she did the same with hers. If they loaded them all, they might just be able to make a show of force when the time came.

CHAPTER 61

SHIRRI

Shirri burst up onto the top surviving floor of the Citadel just behind Guy and Houk, that curious elf, and the black night sky hung over a scorched but flat floor of impossible smoothness. The walls that might once have stood rising above the ground had been seemingly burned off smooth around the edges. The slightest chill prickled at Shirri's skin beneath her robes as she left the residual, clinging warmth of the Citadel's interior behind and stepped out into the burgeoning night.

"We should set up first here at the stairs," Guy said, puffing, his sword in hand. "Choke 'em off before they get up here and have room to work at devouring us." His beady eyes were barely visible in the dark; her half-elven eyes were simply not as good as a pure elf's. With a wave of her hand she cast the Eagle Eye spell on both of them, and she could see his pupils dilate as it took hold. "That's better."

"I agree," Shirri said, swinging Philos experimentally. Singing through the air, it made a sharp whistling sound. It would do. "Eventually they'll push us back to the edge–"

"We go over together, when it comes to that," Guy said with a firm nod – and not a trace of doubt, it seemed.

"I never thought I'd die fighting beside a Machine thug," Shirri said. Below, she could hear the snarls of the scourge. They drew closer by the minute; but also, she could hear them falling off the staircase, the foolish things, raining down to their deaths at the bottom of the great plunge.

"You're not," Guy said, with a twinkle in his eyes. "Funny thing about that – I could barely stand to live with bastards like me. Hell if I wanted to die as one of 'em."

"What about him?" Shirri asked, sparing a glance for Houk, who seemed to be wandering the perimeter of the tower. She kept her voice down, but it seemed irrelevant; if he was to betray them, if he was Malpravus in some guise, well, what of it? What could he do but cut their lives a bit shorter at this point?

"I'm a bit more worried about what's in front of us than what's behind at the moment," Guy said, gaze firmly fixed down the staircase. Even with the Eagle Eye spell, Shirri could not see the scourge yet, because it took a winding turn back around the neck of the tower and out of sight; visibility was so poor here that they could barely see thirty feet down, though when the moment came that would all be filled in with scourge, so it hardly mattered.

Shirri felt a strange prickle at the back of her neck. She raised a hand into the air, chanted words long ingrained in her, and released a burst of fire into the darkened heavens. Counting to five, she did it again, and after a ten count, once more, letting bright flames burst upward into the night sky.

"Trying to catch eyes, are you?" Guy asked, bending his head back down to look down the stairs. "I hope it works, I do."

"But?" Shirri asked.

"Well, I'm not counting on it," Guy said.

"If only we'd found that medallion," Shirri said wistfully. The noises were growing closer now, the thud and squeal of scourge going over the edge more pronounced.

"I don't think the medallion would have been of much use right now," Guy said. "Unless it could conjure an airship out of the bloody ether."

Shirri cocked her head. Could Sanctuary have become an airship? It didn't seem completely improbable.

But that was irrelevant now; no medallion, no good. And with Longwell having made his choice, this was simply the end. Not that him being here would have much mattered. Two of them or three, they were still fated to fight unlimited numbers of scourge until they were crowded to the tower's edge. Then, below:

A sharp drop and quick stop. That was the endgame.

"I hear 'em coming," Guy said, readying himself, settling into a stance with a low center of gravity. He held his sword high, and Shirri tried to match his movement. She was even less practiced at combat than he; best to learn a few things now that she had a weapon in her hands.

The end was nigh. And there was nothing for Shirri to do but clutch Philos tight, shoulder to shoulder with Guy, and wait for it to come.

CHAPTER 62

SHIRRI

*D*own the darkened shaft of the tower, the ravening horde of scourge clamored and growled, rising like water come to a boil around the Citadel's circular edges. But below that sound, Shirri heard...

...Something, that was sure. More than groaning, hissing, angry scourge clawing their way up to them. Guy was poised and ready, but Shirri waited, listening, her head cocked for some sign of...

Longwell burst out of the stairwell in a double bound, hitting the wall just below them and leaping out as though fountaining from the small opening. Guy gasped and took a step back, neatly avoiding catching one of the dragoon's pauldrons in the teeth.

"You came," Shirri said, feeling her heart strangely aglow at his sudden entrance. Then it fell. "You couldn't get in the portal?"

"They're coming," Longwell said, positioning himself with them, abrupt, grim.

She tried to conceal her disappointment as she realized: without her, he could not close the passage to the Realm of Life. Of course. Not a choice he'd have made willingly, coming up here to fight and die with them. It was one forced upon him, and something about that made her heart sink.

But there was no more time to think about that, because the scourge were here, surging up the last twist of the staircase and bubbling out of the rectangular opening in a howling, slobbering mob. Shirri struck with the others, all together, her staff bludgeoning the lead scourge and sending him back. Longwell speared one, holding him at bay while Guy sheared the head – rather clumsily – off another. Together they formed a perfect blockage to the tower entry, one carcass and two stunned scourge.

For a moment, even, it seemed as though that might be enough to stop this madness. The bodies squirmed and bubbled and writhed like champagne trapped in a leaking bottle. They could not get around the cork of the dying. Shirri brought her weapon down again and again like a mallet upon a nail, dashing the scourge's brains out of its skull on the third strike. It twitched and became stuck, being pushed, and finally...

...It popped. And then...the scourge were everywhere.

They exploded from the hatch-like opening, clawing up the sides, fountaining into the open as Shirri and the others fell back, swinging all the while. Her staff fell upon skull and skin and bone, breaking and crushing and cracking and sundering, but none of it seemed to make much difference to the flood-tide of scourge. She was screaming, she realized, a bit tardy, leaping back as the scourge pressed forward, undeterred by their numbers falling to sword and spear and stave.

And their numbers fell. Oh, how they fell.

It was a tide of bodies, for every wave of them coming up seemed to come over the last, pushing Shirri and the others toward the edge of the Citadel.

"Any chance you know Falcon's Essence?" Longwell said over the din of claws and growls from the scourge. Hissing and slobbering had never been at such volume, at least not that Shirri could recall; and in it, her grunts and cries of exertion as she swung and swung were lost in the clamor. "Or is that one of the spells they no longer teach?"

"Yes, I know that one," Shirri said with a careful eye behind her, mid-swing. She connected and sent a scourge flying over the edge of the tower. There was little space left behind her. "But I'm not sure it'll do us much good. It's rather spotty."

"Yeah, I watched Cyrus use it to come down out o' the sky when he got hurled out of this place," Guy said. "Saved his bloody life, didn't it?" The shorter man made the appearance of looking out over the edge. "Not sure it'll do us the same favor, though."

Shirri glanced in the direction he was, and if she hadn't already been gasping for breath, it would have taken hers away.

The streets were swimming with scourge. The ashen city seemed to be filled with them, all the way to the walls. Gray skin mixed with black and gray ash in the dark of the city, the last hints of daylight and rise of moonlight shining down on the spectacle, making it appear like the city ruin was writhing, squirming, an anthill disturbed.

"Anything to give us a little more time," Longwell said. "Give it a cast!"

Shirri swept the stave forward and knocked a scourge sideways, tumbling with its clawed legs flailing as it flew over the edge. Then she swept it back, casting the spell thrice–

Her feet floated off the ground perfectly fine. As did Guy's, and Longwell's.

"See?" Longwell was swinging his spear now, not bothering with stabbing, and it was having a fine effect, sending scourge sideways off the edge with black blood spurting from their wounds. "Sometimes you just need to try something new."

"And excellently timed, too," Houk said from behind them. Shirri turned to look; she'd forgotten Houk in her scramble to fight, and to cast the spell–

But he hardly needed it. For he was already floating a half dozen feet over the edge of the tower.

"You'll need to step closer," Houk said. Something was moving behind him, slipping out of the dark clouds covering the moon–

The *Lady Quinneria*.

It caught the moonlight, metal blades turning in the last orange glow of twilight. Surging toward them on a steady approach, it slewed to the side, unable to get too close to the tower, and drifted in the last hundred feet or so toward them. Shirri stole glances even as she fought the scourge for every inch of ground. They kept coming and coming, geysering out of the hole atop the tower.

"Come," Houk called, somehow glowing in the moonlight. "Two days northeast, follow the coast – you will find me there, waiting."

"Who the hell are you?" Guy asked – because of course it would be him.

"A friend," Houk said, his smile twisting low, as his body itself seemed to discorporate, as though blown away by the wind. "One with answers to questions you have long asked. And one who would give you aid, if you but come to see me." With that, he was gone.

"Go, go!" Longwell shouted. With a glance, he turned to them–

And with a nod from Guy, they all broke and ran, feet upon the air, across the thirty feet or so of distance between the Citadel and the *Quinneria*.

Scourge followed them off the edge, a waterfall of the gray creatures. The *Quinneria* stuttered slightly sideways, making them work just a bit harder for it.

Then they were on the deck, and the Falcon's Essence was gone, as surely as if it had never been there. They thumped to the deck amid the shouts of the crew, the squeeze on magic returned with all its full and voluminous force. Shirri felt a sharp pain at her elbow; a whispered breath of a healing spell did little to assuage it.

"Take us away!" Alixa shouted, and the ship moved. "Are you all right?" She descended from the quarterdeck, green garments fluttering.

"We have to go northeast, two days, following the coast," Shirri said, speaking even as she rubbed her elbow. Another healing spell reduced it barely at all.

"You just gonna take that elf's word 'e's our friend?" Guy looked like he was massaging a spot or two of pain as well, and Shirri added unto him a healing spell as well. He did not stop rubbing his pains.

When she turned, Longwell was looming over her, his spear

planted like he was a guardsman, but blocking nothing but the side of the ship. "You didn't have a problem casting Falcon's Essence atop the tower," he said.

She shook her head. "I suspect 'Houk' removed the restriction long enough for us to save ourselves. Without it–"

"We'd have died trying to get to the airship," Guy said, looking right at Alixa, "because it'd take a madwoman to bring her ship close enough to let the scourge flood the bloody deck."

Alixa stared at him coldly for a moment, then nodded. "Who are you talking about? That odd elf?"

"He says he's a friend," Shirri said. "But I think he's the source of the hobbling of magic."

"For over five hundred years?" Alixa asked. "Where is this elf now?"

"To the north, he said," Longwell spoke crisply in the dark. Already, the *Lady Quinneria* was almost to the city walls; below the city writhed, it squirmed.

It lived. Or rather...it didn't, since scourge were hardly alive.

"Northeast is rather sizable direction," Alixa said. "How are you meant to find this stranger with but that for guide?"

Longwell was looking at Shirri; as was, she realized with a sharp shock, Guy, and finally Alixa. "I...don't know," she said, finding the words somehow within. "But I think we should at least try." She sighed. "The medallion is gone, after all, putting us at loose ends save for this. I would hate to return to the others with nothing to show for all we've lost."

Alixa looked to Longwell; a strange thing, Shirri thought. Had they not just quarreled before? Had she not known what he meant to do? Yet still she looked at him. "And what would you do, Samwen?"

Within his helm Shirri could see his eyes; his eyes in that impassive face, the beard flowing out from beneath the oddly shaped dragoon's helm. His mouth scarcely moved, and neither did his eyes, save to subtly flicker back toward the tower, and all that he had left behind–

"Go northeast," he said softly. And with that he turned, drifting away as if caught on the wind. He moved with a strange grace, yet slow, as if still invisibly tethered to the tower. He took up position at the aft rail, watching the city of Reikonos – and that magnificent, ruined tower that stood above it all – as they flew away.

"Set a course – northeast," Alixa called, loud enough to be heard over the entirety of the deck. She turned crisply on her heel, striding back to the quarterdeck. "After the sea, follow the coast."

Shirri found herself alone with Guy mere seconds later, standing at the place they'd crashed onto the deck. He spoke low, sotto voce, beady eyes scanning all the men around them going about their tasks. "You really think that Houk is a friend?" He turned his head slowly toward her. "You're sure 'e's not just Malpravus in another guise running us to him?"

"I don't know," she said, her hand finding the rail as the adrenaline from the fight began to fade, and she felt suddenly weak; Philos did not seem to help that much. "He could be. But we don't have many friends at the moment, and certainly few enough with power. It seems to me that if this Houk is the source of magic's wane, then he must surely not be a friend of Malpravus's, for he was the check upon the sorcerer's action all these years. And if he's not a friend of Malpravus–"

"Then we definitely want 'im to be a friend of ours right now," Guy said with a sharp nod. "Like how you and I might not be friends – except we're both in the sights of that Malpravus prick."

"Exactly like that," Shirri said with the trace of a smile. It was matched by Guy's, and they stood together at the rail, an improbable pair, watching the ground give way to the Placid Sea as the *Lady Quinneria* turned its course north.

CHAPTER 63

ALARIC

"What are you doing up here?" Mazirin asked as Alaric puffed once more onto the main deck. She took him in with a glance and a frown. "You're supposed to be manning the guns."

"The guns are loaded and ready to fire on both sides," Alaric said, "and I can be back at them at a moment's notice." He stared into the clear blue, searching the skies for the dragon; there it was, off the left side only a few hundred yards away and closing, its bat-like wings black against the bright sun.

"Baynvyn calls that he is ready!" Qualleron shouted, taking his head out of the belowdecks passage. "That the engines are ready to be squeezed like a suckling pig for all their worth."

"That's so strange," Edouard muttered, his hands pale with a death grip on the wheel. "Why would he say it that way?"

"Eyes forward, helmsman," Mazirin snapped. "Concentrate on the task at hand."

Edouard did snap to, putting his attention back to the wheel and where the *Raifa* was going.

Alaric peered into the shadowy silhouette of the dragon. Its wings were flapping, trying to keep itself in the shadow of the sun, and where he could barely see it against the flaming brightness.

"It is drawing closer," Mazirin said, peering with one eye into the tinted spyglass. "No – it's moving away."

"Perhaps it means to leave us be, now that our guns are run out," Alaric said. He truly could not see what the dragon had in mind, what it intended.

An unintelligible shout from belowdecks was followed by Qualleron bellowing, "Movement below the ship!" as he ripped his head out of the hatchway to shout loud enough that Alaric felt almost as though he'd been hit by a Force Blast. When he regained himself, he spun, sensing something–

A dragon's head appeared from behind them; while the one had kept their attention, this one had come up from below and now opened its mouth, ready to breathe upon them, its mouth green with acid.

Before it could draw a breath to strike, Alaric raised his hand and shouted, loosing the words of the Force Blast spell, already to mind. It launched from his hand, barely hobbled at all–

And slapped the dragon in the face, causing it to spew green into the empty sky. It sunk below the side of the *Raifa* and bolted, flying swiftly away in the opposite direction.

"It's skittering off like a wounded rat," Edouard crowed, taking a hand off the wheel to point.

The wind rushed on, and Alaric watched into the sun, Mazirin swinging her spyglass around to do the same. "It's running."

"They want no part of honorable battle," Qualleron said, pointing as it flew away. It was showing them its arse, no hint of wanting to come back for more.

"Let us hope it remains so," Alaric said, though he could tell by the pucker of Mazirin's brow that she, like him, had doubts that it could be.

CHAPTER 64

SHIRRI

*T*hey sailed through the night and into the day, Shirri watching the horizon, the moon sparkling upon the waves. At dawn, with its bright orange beams sliced through sullen clouds that dared to darken the sky, Alixa came down from the quarterdeck to stand with them, her tread steady on the boards.

"The shore of Arkaria curves – a bit – when it becomes the land of ever-frost," she said stiffly. "Things will be turning cold soon."

"What's your bond with him?" Shirri asked, the tiredness making her feel reckless in her query. It just burst forth; it wasn't something she normally would have dared asked, certainly not of the Administrator of Emerald. But things had changed, hadn't they? She'd gone from a debtor to the Machine to, inexplicably, a person who spoke in the presence of rulers and supped with administrators. And asked them impertinent questions upon the decks of their own airships.

Alixa seemed as though she would not answer – but only for a moment. "I am not from this land, as you may know. I am from Luukessia."

"Like him." Shirri nodded at Samwen, standing in the distance, presumably hearing none of this against the roar of the wind.

"No." She shook her head. "He came from the land when it was alive. I came from it when it was long dead, when the last few of us remained in a remote corner of Luukessia, protected from the over-running scourge by a volcano slowly stirring to life. We lived and labored in its shadow until the day came it erupted. Only three of us, on a desperate adventure, made it out alive. Us and Scourgey, as we called her then." Her eyes looked sad. "You know the one."

"Yeah, you don't meet too many scourge that are docile that way," Guy said.

"I was the last survivor of we three who escaped the village," Alixa said. "I'd encountered Samwen on my journey, seeking revenge for what had happened to us. He took me to Emerald Fields, where I began my ascent to...well, what I am now." She stuck out her chin. "So...I suppose he is a friend, a mentor – almost a father figure. Or was, before he faded into the ether, as it were."

"I always thought that phrase was trite," Guy said. "Then I started seeing people actually fade into the ether, and it made a sudden amount of sense."

"He tried to abandon us at the tower," Shirri said, compelled by some unseen force to unburden herself to Administrator Weltan. "He only came back at the last, rushing up at the end through the scourge. He saved our lives, but I reckon it was only because he realized he couldn't shut the portal after himself. That they'd follow him in there, and without our help he'd be stuck with them forever coming at him."

Alixa hung her head. "I should have known he wouldn't give up his dream of returning to that cursed realm of his that easily."

"But 'e did make the right choice," Guy said. "Give the man a little credit."

"I'd be more likely to give him credit if he'd come when we asked, for the reasons we told him he should," Shirri said. "That he realized his end was nigh, that his best option was us...I just cannot forgive him for that."

"Once upon a time, Samwen Longwell might have been the bravest man I ever met," Alixa said, staring at Longwell's shadow looming on the aft deck. "To find out his fate, what's become of him..." She shook her head. "...It's humbling. To watch a great man fall from such heights to...to this..."

She did not finish her description. Indeed, she did not need to, for among them, there was not one that did not know what exactly she spoke of.

CHAPTER 65

ALARIC

"These mountains are thick," Edouard said from his place at the wheel; the hour was growing late, the mountains where Kortran had once been were ahead, and they were all upon the deck in the late afternoon sun.

Alaric stood beside Mazirin, though neither of them touched; still, being close was enough. This was how he preferred it, in the company of others – a comfortable distance between them, yet the glances were plenty to set his heart aflame.

"How far out of Kortri are we?" Calene asked. She leaned against the side rail, staring out to the north.

"A few hours," Mazirin said, "and we may wish to stop, perhaps take on some crew." She gave Alaric a beseeching look. "As you saw in our recent brush with the dragons, if it comes to a real fight...we are not well prepared."

"But it didn't come to a real fight." Baynvyn even was with them, the sun's light emphasizing his faded blue complexion in the late afternoon light. He glanced at Alaric. "You scared them off."

"I am hard pressed to see how I did much other than startle them," Alaric said. "I certainly didn't cause that dragon any injury, not with a mere Force Blast."

"The illusion of your strength was enough to secure your victory," Qualleron rumbled from the main deck. He was still almost at head level with them all, so tall was he. "The mere whisper of your formidable energies deterred your foes from battle. A great victory indeed, to win without fighting."

"I do prefer to win without fighting," Alaric said with a tight smile, "though I wouldn't count on it becoming a regular feature of our lives. What comes now, with Malpravus – it shan't be as easy." A question occurred to Alaric. "'Kortri' – might that be related to old Kortran?"

"Aye," Calene said with an easy smile. "After the dragons destroyed old Kortran, the elves of Amti eventually expanded into the area, built a city on the ruins nestled in that valley. Then they came further south, to the Ashen Wastelands, as the dragons were hunted to their end." She looked out over the vistas of the coming mountains. "I remember when dragons could fill the sky as far as the eye could see. The old, huge ones, and those little drakes and wyverns, too. The wingless wurms, crawling their way across the ash like snakes in the dirt." She sighed. "I almost miss seein' them...sometimes."

"You should not miss such destructive creatures," Mazirin almost spat. "The ruin of navigation in these parts, that is what they are. Preying always upon nearly unarmed vessels. I consider it a blessing that the Firobans sought them for their tallow, their bone, their scale and blood. They have done us all a great service, nearly wiping them out." She spat again, a curious custom, and one Alaric had not seen from her. It seemed to denote a great hatred for dragons, one far out of line with her usual staid, straitlaced and pleasant – to him, at least – demeanor.

"They helped you in the last battle against Bellarum, didn't they?" Baynvyn asked, a bit stiffly. "That was what Terian and my mother told me, anyhow."

"Aye, they did," Calene said. "They'd sworn they would, Ehrgraz and the rest. And when all hope was nearly lost, they swept in at the last and helped us win the day. Told Cyrus afterward not to seek them again, that it'd be his arse if he did. Wanted to live apart, they did." She sighed once more. "Been on a bit of a low trajectory since, relations between all the rest of us and the dragons." Inclining her head to Mazirin, she added, "She's right, though. Bit hard to get along when airships want to come through dragon territory and they wouldn't suffer the sight of them. Made it right natural for the elves of Amti to pay bounties on dragons to Firoban ships that wanted to harvest 'em anyway. And now..." She shook her head. "There's few enough of them left."

"Enough that we just saw two of them," Edouard said. "Two of them tried to bait a trap for us, attack us."

"I wonder if they haven't had something to do with the fall of the telegraph lines in this area," Qualleron said, his hands folded in front of him, massive arms and elbows leanings against the rail so naturally; it was an odd spectacle, seeing a troll so large he could do that. But Qualleron was an odd spectacle anyway.

"If so, they cost us days and forced this trip upon us," Mazirin said.

Alaric thought about that for a moment. "Could that ambush have been part of a well-planned trap by the dragons to draw ships in and destroy them?"

Mazirin shook her head. "Dragons are stupid by all accounts."

"Some dragons are stupid," Calene said. "Drakes, wyverns, and wurms, for instance. They're about as bright as the dullest street tough. But the masters of the dragon race – they're quite smart. Canny, too."

"Ehrgraz, for instance," Alaric said. "He was a master strategist, and general of their people."

"He came to Cyrus, coerced him," Calene said. "Got him to draw the dragons in to Sanctuary's war with the titans. That roused the dragons to rage, and Ehrgraz got what he wanted – the titans wiped out. No more threat on the dragons' border."

"I imagine if Ehrgraz were still around," Alaric said, "they might not perhaps be in as rough a spot as they are."

"Uhm," Edouard said, "I'm not sure how rough the spot they're in actually is." And with a gulp, the pale man pointed straight ahead.

Mazirin gasped. And Alaric could not blame her.

On the twilight horizon, Alaric saw what – at first blush – looked like bats. A sky full of them, silhouettes of their jagged wings. They came by the hundreds, the thousands, perhaps – coming forth toward the *Raifa*.

But they were most certainly not bats.

They were dragons.

And they darkened the skies to the north, blocking the way home.

CHAPTER 66

VASTE

"*H*ey, *gisomari*."

Vaste felt an unsubtle prodding in his belly and stirred within the sweaty confines of the lodge. He stared up into a face looking down into his, with another behind it, aglow with white shading. "Ugh," he said, realizing it was Huaviri – and Rusyl Davidon, still lingering – that peered down at him. "You."

"You passed out, *gisomari*." Huaviri shoved a metal flask into his hand. "You're dehydrated. Which is not the point of this."

"What exactly is the point of this?" Vaste drained the flask easily; it was water, albeit a bit smelly, as befit water from the swamp. His head ached, and so did his body. He didn't know how long he'd been in this sweltering tipi, just that the fire was burning low, and light was streaming in through the flap. "I came to learn from you, not die from starvation or thirst."

"Drink," Huaviri said, gesturing to the flask. "Probably don't eat, though. You need to be a little on the edge of death to really commune with the spirit world, at least at first."

"I've already communed with the spirit world from the edge of death," Vaste said, coming upright with surprising violence, though he felt he lacked a certain energy. "I can see the ghostly figure of my friend's father staring at me over your shoulder, and I find his company ill, much less interesting than even his son. I can only assume that was Quinneria's intellectual influence."

"Eri," Rusyl said in a soft, moaning voice.

"Yes, her," Vaste said. "Also dead, just so we're clear. But much less annoying and also a hell of a pie chef. Still, absence makes the heart grow fonder and all that, so get lost and maybe I'll think fondly of you in time, Rusyl."

"You should be careful," Huaviri said, "once they're gone, they're gone. You should think carefully whether you actually want him gone."

Vaste grunted. "I can't make him go away. Much as I might wish I could."

Huaviri's face got pinched. "You really don't know anything, do you?" He guffawed, low. "You showed up just in time."

"In time for what?" Vaste asked, staring into his wrinkled face. Then it hit him. "Oh."

"Yes," Huaviri said with a smile. "I'm about to die, Vaste. So you might want to put a bit more effort into this." With a clap on his arm that felt like a shock, Huaviri's smile faded. "Because teaching you? I think it's going to be the last thing I do."

CHAPTER 67

SHIRRI

*S*unset, and the wind grew colder out of the north. It blew off the bow with violence and feeling, and Shirri found herself huddling in a boat cloak one of the crew had handed her. She sat watching the bright orb diminish, slipping beneath the waves in the west, a cold and frozen shore to the east running past, becoming an increasingly shadowed land with every passing minute.

It was a mountainous land as well, beyond the domains of the dwarves of old; they had traveled northeast with tremendous speed, as much as the airship could muster. A rattle commenced a few hours before, and the furtive looks exchanged between the crew members, the hushed whispers she caught with her slightly pointed ears, gave Shirri an unsettled feeling.

But they could not go back, for the nearest city was days away. Somehow, the Administrator had staked their fortunes on forward, and forward they went.

Guy came up beside her, shivering, a bowl of something steaming clutched in his hand. He offered it to her, and Shirri accepted, quite grateful. She took a scalding sip from a rude wooden spoon without bothering to ask what it was first, and burned her mouth.

When she looked at him questioningly, perhaps even beseechingly, he said, "Hot salted pork broth. Absent, mostly, the pork." He had a bowl of his own and let it stream down his bearded chin. "Owowowow!"

Owowow indeed. With her tongue, Shirri could feel tiny flaps of mouth-skin burned to blister by this delicacy. Still, she felt compelled to blow on it, trying to reduce the heat so she could drink it down.

"You think that medallion got nicked before Reikonos burned?" Guy asked, mouth contorting under the fury of the broth.

Shirri was a long time in answering, because she was trying to eat around the hot broth as well, and her mouth hurt. "I don't know. You have a theory?"

Guy shook his head slowly, blowing on a steaming spoonful. "I reckoned maybe it evaporated along with Sanctuary."

"Hmm." That was a worthy thought. Except... "But Cyrus still had his."

"I s'pose." Guy paused, opening his mouth, and this time his breath puffed slightly all on its own, the temperature was coming down so swiftly. "I don't understand any of this magic gibberish. Not what you can do with your spells, nor Cyrus his, nor Alaric his...his ghostliness, I s'pose. I don't comprehend the so-called 'hobbling,' save for the obvious bit about how we just ran on air when Cyrus came down like a skipping stone. None of it makes sense to me. Not one whit."

"Magic is hard to understand in these days, I suppose," Shirri said, letting the spoon rest in the bowl, both steaming in her hand, "unless you were raised to it. Raised in it, even."

"And you were raised in it?"

She nodded slowly. "My mother taught me much, for she was a spellcaster, as her father was before her. League instruction had gone away by that time, of course, the hobbling had begun...yet still I could do some. Not as much as those who came before, but enough to keep me from death a time or two. And little more than that, toward the end," she said ruefully, thinking of that moment in the alley when she'd called out because the Machine was closing in, far too many of them for her to dispense with by spellcraft.

"I never ran across magic in my dealings," Guy said, leaning against the wooden rail. Below the sea skimmed past, catching the sparkling orange glow of the sun's dying rays. "I s'pose I ran too much with the low crowd."

"I was in the low crowd myself – or rather, no crowd," Shirri said, leaning beside him. "When you're on the bottom in Reikonos, the only difference is what you do."

"Which is why I went to work for the Machine," Guy said. "Without it...I'd have been nothing. And I was, when Cyrus came across me in the alley that day. 'Course he'd already driven me out, but...I can't find fault in him for it." He sniffed, the chill seeming to get to him. "Funny how I mouthed his name all my life, invoking him without meaning it...and when I came face to face with the man himself, he did end up changing my life. But only after he ruined it, and shamed me. Now he might end up saving the world. Again."

"Maybe we'll help," Shirri said, with the trace of a smile. Rueful, sure, but present.

"Doubt we'll have that much influence," Guy said. "Not if we can't f – 'ey, what's that?"

He pointed, and she looked; to the east, across the shadowy lands, there was a point of light in the growing dark over the mountains. Bright and red, like an angry sun peering through clouds, it was barely visible and at some distance. Still, in a land of frozen mountains and tundra, any light was odd...

"Administrator?" Shirri called out, catching Alixa's attention from the quarterdeck. Shirri pointed into the distance; three spyglasses were aimed at the very spot within moments.

"What do you suppose it is?" Guy asked. Up on the quarterdeck, Alixa was already issuing orders. "You think it's what we're looking for?"

"Perhaps," Shirri said, for she did not want to get out ahead of herself. But...maybe. "Perhaps."

CHAPTER 68

"*I* had such hopes you'd be a quick learner," Huaviri said, as time crawled slowly by. They were still in the damnable lodge, which smelled of sweat and death, and Vaste didn't feel he had any sweat left, in spite of a regular amount of water and the occasional bit of food brought to him. Death, though, that seemed close.

"I had hopes you'd teach me something," Vaste said, his patience finally gone, "other than to drip like I'm in a bloody swamp, and how to stare at a ghost I hate until I want to beat his damned skull in. And he doesn't even have a skull anymore, and probably hasn't in a thousand years." Vaste waved the tip of Letum at Rusyl, who did not react to the vaguely threatening motion.

"Can't teach you what you're not ready to learn." Huaviri looked drawn, tired. His hands were withered, clutching his walking stick.

"'Ready to learn?' Good sir," Vaste said, that last thing holding him back, that small reserve of good sense, "I have traveled across the bloody world – at least the part I've known – to talk to you. I've come from friends in the direst of straits, each going upon their own particular mission to try and find ways to beat this great threat before us. I left them behind, blazed right through the town of New-Whatever, ignoring my diplomatic responsibilities to try and bring them into

ROBERT J. CRANE

this war on our side, in order to get to you faster. Because I thought perhaps what you had to teach me could be the difference maker in the upcoming fight."

"You can't speed up your journey, *gisomari*," Huaviri said weakly. "Knowledge comes to you when you are ready for it. And you," he shook his head, almost sadly, braids swaying as he did so, "you're just not ready."

"Fantastic," Vaste spat. "When will I be ready? Do you have a rough estimate there? Will it happen before the world is utterly destroyed at Malpravus's hands? Just curious, so I can get some idea of whether I should be adding post-destruction day events to my calendar, or maybe just give them a pass. I do so hate to be discourteous in my failure to RSVP, you see."

"You'll be ready...when you see," Huaviri said. And that was it. He settled his head low, sagging over his sunken chest.

Vaste stood, his frame tired, feeling like it was going to sag. "Oh, I see."

"No," Huaviri said, shaking his head. "You don't."

"I see more than you think," Vaste said, and it came out in a roar. "I see a world trending toward death, because Malpravus seeks our deaths. And I see you – you, here, distracting me. Why? Because it amuses you, perhaps?" He turned his back on Huaviri. "Because you see some possibility of keeping me out of this fight–?"

"Why would it matter if I keep you out of this fight?" Huaviri almost whispered. "What do you have to offer your people, except a staff that will do little against the endless armies of dead coming for you, a wit that will damage your foe not at all, and a body that will only slow your enemies as they clamber over it to get at your friends?"

That struck home. Vaste felt a sharp pain in his chest. "I am useless in this, aren't I?" He put a hand on one of the lodge poles. "Just like Malpravus always said. I'm a non-entity in a fight with him. Without magic, with only Letum at my disposal, I'm no more than a stick-swinging troll – the damned thing I always feared to become." He hung his head.

"...You could still be more, Vaste," Huaviri said, almost so softly it couldn't be heard.

"I don't understand what you want from me," Vaste said, hanging his head. Outside, he could hear Aemma and Merrish going at it again, biting at each other like the fools they were. "Listen to them," he said, after a moment. "They fight each other more than they fight Malpravus." When Huaviri did not respond, he picked up the thread again himself. "But at least they fight, if misdirected. What am I supposed to do?" He glanced at Letum, leaning against the pole by the door. "Is it truly down to this? I go into battle like a troll of old, with that as my club? Is all I have to offer to be a bludgeoning hand in the service of Sanctuary – which no longer even exists? All this time, and is this really all I am? A man who couldn't find love except from the pity of a magical force older than civilization? Who can't do a thing to save this world? Is this all there is–"

He whirled on Huaviri, and all thought of the last complaint died upon his lips. The warm, humid air and the puffs of smoke filling the tent provided a haze that clouded the space between them, and he stared at the shaman who'd been trying to tell him something, teach him something...

But Huaviri's teaching days were done, for the old man's head had fallen back, and his mouth was open, his chest unmoving; he had drawn his last breath.

Huaviri was dead.

CHAPTER 69

SHIRRI

*I*t was not what Shirri expected.

She'd thought...perhaps a fire. A nice, glowing fire in the distance, nestled in the mountains, far from the reach of the scourge, away from any troubling sorcerers. Some isolated spot where Houk – whoever he was – waited, fire burning to signal them in, to welcome them with, in her deepest fantasies, chocolate and a warm bed where Shirri could sleep until her eyes stopped burning from fatigue.

What they found instead, as the airship drew closer to the glow...

...Was a battle of magic, already well-joined.

Hellish red light was the fire she'd seen on the horizon, and the closer they got the surer she became that this was Malpravus. For it was the very shade of the spell he'd cast to destroy Reikonos, with hints of black nestled in the red energy. It glowed against the clouds above, like a mythical hell unleashed, and it was only when they crossed the last range of spiked peaks that they could see what force the red spellcraft was loosed against. It was a barrier of pure, glowing blue. And against that hellish red, the blue seemed to be slowly on the wane.

As the *Lady Quinneria* came down into the valley, Shirri could see the barrier holding back a swarm of what looked like ants, moving in the snow, undulating from end to end of the vale.

"The bloody scourge," Guy croaked. "How are there this many here when we left eighteen armies of 'em back in Reikonos?"

"I have a question of my own." Longwell stepped down off the last rise of the quarterdeck. "Who is it that holds back Malpravus in all his violent tempest?" He planted a mailed hand upon the rail and leaned forth. "For I want him as an ally."

"Probably we have to get to him first," Shirri said. The ship was slowing. Alixa was speaking to her crew; caution was, presumably, warranted. The engines sounded a bit better, but hardly up to the task of plowing headlong into whatever that red spell was. Though, Shirri amended her thought, the spell would probably be worse for those of them onboard than the struggling engines.

Shirri stared down at the terrifying red glow, lashing away at the blue shield; there seemed a definite contraction in the strength of the cerulean magic covering...whatever lay below. It was hard to make out with the crackling energy in the way. Something certainly seemed to be down there.

"What exactly is that? Beneath the blue?" Guy asked, peering down. "It sort of looks like a...a house, maybe. Or a cabin? Never seen one of those before. Only 'eard of 'em." He squinted harder. "That's what living your whole life in Reikonos gets you, I suppose. Not very worldly."

"You know, I think you may be right," Shirri said, squinting slightly less than Guy. Was it Houk's house down there? If so, who was Houk to have a home in the middle of nowhere in scourge country? The snowy peaks hemmed him in, but plainly did not make him inaccessible to the creatures. They raged around the edges of the blue spell, though it seemed little affected by their swarming presence.

The airship drew ever closer, slow and drifting. Distance was hard to gauge without knowing the size of the house, though Shirri felt they must surely be only a few hundred feet away now. Alixa's maneuvering kept them firmly away from the lashing red energies, keeping the blue bubble well between them, the ship reducing altitude gradually.

Coming down off the top deck, Alixa nearly bumped into Shirri. Brusque and business-like, she said, "How are we supposed to get in there? I'm not chancing my ship against the spell."

"I...don't know," Shirri said, confused again that the Administrator was talking to her as if she were somehow in charge of anything. "Houk just said to come northeast."

Alixa blew air impatiently between pursed lips. "This isn't even northeast, not truly. Are you sure we're in the right place?"

"No," Shirri said, feeling her eyes widen as her uncertainty rose. "Though the red spell-light would suggest that we've found Malpravus, and that might indicate–"

As if summoned, the red spell came at them just then, striking the bottom of the *Lady Quinneria*. Shirri cringed, bracing herself as she seized the rail; if this was the same spell as in Reikonos, it would pass harmlessly through the wooden hull and course directly into the crew, killing them instantly–

It did not.

On either count.

The red spell-magic struck the ship and the whole thing rattled, the bow disintegrating, splinters of wood and shards of metal blasted back at them as surely as if a barrel of Dragon's Breath had been lit off at the forecastle. The crimson spell-light refracted upward like lightning, leaping from the bow to the forward blades, severing the upper shaft just below the blades. It spun off wildly...

...and the *Lady Quinneria* began to list.

The spell-light faded, the brightness of it now a dark afterimage in Shirri's vision, like faded lightning after the strike. The ship lurched again, rattling, turning to a forty-five degree angle and beginning a decline, the ship's lift unequal to the task of holding the vessel aloft.

"There are bloody scourge everywhere," Guy said, hanging onto the rail. "And we're going down in the middle of them!"

This seemed to be true. The ship rattled again, and began to plunge...

...with nowhere to go but either into the blue spell...into the red...

...or into the scourge waiting below.

CHAPTER 70

VASTE

*H*e burst from the lodge into the cool, morning air, humid but not nearly as stifling as it had been in the tent. His skin prickled with goosepimples as he stepped out, and Vaste looked over the camp, sucking in a fresh breath and catching a tang of that sulphuric stink that made him almost gag.

The world was a bit blurry around him, the tipis, swamp grass, hummocks, fires, all of it blurring together. Someone rose in the middle distance, and his eyes didn't quite adjust fast enough after days of darkness in the lodge.

"Vaste?" Aemma's voice wafted over to him, soft and questioning. Merrish was beside her at a fire, he realized. That's right; he'd heard them bickering from inside.

"Or what's left of him, at least," Vaste said, stomping through the soft, loamy soil over to a stew pot that was emitting a beautiful aroma. He seized the ladle, prompting a grunt from Asa-tee, who was minding it, and sipped it down, burning himself slightly in the process.

"Hey, *gisomari*, you're supposed to be fasting," Asa-tee said. He didn't quite snatch the ladle back, but he did take it rather resentfully once Vaste was done draining the contents.

"My fast is over," Vaste said, "and it was a total lie – because it was actually slow. Agonizingly slow – and pointless." He wiped his hand over his forehead and found it sticky with days of dried sweat.

"It's not pointless until you give up," Asa-tee said.

Vaste slowly turned to look back at him, realizing that Niamh had been lying down in the space between the fire and the sweat lodge, as if waiting for him but trying to remain close to a fire. "Oh, it's pointless. You see, Huaviri is dead, and I've learned nothing from him, except perhaps that the rumble of my stomach can occasionally sound like an angry old man when I haven't had anything but water and broth for a long while."

"He's dead?" Merrish chimed in at last, rising to his feet. "But you came to learn from him."

"Yes, and now you see the problem," Vaste said. "I'm surprised you had time to come up with that keen insight, though, in between your verbal spats with Aemma. You must be devoting most of your energy to coming up with insults for this feud. Where is Aisling?"

"Back at the ship," Aemma said softly, waving a hand in the direction of the airship, which was hovering a few hundred feet away, to Vaste's left. "They had a messenger vessel arrive this morning," and here she waved her hand at a smaller vessel that was beside the dark elven one. "She went to compose a report on our progress."

"What progress?" Vaste asked, kicking over a bucket that had been sitting by the fireside. That drew a sharp rebuke from Asa-tee in his own language, but Vaste did not care. "I've been here for days, and nothing has happened of note except I've starved myself and talked to the ghost of my friend's dead father. Oh, and I outlived my teacher, albeit not for long, because we're all going to die. I feel disgusting enough that wading into the swamp might qualify as a bath at this point. I swore I'd never come back to this place and yet here I am, on this errand of a fool, and indeed being made a fool of in these accursed swamps again!" He kicked the pail, causing Asa-tee to throw up his arms.

"We never should have come here," Merrish said, nodding. Then he cast a hard look at Aemma. "You should have worked harder on the people of New Idiarna, gotten them to come to our side. Then at least we might have seen a little profit from this venture."

Aemma flushed to her blond-brown roots. "I didn't know them. Why would they listen to me? It'd be like you trying to marshal the people of Amti to your cause."

"With the world hanging in the balance," Merrish said primly, "I expect I could get the people of Amti to listen to me – wait, Vaste, where are you going?"

"The people of Amti might listen to you," Vaste said, stomping away from the campfire, away from all of them, and into a patch of sawgrass that blocked the way into a hummock, "but I damned sure have no desire to. Not now – not ever." He whirled around, intent on issuing one last cutting remark before he endeavored to find the least polluted pond in this swamp to submerge himself in. "Bringing you along – the two of you, arguing like children with burrs in your undergarments – has been one of the worst mistakes of my life. And I just led an entire airship of people on a dayslong excursion into the bloody swamps for no reason when the world hangs in the balance."

With that, he left Merrish red of face and sputtering, and turned away, using Letum for balance as he stalked off into the swamps, cheeks burning from his towering temper, intent on getting as far away from these people as he possibly could.

CHAPTER 71

SHIRRI

*T*he *Lady Quinneria* lurched, going into a flat, slow spin as the back started to come around. The front blades were missing, as was the bow, Shirri standing only twenty feet away from where the ship came to an abrupt end. Singed ropes and scorched planks hung over the edge, burnt off by the glowing red spell that was dashing itself against the blue barrier in front of them.

And Shirri hung on, against the sudden, dramatic drop of the ship. Before her, so did Longwell and Guy; beside her clung Alixa, hanging on to both the rail and Fulmenar, the Claws of Lightning, whose odd sparking was still strangely noticeable next to the growing blue and red flares of light doing battle ahead.

"We're going in!" the helmsman shouted from the quarterdeck. There was no mistaking the truth of that statement; gravity had them, and soon the scourge would, too.

Or perhaps not. The blue barrier of that spell loomed before them, larger and larger. Would they skip off it, bouncing back against the ground and into the waiting mouths of the scourge? Or would they disintegrate against it like the front of the ship had when tested against that crimson spell?

It seemed they would soon find out. Shirri knew which she preferred, and it was not the devouring.

It was a shame it had to end like this. But hardly surprising; Shirri felt as though she'd been dodging death since that alley in Reikonos. All that Cyrus and the others had bought her was time. Time in which to feel harried by the Machine, to put the pain to them, to see Reikonos destroyed, and so on.

Wasn't that a funny thing to think about now, as the ship twisted beneath her, surging toward the implacable spell barrier? She should have regretted all that had come from the last few months. It had hardly been a life of the sort she'd have chosen for herself, if given a catalog and a choice. She would have assumed she'd have selected the existence of a placid housewife, perhaps. Maybe a mage in Pharesia who plumbed the remaining secrets of magic over a life's long and solitary study.

Instead, she'd joined a rebellion and seen herself become one of only a dozen or so leading the fight against Malpravus, the worst threat Arkaria had seen since the days of her grandfather.

And the funnier thing was...she didn't regret a minute of it. She only regretted that it was coming to such an unsatisfactory conclusion.

The blue barrier swelled closer in her vision, inescapable now. It would be upon them shortly, and then the tale would be told – destruction and devastation or a bounce to an even worse fate. She held tight to Philos, glanced once more at those around her – Alixa seemed tensed for a fight, as did Guy, with Praelior in hand.

Longwell, though...he seemed strangely at peace in spite of clutching Amnis. They all held to the rail, and Shirri looked ahead, at the spell-barrier, wanting to look death squarely in the face. It glowed and coruscated, crackling with little hints of black in the cerulean glow. They grew in size as the ship drew closer, now large enough she could see them up close–

And then the barrier simply...parted.

It was a subtle thing; it was there one moment, then gone the next, at least from directly before them. The *Quinneria* surged through, still falling out of the sky toward a cabin nestled in a thicket of pines.

Shirri looked back; the barrier had a hole in it, one that was swiftly closing now that they were through. The hellish red glow seemed black where it was striking the barrier, and Shirri stared at that area. The air had a discordant tone coming from that direction, and the blue seemed strained there, damage clearly being done.

The wreck of the *Lady Quinneria* came to a rest, though not nearly as rough as it should have. It seemed poised to remain upright for a moment, then slowly started to tip to its side. Shirri held fast as the crew scrambled for handholds and found them placed all over the deck. Lumber groaned, metal squealed.

And then the ship settled into the bondage of gravity, a great groan running through it as it finally gave up the fight. The last blades spun down to an abrupt stop, and a glow of blue was visible upon them. The timing was fortuitous, and, Shirri knew, intentional; if left spinning, they would have churned against the rocky ground, sending fragments in all directions as it shattered against an unyielding surface.

"Well," Guy said, letting loose of the rail and tentatively crawling onto the grass-covered earth. Snow existed beyond the barrier, but here the soil was covered in verdant green. "Here we are." He dusted his hands off as the rest of them disentangled themselves from the ship and rail, respectively. "...What now?"

Shirri turned. The cabin was there, a small two-story house with a curious look to it. She was hardly as much of a city mouse as Guy, but this style of structure was entirely new to her. It waited, though, in the midst of the crackling, beleaguered blue shield, the only thing of interest in the boundary. "We go see 'Houk,'" Shirri said, because the answer was obvious, at least to her. "And we find out what this is all about."

CHAPTER 72

VASTE

*H*e stomped through the grass, ignoring it biting at his flesh, ignoring the branches that snapped at him as he crossed the hummock and plunged through the paths of the swamp. His bare feet submerged as they had on the rare occasions he'd stalked through the swamps as a child, bugs chittered near and in the distance, and yet Vaste kept walking, heedless of his tiredness, feeling the hard bite of annoyance as he went on, away from camp, into the depths of the Great Dismal Swamp.

Wasn't this a well-named locale? He battered at a low-hanging branch that tried to thwack him between the eyes, snapping it cleanly off with Letum. "To hell with this place," he muttered. Nothing good had ever come to him in these swamps, nor in Gren, either. He may have been born here, but it was hardly home.

He reached a high hill and stopped, surrounded by a circle of trees, blotting out the faint sunlight that was trying to shine through them and the clouds. It was a losing battle; there were clouds everywhere. Patchy fog was layered in the low-lying areas of the swamp; he'd crossed through it without paying much attention, and now as he stood on a hilltop, he found it at bay at last.

"Screw it all," he muttered, and tromped over to a fallen log.

Giving it an experimental prodding with Letum, he found it sound, and plopped his precious bottom onto it. It did not collapse. Which was fortunate, because he doubted he could weather even one more setback right now.

How had this all gone so terribly wrong? Asa-tee for one, probably. He could have led them to Huaviri while they were aboard the airship, sparing the miserable, multi-day walk through these swamps. And Huaviri, for another. If he had such important information to impart, why not just get to it? Vaste had spent days in that stupid sweaty lodge and received only such instruction as, "Concentrate," and, "Focus," as though this were specific information. What the hell was he supposed to do with that? And how was he to ignore the rumbling in his belly and weakness in his limbs?

What was the purpose of it all?

And there was Aemma and Merrish, constantly quarreling outside. Was there ever an agreeable word between the two of them? He wanted to take them and...well, really he just wanted to thump Merrish to reasonable behavior. He felt no such inclination with Aemma. Trying to tell himself that it was because she was not annoying, that perhaps it was because she was a woman, that somehow it was different...all those explanations failed to find footing in his mind.

The truth...well, he didn't want to think about that. The wound from Birissa was still too raw to invite such rejection as he could imagine from Aemma. He had helped the tall human, saved her life. That was all, she was merely grateful.

"The world is coming to a bloody swift conclusion," Vaste said, "and I'm sitting here in a swamp thinking about a woman, about my failures, about how useless I am."

"Maybe you just haven't found your use yet." The voice was soft and feminine, though he didn't hear it well with the thudding of his heart from the hike to get here.

He caught a glimpse of movement out of the corner of his eye; long hair swaying with her walk, and he turned his face away. There were tears in the corner of his eyes, and he hated himself for it.

"Go away, Aemma," Vaste said. "I don't feel like talking right now." Certainly not to her, for fear he might say something about her, about the feelings churning his gut along with the rising worry for the coming apocalypse.

"Don't matter what you want," came the voice, distinctly un-Aemma. "You're playing a bigger game than just 'what Vaste wants.'"

He turned to look, and what he saw was...impossible. A flash of crimson. Hints of green.

A red-haired figure was tromping through the swamp in bare feet and emerald robes. Her face was pale but lovely, and he had not seen it in more than a thousand years, not like this.

Not since the night she died in old Sanctuary.

His voice cracked as he spoke, barely a whisper. "...Niamh?"

CHAPTER 73

SHIRRI

"Hello?" The door to the cabin was unlocked, and Shirri – for some reason – was the one who was first to open it. It did not squeak on the hinges, but she almost wanted it to. For ominousness's sake.

Blue light glowed into the entry, revealing a cabin that was much larger than it appeared from the outside. And – surprisingly – quite homey.

"Gotta be the God of Good," Longwell said, looking around, only a step behind her. "That's the only explanation for who Houk is."

"I would have razzed you for believing in gods still," Guy said, third to come inside. He walked tentatively, sword clutched tightly in his stubby fingers. "But then I met Cyrus Davidon, and since then...things have taken a bit of turn in my life."

"Come in," a voice boomed over them. Ahead, beyond the cozy, homey sitting area, was a staircase shrouded in pure, white light. It led up, out of the comfortable space like stairs to the heavens. "Come up."

"You were saying about your life taking a turn?" Longwell asked, keeping his grip on Amnis firm and the spear tip pointed up the stairs. "When I met Cyrus Davidon, I went from skirmishing with men on horseback to jousting with bloody gods. And things have never really been the same since."

Shirri found herself walking up the stairs, Longwell behind her a step, Guy behind that, and Alixa bringing up the rear. The men of the *Lady Quinneria* remained firmly out of doors, apparently quite content to be kept company by the flaring blue shield and the black coloration of the spell warring against it. Either the voice or the atmosphere of the cabin must have left them cold, which Shirri could sympathize with.

But she couldn't allow herself to indulge those feelings. Not anymore.

Reaching the crest of the stairs, she found more of the same – soft, white light glowing from the surfaces around here, a figure shrouded in it ahead in a seat, a window upon the world outside beyond. The blue shield was under attack, red-tinged black battering away at it before their host's eyes.

She saw him plainly now, Houk, though he looked...older. His ears were softly rounded, lacking any hint of elven ancestry. He had his back to her, but his head angled slightly so she could see him as she came 'round. Longwell followed after, and bristled as he came into view of the man's face–

Longwell loosed a curse so vile Shirri almost took a step back from him. "Of all the people I might have expected to find here, it wasn't you."

"You never did see my hand at work, did you, Samwen?" the old man asked. His face was deeply lined; he seemed to be growing older by the minute. "Not when I opened the Realm of Life to you to save yours, nor when I closed it behind you to keep you safe. I opened it again for Vara and Isabelle, to give you a chance at some rescue after all those years alone." He stared up at the dragoon with a strangely satisfied smirk. "My hand has been at work all these years...guiding and steering you. Guiding and steering all."

"'*Hand?*'" Longwell raised his spear as if to strike. "All these years, you still hang your helm on that? The gods are dead; someone should have lopped you off a millennia ago, Gatekeeper–" And he raised his blade to strike.

Shirri struck the tip of Amnis with Philos and knocked it down, sending Longwell pitching off balance. He recovered quickly enough and spun back, finding Shirri between him and the man they'd come here to see, this man who'd steered and saved them–

"Get out of the way, Shirri," Longwell growled. "This one's not worth saving. He's a relic of the old days, the bad ones – and he was the worst. 'Hand of the Gods,' they called him then. And 'Gatekeeper,' for he was the one who treacherously walked souls through the Trials of Purgatory – seeing countless die along the way."

"You can just call me Stepan," the Gatekeeper said, his voice little more than a rasp. "And you might want to take a few moments to listen to me." He coughed, and it was deep, wet, and hacking, the sound of a man in his last days, last moments, even, perhaps. "After all..." and out of the corner of her eye, Shirri saw a rueful smile on his lips, "...they're going to be my final ones in this life."

CHAPTER 74

VASTE

"My favorite troll," Niamh said with a whisper. She was almost aglow, a strange visage of pale light, like Rusyl Davidon, existing in that curious interstitial space between life and death, her ghostly form shading the trees. "Of course, also the only troll I ever really liked...but still." She smiled, ephemeral. "You don't look like you're doing so well, my friend."

"Noticed that even with your limited capabilities?" Vaste peered at her; behind the white glow of her spectral form he could see – dimly – the one she truly inhabited in these days, that dark and gray, hunched-over creature with the elephantine skin and black eyes. It was so vastly different from this spectral beauty as to defy reconciliation. The elven druid was more lively in death than the scourge creature was in life.

"It's not my capabilities that are limited, Vaste dear," Niamh drawled sweetly. "Just the form." She ran a hand over her ghostly, human form. "I'm not so pretty anymore, and that's a real shame. Being a wise and fair elf was a trip; being a low and guttural growling scourge for the last millennium...well, it's been hard to socialize, because let's face it – I hate my kind. I'm a self-hating scourge. Killed more of 'em than you have, even, probably."

"But...you can speak," Vaste said. "You're talking now."

She laughed, a great, silvery laugh. "I'd have spoken before, but the scourge body isn't suited to it."

"But you're not a ravening beast," he said. "You're...you, more or less."

"More or less," she agreed. "I wasn't trapped by Mortus for long before you all ended up killing him, so I didn't have the madness that so many others did, stuck in his tower prison for years and decades." She bowed her head. "It was terrible, but that's where the torture was." She glanced up. "Being a scourge was no joy, but the reason they're so damned mad is because of the imprisonment in the Eusian Tower. Given long enough, it leaves you feral, angry at life, and at all things alive."

"Why can I see you now?" Vaste asked, staring at her. "Why couldn't I see you before?"

"You've changed," Niamh said, "while you were in the lodge." She brushed closer to him, and he could feel her presence. "I don't think you realized it, you were so busy starving, thirsty, suffering, and, well...you know." She leaned closer, almost conspiratorial. "Complaining."

"Ah," Vaste said. "I do that sometimes."

"All the time, Vaste dear. You do that all the time."

He gave her a beseeching eye. "Did you come back to life and follow me out here just to deliver that critique?"

"No," she said with a smile. "I came because I sensed you needed a certain amount of help with what you're here to do. And because, of all my friends in Sanctuary, you're the one who's going to finish this, Vaste." She smiled at him. "You have to. But first..." And she stepped back, waiting.

And a moment later...Vaste was not in the swamp, not in the woods.

He was somewhere entirely and completely different.

CHAPTER 75

SHIRRI

*L*ongwell looked as if he wanted to knock Shirri aside, bowl her over, and impale the Gatekeeper, the Hand of the Gods squarely through the chest with Amnis's wide point. He tensed, his blued armor making him look like a metallic statue, ready to leap into an action pose.

"Maybe we should listen to the old bird," Guy said, brushing a hand on Longwell's vambrace just above the elbow. He was delicate, and Longwell did not stir at his touch. "'e doesn't look like he's long for this world."

"One can only hope," Longwell said, and did not lower his blade's tip. "Talk then, Gatekeeper. Spin us a tale. And make it a good one, lest your exit from this world come somewhat faster than this natural end you speak of."

The Gatekeeper coughed again, and a hint of crimson brighter than the spell-light that played against the barrier appeared upon his lips. "Nothing natural about my end, I'm afraid. It's a simple one, and one you've seen before – man with magic uses it all up, then taps the store of his life's energy to finish whatever task he's set on." He brushed a hand against the sleeve of his white robe; deep wrinkles had appeared up and down his arm, scattered age spots seeming to darken even as Shirri watched. "I'm afraid I'm almost out of it, though, and that's going to make this conversation rather shorter than I might have preferred." His eyes were becoming whiter and rheumier by the moment.

"I've heard of you," Alixa said, stepping forth. "You served the gods when they walked this land?"

The Gatekeeper nodded; there was a weary quality to his movement. "For ten thousand years. You see, I came to this land with your friend Alaric Garaunt – though he was not called that, then. A rift between us drove me into their service – and I served them well, until his protegee, Cyrus Davidon, unintentionally freed me when he culled the last of the gods. Since then...well..."

"Let me guess," Longwell said, his voice dripping with disgust, "you've whiled away the years being a benevolent sort of prick. Making up for your sins by doing good where once you did evil?"

The Gatekeeper stared up at them. "Hardly. I've been a self-serving bastard – which is why I've chosen to be a recluse." He grimaced. "But you're not wrong about me making up for my sins. I've done my best – and my best was putting the choke on magic by draining it all so that Malpravus couldn't achieve his goals." He grimace grew deeper. "Until someone came along and gave him enough power to do what he'd been seeking to do all along."

"You can't possibly blame Cyrus and the others for that," Shirri said. She stood beside him now, looking down upon this pitiful figure.

"I don't," the old man said. "I tried to help them, even, once I realized what they were up to. I've fought a lonely and long-ranging battle against Malpravus on a number of fronts this last thousand years." His eyes were white, like looking into a saucer of milk. "He crushed or co-opted every opponent I tried to stir against him. An utter tyrant, one who learned the lessons of the gods' fall well. Until Cyrus and Alaric returned, there was no one willing to take up arms against him." He favored Shirri with a smile. "Though I did have high hopes for you and your mother."

"...How?" Shirri asked. "You can't possibly have meant to put me against Malpravus."

"Not immediately," the Gatekeeper said. "But every age needs its champion. A tyrant always rises, you see, and heroes must rise to combat them. But Malpravus, he lived too long, got too powerful, too good at catching those heroes when they were young, impressionable. He would kill them, or convince them to join his Machine." And here he looked at Guy. "Like you, you improbable fellow. I wouldn't have placed a single bronze coin on the odds of you being the one to throw off those shackles. But then – I wouldn't have bet on Alaric Garaunt becoming what he's become, either."

"You're about to die, though," Alixa said. "Why did you bring us here?" She knelt on the other side of the Gatekeeper, at the opposite arm of his seat. "You've doomed us."

"Doom was always in the cards," the Gatekeeper said, turning his rheumy eyes back to Shirri. "You knew that when you went down that alley with all those Machine thugs on your tail. The end...is nigh. But," and here his eyes sparkled, "maybe not. Hope still breathes while Cyrus and Alaric still move. I've learned that much even if Malpravus hasn't."

"But how?" Shirri asked, taking up his hand. It was already cold, as though he'd plunged it in the snow outside. "You've been here a thousand years. You have powers none of us possess – yet still he is going to defeat you. How are we...so much less than you, supposed to defeat *him?*"

"I would suggest," the Gatekeeper said, his voice taking on a tired, dream-like quality, "*together.*"

"We're in the bloody north with a crashed airship," Alixa said irritably. "Your shield is about to fail, allowing Malpravus in. You want us to fight him together? That seems like a rather short fight."

The Gatekeeper slowly shook his head, gray strands delicately falling out. "Not the four of you." He looked right at Shirri. "All of you. All – Cyrus, Vara, Alaric, Vaste, you – and any others you can muster.

All your merry bands, all of you against *him.*" His voice scratched. "It's your only chance."

"But they tried that," Guy said softly. "And didn't have what it took. And if you've lived longer than all of us–"

"I've been a brake on Malpravus's ambitions for a long time," the Gatekeeper said, the cadence of his words slowing. "When I'm gone...he'll be able to use magic in a way he hasn't for a thousand years. Stronger. More powerful. Easier." His dull eyes flashed, looking to Shirri. "But so will you."

"But none of them are the sorcerer that he is," Longwell said stiffly. "Only Curatio – and he's dead."

"Yes." The Gatekeeper nodded slowly, almost imperceptibly. "You're going to have to figure out a way...to beat him...absent all that...and in spite of...well...him." The eyes were so faint, now, so rheumy as to be like milk. "But I believe...there is a way."

"It'd have been nice if you could have laid that out for us centuries ago," Longwell said. "Appeared to us then, as clearly you were capable of. Let us know what we were facing."

He stared over Shirri's shoulder at Longwell. "In spite of what you might think...I don't want to see you dead, Samwen. I have...watched over you all...for so long now." His head lolled. "The distance...made it easier for me...not to be a bastard. Made me...almost fond of you lot." And here he looked up at Shirri. "Some more than...others."

"You have a chance...but that's it," the Gatekeeper said, his voice fading. "A better one now than two hundred or six hundred years ago, even with me at your back. I've leeched the bastard...made him...work for this."

He seized Shirri by the shoulder, a weak hand upon it. "You have to go back...to the beginning. Where it all began...Sanctuary. You'll know soon enough. Tell them all. There's still a chance. A good one, even." His eyes started to fade.

A crack outside made Shirri turn her head. The red light was bright now, all trace of blackness gone; it was nearly through the barrier, the blue fading rapidly.

"You surely can't mean we have to all face him on our own," Longwell said. "Armies of elves and men against scourge. All of us against bloody Malpravus, the strongest sorcerer on the planet. He's a god now."

"Worse than any of them ever were," the Gatekeeper said.

"How do we survive this?" Alixa asked. She was watching death, in that red spell-form, coming for them. Tendrils of it had started to snake through the last vestige of the blue barrier. "How are we to fight when that is certain to doom us?"

"Nothing is certain except death." His grip on Shirri's shoulder was still present, though barely. He lifted a hand, and a tinge of green shaded them all. He smiled, toothy. "But not today."

Green light washed over them all, and suddenly Shirri was somewhere else, in the deep darkness of a place she did not recognize. Mouths spoke in a tongue she did recognize, and a shiver crawled up her spine for the feeling of chill, and the sight of rocks, and a portal of ovoid shape, with glowing runes stitched in its rocky surface.

"Magic...has returned...to Arkaria," the Gatekeeper whispered. He lay against the stony ground in this dark place, voices all around speaking the dark elven tongue.

"What in the hell is thi – LONGWELL?!" A man wearing armor that looked exactly like Alaric Garaunt's, but bearing a broad headed axe, pushed through the crowd of dark elven guards now circling them in the midnight dark. They were in a courtyard sort of area filled with dark elves and with a pile of broken stone in its center that reached the ceiling of the chamber.

"Terian?" Longwell asked, cocking his head curiously.

"Did you just teleport into Saekaj Sovar?" the one called Terian asked, stepping past them all to run a gauntleted hand over the portal's smooth, ovoid surface. It was leaned against a cavern wall carelessly, as if forgotten in this place. Dark elven guards in armor ringed them, and, behind that, a curious mob of dark elven civilians – laborers and the like. He looked down at the man at Shirri's knees. "And who is – is that the Gatekeeper?"

"It is," Longwell said. "Or it was." He did not sound nearly so angry as he had been before.

"Not sorry to see him go," Terian muttered.

"You will be," Shirri said, feeling a strange mournfulness in her soul. "When you realize what we've just lost because of his death..." She stared down at the fallen figure, who'd spent his last breath helping them and then giving them an escape from Malpravus, "...you will be."

CHAPTER 76

CYRUS

*T*he passage of days filled Cyrus with doubts; time seemed to roll by. Wandering the halls of the palace filled him with the most curious sensation; worry and wonder.

It had scarcely changed at all from the time when he'd been here before, and that was vexing in itself. How could a place last a thousand years without any appreciable change? The gardens seemed the same, the hallways. On one day he even managed to trace his way to the suite of rooms they stayed in during those days a thousand years ago. They were unchanged.

No word had come from any of the others. Alaric had seemingly vanished into the mists of the south, not a hint of presence. As if they'd simply disappeared. No sign was to be found of Shirri Gadden, or Guy and Longwell, either. An expedition sent from Termina brought only terrible news – fragments of the airship were found in ruin by the wall, a tremendous explosion left behind, and numerous scourge swarming the streets.

At least Vaste was still to be found, though somewhat incommunicado. Their airship remained firmly parked in the swampy hinterlands, accepting regular resupply from messenger airships.

Finding himself sitting across the breakfast table from his wife on that clear day, Cyrus stared past her, taking only slight notice of her bleary facade. A cup of tea steamed quietly in her hand, and her gaze, too, was well-drifted past his. Like arrows that seemed fated to pass on the way to missing their respective targets.

"You seem...distracted," Cyrus said, finally, when he'd had enough of the silence and his thoughts of self-pity.

"I am incredibly tired," Vara said, drowsing. "I cannot remember a time when I have felt more tired."

Cyrus nodded. "With what little we've done, you'd think we'd be swimming in energy."

"Given the course of recent events, I'm surprised we can muster the strength to get out of bed." She shifted her bleary gaze past him once more. "It's not as though we've had much inclination to do anything in it of late."

He grimaced. That was true. "Too much bad news. Too much on the mind."

Here she mustered a very slight smile. "Even when we were in the darkest days of Sanctuary, when everything was falling apart, your lust for me was a never-ending wellspring."

"Unfortunate choice of words," Cyrus said, catching a flutter of eyelids, Vara's face very much set in the temptress mold. "It's still there. But I don't think we've been in quite such dire straits before."

"You maintain Malpravus is worse than the gods?" Vara asked.

"Other than a couple exceptions, I generally faced down the gods after you died," Cyrus said. "The ones before that weren't concerned with destroying the world – only me, and perhaps Sanctuary."

"Yartraak intended to invade all of Arkaria. He would not have been merciful, had he won."

"True enough," Cyrus said. "But we also had the option to flee beyond his sight, though we chose not to exercise it. Now...the world has grown small, though I haven't seen but a portion of it. There is nowhere to hide in the age of airships."

"We will endure," Vara said, that tired look once again in her eyes. "You will see."

"I hope so," Cyrus said, a knock sounding at the door. Loud and urgent, it brought him to his feet. "Come in."

The door burst open, and in came Ryin, Glaven trailing a step behind, as though trying to slow the druid or perhaps stop him. "Have you seen?" Ryin asked, "Have you taken note?"

"Note of what?" Cyrus asked, scowling. He'd not been kindly disposed even before breakfast had been interrupted. Now he was even less so. Ryin smiled, gesturing him to the balcony. "I don't want to deal with crowds right now," Cyrus said, feeling a pit in his stomach. "Later, all right? I'm scheduled to go out at—"

"There are no crowds," Ryin said, throwing the balcony doors wide. Sun shone in, and brought with it a nip and a chill. "I want to show you something out here."

Cyrus trudged out on the balcony, Vara trailing behind. "Show me, then. I hope it's good, though, because my wife just offered herself to me and you're kind of intruding on my opportunity—"

Vara caught him in a glare. "I did no such thing."

"Well, you implied."

"No, I merely stated it's been a while. That's an observation, not an invitation. The only thing I want right now is a nap."

"You just got up," Cyrus said.

Ryin cleared his throat. Glaven stood beside him, looking daggers at the druid – or as much as the butler could look daggers. His demeanor was so mild for a killer of men. "Cast a spell," Ryin said. "Any spell will do, so long as it has some punch."

"How about the Return spell," Cyrus deadpanned. "To send me far, far from here."

"Probably don't try that one," Ryin said with a grin. "Flame. Wind. Water. Try something, please – over the balcony, of course."

Cyrus looked at the druid warily. "Maybe a Force Blast right into you?" But he stuck his hand off the side of the balcony, recalled the words for the fire spell, and–

A blast of heat washed over Cyrus, making him take a step back from his spell. One which did him little good, as it was coming from his hand, so the heat simply remained.

"Magic is back," Vara whispered. She lifted her own hand, sending a Force Blast over the balcony that almost knocked Cyrus over in its backwash of wind. "Magic is back."

"It is." Cyrus cut off the flow of fire. Glaven, watching them carefully, said nothing, but a smile broadened out on his face. "But the question remains," Cyrus said, "is this good or bad?"

"Good in the sense that it might indeed give us a fighting chance," she said. "Bad in the sense that–"

Someone burst in the door, and Cyrus turned. "Dioro?"

The elder hurried in, a retinue of servants behind him. Nearly breathless, the older man gasped out, "We've had a messenger – from Termina." His eyes wild, he gasped. "Scourge are gathering on the far bank of the Perda."

Cyrus felt a cool chill prickle at his back. This was not unexpected, yet it hit him hard nonetheless. "Malpravus is coming."

CHAPTER 77

CYRUS

"*R*yin," Cyrus said, and the druid nodded, leaping over the balcony's edge without another word. He ran upon the wind, like in days of old, heading toward the distant wall beneath the shade of the mighty trees that sheltered Pharesia's palace. His speed was incredible, and Cyrus had to wonder what spell-magic he'd discovered to give that aid. "He'll be there, and swiftly – but not as swiftly as an airship." He turned his gaze to Dioro. "You have one awaiting us?"

"We do," Dioro said, coming to the rail. "It is spinning up now, and a motor carriage is being brought around."

Cyrus watched off the balcony, unhurried. Now that magic had returned, he could simply leap over the rail and down to the ground below to meet the motor carriage that would take him to the airship. Ryin was already out of sight beneath the trees, melded with the shadow to become indistinct. In moments he would join his army. Would they make it to Termina in time? Hard to say.

"Now we're coming to it, aren't we?" Vara whispered. "The moment is nearly at hand."

"Yes," Cyrus said. "Dioro, what was the message from Termina exactly? Just the scourge?"

Dioro nodded. "Yes. They are back to the banks of the Perda, as they were before the...incident...at Saekaj Sovar."

"You're thinking," Vara said, watching him chew over that response. "And quiet. Never good signs, husband."

"Just recalling that we have much ground to protect," Cyrus said. "And so little to protect it with."

"But it's not the ground that's important to Malpravus," Vara said. "It's—"

"The people, yes," Cyrus said. Something about that bothered him, too, though he could not quite put his finger on it. "I suppose Termina is a rich enough target. Lots of elven lives to take there." A cloud moved in front of the sun, casting a bit of shade upon the day. The motorcar rumbled in the distance. He could see it make the turn at the corner of this wing of the palace, rattling slowly toward the portico below.

"People have never interested me very much." Malpravus's voice hissed from somewhere in the distance. A great many somewheres in the distance, as near as Cyrus could tell; it seemed to reach him distantly from several directions. "Not as a whole. Not as a lot. Other than as fodder for my considerable ambitions."

"Shit," Vara said, turning to look; the voice was not coming from within their suite of rooms, but from without, both off the balcony and deeper within – from other open balconies besides theirs, from down the hallways. She wheeled on Dioro. "You didn't dispense with all the dead things in this palace after the last incident?"

Dioro blushed terribly. "It would be a nearly impossible task, and so many of them are ancient—"

"So are you," Vara said tightly, "though I fear because of your error you will not make it much longer."

"Do not blame kind Dioro," Malpravus said, voice still coming from everywhere. The sky was darkening now; Cyrus looked up to see a distinct shadow covering the sun, though he could not tell what exactly it was. The effect was terrible, the morning turning dark like dusk. "He knew not what he did, and he always spoke a language I understood well – power."

"I – I didn't," Dioro stammered to little effect.

"You were one of the few I would call friend in this world," Malpravus said. "Though I doubt you would agree now. For what is a friend but one who is able to provide mutual use? I learned from you, and gave you aid in return. Now, though, we find ourselves in an entirely different position."

"Get behind me kindly, sir," Glaven appeared by Cyrus's side, that long rifle clutched in his hand, pointed up at the sky.

"I don't think that's going to do much good, Glaven," Cyrus said. Now the horizon was black, the city covered in night.

"All the same," Glaven said, inserting himself between Cyrus and the rail, and raising his weapon to aim at the sky. "Sir."

"I have only one use for you now, Dioro," Malpravus said. "You have outlived all others. Taught me everything you knew."

"Not – everything," Dioro said with a panicked gasp.

"As near so as not to matter," Malpravus's voice said airily.

"I don't even want to ask about the 'one use' you have for Dioro," Vara said tautly. Ferocis was in her hand, and she was looking around the room as if Malpravus was certain to sweep out of one of the increasingly darkened corners of the ceiling.

"It's obvious, isn't it?" Cyrus had his own weapon drawn, and now it was as though night had fallen on Pharesia and the old palace, the trees in the distance dark shadows barely visible in the lack of light. "Dioro's reached the end of his use, so all he is to Malpravus now is but another small bite of power."

"You may be the only one who ever truly understood me, lad," Malpravus said. "Such a shame you never came around to my way of thinking. But that's all right; this is your last chance, though. Decide quickly."

"Sure, I'll join you," Cyrus said, utterly deadpan. Dioro's head snapped around. "Kidding, Dioro. Malpravus – go to hell." And he clutched the hilt of Rodanthar tightly, waiting for the inevitable.

It came, and quickly.

The darkness turned red, an evil tinge that Cyrus had seen all too often of late. From out of the blackness came that horrible crimson glare, crawling forth to brighten the sky and paint it the color of blood. Tendrils of red light snaked across the sky and dipped down like crimson spikes, penetrating through the branches of the tall trees first.

"It's Reikonos all over again," Vara breathed, and it was, for the red light came down, without even a hint of Malpravus in sight, blackening the boughs of the immense trees as the light crawled down them, casting them in a terrible scarlet.

"No," Dioro said, shaking his head furiously, unaccepting. "No, I won't allow it—"

The old wizard lifted his stave and pointed it to the heavens. A spell of perfect blue light sailed forth from the tip, slashing into the coruscating red spell-light crawling down toward them—

Suddenly it was as if the red had turned to lighting. Conducted by Dioro's blue magic, it rode the beam down so fast Cyrus's eye barely registered it, crawling over the elf. His skin blackened in an instant, and he looked at Cyrus; frozen in the moment, mouth open, spittle flecking across his parched lips, panic writ across his face.

In a moment he was gone, and the red light leapt to the next nearest target—

Catching Glaven in the side he grunted in pain, and his face twisted in agony. It did its work swiftly, and Cyrus could see it happen, all the life drain from his face. The room was drenched in demonic red, spikes of that crimson light descending out of the sky into Pharesia like lightning strikes of scarlet, crawling across the city and the palace and all points between—

It was like looking at a world aflame, a world in the throes of death—

Malpravus's world. His, and wholly his.

Vara raised her sword, starting to charge toward Glaven, but the elf shook his head once, and hard, before the last of the light consumed him, and his eyes rolled back in his head.

Cyrus knew what came next, knew and was not prepared to face it, not prepared to weather or endure it.

He reached out and grabbed Vara's hand as Malpravus's voice lashed out at them from Dioro's blackened lips. "Such a shame, dear boy, that it has to end this way." The world outside was red, like blood, not a hint of blue, of green, or even black. "But it's probably better that this is your end. After all," and Glaven was speaking now, too, his skin ash, his body slackening, falling to his knees, gun clattering against the ground as the light danced, preparing to jump to Vara, the next nearest target—

Cyrus pulled her close, ripped her off balance, yanked her against him, the words already flowing from his mouth. He knew them well, knew them perfectly, but had not spoken them in a thousand years for fear of what they might do, where they might lead him.

Even now, with magic restored, he wondered where the Return spell might take him. For the last time he'd bound his soul, it had been in the tower of Sanctuary—

And there was no Sanctuary anymore. Not really.

The red lightning leapt toward Vara, a beam of death like a crimson spear for her heart. He bellowed the last word of the spell, and the hobble on magic was gone, so it took immediate effect, blue light covering them both and dragging them away from Pharesia, away from the scarlet cast, away from Malpravus's world—

Away from death.

And sending them onward, into a pale glow, and the unknown.

CHAPTER 78

CYRUS

*S*oft white light surrounded Cyrus as he opened his eyes; the space around him was formless, empty, a great void. There was no horizon, no scent, no breeze. All was still, quiet, the silence eternal and all-encompassing.

Just him, alone, bathed in the light.

And then...not alone.

"Where are we?" Vara asked, her form coalescing out of the light as though she'd appeared from beneath a veil of alabaster. Her armor was still shining, silver, and the gold of her hair and pale cheeks tinged with red gave her color against the ivory surroundings. Her eyes swept to and fro, seeking as his had, and finding nothing.

"We're in Sanctuary," Cyrus said, for this was the conclusion he'd come to. "Or what remains of it, at least."

"This?" Vara extended a hand, making a slow turn through the white light. It didn't shimmer, didn't move, just faintly glowed. She stopped, putting her hands on her hips. "It doesn't feel like the ether."

"Maybe it's not," Cyrus said, glancing around. "But it's not anywhere physical, either. We were just in Pharesia, if you recall–"

"My powers of recall are not diminished," she said, eyes narrowing. "I watched Dioro and Glaven die, just as you did."

"Yeah," Cyrus said quietly.

"Whatever the case," Vara said, setting herself once more to surveying the white light around them, "we have to find a way to get out of here. Preferably with Sanctuary. Return it all to the real world, to Arkaria – why are you shaking your head?"

"Remember where Sanctuary was when it went into the ether?"

Vara's face became pinched. "Reikonos. And – oh."

"Reikonos is currently covered over in scourge. At least according to the airship that came in this morning."

"Damn," Vara said. "Well, we'll find a way to bring it out somewhere else, then, and – why are you making that face?"

Cyrus wasn't exactly aware he'd been making a face. "Vara...I think this might be the end."

"A very distinct possibility, if we don't find a way to rejoin our comrades and stop Malpravus. Now – how do we get this thing out of here?"

"I don't...see a way to stop Malpravus," Cyrus said, and it felt painful to say it to her. "I think...this genuinely might be the end. No way forward." She was staring at him, almost no reaction except pursed lips. "No solution. No–"

She stuck a gauntleted hand over his mouth, and he realized he couldn't smell the oil from the joints. "Cyrus."

"Vara," he managed to mumble around it.

"This is Malpravus we're talking about," Vara said. "Not one of the gods, who you have already beaten. Not Bellarum, who stripped the very powers of the God of Evil and then turned them against you. Malpravus. Who we have defeated multiple times."

"Not this time," Cyrus said. "Which is, it seems the last time." He took up her hand. "Vara...this is the time that counts. Gods don't matter; we beat them with magic and all of Sanctuary, and none of them had access to the amount of spell energy Malpravus has. We had help from my mother, and Curatio – both dead. And above all, we had Sanctuary. Not just the people – Sanctuary itself, the entity. It was there, it was aiding us all that time. It kept Bellarum from harming me with the God of Evil's magic. All those advantages...they're gone now. As a warrior, as a general...I cannot beat him." Cyrus clutched his hand. "I can't beat Malpravus. I can't see a way...and for me that means...it's over."

"I have never known you to quit in the face of a fight," Vara said softly. "Never known Cyrus Davidon to give up when there is battle ahead."

"There's no hope, Vara. No strategy. No...we have nothing. An army of scourge against us, and at the end of it, Malpravus. The two great foes I could never quite finish." Cyrus shook his head. "No matter how much I believed, no matter how hard I tried...even with all the help we ever mustered, we couldn't end either one of them. Now we have less help than ever...and I still see no way to beat them." He sagged in the face of the white glow. "*I* can't beat them."

"Then, perhaps, General," came a voice – strong, familiar, "you should let your army beat them."

A figure was advancing toward them out of the white, clad in shimmering robes of purest ivory. His face seemed to be shrouded in the glow, but as he grew closer they could make out elfin ears, and a satisfied grin.

"Curatio," Vara breathed.

For it was truly him. "Hello, my old friends," he said. "And welcome home."

CHAPTER 79

CYRUS

"Curatio," Cyrus said, scarcely believing that the healer could be here, could be before him. Vara clung to him, her own breath seemingly caught within her. "But you died."

The white glowed upon the face of the elf, the healer, the sorcerer. "I did," Curatio said with a curt nod. "And suffice it to say...I am not alive now. I am in much the same condition Vara was after Bellarum's attack on Sanctuary. Perhaps even," and he grimaced, and a momentary flash seemed to reveal him as he was now; a very old face, weathered and wrinkled beyond belief, "worse. I doubt I will ever be capable of regaining physical form as you have, my dear." And he nodded at Vara. "But...I am here, in the ether, and that is not nothing."

"But Curatio," Cyrus said, shaking his head, "Malpravus...he absorbed you. Took everything you had, all your unnaturally long life—"

"And promptly used it to steal even more life, laying waste to whole cities," Curatio said ruefully. "Yes, I know. I wish it were not so. I would not have cared to leave you, my friends, in such terrible straits. It will continue, you know, unless you do something to address it. Not only Reikonos and Pharesia, but Termina, Emerald, Amti – it will go on and on."

"Yes, I've just told him that," Vara said, giving Cyrus a light push to the arm. "He doesn't seem to be listening, though. A terrible affliction of his sort."

"I listened," he said, but looked at Curatio. "But Curatio, you must surely see – it is hopeless now. Without you, without Quinneria, without Sanctuary–"

"Hope is a funny thing to lose," Curatio said, "for a man who has overcome as many hopeless situations as you have."

"Listen to the elder elf," Vara said. "He knows of what he speaks, having probably seen more hopeless situations than both of us combined."

"I saw more in my days with Sanctuary than all the other years of my life combined," Curatio said with a smile. "Yet still, somehow, we managed to make it through."

"It's different now, Curatio," Cyrus said. "Malpravus firmly has the whip hand. Magic may have returned, but it seems to me without you or Quinneria, that is an advantage reserved to him as the rest of us are hardly masters, and he just devoured the remaining masters of spell-craft when he destroyed Pharesia."

Curatio's eyes narrowed, almost in amusement. "No. One survived, and is happily on your side, still contrary as can be."

"Ryin lives?" Cyrus asked. "And his army?"

"It stands ready to join you in battle," Curatio said.

"Great," Cyrus said. "Now we just need to find a way to get in contact with him, then choose a battlefield where we can spend our lives against the never-ending waves of scourge while we wait for Malpravus to kill us all with one good spell."

Curatio sighed, though Cyrus had a feeling he did not actually breathe anymore. "Cyrus–"

"Curatio," Cyrus said, catching a disappointed look from Vara out of the corner of his eye, "I have been the General of Sanctuary for many years now. I am well aware that I have occasionally become 'Mopey Cyrus.' I want to assure you that in this moment, I am not being 'Mopey Cyrus–'"

"Could have fooled me," Vara muttered, "and I am not easily fooled these days."

"–I merely see the truth," Cyrus said. "I have no way to beat him. No spell at hand, and my skill with a sword is inadequate to the task. Fly every airship we have at him, shoot every gun – none of these will halt him. Hell, kill every scourge – which is a rather tall order, taller than a titan – and we still have *him* to deal with." Cyrus slumped. "This is indeed my worst nightmare. The two foes I never could quite beat, combined together in one hellish admixture."

"You don't have to beat them, Cyrus," Curatio said simply.

Cyrus stood very still in the white light. "...I don't think you understand how this works."

"Beg pardon?" Vara asked. She too, stood with her head cocked.

"You have been a sword-swinging warrior for so long," Curatio said, undertaking to pace around them, "that sometimes you forget. What does a *general* do, Cyrus?"

"He fights," Cyrus said.

Curatio chuckled. "No, in fact. Seldom do generals fight. Only the most young and energetic, some might say foolish. The general *directs* the battle." He leaned in close to Cyrus and Vara, who already stood together. "You don't have to win by yourself every time. You seldom have. And you certainly don't have to now."

"They're almost all gone, Curatio," Cyrus said, feeling dry in the mouth. "Alaric is missing with his crew. Shirri – the same. Vaste hides in the swamps, doing gods-know-what. Pharesia is destroyed, our army at Termina is surely next – what do I have, Curatio?" He threw a hand up, waving it about in the white, misty light. "I don't even know where I am."

"Just because they are not with you in person," Curatio said, "does not mean they are not with you in spirit, and in purpose." He waved his hand, the flourish of a magician. "Behold."

And there around them were suddenly Alaric, Shirri Gadden, and Vaste.

"Together once more," Curatio said with a small, satisfied smile. "And united, nothing can stop Sanctuary...not even Malpravus and the scourge."

CHAPTER 80

CYRUS

"*T*his is a most curious turn of events," Alaric said, speaking for all of them, really. He was looking around with his one good eye, as was Vaste, who looked particularly pale and sweaty. Shirri looked nonplussed, as per usual. "Is it truly you, brother?"

"It is I, albeit in diminished form," Curatio said. "Cyrus and Vara have joined me...and they bear news."

"Pharesia is destroyed," Cyrus said, focusing on Alaric. Why? It was as though he sought absolution, and the old knight was only one who could grant it. "Malpravus came upon us, unencumbered by the restrictions on magic—"

"That's – I found the secret of that," Shirri said.

"You found the secret as to why magic now is terrible and useless?" Vaste asked. Truly, he did look simply awful. Cyrus peered at him, and the troll looked back, quirking an eyebrow. "What? I know I don't have food on my face, because I haven't eaten anything but broth in forever."

"You look like you've seen a ghost," Vara said, frowning at the troll, her arm clinging to Cyrus's back.

"Funnily enough, I've seen more than one of late," Vaste said, "and I'm not speaking of you people here. What was the block on magic?"

"Someone you all knew from before," Shirri said. "A man the others called the Gatekeeper–"

"That bastard," Vara exploded. "I should have known he'd be responsible for this atrocity–"

"He was keeping Malpravus in check with it," Shirri said, leaping right between Vara and one of her favorite targets. The blond elf cut a daggered look at Shirri, but the half-elf seemed undeterred by the paladin's fire. "Now he is dead, and thus–"

"The hobble is gone, and the horse's arse runs free," Vaste said. "Marvelously timed." He gave Shirri an appraising look. "You saw this happen, did you? How did you survive?"

"He teleported us away at the last," Shirri said. "I am now uncomfortably ensconced with the dark elves in Saekaj, a guest of your old friend Terian."

"Stepan," Alaric whispered, almost mournfully. "At least you went out a hero, my friend."

"Speaking of old friends," Vaste said, turning to Curatio, "any chance you could save us some time and widen this circle a bit? Maybe suck in a few people outside the inner circle, give us a chance to confer about how bad things are, how bad they're about to get, maybe strategize, feed ourselves a classic Sanctuary meal – something to really satisfy the palate, given we're all, it appears, about to die?"

Curatio shook his head, laughing lightly. "Is hope truly so thin on the ground without me that you're all given in to despair?"

"Glaven is dead," Cyrus said, looking straight at Vaste. "I thought you should know."

"Hiressam is dead, too," Shirri said. "He died in the crash of our airship in Reikonos."

"This is not instilling a great deal of hope in me," Vara said.

"You know who's sort of still alive?" Vaste asked. "Niamh. I was just talking to her, in her ghostly, red-headed form. A bit pale of cheek – and everything else – but cheerfully non-scourgey. Oh – and I talked to your father," he added, looking at Cyrus.

Cyrus blinked, unsure whether Vaste was actually talking to him.

"Whose father?" He glanced 'round; Vara's was certainly dead, as was Alaric's, most probably Curatio's – Shirri's father was the only one he could possibly mean in this group.

"Yours, nimrod," Vaste said. "He wore your armor, carried your sword, had your mopey bearing. Unmistakable, really."

"He's long dead," Cyrus said.

"Yet I spoke to him – and Niamh, too," Vaste said, waving a clawed hand vaguely. "It's really the only thing that's come out of my little sojourn."

"I – what?" Cyrus shook his head, trying to get the confusion out of it.

"Could you bring the others into this space?" Alaric asked, focusing on Curatio. "Any others who might be in on this fight with us, so that we might coordinate? There are allies out there still who might willingly give aid." He smiled tautly. "I found a few, for instance."

Curatio shook his head. "I am at my limits here. Sanctuary is desperately wounded, still, after what Malpravus did. The magical energies of the Ark are at a low ebb and need to be replenished. Until then, I can perhaps envelop one or two more people, ones who have had a strong connection to Sanctuary in the past, but that is it."

"Ryin," Cyrus said.

Vaste did a double take at him. "'One or two,' he says, and you immediately decide to bring in the contrarian eggplant? Why not someone useful, like Dugras? He might at least bring a fleet to the battle."

"Ahh," Curatio said. "I feel the pull of one who wishes to join us."

And with a wave of his hand, and a flash of red hair...

...Niamh was there with them, in all her former glory.

"How?" Vara asked, gawking at the red-haired elf. "She died. Even as her current...form...how is she here?"

"I've always been tied to Sanctuary," Niamh said with a wan smile. "I was here so long, I got pulled in a little. Now I'm bonded to you all." She looked to Cyrus. "It's how I found you, both on the parapet of

Reikonos that first time, then followed you to where your airship crashed." She brushed a hand across her heart. "I can feel you here." She looked at each of them. "All of you."

"I'm glad you broadened your statement to encompass us all," Vara said tautly.

"For she was starting to get jealous of a dead woman," Vaste said.

"You're so close, all of you," Niamh said, taking a step toward their circle. "You're still in the fight – and you can win this. I truly believe it."

"I wish I did," Cyrus said.

"Take heart, old friend," Alaric said, the Ghost offering a slight smile. "Malpravus may have risen, but our end is not yet here."

"He's coming for us, Alaric," Cyrus said, "and we may be united here, but we're divided out there."

"Then the time has come for us to reunite," Vara said, "to stand together against Malpravus. Pool our magic, our resources. To prepare our defenses and fight with everything we have."

"But what do we have?" Vaste asked. "Forgive me for joining Cyrus in the realm of mope, but I went north and found nothing." Niamh cleared her throat. Which was funny, for she no longer had one, in the strictest sense. "Nothing besides a damned ginger elf."

"We lost Pharesia," Cyrus said, "and Malpravus added more magic to his stock than we could possibly have fathomed. If he hits Termina before he comes to us..." He shook his head. "...There won't be much left of Arkaria."

"There is so much left of Arkaria," Shirri said. "The people of Termina, of Emerald, of Saekaj. The men of the North–"

"Oh, right," Vaste said, "they are definitely not with us. They said to tell you so."

"It doesn't matter," Shirri said. "We are enough. Us. Standing firm. Malpravus is not invincible–"

"He certainly looks the part," Cyrus said. "Sword doesn't harm him, and no spell we can cast can block his."

"Cannons have little effect, I would imagine," Vaste said. "So what's left?"

"Much is left," Alaric said. "An entire final battle, in fact. This is not over, so long as we stand together."

"I have fought these massive battles before, Alaric," Cyrus said. "I don't have anything to bring to it this time. No strategies, no surprises, no additional armies—"

"I have an additional army," Alaric said.

"As do I," Shirri said. "The dark elves are but waiting for word. A single location whispered to Terian Lepos, and within a day his forces can surface almost anywhere in eastern Arkaria. Send us wizards and they will be anywhere in minutes, he assures me."

"Ryin's army is at your disposal," Vara said, "as well as Isabelle, with our forces in Termina. You have armies."

"But no strategy," Cyrus said, seeing Vaste nod along with him, "save for to march them into the scourge and hope for the best. To say nothing of Malpravus and his spell-craft that kills entire cities. Having people to throw into a grinder is not a strategy. It's the equivalent of putting an army of ants against a wizard. That first fire spell is going to make swift work of the entire hill."

"Cyrus," Alaric said, "all my life I have left when the trouble became too much. When the gods first came to power over the so-called lesser races, I entered the ether for the first time. When you began to face them down, I let myself be captured and told you not to fight." He lifted a mailed, clenched fist. "Those days are over. I know you despair, but I tell you this – we must fight Malpravus."

"I, too, am done running from troubles," Shirri said. "I was the mouse, in action. Now I choose to be the lion, and if I die in the fight...then I die a lion."

"That's cute," Vaste said. "I can almost hear you roar."

"I am fighting," Vara said, taking hold of Cyrus's arm. "You may join me, or not. I will not remain in the ether hiding, waiting for Malpravus to crack his way through, as surely he eventually shall, even if he waits until he is done with the rest of the world. I do not care for the shape of things, and do not wish to raise our child in those circumstances – so I must defeat him."

"But he's – what the hell did you just say?" Cyrus had started to make his argument to the others, but his head snapped back 'round to Vara, and found her smiling in a very self-satisfied way.

"Congratulations, lass," Alaric said, wearing a broad grin.

"Even as our lives come to their close," Curatio said, "another begins. Very good."

"Ooh!" Niamh clapped, then leapt at Vara, wrapping her up in a ghostly hug. "This is the best news I've had in a thousand years!"

"Your father will be so proud," Vaste said, a touch acidly, "if I can bear to face having a conversation to tell him."

"Seriously?" Cyrus asked, caught between asking that of Vaste, but also Vara.

"Cyrus," Vara said, taking hold of his hand, her gauntlet clinking against his. "There are terrible obstacles before us. But we can defeat them, if we work together."

"How?" Cyrus asked, throwing arms wide in despair. "How the hell are we supposed to beat him? We have no strategy, no plan, and I'm sorry, but standing together in one place is not a strategy. And we don't even know how to exit this ether! If it's even possible."

"It is possible, in fact," Curatio said. "You can exit the ether...in one very specific place, and one place alone at present." His eyes twinkled with amusement. "And I would suggest you conduct your battle at that very site, for a number of reasons."

"You have a strategy?" Cyrus asked, feeling quite jaded.

"It is perhaps all I have left," Curatio said, "General. But if you would allow me to assist...I think I can help you."

"And you won't be alone," Vara said, wrapping her arm in his.

He could see them gathered around him – Shirri, welling with hope; Alaric, confident, determined; Niamh, with a glow of excitement. Even Vaste – poor, dour Vaste – seemed almost like he could believe again. "All right," Cyrus said, with a touch of reluctance. "We'll do this together. One last time." And he nodded, resolute. "So...where, when, and how are we doing it?"

To that, Curatio just smiled.

CHAPTER 81

VASTE

*C*oming back to himself upon the hilltop, Vaste blinked into the shaded light...

...and found himself drenched. Water was coming down from above, soaking him through the robes and chilling him to the skin. "Gyah!" He leapt back, but it did no good.

Rain poured from the sky, and he turned to find Niamh standing there, effervescent beneath the liquid assault, smiling at his discomfiture. "You're not afraid of a little rain, are you?"

"I'm uncomfortable at a lot of rain, because it wets me and makes me chilly," he said, brandishing Letum. "Now if you'll excuse me, I'm going to gather myself, my people, and get the hell out of this swampy hellhole, since I have nothing else to do here." And with that, he gathered his soaking robes and ran for it.

It wasn't hard to follow his own trail, even in this downpour. He ran barefoot through the swamp, crossing mud and water and even, occasionally, patches of dense soil. A series of puffs of black smoke in the distance were his guide, and he followed it until he burst out of the last patch of sawgrass to find them all standing there, in the rain, even Aisling. They looked at him, almost beseechingly, and she was the first to speak. "Oh, good, you came back," Aisling said. "I was beginning to think I'd have to bring down a search party from the ship to find you."

"Why would you think that?" Vaste asked. "Where did you imagine I would go?"

"Hell if I know," Aisling said, her white hair plastered to her face and shoulders. "Figured maybe you stumbled into quicksand, and wouldn't be able to get out without the airship's steam winch."

"You think I can't climb out of a pit myself?" Vaste asked, and she made a show of looking him up and down. "That cuts deep," he said, watching her look him over. "Listen – we have to go now. The final battle is set to begin in the south, and unless I miss my estimate, we're at least a day and more away."

"The final battle?" Merrish scoffed lightly. "And we're simply going to fly back?"

"It's either that or keep sitting here," Vaste said. "And I hate this place and don't care to die here, so..." He clapped his hands together. "Let's get ourselves packed and get moving. I don't want to miss this fight."

"But you finally have something to contribute to it?" Aemma asked.

"Shit," Vaste said, glancing at Asa-tee, who watched with vague interest from beneath a leather awning. "No. No, Huaviri died before teaching me whatever it was he wanted to impart. I don't suppose you know–"

"I'm just the helper," Asa-tee said with a broad shrug. "Not a protege. His gifts were his own, never mine. I only kept him fed and cared for. I could never do what he did." There was a quiet awe in how he said it.

"Well...damn," Vaste said. "I don't suppose you can fight? Because we've got one coming up."

Asa-tee shook his head. "This one's your fight, friend. I wish you well for all our sakes, but I'm afraid I'm not of any particular use in this. Besides, I have to start breaking down camp, take care of Huaviri, prepare to leave. I've got days of work ahead of me before I can even think about leaving. Then I'm gonna have to walk to the nearest town with an airship port."

"If you come with us, your journey will be either much quicker or much shorter," Vaste said. "Definitely one of those."

Asa-tee frowned. "I think I'd rather take my chances walking, *giso-mari*. And I can't leave Huaviri unburied." He shook his head. "It's bad medicine, friend."

"Fine. Everyone else," Vaste waved his hands to encompass the whole camp, "get your things together – and let's get out of here. I'm just going to get my boots and I'll be ready to go." He ducked into the lodge, ready to snatch them up and go.

But there, standing before him, and before his own dead body...was Huaviri.

CHAPTER 82

VASTE

"*Ah, gisomari*, there you are," Huaviri said, as casually as if Vaste had just strolled in after breakfast. He hadn't eaten breakfast, of course, because he was still starving, but still...as if he had.

Vaste stood in the steam of the lodge and stared at the spectral figure. Yes, he looked exactly like Rusyl Davidon had, and Niamh. "Uh...you're dead."

"Yes," Huaviri said, taking a step toward him, right through the crackling fire. "I am."

"Shouldn't you, then..." Vaste stood there, quite flustered, "...move along or something?"

Huaviri chuckled. "Has Rusyl moved along? Has your friend wearing that awful, gray skin over her pretty face? Death's not always the end. Sometimes it's a new beginning, or an uncomfortable, interminable middle. You should know that by now."

Vaste sagged, letting his haunches find the floor. "Is this what you were trying to teach me?"

"It's the lesson I had to be dead to teach you," Huaviri said, his old eyes sparkling with amusement. "Truthfully...this is what we were waiting for, friend."

"And all the other stuff?" Vaste asked. "The starving me, the denying me water, making me sit in this heat?"

Huaviri laughed. "I can't pretend it wasn't funny to make you whinge. You could stand to skip a few meals. It won't kill you. But no – I've been keeping you here until this very moment." He leaned forward, long braids stirring as he did so. "This is the moment you're here for, Vaste. This is the lesson you needed. Not just to see the dead, though you did need to get a bit better at that."

"To communicate with them," Vaste said, staring at him.

"To send them along," Huaviri said. "We don't belong here, we dead. Your friend's father," and he waved a hand at the lodge flap, "he's been here long past the time when his son should have died. And why? It's not like he knew this Cyrus was still out there. He sticks around because he has the sense his life is unfinished, because he thinks he still has something he needs to do." Huaviri touched a withered hand to his chest. "As I do – though not for long."

Vaste stared at him through narrowed eyes. "That's why you stuck around?"

"Well, yeah," Huaviri said with a chuckle, "but in my case it's actually true, assuming I can get this one last truth through your thick skull. People don't stick around just to stick around. They do it because they feel their purpose is unfulfilled, and there's a lack of peace in that. Ask your friend with the red hair. That rage those creatures have? They weren't always like that; they had any chance of completion or peace ripped away from them. And you can't go on like that."

"How do you...fix that?" Vaste asked. "How do you fix a thousand or ten thousand years of rage?"

Huaviri leaned in a little closer. "You gotta ask yourself why people are sticking around to begin with."

"Because...they're worried about the people they left behind?"

"In some cases," Huaviri said. "But it goes deeper than that, *gisomari*. They've been part of the stage drama and a lot of them want to know how the play ends. That the characters that they care about...that they're going to be all right." He lifted a spectral hand. "Do you know what I mean?" And he looked at Vaste hopefully.

A small tingle ran up Vaste's scalp. "Yes. Yes, I know what you mean, now."

Huaviri looked at him expectantly. "...And?"

"Thank you, Huaviri," Vaste said quietly, drawing to his feet. He put only a bit of weight on Letum, for now he felt almost as if he did not need the godly implement any longer. "Thank you. For everything. I think...I think I'm going to be all right now."

The Azwillian smiled. "Yeah...I think so, too." And he faded away, as though he'd never even been there.

Plunging out of the tent, Vaste almost ran into the spectral shade of Rusyl Davidon. "You," Rusyl said, blinking at him in surprise.

"Yes, Rusyl, it is I, the greatest and last of the trolls of Gren – for now," Vaste said, drawing himself to his full height and looking down on the shade of Cyrus's father. "Your son – he turned out fine. Married a spunky elven woman, won many battles, and stands on the precipice now of defeating the greatest foe our land has ever seen. He's a general greater than any that has ever walked Arkaria, and he carries your sword and wears your armor into battle."

Rusyl's shade paused, a confused look that turned, gradually, to pride. "Truly?"

"It is so. And also," Vaste said, "if I'm not much mistaken, that elven wife of his has a bit of a glow about her. If you know what I mean."

"Well done, Cyrus," Rusyl said, and he faded like mist in the sun. "Well done, indeed..."

"Vaste?" Aemma peered at him through where Rusyl had been standing. The others were moving about the camp, though none save Merrish seemed to have taken note of his conversation. "Are you all right?"

Vaste smiled. "You know, Aemma...I think we might just make it now."

CHAPTER 83

CYRUS

"*I* can't believe we're back here," Cyrus said, looking over the desolate landscape. There was barely any grass upon the ground, and not merely because of the season. The earth was upturned, scuffed, as though every seed and weed had nearly been burnt away by some cleansing fire. It had not, though; it was not fire at all that had despoiled this shadowy land, the clouds hanging thick overhead, barely a hint of sun to give it light.

Vara took his hand, gauntlets clinking together. "It all comes full circle, doesn't it?" A small wind like a breath stirred her hair where it had come loose from her ponytail. "And now we are back at the beginning."

A hint of sun, a tiny beam of illumination, reached between the gap in the clouds to shine down at the crater at their feet. It was not much of a crater anymore; time and weather had done their bit, filling it in over the last thousand years so that it was a much shallower dip than it had been in the last days before Cyrus had left Arkaria.

Yet the great crater of Sanctuary still endured in spite of all that. It stood before them, squarely in the middle of the Plains of Perdamun, the once-vibrant land, and it waited.

They'd exited from the ether as Curatio had promised, tossed out here at the edge of the crater, and now found themselves looking down into it as Cyrus once had a thousand years ago.

"Come," Vara said, snaking a small hand beneath his armor and bringing out the medallion that still hung there. She let it loose to clank against his breastplate, and it swayed, unleashed now, no longer restrained by his chainmail and undershirt. "Let's have it – how does it go again?"

Cyrus loosed a mighty sigh. Casting back in his memory, the words occurred to him, and he spoke them, closing his eyes as he did so.

"I invoke thee who hear my plea,

I request thy aid,

For those who are soon to die."

Vara gasped.

Lightning rumbled, albeit weakly compared to how it had been before. A few flashes under the leaden sky, the wind picked up, and then the crawling sensation of electricity ran over Cyrus's skin beneath the armor. He stared at the afterimage burning its way into his eyes, and there, before him, where the crater had been–

A ghostly afterimage, like a dream taken into the waking world.

It was Sanctuary. But not whole, not as it was. It was shrouded, partially in ether, wavering, its pretty lines blurred.

But it was there.

"There's your bloody hope," Vara said, putting a hand on his shoulder. "There's the start of your strategy."

And, Cyrus had to admit...

...it was not a terrible start.

CHAPTER 84

CYRUS

*T*hey sat looking at the twisted, spectral shape of Sanctuary as the sun sunk low in the sky. Its soft glow shed light like an aurora in the night. She lay against his side and Cyrus sat upright, watching the shape of it, old and familiar, large as it had ever been when it stood in this very spot, twist like smoke from a fire.

"I never thought," Vara said, a touch sleepily, as she always seemed to be these days, "we would see it again here, in this very spot, as it was in the days of old."

"Well, it's not...exactly," Cyrus said, looking at the entry gate to the wall, translucent before them. "It's not what it once was, and I don't know quite how to bring it back."

"It lacks energy," Vara said. "So...you feed it."

"Oh, all right," Cyrus said with mild sarcasm, "that sounds simple enough – save for I don't have any energy to give it, and none seems readily at hand."

"Have you thought about trying to cast a healing spell on it?" Vara asked, and raised her hand. It glowed white for a moment, then fell upon Sanctuary with a sparkle of light.

Cyrus stared at the old keep. It seemed...perhaps a touch clearer.

"Fantastic," he said. "Do that about a thousand times and perhaps we'll be able to at least set foot in it without tumbling to the bottom of that pit."

She gave him a puckish smirk. "I don't see you coming up with any ideas."

"Save your life energy, will you?" Cyrus said, placing a hand on the plate covering her belly. There was no hint of any bulge there, as yet. "You need it."

She smiled at him, and it warmed him upon those chilly plains. "Yes, I do, for growing any offspring of yours is bound to be a frustratingly energy-inefficient task. Why, the sheer allocation to growing that arse alone–"

He twisted her ponytail in his fingers playfully, and she laughed. Bringing her face to his with a guiding hand, they kissed. "I am a bit confused, though," Cyrus said once they parted, "as to how this happened."

"Need I draw you an illustration?"

"I mean–"

"I have not been on Ventra'maq in a thousand years, Cyrus," Vara said. "The last of it was purged in the ether, thus–"

"You didn't say anything."

"I didn't think about it," Vara said, lying back, breathing slow, contentedly. "Out of mind, I suppose. Or perhaps..." and here she turned her face to him, "...I was simply ready."

"You could have said something," Cyrus said, feeling his own face redden. "The timing is–"

"It wasn't a conscious decision," Vara said. "I did not consider it and conclude, 'You know what would be excellent right now, in this time of crisis? Something else to worry about.' It simply...I suppose I just let it happen."

"I'm glad you let it happen." Cyrus turned his gaze once more to the wavering, ethereal keep before him. "This seems to be our last stand either way. Might as well imbue it with extra meaning, since failure will take all we have in any case."

"Yes," Vara said. "You think this will draw Malpravus, then?"

"My dear," Cyrus said, letting his fingers twist within her own, and covering her small hand with his mighty one, "I think he is surely already on his way."

CHAPTER 85

VASTE

*M*orning dawned to the airship already in motion, the sun coming up to Vaste's left, chasing the darkness across the sky with the first beams. He sat cross-legged on the forecastle, listening to Aemma and Merrish lashing away at each other on the quarterdeck while Aisling sighed and harrumphed between their traded volleys.

"Those two are going to end up killing each other." Niamh's voice came as a sigh, and when he looked, her ghostly figure was lit by the dawn, giving her red hair a fiery quality like he remembered it bearing in life.

Stirring out of the deep thoughts in which he'd been wading, Vaste deigned to toss the two of them a look. "No," he said, regarding them ever-so-briefly; he had barely noticed them feuding, "I don't think so."

Niamh settled on the deck next to him, strangely corporal for such a ghostly form. How was that? "You don't think the elf and human, who were at deadly war not so very long ago, are going to kill each other?"

"I doubt it," Vaste said, feeling a little uncomfortable in his abdomen and back. All that extra weight seemed to have thrown off his balance, and lack of proper sitting and exercises made it difficult for him to stay in this position overly long. Well, perhaps he'd have to do something about that – at some point. "As you point out, they were at war, and not so long ago. But Aemma lost all she knew, and Merrish now knows he did infinite wrong in the course of his fight." He opened his eyes to find Niamh staring at him. "He feels guilty and lashes out; she feels mournful and strikes back. I've seen murder in the eyes of those who would commit it. Neither is there. Neither is particularly close. They nettle one another, no dagger is present."

"Hmm," Niamh said, her spectral figure matching Vaste's cross-legged posture. "Look at you, brimming with insight. What are you now? Not a healer anymore, exactly."

"I haven't been 'exactly' a healer for a thousand years, my dear," Vaste said, staring at that blazing orange sun cresting the horizon. "Perhaps not even since Oroguuk saved me from that mob in Gren."

"But you're different," Niamh said. "You're no mean sorcerer like so many of the others these days. You're something else. Something new."

"Or more likely something very old," Vaste said. "The oldest sort of magic user among my people, I think: a shaman."

"And what is a shaman, pray tell?"

"I sit at the crossroads between a healer and a necromancer," Vaste said, pursing his lips and giving it some thought. "My wizardry is minimal, though potent when I have unleashed it. Death magic is at my disposal – which is, I think, how I was able to overcome, in Termina, some of the block upon magic that the Gatekeeper had imposed, and how Malpravus was doing a better job of slipping its bounds than anyone else. He wasn't using traditional magic – or at least not just it."

"You were casting the remnants of the souls of those who passed in Termina," Niamh said. "Outside Malpravus's reach."

"Exactly," Vaste said. "But...little is outside his reach now, with the fall of Pharesia and Reikonos. They are in his belly, and now he is full of power."

"So...what are you going to do about it?" Niamh asked.

He started to answer, but sensed movement behind him. When he turned, there stood Aemma, tall, looming over him, such a strange feeling from a human woman.

"I cannot stand that elf," Aemma huffed, her arms wrapped around her slender form. He took note for the first time that her teeth were slightly larger at the top, and her jaw hung a bit back in an overbite. He wasn't sure how attractive that was for humans, but for trolls it was very much an adorable quality.

"He does enjoy twisting your tail," Vaste said, rising so that now he towered over her. She glanced up, not exactly in surprise, for she obviously knew he was the larger, but there was something in her eyes as she watched him rise, some flash of admiration. "I think it's a strange brew of guilt and malice toward humans writhing around inside him." He felt a prickling across his forehead. "As though he loathes himself, yet self-preservation cannot allow him to turn inward, and so instead he turns his anger outward, toward you, the convenient target. Very curious."

"Why am I the convenient target?" Aemma asked, looking quite exhausted.

"Because neither Aisling nor myself would take such abuse without lashing back," Vaste said, reaching out and plucking up her hand, which caused Aemma to blink in surprise. "But you, buried in guilt for what happened to your people, you take his remonstration with but a small amount of snap back."

"I suppose I do," Aemma said, watching his hand upon hers. She looked up into his eyes, and he saw some curious mix of feelings there. "Do you know what it is to feel the guilt of those you have lost weighing upon your shoulders?"

"You know I do," he said, rubbing her palm with his thumb. It was a strange feeling; warm. He felt warm.

"How do you...get past it?" she asked, her voice low and hopeful.

"Redemption is a path we must walk every day," Vaste said, taking up her hand, lifting it so that it was even with his heart. "Also..." and here he leaned in, bringing his face to hers, "...distracting yourself can help."

He kissed her, taking great care with his protruding fangs. She kissed him back, passionately, her hand finding the nape of his neck and leaning into it with great enthusiasm.

"That's my troll," Niamh murmured softly.

He did not let it stop him, and they continued to kiss as the ship flew onward into the breaking day.

CHAPTER 86

CYRUS

There was a sound behind Cyrus that stirred him out of a faint slumber. They lay in the sun shining down upon them, Vara curled against his side upon the desiccated plains. No hint of green lay in sight, and the air smelled of dust that coated Cyrus's dry tongue where he'd fallen asleep with his mouth open.

He disentangled himself from the delicate arm of his wife, letting her vambrace down gently to the bare earth. Cyrus hadn't intended to fall asleep, for fear that the scourge might fall upon them. Still, he had drifted off, and now he sat up, staring into the dry, almost desert air of the Plains of Perdamun.

Drawing up to a knee, he looked once more at the ghostly Sanctuary, writhing and coruscating in its position, all faint lines and barely-there wisps of what was once a mighty fortress. The outline of the tower caught the midday sun's light, and Cyrus moved to stand, looking for the source of the faint scratching he could hear.

A little dust kicked up a few feet away, caught by the faint breeze. The grains flew past, motes on the breeze, and Cyrus blinked at them. Looking back to where they'd entered the air, he stared.

The earth...moved.

It was a subtle thing at first, as if they'd been stirred by some unseen foot. He approached the disturbance slowly, watching as dirt seemed to drain into a funnel before him, as though it were a bottle and someone had removed the stopper to let all the dust out–

A flat metal spade tip burst from the ground, and Cyrus took a step back, drawing Rodanthar and feeling strength course through him as the last grains of dirt wafted past his face. The hole widened; the spade tip disappeared, and others chipped away at the dirt around, breaking the earth open, blue faces peering out with squinted eyes into the sunlight.

Shouts in dark elven echoed in the newly exposed tunnels below, and Cyrus let his sword drop. The hole widened, and widened again, a host of dark elves working their best to open it up, revealing within a darkness, and then a face–

"Oh, good, you are here," Terian Lepos said mildly, taking Cyrus's offered hand and climbing out onto the Plains of Perdamun. His metal boots crunched into the plain's dirt, perhaps the first feet to find that particular spot in a thousand years. "I'd been told, of course, but you never know how reliable these rumors are until you see them with your own eyes."

"I happen to be very reliable." Shirri Gadden emerged next, smudged with earth, her hair a mess, but still...alive, and well enough. "Especially in all matters Sanctuary, apparently."

"You are a veritable expert," Cyrus said, offering her his hand. She took it with a grateful smile and he lifted her out of the hole. Within, he could see Longwell in the darkness, half-covered in shadow. Behind was Guy, and – if Cyrus was not much mistaken – Alixa Weltan, the Administrator of Emerald. Curious, that. "In matters of Sanctuary, and much else. As befits one of your lineage."

She flushed at that, and dipped her head. "Thank you," she muttered, then raised her eyes upon the insubstantial keep covering the southern horizon. "Behold," she whispered in awe, "that which I am supposed to be expert on."

"So it is back – sort of," Terian said, putting his hands on his hips and inspecting the old keep. "How?"

"Hope is a hard thing to kill," Vara said, shuffling through the dirt behind them. Terian turned to look, and offered a puckish grin. "Dark knight."

"Not so dark anymore," Terian said, punching Cyrus lightly on the pauldron. "Thanks to this husband of yours and his redemptive qualities." He pointed at the ephemeral form of Sanctuary. "How do we fix this?"

"Don't know – yet," Cyrus said, for he was moved to add that last bit. "Hopefully the answer will come to us, you know–"

"In the fullness of time," Vara and Terian chorused, each offering the other a mildly reproachful-bordering-on-amused look at the finish.

"Well, while we wait for time to get full," Terian said, "and your other guests to arrive – I brought you an army." He waved a hand behind him, where dark elves in armor and bearing swords, lances, and flintlocks were already swarming out of not only the hole he'd emerged from, but a half-dozen others that were being burrowed out of the plains dirt as Cyrus watched. "Hopefully it won't get absorbed in one good spell, but if it does, I reckon we're not going to be around to bitch about it."

"To that purpose," Cyrus said, turning to Shirri, "have you, by chance, any ideas for how to either restore Sanctuary or drain Malpravus of his power?"

"I'm sure it will come to us with the others," Shirri said, a touch nervously, "in – well, you know."

"I do hope you're right," Cyrus said, turning his gaze to the horizon. To the northwest he saw airships, presumably those of Isabelle, and the force from Termina. But also, on the northern horizon, a cloud as black as night, that he knew, somehow, was Malpravus, and dust upon the ground below that heralded the coming of the scourge.

CHAPTER 87

CYRUS

"*R*emember when the Waking Woods was over there?" Terian asked, when they were lined up in a proper formation. The dark elven army was still exiting the earth; the airships from Termina had arrived and offloaded their armies; now they circled overhead, while a ring of black clouds covered the northern sky like a hurricane coming toward shore.

The corner of Cyrus's mouth tugged up, almost imperceptibly, a tickle at his cheeks. "I do."

"You can see the temple now," Terian said, sounding almost wistful as a stiff breeze came hard out of the north, bearing that smell of rot that always preceded the scourge. "With the earth so bare. I wonder...if we beat them, destroy the scourge...how long will it take to grow forests in eastern Arkaria again?"

"We will see the first done," Vara said with serious confidence. "As to the second...well, one can hope we see it, as well."

Terian nodded. "You found Ryin?"

"We found him," Cyrus said. "He's on his way...along with his army."

"You found us all," Longwell said, voice scratchy. "And here we are again, at the end of the world."

"It's different this time," Terian said.

"How's that?" Cyrus asked.

"Because this time...you're here," Longwell said.

"I'm flattered," Cyrus said, casting a glance back. Shirri was there, clutching Philos in her hands. He nodded approval, and she seemed to take strength from that. Dark elves in endless ranks were back there; to his side were Isabelle, Gareth, and that odd fellow, along with Birstis and his trelves on catback. There were humans, too, from Emerald, bearing muskets and spears, and they, too were lined up against the backdrop of the whispering, shimmering Sanctuary. "It remains to be seen if I make a difference, though."

A light shone down from those dark clouds; not quite blood red, but close. It seemed to illuminate the whole world, bright and glowing across the whole of Arkaria.

"Not very inconspicuous, is it?" Pamyra asked, huddled beside Shirri. She was giving Shirri's weapon an admiring glance, but her eyes swiftly flicked back to the red horizon.

"Malpravus has never been one for subtlety," Vara said.

"My ways are obvious and straightforward." Malpravus's voice crackled over them, seeming to touch Cyrus deep down in his bones. "Shouldn't that appeal to you, Cyrus Davidon?"

"Why is it always Cyrus?" Terian grumbled.

"You had your opportunities, Terian," Malpravus said. "I offered you many chances to become more than the rather limited soul that you are."

"I shudder to think what your soul would be like if you'd followed Malpravus's path instead of your own," Vara said. "Why, I imagine you would have followed through on your initial instincts and killed my husband upon his return."

"I thought he was a fake," Terian said.

Cyrus frowned. "You tried to kill me after that, too."

"I was in a bad place. You try spending the better part of a thousand years buried in the earth and see how your mind holds up."

"I'm so pleased to see all of you here again, against the scourge,"

Isabelle said dryly. "I always try to go forward in my life, yet here we are, back again. And against Malpravus once more."

"This is what happens when you leave unfinished business," Guy piped up. "So...let's finish it, shall we?"

Cyrus felt a certain tension in his gut and tried to put his fears aside. They were all together now, after all, and the others were riding in; if ever there was a chance to put this right, this was it. "Let's finish it," he agreed.

"You will not find me easy to finish." Malpravus's cloud was now nearly upon them, and glowing redder by the moment. The airships of Isabelle's combined fleet were behind them, hovering in the air, holding position with their sides exposed, cannons out, primed to fire. The dust cloud of the scourge grew closer, too. It was now possible to see the black of their eyes, less than half a mile away.

"His spell is going to be arriving directly," Vara said. It was true; the cloud was growing redder, and was above them now, the leading edge less than hundred feet away. "Shall we try something old? A classic, perhaps?"

"Indeed. Isabelle," Cyrus said mildly, "if you'd be so kind as to cast a cessation spell over the area."

"I'm a healer," his sister-in-law – bit more like a sister, at this point, though – said crossly. "I'm hardly your best option for that."

"But you're simply the best at so many things," he said, turning and giving her such a winning smile. Truly, she had aged; the spell she'd cast to save herself and Vara in Reikonos had leeched the life from her skin, the color from her hair. This was a vision of what Vara might look like when she grew old. Or rather, Cyrus thought as he looked at the glowing red sky, *if* she grew old.

"I can handle such a modest request," Shirri said, lifting her new stave high. Philos glowed at the tip, and a wave of light swept over their entire army, her unrestrained magic carrying it an incredible distance.

"My mother's legacy is in the best of hands," Cyrus murmured; Shirri's cheeks flushed, and he knew he'd been heard.

"What an adorable notion," Malpravus's voice crackled over them, like thunder on the wind, "thinking your spellcraft can stand against mine? How old are you, girl? Thirty? Forty?"

"Five hundred," Shirri said without appreciable strain. She sounded good; strong. "Give or take."

"Have I mentioned you look damned good for your age?" Guy asked.

"No," Shirri said, murmuring words too soft to be heard between the ones she spoke aloud, "but thank you, Guy."

"It matters not," Malpravus said. "There is no stopping my spell with yours. It simply cannot be done."

"He may be telling the truth," Pamyra said.

"If so, we're dead anyway," Terian said, eyes locked on the scourge coming. They would be arriving in mere moments. "Army – ready yourself! Watch for flankers!"

"We're going to get surrounded, swallowed up," Alixa said. "That much is a foregone conclusion. Prepare your defense! Watch out for those next to you as well as yourself!"

"You will be swallowed up, it is true," Malpravus said. "You will become part of the greatest whole you could imagine–"

"More like part of the greatest asshole I could imagine," Terian said.

"And he can imagine quite the asshole," Cyrus quipped, "being one of the greats himself."

"I will not miss the repartee," Malpravus said, the red sky flashing, "when you are all dead. The silence shall, truly, be golden." The red cloud flashed in its dark, crimson depths, and Cyrus could feel the magic crackling within, ancient and terrible. "This, it would seem, is our final farewell." It seemed to swell, and then–

"Don't say goodbye just yet, Malpravus," Cyrus said, watching the darker cloud above the armies; something was rippling at the edges, moving toward Malpravus's red cloud–

And from the edge burst a dark figure on black wings, scaled and terrible, the shape oh-so-familiar–

A dragon.

With a belted breath of flame, it tinged the red glow a fiery orange, and the scarlet cloud shrunk. Malpravus grunted somewhere within, and then from out of the clouds burst a host of other dragons led by a familiar airship–

Alaric's. It was the *Raifa*.

And the dragon at the fore, the one who had struck Malpravus in his heart...

...was the old legend, Ehrgraz.

CHAPTER 88

ALARIC

*T*hey swept in behind Ehrgraz, not quite able to match pace with the elder dragon. He struck true at the heart of Malpravus, his magic clearly a match for the necromancer-turned-sorcerer, and Alaric could feel the terrible duel going on at the heart of the clouds, where the dragon struck in a way Malpravus had not expected.

But that was hardly the only worry before them. The dragons swept in around the coming scourge as the airships waiting in formation released their first volleys.

"This is battle," Qualleron said as the cannonades landed amidst the gray-flesh creatures swarming toward the ghostly remain of Sanctuary and all its defenders arrayed below. "This is what I have longed for." He turned to look at Alaric. "Deliver me unto the field and I will kill countless for you."

Alaric breathed the words of the Falcon's Essence spell, then waved his hand. "You are as unto a falcon, my friend. Descend and do your fine work."

"I shall," Qualleron said, and leapt over the edge with his blade already drawn. Alaric watched him run on air down toward Cyrus and the rest, formed in their octagonal line around Sanctuary's glow beneath the thunder of the airship guns and the screech of dragons loosing flame, ice, poison, earth and water breath.

"That's not enough to stop them," Mazirin said, huddling behind Edouard as the *Raifa* went into a hard turn. The former executioner seemed to have a good grasp of the wheel, and though he was pale and a bit sweaty, he turned it with confidence. "Not the dragons, not the army." She pointed a finger into the distance, where the ground was covered in gray all the way to the horizon. "Certainly not the airships."

"This is not a battle that will be won by armies," Alaric said, holding the rail as the *Raifa* pitched into a tight turn, anticipating the release of a broadside. Alaric vanished into the ether, preparing to join Calene below to do his meager part.

"Then what will it be won by?" Mazirin asked; but he was already gone, and did not get a chance to answer.

CHAPTER 89

CYRUS

*F*ire and thunder greeted Malpravus and his seemingly endless army of scourge. They were upon them now, the great gray mass meeting the first line of sword and blade and spell, and Cyrus's band was equal to the task – for now. Black blood flew along with scourge heads and limbs. Cyrus's muscles strained as he turned loose his full strength upon the enemy at hand and trusted Ehrgraz and Alaric would deal with the – perhaps infinitely worse – one above.

"How long do you reckon Ehrgraz can keep Malpravus from casting that death spell?" Terian asked, splitting a scourge in half with Noctus as he stood shoulder to shoulder with Cyrus.

"Don't know," Cyrus said, slashing apart a scourge's head with Rodanthar. Black blood flew in a line across the dusty plain.

"Alaric is dealing with it as needs to be dealt with," Vara said, Ferocis flashing as she turned loose her own weapon. The scourge were already overwhelming, attacking at the edges of the formation where no godly weapons could be found. The only thing keeping the combined army of dark elves, elves, and men from dissolving into chaos was the dragons flying crisscross patterns and unleashing lines of destruction with their very breath. Flames, ice, acid, and rock showers danced across the formations of scourge, leaving scars in the land and ruin where their breath touched.

And, Cyrus knew within moments of the battle being joined...it was not nearly enough.

Not enough to stop Malpravus, though the sound of Ehrgraz flying and fighting with the red, glowing cloud above heralded a great fight being fought just out of Cyrus's sight. Not enough to stop the seemingly endless army of scourge, either, stretching all the way to the horizon and beyond, waves of gray enemy that would bring sure death to the combined army.

As general, Cyrus knew all of this...

...yet still he fought on.

Time. They needed time.

And with every hacking blow of his sword, every scourge he cut through, decapitated, slashed apart, he bought that time...

...even though he doubted the ultimate worth of the seconds he paid for.

"They're coming in!" Pamyra's voice cracked over them. "Breaking through against the humans!"

Cyrus turned to look and found...yes, it was true. "Perhaps cessation is a bad idea," he muttered, swinging his blade sideways, half-distracted by what he saw.

In spite of a flame drake running down the line and scorching black a line of scourge wide as three wagons, in spite of a cannonade that blasted to pieces countless scourge on that front...

...they tore into the front line, blood spurting and spraying as their teeth and claws found vein and artery, turning the green-clad army of Emerald into a red mess. They wormed their way into the formation, and already Cyrus could see it flagging. "Longwell, Guy–"

"On it," Longwell leapt as Vara used to, Amnis sweeping behind him. He plummeted into the midst of the gray onrush of scourge, sweeping with his spear and attacking with vicious fervor.

"I don't know if I can jump like that," Guy said, considerably squatter and less athletic than the dragoon, "but might as well give it a

– WHOA!" He leapt, small, fat legs pinwheeling beneath him. He came down in the midst of the scourge, just shy of Longwell's swinging spear.

"Cyrus," Vara said, voice iron, but infused with worried urgency.

He turned; now the scourge pressed in on the right, tearing into the octagonal formation of the dark elves. They bore a terrible brunt, and dragon breath and cannonade could only mitigate it.

"We're going to fail, aren't we?" Pamyra asked quietly.

"No," Cyrus said, steely determination infusing him. This he was certain of.

For out of the west, he could see at last, beneath the shroud of Malpravus's evil-looking cloud, hints of green in a land of gray, of dead ground and writhing scourge. Green churning its way through the land on a terrible march through the enemy, destroying its way toward Cyrus's army–

"By the gods," Longwell called, over the entirety of the army.

"No," Cyrus said, watching a ripple of worry pull the scourge off their line, just for a moment, as they turned to see what mighty, unstoppable force was crashing through their ranks, shuddering the ground of the southern plains beneath them, "not a god, but a druid."

"I believe he's called a Hierophant, now," Vara said, watching the onrush of green come ever closer, the edges of their own formation taking advantage of the breathing room afforded them by the assault of Ryin's army into the scourge's flank. It was a towering force, taller than any man, troll – hell, almost as tall as a dragon.

"The woods of old," Terian said with a smile, "they are awake – and they return."

For at the head, running upon the air itself, was Ryin Ayend...

...and behind him, very much alive, very much enraged at the army of death, and striking down with branch and root, was the moving, breathing, fighting remnant of the Waking Woods.

CHAPTER 90

ALARIC

The guns thundered as the trees came charging in, Alaric triggering the *Raifa's* cannons one by one, the fire coming to bear on the wall of scourge surging across the landscape, turning the gray plains even grayer, with spatters of black as a cannonball struck home.

"This is a side of you I don't think I ever really saw in the days of yore," Calene shouted as she triggered another cannon. The explosion of gunpowder recoiled it back on its rails. "You know, the fighting, vengeful, destructive side."

"Were you not there on the Endless bridge when I brought it down?" Alaric asked, triggering his own cannon, then running to the next. These were drops of sweat applied to a raging fire, but it was all they had, and so he fought with them.

"Yeah, but that was different," Calene said. "Or at least it felt so. Might have had something to do with my youth at the time."

"I suppose you never heard about my upbringing?" Alaric asked, placing flame to the small hole at the back of the cannon. Another boom thundered in the confined space, setting his ears to ringing within his helm once more. A healing spell seemed to be in order, and he used it, though it did nothing. With a sigh, he realized: a cessation spell must be in effect. "How, upon the age of my majority, I chose the words that were to define my reign as king of Luukessia?"

"We never really talked much before you, er, 'died.'" Calene had worked her way almost to the end of the line and was shouting back at him. "So no."

"They included 'strong,' 'unyielding,' and 'merciless,'" Alaric said, "feeling that they would well define, in my youthful idiocy, my intentions toward governance. While I rescinded them later, I am feeling them apropos in this moment."

There was a screech and a howl overhead, albeit muffled, and Alaric stuck his head out the gun port. Something huge and black flashed past–

Ehrgraz.

And he was falling out of the sky.

CHAPTER 91

CYRUS

*E*hrgraz landed upon the scourge before Cyrus, claws down, tail lashing furiously, and black blood and gray limbs flew everywhere. Great gashes of scale were gouged from the dragon's back and sides, and his pointed, spiked face was unmistakably twisted in pain. He lashed his head around on his long neck, using his teeth to gnash and chew; his wings, bat-like and covered in scaly flesh, had holes in them wide enough to drive a wagon through.

"Nice to see you land on your feet, Ehrgraz," Cyrus said, advancing the line a touch while avoiding the dragon's tail. The dragon lifted it as Cyrus approached, keeping it from smashing Cyrus across the plains. "Rather cat-like, I must say."

"Your wit has not been missed, Lord Davidon," Ehrgraz said, rearing back on his hind legs and slashing madly through the scourge trying to swarm over him. Vara and Terian had advanced as well, taking up flanking positions with Ehrgraz in the middle of their line on this facing of the combined army.

"Not by you, perhaps," Cyrus swung and cut a scourge in half at the ribs, "but there are those who did miss it. What about my leadership, though?" He struck again, cleaving a scourge's shoulder, then stomping its spine when it crashed down before him. "Did you miss that?" The crack was pronounced.

Ehrgraz breathed fire in a wide swath, the heat forcing Cyrus to avert his face lest his skin blister and burn. The flame was so intense that when it stopped, there was nothing left of the scourge that had been coming toward him in a wide arc for a hundred yards. They were just gone; only ash and limbs that hadn't been caught in the sweep of fire remained. "No."

"What has brought you to us this day, then, Dragonlord?" Terian asked from Ehrgraz's other side; Cyrus could barely see him between the tree-trunk legs and the lashing claws. "Surely it's not the company, or the mere desire to do harm to Malpravus for the sake of a good time?"

"Your friend Alaric has served you well," Ehrgraz said, voice straining as he breathed another gout of fire, though this one much less impressive than the last. It licked over the blackened, glassy grounds he'd just scourged of scourge, removing again the flood tide of gray that had surged into the empty space. "My people have been hounded and near-destroyed. He offered us a fine bargain in exchange for our help...which I might have given in any case, for Malpravus is wretched, and his plans affect us all." He turned his face to Terian, and his voice became pure malice. "And if you call me Dragonlord again, Sovereign, I shall turn you into a char that shall not be distinguishable from the pan drippings of one of your spiders."

"Heard," Terian said. "Noted."

"Malpravus is not going to be easily stopped, Davidon," Ehrgraz said, turning his long neck and head skyward. The glow had begun again. "He has crippled my wings; I cannot delay him any longer."

"That's not the best news I've heard today." Vara buried her blade in a scourge's back, chopping it in two as it tried to strike past her at the row of mages behind them. She stopped it, though, kicking the front half, with snapping jaws, back into the onrush of scourge.

"What is your plan to stop him, General?" Ehrgraz looked to Cyrus.

Cyrus could feel the cool sweat on his palm as he swung his sword. "Let me get back to you on that." He struck, another fine shot that killed a scourge but did little else. Another drop mopped up from an endless ocean.

"Do you not have a plan to defeat him?" Ehrgraz asked. "To carve his bony heart from his chest with your blades?"

"I am the general," Cyrus said. "I don't really do that myself anymore."

"Then who is going to kill him?" Ehrgraz roared, turning loose his claws upon the scourge. The zone he had cleared with his fire breath was now alive again, entirely filled in with the scourge and their writhing, stinking bodies.

Cyrus's eyes alighted upon the shadow of an airship coming from the north. "I don't know yet. But I do know who's about to kick him right in the bony arse."

CHAPTER 92

VASTE

"Well, we're a little late," Vaste said, hanging onto the rail of quarterdeck of the...the troll blinked. "What's the name of this ship?"

Aisling was at the helm and cast him a wondering look. "We're about to ride into battle against Malpravus and an army of infinite scourge, and you want to know the ship's name?"

"Yes," Vaste said. Aemma and Merrish flanked him on either side, and both were looking at him strangely as well. Niamh, in her ghostly shade, was just to the other side of Aemma, though he could see her clutching the deck with her claws in her shadowy, scourge form. "It's not as though we're right there, about to jump into it. Humor me."

Aisling sighed, shaking her head. "It's *Nemh'ash Khalour gev'Amanraniy.*"

Vaste thought about that for a moment, running through his – admittedly limited – understanding of dark elven. "'*The Anger of Old*'?"

Aisling grunted. "That's not quite what it means, you ignoramus."

"Look at that," Aemma breathed, raising her hand to point. A dragon was raging in the front line, surrounded on one side by Cyrus and Vara, on the other by Terian, that old dog. The army's hexagonal formation surrounded the pit in the earth where old Sanctuary had stood, and now–

–now Sanctuary stood again, albeit a shimmering, faded ghost of its old self.

"Never thought I would lay eyes on that again," Merrish said under his breath.

"There's another fleet coming in," Aisling said, pointing over the wheel. "Looks like Amatgarosa is arriving."

"The more, the merrier," Vaste said, spying Qualleron churning through the scourge at the back of the army, his form still visible through the shimmer of Sanctuary.

"Then Malpravus must be pretty damned merry," Aisling said. "Look at all those scourge. They go for a hundred miles, easy."

Vaste nodded, clutching the side of the ship. "I think it's about a thousand years past time to do something about that – and him. Aisling – I need you to take us down low, and slow enough I can jump off."

Aemma caught his arm, her eyes flashing. "You're not leaving without me." She had a sword, dark elven in its provenance.

"Nor I," Merrish said haughtily.

"Do I even have to chime in?" Niamh asked.

"Fine," Vaste said as the ship slowed, coming low over the formation of the allied armies. "You, try not to get mistaken for the enemy and killed." He gave Niamh a look.

"Like anyone could mistake me for one of those brainless, mindless things," she said, though the reply was surely lost on the others.

"We'll try and lay down cannonades to protect you," Aisling said, handing off the wheel to one of her crewmates. There were so many. "Don't see how an old rogue could do much good on the ground down there, though."

"I don't see how nearly anyone's going to do any good down there," Merrish said with a slight shudder. But then he leapt overboard anyway, pistol blazing as he descended into the fray.

"The elf's not wrong, you know," Aisling called as Vaste leapt the rail. "This is madness."

"Then it's just where I belong," Vaste said, and down he went, rolling as he landed in the space the dark elves made for him.

"You suck at dark elven," Niamh said, her spectral form descending a little more gracefully than he had. Perks of being a ghost, Vaste supposed. "The ship name, I mean. It's not *'The Anger of the Old.'* It actually means *'Rage of the Ancients.'*"

"How poetic," Vaste said, his boots kicking up dust as he came back to his feet. The smell of scourge was strong, making him nauseous, the stench like rot, triggering instant nausea.

"It's a reference to when Sanctuary and her allies took on the might of the gods," Niamh said. "Acknowledging the great fight, you know?"

"Then it's about the rage of the gods," Vaste said. "Odd choice for a dark elven ship name."

She shook her spectral head, trace of a smile. "It's a new ship, Vaste. The 'ancients' in it...they're you. Or us, if you prefer."

"Well," Vaste said, slightly annoyed and using it to add fuel to the speed of his run, "I object to being called 'ancient'...but I suppose I am feeling a bit angry." He clutched Letum and saw the scourge coming forth against the line of battle. "Let's go show Malpravus how much."

CHAPTER 93

ALARIC

"*T*his is doing nothing," Alaric said, watching the volleys from the newly-arrived Amatgarosan fleet land against the scourge. Dugras was on the quarterdeck of the lead ship, gesturing frantically as they fired, the thundering volleys landing among the seemingly infinite gray-skinned beasts to little effect. Hundreds would fall, hundreds more surged in.

"Aye," Calene said, hurriedly reloading another cannon, the Bow of Life clutched in her fingers to give her speed. "But what else can be done?"

Alaric stuck his head out the gunport; the glare of red looking down upon them was extreme, and growing brighter by the minute. "Something. Something should and must be done." And with that, he decided to do it.

Materializing on the quarterdeck a moment later, he appeared beside Mazirin, causing Edouard to jump. Though perhaps not nearly as much as he might have only a fortnight before. "We need to attack Malpravus," Alaric said grimly.

Mazirin looked up at him and gave him a tense nod. "Push the throttle forward," she said to Edouard, "and crank the wheel around to here." She gestured.

"Throttling up, changing course," Edouard said. His voice had only the slightest hint of quake to it. "Time to poke the bastard in the eye, huh?"

"Something like that," Alaric said, looking at the evil red clouds above. They'd be there shortly, but...what then?

CHAPTER 94

CYRUS

*H*is arms were growing tired, swinging Rodanthar as he stood in the shadow of Ehrgraz, Vara beside him huffing slightly with each blow thrown. "No end in sight," Cyrus muttered, and the words felt right. For there was no end in sight, only endless gray scourge as far as his eye could see. Well, that and red, glowing increasingly bright above them.

"His spell will soon be cast," Ehrgraz wheezed, laying down tongues of fire only a fraction of the size of what he'd breathed at the beginning of the fight. "If you have any ideas, Davidon...now would be the time."

"You can't fly up there and piss him off further?" Cyrus asked, eyeing the cloud as he attempted a fire spell; Shirri's cessation held, though she was somewhere behind him, where he could no longer see her. Perhaps it was futile; they were so busy killing the coming scourge that there was no one capable of dealing with Malpravus above. Or maybe just no one willing.

"My days of flying are at an end until I receive a healing spell," Ehrgraz said. Boiling blood was seeping from his wounds, sizzling as it touched the plain's dirt where it fell. "At least for now, I am ground-bound, like you fools."

The trees of the Waking Woods were pressing hard against the scourge, but somehow Ryin's army was making only the slightest dent in this unstoppable force of the dead. Cyrus watched a battered scourge go flipping through the air and land about thirty feet from him, crushing another scourge, rolling another. It had little effect; the ones that died were but a drop in this ocean, and more came with every minute.

Cyrus turned to find snapping teeth descending upon him and brought his blade around. Too slow; they caught him upon the vambrace, the scourge wrapping itself upon the metal protecting his forearm. "Ungh!" Cyrus grunted, shoving against the mouth that clenched him. He felt teeth break, but only when he brought his sword over and smashed the beast with his hilt did it let loose.

But it gave time for three more to jump him, and one of them slammed into him with the force of a hundred pounds, driving Cyrus to his knees. Another hit him crosswise in the back, slamming him to the ground.

The drip of warm, wet, stinking saliva through the armor on his neck felt like a horrifying rain. As Cyrus tried to move, the scourge struck, sinking teeth in where the armor didn't quite reach, giving him a stabbing pain in the base of his spine.

CHAPTER 95

SHIRRI

*S*he'd begun to feel the strain, and also to question the order. The cessation spell held, but the front line was buckling, and the red glow above was casting deep worry in Shirri's heart.

The snarling of the scourge was loud, and Shirri stood with Philos planted, eyes squinted as she chanted in her head a particularly tense passage – the spell endured another round, and she kept the chanting going in her mind.

When she opened her eyes, she saw that the front was collapsing on her left. Longwell and Guy had fallen back, leaving them with a margin of only ten or so feet from her. A hand on her shoulders guided her back, gently, small steps at a time, her mother's voice in her ear. "This way...like that, daughter...careful."

"We're not going to make it, are we?" Shirri asked softly, looking up. The glow was angry, angrier than Malpravus had any reason to be. However could he hate them so much?

"You think your spell can stop me?" Malpravus's voice seemed to ascend from below her, like mist wafting out of the ground. "You, the little mouse of Sanctuary?"

Shirri did not reply.

"You are no one," Malpravus said. "You were not of notice before you were rescued by these better people. How do you not realize that they pay you little mind because they know...you are nothing but a small thing, a failure in search of notice."

"I'm not a failure," Shirri whispered.

Her mother was beside her in an instant. "Who are you talking to? I know you're not a failure."

Shirri felt the sweat beads come up on her forehead, and when she opened her eyes from a squint, she found Longwell looking back at her – just a glance, before he returned to fighting off the scourge. "No one," she murmured. But it was not no one, and she felt bad for saying it.

CHAPTER 96

ALARIC

The *Raifa* burst out into the interior of the glowing red cloud covering Malpravus to find an orb like a living sun in the center of it, shedding a crimson glow across the wide, empty space within. The *Raifa* shook slightly under the pressure of whatever energy the orb threw off, and the brightness was terrible, forcing Alaric to squint against its intensity.

"Something is buffeting the ship," Mazirin said as they broke from the cloud.

"That would be the spell of death he's about to cast," Alaric said.

"Spell of what?" Edouard asked.

"Calene – fire!" Alaric shouted, and was rewarded with a cannonade from belowdecks. It struck the red orb in the distance, sending ripples through some shield or spell, Alaric could not tell which it was. The black cannonball fell, halted in midair by the screen, then the next, then another–

"This is doing nothing, Alaric," Mazirin said. "Take us–" She had turned to Edouard, started to point to him.

"How kind of you," Malpravus's voice lashed over them, "to bring yourself so conveniently to me, Alaric. Your soul is a bit old, your power diminished, but that you are willing to sacrifice yourself to my hunger...well, it means something."

"Brace yourselves," Alaric said, hurrying to the side of the ship nearest the red orb. That an attack was imminent seemed obvious. Whether they would survive said attack...well, that was considerably more in question...

CHAPTER 97

SHIRRI

"You will always be nothing," Malpravus's voice pervaded Shirri's ears. "How do you suppose you came to this company, but for as a thing for them to protect, to save?"

"What's happening?" Longwell was looking at her again. Three scourge were impaled on his spear, but his head was turned to her.

"He's in my head," she said, resisting the temptation to lie. "Talking to me, directly in my ear."

"Who?" Guy asked, the man sweating profusely, his sword moving as though it had a mind of its own, barely giving her a look as he struck blow after blow. He was doing his best, credit to him, but none of their best was enough. Not today. Not for this.

"Malpravus," Longwell said solemnly, striking once more as he shed the dead scourge from his spear.

"Oh," Guy said. "Well that's probably not good."

Shirri hit a knee, couldn't hold herself up anymore. The pain in her mind was intense. The doubt seemed to weigh her down like a motorcoach upon her chest.

"Shirri," Longwell's voice crashed through her weary facade, and she felt the haft of his spear bump her. She looked up, and he was there, fending off scourge with one hand and offering the other to her. "Get up."

"Can't," she said, not even bothering to strain against it. She was keeping up the spell, but only barely, by rote memory.

"You know you are doomed and certain to fail," Malpravus said. "He knows it, too. That's why he tried to escape before. He knows you, knows what you're capable of, what I'm capable of." He was practically crowing. "He knows what's coming."

"Shirri," Longwell said. "He's just trying to get you to drop the spell because he knows he can't win unless you do."

"I can't keep it up," she said, and her voice sounded so small to her. Like it truly was coming out of a mouse, a mere squeak.

"You can," Longwell said, and how did he sound so sure when she was so certain she couldn't?

"I can't," she said, "and you know I can't." She opened her eyes, the words still drifting through her mind in a sublingual cast. "It's why you left." She looked up to find him staring at her, Guy absorbing the trouble at his back while he spoke to her. "You knew. You knew we were doomed. That I couldn't—"

"I chose to come back," Longwell said, and he thrust his arm down at her, pausing to spear a scourge leaping at him. He flung it back and knocked three more over, then turned to her. "I chose to follow you to the top of the Citadel."

"No," she said, shaking her head. "You only did it because you couldn't get into the Realm of Life – or couldn't seal it, and you realized it—"

"I didn't even try," he said, and he sounded so strong she opened her eyes. He stood above her, his beard stirring in the light plains wind. "I came back to you before I even made it down the stairs, no thought of sealing the realm, or accessing the realm. Maybe I could have, maybe I couldn't – I didn't give it a go." His hand was there, offered, strong. "I came back because you were *right*. I don't want to live another two minutes in fear for my life while thinking about all those who are dying. Including my friend." He turned, and with both hands, whipped one scourge and brought the blade tip around to send another flying. "I am through running from Malpravus, one way or the other. Now – let's finish this...together."

She took his hand, and never let up the cessation spell.

Because she couldn't fail them now.

CHAPTER 98

VASTE

"I used to tell you these trees would speak to me," Niamh said, "but did anyone listen? No, the druid was stupid, you all thought. Well, ha!"

"I don't see any speaking," Vaste said, watching the trees club and crush their way through the scourge army. Impressive, but not nearly enough. "I do see a lot of thwacking. Did they ever thwack you?"

"I'd thwack you now if I could," Niamh grumbled.

Vaste took in the scope of the scene before him. The trees of the Waking Woods did go all the way to the horizon in the northwest, but...the scourge went to the horizon on a wider distance. "This is going to take forever."

"And take our focus off of Malpravus," Niamh said. "Uh, you might want to help Cyrus."

Vaste turned, already on it. The warrior was down, a scourge upon his back, just twenty feet away, his place in the line between Vara and Ehrgraz the dragon already being overrun. They were making a dogpile – or a scourge pile, rather – of him, and Vaste didn't need to think very hard to guess what was happening down there.

The rest of the formation was flagging, too. There was no holding back this floodtide of scourge, perhaps not even with the trees. And

Sanctuary just sat there, half in the ether, helpless against what was coming.

Though, truthfully, they were all helpless against what was about to come. The red sky glared down, the brightness growing by the minute. That spell was going to come, though Vaste didn't know quite when.

He slammed Letum down on the scourge atop Cyrus, crushing its neck instantly. Swinging his staff in a broad arc, he cleared a space around him with one hand and picked up the dead scourge and threw it off Cyrus with the other. "Your savior is here, Lord Davidon. Chop chop."

Cyrus lifted his head, pulling to his knees. "Vaste?" Beneath his helm, his eyes were tight and squinted.

"Is it truly so surprising I would be the one to save you?" He kept swinging Letum, sending the scourge scrambling back from the whistle of the staff's tip. "I've saved you before, obviously."

"I'm not Malpravus," Cyrus said, and it was obvious his ears and head were ringing. Not a great sign. "I'm never surprised when you do something amazing and save us. Any of us." He was blinking, bleary-eyed, looking around. "Wish you'd do something along those lines right now, in fact."

Vaste sighed. "Of course you do. Because why be satisfied with me saving your life?"

"I think it has something to do with the fact we're being overrun, you grotesque," Vara said, sweat pouring down her face. She was fighting with all she had, and there was a mound of scourge bodies before her, ever-growing, and forcing her to retreat bit by bit.

"Vaste..." Niamh's quiet voice reached her from just ahead; she was standing there, over the first rank of the battle.

"You brought Niamh into this?" Cyrus had taken up his place once more and was swinging wildly, destroying three scourge with Rodanthar as he slipped back into line beyond Vaste. "Are you mad? What's to keep her from being killed by a well-meaning soldier with one of those autorifles?"

"Vaste," Niamh said again, gently. He did not dare look at her. Instead he swung Letum down on an approaching scourge and cratered its head, sending a spray of black blood in all directions.

A second later, another scourge darted in beneath the first as it started to fall. It came for Vaste's leg and almost got it; he managed to use his Letum-enhanced reflexes to slam the end of his stave down and crush its skull, too, but it was a very near thing. Black blood drenched his robes, making him feel even more sticky than the swamp had.

"I wanted to believe," Cyrus said, straining as he swung for all he was worth. "That without a plan, without a strategy in hand, that just bringing everything we had to this battle...that it'd be enough." He looked to the sky, just for a moment, and the red death that waited there glared down upon them all. "That as general, maybe I was enough to beat this bastard, though I seem to have exhausted all my tricks." He swung wildly again, clipping a scourge at the shoulder as it descended in a clawing attack and sending it under Ehrgraz's foot. The scourge's blood squirted out from all sides. "I was wrong. We'll fight this battle for days, and still lose."

"Vaste," Niamh said, still hovering above the battle, her red hair gleaming in the crimson light, "it's time, my darling."

There was a crackle in the air, a hum of anticipation that made Vaste shiver. "I wish you hadn't called me that," he said.

And he took a step forward.

CHAPTER 99

ALARIC

"You always were a fool, Alaric," Malpravus's voice reached him over the crackling of the energy about to be unleashed. "But a useful one. You helped me form the alliance that did so much to advance Goliath's cause, my cause, gave me a well of souls to tap into once I began my true ascent. And now..." There was no face to smile on that glowing red orb, but Alaric could hear it nonetheless. "...you bring me an entire fleet of Amatgarosan airships, and all their occupants to feed upon."

"No," Mazirin said numbly, for out of the cloud in the distance the first of the Amatgarosan airships burst forth. Though it was hard to be certain, Alaric could have sworn he saw Dugras upon the quarter-deck, gesticulating furiously, a half dozen ships following hard behind his. Mazirin turned, and there was a hint of tears in her eyes. "I've led them into destruction."

Alaric said nothing, for there was nothing to say; the glow increased, the spell coming imminently.

CHAPTER 100

CYRUS

"What the hell is he doing?" Vara asked as Vaste stepped forward. He did not swing Letum, but rather kicked a scourge out of the way, taking a place before the line, the scourge a second from streaming around him, flanking him, devouring him.

All Cyrus could do was swing, trying to keep clear the troll's back. "Vaste!" he shouted, "get back here before you die!"

But the troll did not heed him.

CHAPTER 101

VASTE

"Death," Vaste whispered, barely hearing Cyrus's invocation. He was walking into the streaming scourge, the grayscale figures with elephantine skin and terrible, sharp claws and teeth. They slashed and gnashed, bottomless fonts of rage, separated from life, harbingers of death seeking to devour life wherever they went.

And now...he could see them plain. Just like he could Niamh.

"I see you, Verner Braundeis," Vaste said, pointing at the scourge nearest him. Its spectral form was a small man with twitching eyes and a small face, and it started at his calling its name. "Why are you here?"

"Huh?" Braundeis's specter asked, looking around, as if Vaste could possibly be talking to someone else.

"You died a thousand years ago," Vaste said, cocking his head at the man. "In your bed, in the village of Hamwerne, your children in the next room and your wife beside you. Why are you still here?" He raised a hand. "Why are you trying to kill the last of this land?"

"I...I..." Braundeis said.

"You!" Vaste pointed his stave at the spectral form of another scourge, this one a squat dwarven woman with her hair bound.

"Delorous!" She looked up at him, seemingly poleaxed at being called out. "You left behind fifteen children when you died, forty-two grand-children. They were your legacy, the life you left behind – why do you try and destroy life now?"

She shifted away from him, as if assailed by his words.

"I see you all!" Vaste shouted, quelling the noise of war around him, looking over the endless army of squirming souls that stood, in his vision, before those shaded forms. "You dead, you miserable! I know who you were – and I see what you have become! You were men once, men and women of Arkaria! And now, what are you? Blood-ravening hordes! The end of life and this land! You have destroyed your own lands and kin, your own progeny in your mad quest for death! Have you no shame?" He looked out upon them, and every scourge – every damned soul – had stopped upon the field. "You may have lost your lives, but have you no decency left? Look at what you've become!"

He waited a moment, and then he cast a spell – a strange one, admittedly, and not one he'd known before, but something that tugged at his heart as a shaman. Not words, for words were no longer necessary. A thought – a concept – magic as it was originally meant to be, whispered right into his heart...

...by the voice of Huaviri.

CHAPTER 102

CYRUS

"What in the seventeen hells is going on here?" Ehrgraz rumbled. The battle had stopped, the scourge had stopped coming, and now every black eye was fixated upon Vaste for miles around.

"At least sixteen of those hells appears to be freezing over as we stand here," Vara said, holding tight to her blade. The scourge-tide had ebbed, and the nearest of them was ten feet away, with no eyes nor appetite for anyone in their line. They stood, gray-skinned, black-eyed, and seemingly cowed by the green figure in black robes that spoke to them now, some mad piper catching the attention of the rats like the tales of old. No one seemed eager to wade into the mass of scourge; they leaned on their weapons, breathed hard, and watched the scene unfold.

Cyrus waited, too, for this was the sort of madness he had come to expect...perhaps not from Vaste, but from Sanctuary in general. Both the people and the entity, really. He turned and cast an eye upon the faded, spectral form of Sanctuary, and it was still there, shimmering in the midday, clouded, red-tinged light. Though how long it might stand if the assault of the scourge resumed...

He turned back to watch Vaste as the troll cast some sort of spell, and a wave of white washed over the assemblage. Cyrus blinked; he felt nothing, but then, he looked to Shirri–

She stood behind him a few ranks, eyes closed, mouth moving in the slightest motion. Pamyra caught his eye, shook her head – it shouldn't be possible to cast a spell here, now. Cyrus raised his hand, tried to cast Nessalima's light–

Nothing happened.

"What in the eighteen hells?" Cyrus muttered, turning his attention back to the army of the dead, and his friend, who stood before them, almost ministering to them. For something seemed about to happen.

CHAPTER 103

ALARIC

"...**W**hat idiocy is this?" Malpravus's voice crackled in fury. He'd been all set to unleash his spell upon Dugras's unsuspecting fleet, and then...

...he'd stopped. His attention seemed elsewhere; not on Alaric, not on the *Raifa*, not on the Amatgarosan fleet. The red light waned in intensity, the impending spell dying down as his focus shifted–

The red light surged, moving out of the clouds, plummeting down, down to the earth, disappearing but to leave behind a glow of red penetrating through where it had been but a moment before.

"Follow him!" Alaric shouted, and Mazirin thumped Edouard on the back; he was already throwing back the throttle and tilting the wheel, and below the deck rattled as Baynvyn applied power to the engines as they dove to follow the sorcerer.

CHAPTER 104

VASTE

"*D*on't you see what you have become, my friends?" Vaste asked, wondering only for a moment why he was calling the scourge 'friends.' They were all listening to him, though, this once ravening, mad horde. He didn't see their physical forms anymore; instead of gray all the way to the horizon, he saw bright, glowing figures, some distorted by the ravages of time and being trapped in these awful shells. But men and women, humans, elves, dwarves, dark elves, gnomes – even a few dragons, titans, and goblins.

"Good," Niamh whispered to him soothingly. She was right there, beside him. The spell had awoken them, let them go beyond hearing him to feeling him reverberate through what remained of their souls. Cast from death magic, not his pool of magical energy, it had bypassed the cessation spell as though it were not there, because it did not bind shaman magic anymore than it did Sanctuary. "Keep going."

He glanced at her. "This affects you, too, you know."

Her green eyes glittered; they seemed to shine beneath the white glow. "Keep going."

"You are now the instrument of a man who wishes us all – your progeny, your successors, your legacy – all of us to die." He clutched

Letum, looking out over the sea of faintly glowing faces. "You were done wrong by Mortus. Monstrously so, I would say. But what you have done since...it is a thing of rage. A thing of regret. Look upon this land, what you have made it. Can you honestly say this is what you wanted for those you left behind when you died?"

"No," came a whisper from Braundeis, then Delorous. The ones behind him echoed his sentiment, and in them he could hear infinite regret stirring, along with something else.

"It's not too late," Vaste said, his voice echoing for miles and miles, all the way back to where the scourge ended, halfway to Reikonos. "This does not have to be your final mark upon this world, helping Malpravus to destroy it."

"I can feel him in my soul," Braundeis said, looking up, a wrenching look in his ghostly eyes. "He comes, even now!"

Vaste looked up and raised his staff. Taking aim at the red glow, its intensity growing inside the clouds; he was, indeed, on his way. "You want to stick it to him? I mean, really shove the dagger into his bony back?" He looked at Braundeis conspiratorially, but truly, he was looking at them all.

Braundeis nodded. "Yes." There were other nods; plenty of them, nearly all of them, Vaste thought, all the way back to the end of the scourge line.

"Help me destroy him," Vaste said.

"But...how?" Braundeis asked. It was, clearly, the sentiment of all.

"Let me show you," Vaste said.

385

CHAPTER 105

CYRUS

*T*he red glow of Malpravus burst out of the clouds like a meteor streaking to earth after Vaste's request to let them show him. Cyrus watched, clenching Rodanthar, not that it would do any good. With the glowing red orb that held Malpravus, that perhaps was Malpravus, so far up in the sky, and a Cessation spell over the entire area, there was little enough he could do...

But, as it turned out, that did not matter.

"I release you from this life," Vaste said, to the closest few scourge to him. "You have done all you can here; it is time to move on." Letum was still pointed at Malpravus's orb, as it shot from the sky, aimed very definitely at the troll, and mere seconds away from landing upon his robust green figure–

A white glow rose from the front rank of scourge; it was as water in the hot sun, a hint of steam coming off warm cobblestones after a drenching summer rain. It seemed to waft up, swiftly, into the troll–

And then a white glow burst from the tip of Letum while a second shot out of the bottom, over Cyrus's shoulder–

A primal, guttural, pained scream burst forth from Malpravus's orb that nearly brought Cyrus to a knee. The entire army staggered from the wail and Cyrus opened his eyes to find–

There was a beam of perfect white light that connected Malpravus's red orb to Vaste's staff, and then, from out of the back of Letum, another reaching back to–

Sanctuary.

For it was aglow now, shimmering brighter, and that connection of light between the three of them – Malpravus, Vaste, and Sanctuary – seemed to glow like a second sun.

"My friends!" Vaste shouted, voice bellowing out over the scourge with his magical aid. "If you mean to save that which you have laid asunder – it is not too late! Give your assistance now to your progeny, your legacy – to us! To me! And by your hand, by your act – you will see this renewed!"

There was a moment of silence...

...But only a moment.

And then, with a shuddering groan, unearthly, a million souls filled with anger and regret, reminding Cyrus of the time he entered the portal in Luukessia that had birthed the scourge...

...The scourge lurched forward toward Vaste, not in their usual slobbering, rage-filled, blood-seeking manner...

...but in a mass, almost eager...

...And the glow of magic was coming off them all.

CHAPTER 106

ALARIC

They dove out of the clouds at a steep angle, Alaric holding tight to the *Raifa*'s rail as the ship lurched in the atmospheric soup that Malpravus had left behind. The descent was like rolling down a mountain, and threatened to dislodge Alaric from his post should he but waver a little in his grip.

From the last vestiges of the clouds they burst into an extraordinary scene. There was Malpravus's red orb, hovering in midair, impaled by a white light coming from below, and all the ranks of the scourge nearest the front line aglow and seemingly...

...dissolving?

Alaric stared over the railing at the black-robed, green-skinned mammoth figure at the center of it all, a white chord of magic binding him to Malpravus and back to Sanctuary's shimmering, translucent form.

"Vaste," Alaric said, and he smiled. "At last."

CHAPTER 107

VASTE

*T*he scourge were hurling themselves at him in waves, and he was doing his part, sending them beyond this world into the next, in silence, crossing them over as their bodies dissolved into energy and magic and became...

...A weapon in his hands.

The tether to Sanctuary was strong, and he could feel the voice, the vibrato like a chord being struck in his very soul as the Ark strengthened. He was using the souls of the scourge as a spear, exorcising them from their cold and broken mortal forms and stabbing their remaining life energy into Malpravus, but also feeding as much or more back into Sanctuary.

"HOW?!" Malpravus's voice roared over what felt like the entire continent.

Vaste felt a trickle of sweat trace a path down his temple. "Remember when Quinneria warned you against underestimating me? She said I could be the one that brings you low."

"I – do – not waste time – with trifling things – such as YOU!" Malpravus roared, the red orb speared straight through. The scourge were pouring toward Vaste, and he was absorbing them and dispelling them from an army of death into magical light as quickly as they showed up.

"You think I am unworthy of your notice?" Vaste asked. He was but a conduit for this magical energy, but a worthy one, though it was taking its toll. "I think about that moment a lot. Usually when I wondered if I had any place in this world, the words of the Sorceress would come back to me and I would think...'She thought I could be the one to destroy Malpravus.'"

"YOU ARE A FOOL!" Malpravus raged, though there was pain in his voice now.

"Who's the greater fool?" Vaste asked, readying himself. Still the scourge raced to him, by his hand leaving this world of torment by the thousands, and he felt the power grow within. "The fool? Or the fool who is beaten by him without even seeing it coming?" And he readied his final blow–

CHAPTER 108

CYRUS

*V*aste was aglow, brighter than the light of all the scourge dissolving around him as they raced toward him in a mad effort to annihilate themselves. Malpravus's orb of crimson was straining, white cracks lacing their way through the outer surface like an egg breaking.

Then it shattered.

From within came a dark figure, cloak flapping unnaturally as it fell the last thirty yards toward the earth, something sharp clasped in its hand. It moved with unnatural swiftness, like a bullet in flight, directly toward the unprotected Vaste as the white beam speared its way through the red orb, dissolving it like parchment burning in fire, all the way to the edges. The figure came toward the troll, though, and too quickly as Cyrus and Vara both leapt forward–

There was a flash as the black figure struck home, eclipsed by the one all in white glow; Cyrus had to turn his face away from the pain of the brightness, but Vara's voice crackled pain and emotion over the army–

"VASTE!"

CHAPTER 109

VASTE

here was no stopping Malpravus as he burst from his crimson shell; he shot toward Vaste with a godly weapon in hand, misshapen by the forces of magic that he had been liberally applying to himself. The flash of a blade pointed at Vaste's heart was clear, but there was little he could do. The sorcerer was entirely too fast, and the white light pouring out of his tip moved too slow, and so the blade came, unerringly, at him—

And stopped as the light around him flashed, and something stopped it before it could strike home. The mighty clang of blade against blade was a shock to his ears, and he was forced to grimace away from the sound, from the power of the strike...

...But something had saved him.

Something...large.

Something...green.

Someone...who looked back at him with dark eyes and a lovely face, and armor that he had not seen since it dissolved during the fall of Reikonos.

"Birissa," he whispered.

"My name," she said, and there was more to her voice now than there had ever been before, something deeper and stronger, something more forceful as she pushed her blade against Malpravus's, where the two met in the air before her, "...is Sanctuary."

CHAPTER 110

ALARIC

"*I* can't fire," Calene shouted from belowdecks as Edouard racked the wheel to the side when the orb of red broke and Malpravus's shadowy figure leapt out. "He's moving too fast! We'll hit the others!"

"Do not fire," Alaric said, clinging to the rail. He watched the flash, saw Birissa appear, blocking Malpravus from striking down Vaste. He could not hear what was said, though he suspected he knew the gist. The scourge still surged in, and Malpravus strained against Birissa. The *Raifa* entered a slow circle as Alaric watched, trying to decide what he should do.

But with a glance at Sanctuary – wavering, almost solid now, growing in strength by the moment – it felt to him as though the tide seemed to be turning.

"Bring us close to the keep," Alaric shouted over his shoulder to Mazirin. He felt a shudder through the ship, and it began to dip once more, circling around toward the almost opaque form of Sanctuary.

CHAPTER 111

VASTE

"Sanctuary," Vaste breathed, his mind still consumed with the task at hand, absorbing the scourge and sending their souls beyond the veil of this world while retaining that magical energy to pour into Sanctuary. The keep was taking shape, the Ark returning to solid form, and he half expected the sudden thunder to hail its full reappearance out of the ether, but it seemed to be infinitely sponging the power of the scourge as they waned.

"Keep going, Vaste," Birissa whispered, her blade blocking Malpravus, a battle of strength and wills. She shifted her balance, driving Malpravus's jagged blade away, but the sorcerer was straining in his amorphous, shadowy, malleable shape, trying to drive it back toward her and nearly succeeding.

"Vaste," Niamh's soft voice penetrated his consciousness. The sheer amount of energy passing through him was colossal, not anything he was trained for, meant for. He could feel the voices of the scourge fade away as their souls and essences parted from the magical energy imbued within them; the souls moved on, but the energy was channeled through him, his body, his mind, and his staff. "It's time."

He turned his head very slightly, beads of sweat dripping into his eyes. His arms shook under the burden of all the power surging through him. "Time...for what?"

She slipped into his view, and she was as ephemeral and bright as ever he'd seen her. "It's time for me to go."

"No," he whispered. His eyes burned, and not from the sweat, nor from the pain of all this power coursing through him. "You can stay. We can finish this, find a way for you to–"

"I'm dead, my dear troll." Her fiery hair dipped close to him, and for a moment he felt the brush of what felt like her lips, ghostly, upon his forehead. "There's only this way forward...and it's for me to depart this stage."

"But we just got you back," he said.

"This is what we're here for," she said. "What Sanctuary is here for, remember? To protect Arkaria, remember? To ready ourselves for the battles no one else sees. That's our purpose." She smiled at him through the veil of white light. "My days are finally at end, Vaste dear. My purpose fulfilled."

"I don't want you to go," Vaste said, the glow of white light expanding around him, devouring more willing scourge with every passing moment.

"I know you don't," she said. "But this is what we do. And now, you know what you have to do–"

CHAPTER 112

CYRUS

$\mathcal{H}$e struck while Malpravus's back was turned, because he was a warrior and damn the sorcerer, damn honor, and damn giving the bastard half a chance. Chunks of Malpravus's cloak came tearing off like flesh, thudding to the ground below in clods, like dirt.

"It's like fighting Mortus again!" Vara shouted, landing beside him, chunks of Malpravus landing at her own feet.

"Dishonor," Cyrus said, trading a look with her and feigning shock. "A paladin striking while her foe's back is turned?"

"Alaric can scold me later," she said, "but you struck first – and I have other concerns that invest me in the idea of not being hit myself." She leapt back as tendrils flew out from Malpravus's cloak, spearing Cyrus in the chestplate and bowling him over.

"I can sense the sweet taste of new life growing within you." Malpravus's voice echoed over the plains. "What a happy occasion this must be for you, Cyrus." His voice hardened. "And how I shall enjoy ripping that happiness from you."

Something slammed into Malpravus, dropping him down and peeling inches of black from him, from the cloak that seemed to have become part of him. Black ichor oozed out of the sorcerer, and his face was shrouded in the spasming madness of the cloak.

"I think not," Alaric said, landing on his feet. The *Raifa* buzzed overhead, turning in a slow arc. The old knight rose to his feet, Aterum clutched in his grip. "Necromancer."

"I am so much more than that now," Malpravus said, rising up like a flood of ebony. "I am the last voice of account. The ruler of all things. The inevitable end of this world—"

"A stale turd with a glowy hole in his center," Vaste said, voice straining.

Malpravus strained to look at the troll. "...What?"

A glowing spear of white shot out from the tip of Letum and pierced Malpravus squarely through, shining light into the darkness of his cloak. The sorcerer screamed, flailed, and began to shrink.

"Now," Vaste said, sweating and straining, "do you recall how you stole the life essence from the entire city of Reikonos, Pharesia, and that very dear elven friend of mine?" Cyrus stared in muted shock at the screaming, spasming mass of Malpravus. "Well...we would like it back." His jaw was set. "Every last bit of it."

CHAPTER 113

VASTE

*T*he scourge threw themselves upon his dispersal magic without hesitation, like moths into a bonfire. Which was fortunate.

Because in the face of the dark magic pouring off Malpravus, the resistance he was trying to mount using the channel of magic between them...

...it was the only thing keeping him from being utterly destroyed.

Traditional spellcraft may have been exhausted here, but Malpravus straddled the same two worlds that Vaste did. Admittedly not as well, admittedly he'd been sat on for a great deal of time by the Gatekeeper, who'd kept him from reaching his full potential, but there was nothing preventing him from using it all now.

Nothing except Vaste.

And in this task, appointed to him by life, the universe, and Sanctuary...

...he would not fail.

CHAPTER 114

CYRUS

*T*he strength of the white glow penetrating the depths of Malpravus grew and then seemed to explode, knocking Vaste back on his haunches as the spell rocketed outward in a ring of white, in all directions–

Cyrus staggered; it was an almost physical blow, the shockwave that raced out from it. He turned his face away as the glow went blinding, and as it faded...

...the scourge – every last single one of them – was gone.

Malpravus was reduced as well, a flapping, billowing cloak and a skeletal figure concealed within it. He was on a knee, upon the plain, head bowed. He looked different than Cyrus had seen him, different than he'd been even in their last encounter a thousand years before, when he'd annihilated his own army for no reason other than ambition.

"Ah," Alaric said, a few steps back and on a knee himself, "there you are, Malpravus."

The sorcerer lifted his head, and there was a hollow, sunken quality to his eyes. His cloak draped lifelessly over him, though he still had a small blade clutched in his bony hand. There was spite in his eyes, and he looked behind him, where nothing but dusty plains stretched for hundreds of miles, the scourge gone like they'd never even been there. "Here I am, Alaric," he said, looking up at the airships hovering overhead, the armies arrayed before him, and there–

Sanctuary, shining as it once had been, a keep with an immense stained glass window, tall, swaying trees covering the lawns, four great corner towers and one in the center that stood above all else, stretching up to the clouds that had begun to part, allowing the glowing sun to shine down upon the scene.

"I suppose I expected less of you, Alaric," Malpravus said, looking so very...small. "To simply fade away as you always have when the threat grew too mighty for your undertaking. And who was mightier than me?"

"I have had enough of being a ghost," Alaric said, raising Aterum to a high guard and setting his feet. "And I have had enough of you."

"You never were much of a fighter, though," Malpravus said.

"I didn't need to be," Alaric said. "I trusted my general to defeat you. But not alone." He raised his sword.

Malpravus chuckled. "And you, Cyrus," he said, turning to face the warrior. "The General who didn't have a plan."

Cyrus shrugged, keeping his own sword up, waiting for the last, inevitable surprise. Surely Malpravus was holding one in reserve – either that godly weapon in his hand, or something else. "As you said, I'm the General. And I didn't have to beat you alone. I have an army, after all."

"I had an army," the sorcerer said, almost wistful.

"But I had one that could think," Cyrus said, "one that was with me, heart and soul. You had one that you rode by rote force, with no desire that you didn't give it. My troops gave me a way to beat you; yours were ripe for turning on you at the last. In fact, it was inevitable – because you don't build armies or alliances. You take and take, and thus you never get the best of people. Indeed," and Cyrus raised his blade as well, "I doubt you've ever even seen the best of people, except when they're turning it against you."

The armies were edging closer, surrounding Malpravus now.

Alixa, with her lightning-flashed blades, had snuck around his flank, as had Qualleron with his mighty sword. Birstis and his catback troops were sauntering in to the right, Guy and Terian had snuck under Ehrgraz, who watched the proceedings with both pain and wariness across his immense, scaled face. The Amatgarosan fleet circled closer overhead, and Aemma and Merrish were at Vaste's side, helping the fallen troll back to his feet, one at each elbow.

"I see you all now," Malpravus said, voice dripping with loathing, "as I have always seen you. Chattering insects. Quibbling fools. Idiots bereft of the one thing that would serve you...power...and unity of purpose. I am unified, you see. Free of the squabbles that sunder you. Spared from the thousand small minds that drive you in all directions."

"We're all looking in one direction now," Cyrus said. "And it's yours."

"And I am looking in one direction as well," Malpravus said, malicious smile creasing his thin, pale lips, "and it is not *yours*."

With a flash he seemed to leap back to life, slamming into Ehrgraz at the ribs and sending the dragon toppling over. Bouncing off, he sailed past Birissa's waiting sword and over the heads of more than a dozen dark elven and human soldiers toward the back of the battle lines–

Toward Sanctuary.

And Shirri, who stood beside the monument of old.

CHAPTER 115

SHIRRI

*S*he sensed the trouble coming and her eyes snapped open; the stir of the armies, the conversations between Cyrus, Alaric, Vaste, and Malpravus like the buzz of insects in her ears. Sweat poured down her brow under the unveiled midday sun, beating upon her and combining with the strain of maintaining the Cessation spell to tax her entire world.

Now the sun seemed to fade as she opened her eyes, and the old sorcerer – looking very much like a cloak caught in a strong wind, was whipping toward her over the heads of stunned and slow-moving soldiers.

"Shirri," came the soft whisper of Curatio's voice in her ear, "it is time."

"Time?" she murmured, the black figure coming closer and closer. A blade glinted in his hand, and she knew it was meant for her. "Time for what?"

"You are the only hope, Shirri," Curatio's voice came to her, strong, though he was nowhere in sight. For a moment she felt as though there were fluttering white shears all about her, an easy breeze blowing through on a perfect day...

...And she knew in that moment what she had to do.

She dropped the Cessation spell.

And cast something entirely different.

Something that was breathed into her heart like the wind across those white curtains.

From her hands sprang a flame that burned nearly white, rippling across the surface of Philos and bursting from the tip like a tornado of fire. It crossed the distance between her and the black-souled lich, catching him in the blackest part of his soul, lighting him like the fires that had consumed Reikonos.

He screamed and halted in midair, fell back, and Shirri knew...

...She had just done something that she had never done before.

"The Heart Afire," Vara said, loud enough in the shocked silence that all heard it. "Look upon that holy warrior, armies – and take your cue."

"KILL HIM!" Cyrus shouted, and the world – and the army – around Shirri erupted in a fury of righteous vengeance.

CHAPTER 116

CYRUS

*T*he army spasmed, the idea that they were a disparate collection of individuals put to lie in the surge to action. Rage, rage boiled over in a thousand, ten thousand screaming voices. They came from all around, from the trees in the distance, the elves with their normally stead faces dissolved in anger, the new rage of men with swords of steel and tunics of Emerald green–

And from the old guard of Sanctuary who, with their godly weapons, moved faster than them all.

Cyrus leapt and felt Vara do the same beside him. They both landed at Malpravus's fallen form almost simultaneously, each spearing him at his bony arms, ramming through to the thirsty plains below. Malpravus took the blows with but a grunt, and Aterum landed a moment later in his right leg, followed by Praelior from the hand of Guy on the left, pinning him to the earth.

"Your swords are hardly enough to finish me," Malpravus said, and his cloak knocked them all back, the weapons pinning him in place but knocked from their masters' hands. Spell light glowed at his, red and terrible–

But a blast of purest green magic struck him, and Ryin Ayend was there, running on air toward him, hand extended, followed by another of blue, Isabelle coming from above the army, and then yellow, and Pamyra was there, too–

And finally, then, Shirri joined in, and hers was white, and pure, like Vaste's. Magic as it had been once, before the gods bent it to their cause, controlling it. Pure, and dangerous, nature's own righteous fury, and it speared into Malpravus, drawn by the blades piercing his flesh.

"I am not finished," Malpravus said, bones rattling against the weapons. Cyrus tried to get back to his feet, but the spell energy coursing around him knocked him back. Without Rodanthar in his hand, he seemed unable to resist the current of energies pulsating around the sorcerer–

Something flashed through just then, a blued streak of metal, and a spear struck Malpravus in his center, jutting from his belly with a dragoon ornamenting its end, Cyrus's eye registered Amnis–

And Longwell. His face suffused with rage, spear penetrating Malpravus, the flap of his cloak insufficient to the anger on the dragoon. "You did your evil blackening my name," Longwell said, "and destroyed my city, did ill to this whole land–" He turned his head. "Vaste! It's in his heart!"

"If such a thing still exists," Vaste said, and he was there, with Letum before him, standing against the current of energies coming off the sorcerer in sheer, powerful waves. He extended his staff, and the glow of white channeling in from Sanctuary behind him was matched by the glow at the tip, and it burst forth into the haft of Amnis–

It was like all Malpravus's defenses collapsed at once, like the red orb versus Vaste's magic once more. Amnis glowed, and Longwell held fast, keeping it in place against the rage that the sorcerer tried to turn back on him. Cyrus clawed against the ground, against the force, trying to get to Rodanthar–

But he was not the first to reach his weapon.

"I will see you destroyed, Malpravus," Alaric said, and he had Aterum now again in his grasp, "if I must see you taken piece by piece!"

And he struck the sorcerer's leg clean from his body.

The force pushing against Cyrus seemed to lessen and Malpravus howled; with his leg gone there seemed less magic in the sorcerer, less radiating off him, more spearing him in the heart. Friendly magic, too, and Cyrus pushed against the last of that which was hostile to him, taking up Rodanthar, lifting it–

And he cleaved Malpravus's arm off.

Thrown back, Cyrus rolled, coming up in time to see Guy reach Praelior. Magic was still striking Malpravus, dancing over him in all those colors – white, green, blue, and yellow. Guy raised his sword and struck; with a subtle quake at the ground the smaller man was thrown back.

And then Vara took up Ferocis.

"I have hated you for as long as I've known you," she said, "I know you've felt the same. Let's put an end to this, lich–" And with a swift rise and quick strike, she took his last remaining limb and was knocked back like the others.

"I am infinite," Malpravus shouted, screaming into the void around them as the magic tore at him, pieces of his cloak flaking off, like flecks of darkness in the heart of this storm of light. "I am to be *the* God, and none of you can stop–"

The subtle movement at the necromancer's head caught Cyrus's eye; it was an axe blade, barely visible behind the magics crawling over Malpravus's figure.

"Try being a god without a head," Terian said – and brought down Noctus with certainty–

Malpravus's head was sundered from his body, and his cloak burned up like kindling undone by fire, his body going along with it.

The head, though...that skittered along, coming to rest at the green and clawed feet of a certain troll.

"I was to be forever," Malpravus whispered, the spell-light dying all around them.

"Afraid not," Vaste said, staring down at him. "Because you see...you're not a legend. And according to a very great rock giant...it's only legends that never die." And he lifted Letum to point the haft at the severed head.

With a blast of white magic, pure, and channeled from the heart of Sanctuary itself, so bright it forced Cyrus to look away, he unleashed upon the severed head.

And when the glow faded...it was gone, nothing but ash and dust where it had rested a moment before.

Malpravus...supposedly infinite, timeless, and all-powerful...

...Was finally dead.

EPILOGUE

CYRUS

One Year Later

"We stood together at the end of the world...and together we were enough to stop it."

Alaric's words rang out over the circular table in the middle of Sanctuary's Council Chamber, the whole lot of them clustered around it with the sun shining over the Plains of Perdamun outside. It came in through the open doors along with a breath of spring out of the north...

...and it smelled of new life.

Cyrus leaned back in his chair at the left hand of Alaric. It was a far cry from being the guildmaster, as he'd been in days of old, but it was plenty enough for him. He smiled as he watched the old knight speak before an audience of...so many. The round table had swollen, so many around it as to nearly defy belief.

Once this room had ruled the whole of Sanctuary, an army of thousands.

Now this room helped rule all Arkaria, and a city of a hundred thousand just outside its walls.

"Hard to believe it's been a year already." Terian Lepos sat across the way, the Sovereign of Saekaj and Sovar still wearing the same exact armor as Alaric. There was a new sparkle in his eye that had not been present when Cyrus had first encountered him again that day upon the tower of Saekaj.

But then...there was a lot of that going around these days.

"A momentous year indeed," Isabelle said, the gray showing in her hair now. Still, she too was lively...and an officer of Sanctuary.

"But in spite of all this," said the droll voice of Merrish, eyes slightly less gleaming, "we have business today, do we not?" For he was the representative of the city-state of Termina to this august body. Cyrus's distaste for the man had mellowed in the intervening time, though, and when he looked across Alaric to where his wife sat at the knight's right, she seemed barely interested in what Merrish had to say.

"We do indeed," Alaric said. His eye scanned the room and came to rest on one lone figure, still in her brown coat that hung to her knees. Cyrus watched the smile creep onto the face of the Ghost, and knew what he was thinking before he spoke. "Admiral...would you be so kind as to report on the state of the Arkarian fleet, and the status of our patrols?"

Mazirin rose, that long, curved sword hanging at one hip, her pistol at the other. Her hair was neatly bound back in a carefully threaded queue, and when she acknowledged her husband – such an improbable match, the staid Ghost and the solemn yet fiery airship captain, yet Cyrus had been there at the exchange of their vows, and deemed it good – she also nodded to the shorter man next to her. "I am going to pass this off to the Commodore of the fleet, as he has just returned from an early morning sortie protecting our borders to the north. Dugras?"

The dwarven captain stood, his beard long but well-groomed. "Thank you, Admiral. I did just return from the northern reaches above old Fertiss, yes, and spoke with Ehrgraz yesterday. He wishes to convey his thanks for our continued efforts to slap back the Chaarlandian incursions into their territory, and to let you know that only two Chaarlandian ships have been sighted in that area this month, and both were destroyed. The number of his people felled in the last three months...is zero." That prompted an outbreak of applause around the table. "Those pirates are starting to get the message that if they come for our dragons, or to raid our new villages along the coast, they will find themselves facing the overwhelming response of all our forces."

"I think I speak for all when I say – excellent news," Alaric said. "And the Firobans?"

"Have not attempted to reach the dragon enclaves in eight months," Dugras said, and looked to his right. "Furthermore – Captain?"

Cyrus glanced at the man seated to Dugras's right. Once he'd been thin and pale, but now he was handsome, sinewy, and strong. The captain of the *Raifa* stood, ribbons on his shoulders gleaming in the light streaming in from the open door, his bearing straight and head held tall, Edouard Boswin looked like a man confidently in his element. "Since our last engagement with the Firoban dragoneers, they have respected our borders fully, and we have received multiple treaty offers for trade with the major powers. The only abstention has been from Binngart, in the south, and they were never a force in dragon-hunting in any case."

"I would like to say," Alaric spoke as Captain Edouard sat, "that the transformation of you, my friend, into one of our best and brightest has been a pleasure to watch."

Edouard met the Ghost's gaze steadily, and his thin lips curled into a smile. "Thank you...Guildmaster."

Alaric gave him a nod in return. "Other business?" A cleared throat drew every eye; a small man stood from his place before the hearth, a full beard and dress armor a strange combination on the formerly grubby specimen. "Castellan?" Alaric asked.

Guy cleared his throat again, and brushed his hand against the scabbard where Praelior still rested, a permanent fixture on the man's belt. "A little city business," he said, his lower class accent a bit faded. "We're still seeing obscene amounts of growth as humans leave the confines of the Northern Confederation to take advantage of our offerings of arable land here in the east. Housing is a bit behind, even with Sanctuary's full efforts at making temporary houses and tents." He looked around the table and settled on one face in particular. "We could use a bit more raw material when it comes to wood."

Ryin Ayend raised an eyebrow in amusement. "Are you asking me to sacrifice my friends?"

Guy's jaw dropped. "Errrr..."

Cyrus laughed; he couldn't help himself. "He's getting your goat, Guy."

"Never get a man's goat," Vaste said, shaking his head. "That's just bad form."

"I think we might be able to supply some lumber for you from the west, or south of Amti," Ryin said, still smirking. His was less insufferable, at least. "I'll see it done this day, start moving up a herd of trees."

Cyrus blinked. It was still strange to hear the Hierophant call trees a herd.

"We could also use a bit more stone," Guy said, and here he turned to...well, not quite Terian, but close.

"Boy," Aisling said dryly, "have you come to right place." And she turned to her left.

Where sat a spectacle-wearing dark elf with the pale blue complexion. He glanced up when his mother tapped him on the wrist, found everyone staring at him, pinpointed Guy and said. "Stone? Yes. Okay. We have plenty of that."

"You'll see to it, then?" Terian asked.

"I'll see to it personally," Baynvyn said, tapping the side of his spectacles. He looked 'round, and his gaze settled on Cyrus for a moment. With a short nod, Cyrus acknowledged him back. For there was peace between them. Peace...and more.

"Great," Guy said. "One other item of note...we've got almost a hundred thousand in our shadow here. Food...is still a bit of a challenge."

"That won't be a problem," Calene said airily, her burnt cloak still over her shoulders. And here she turned down the table to the representative from Amti. "Will it, Gareth?"

"No," said the ranger, his bowler hat gone, pinstriped suit replaced once more by a green cloak of the last of the Iliara'douran woodsmen, though now he carried a rifle rather than a bow. "If they're not particular, that is. We've plenty of meat coming from the last of the man-killing predators in the south. Putting them on an airship by the ton would not be difficult. Waste not and all that." He smiled.

"Thank you," Guy said, nodding at each of them in turn. "Both of you – and Amti."

"'Tis nothing," Gareth said, waving away the thanks with a grin. "After all...we are all in this together."

"Which begs another question," Alaric said, and now he turned to the pale-green soul sitting halfway down the table. "Birstis...what has the Brotherhood of the Savannah Cat seen in the way of the banditry at the east?"

"Hopefully its dying throes," Birstis said, "and largely confined to the basin of the old Riverlands and the new settlements springing up along those fertile banks. We are striking back, though, against the – well, the troubles coming from there. Perhaps Qualleron would like to speak to that." And he turned to the yellowish troll.

"My order has hunted the troublemakers," Qualleron said, rumbling from his place. "A motley mix. For some reason, they don't wish to stand and fight with us." He shrugged the broad shoulders, nearly overturning the chair as he did so. "But they will continue to regret their decision, for we are honor bound to chase them unto the ends of this, our adopted land." He thumped his chest and bowed his head.

"I love the loyalty of the Baftshan troll order," Terian said. "And I love the look on the faces of human bandits when they realize who they've crossed. It's magic. If you haven't ever ridden with them in a pursuit, I highly recommend doing it at least once."

"Noted," Alaric said, "though I must admit...I have become rather enamored of travel by airship."

"And here I thought it was just that you enjoyed traveling with an airship's captain," Ryin said.

"That too," Alaric said.

"Is that all the business for today?" Vaste asked, sliding his chair back. His frame looked slightly thinner, his eyes alive and eager, his face more alert, his jokes slightly less...jokey.

Cyrus felt a glimmer come to his eyes. "Why? Are you in a hurry to return to your pink-cheeked blushing bride?"

"You're just jealous of her," Vaste fired back.

"Why?" Cyrus asked. "Because she's almost as tall as me?"

"And she's with me, and I am a loyal husband," Vaste said matter-of-factly, "which means you are now permanently saddled with a perpetually exhausted elf and her squalling rugrat." Here he looked at Vara, who barely stirred.

"At least part of that might be true," Vara said at last, lacking her usual fire.

"Fine," Alaric said, chortling as a chuckle moved around the table. "One last thing, and then Vaste can get back to his tall drink of human–"

"She wanted to be here, really she did," Vaste said. "As the representative for the Northern Confederation and all that – she's just...more tired than Vara, almost. And perhaps slightly queasy."

"I would be queasy as well if I were carrying your child," Vara said, "she need not apologize to any of us for failing to attend." A spark of mischief flashed in her eyes. "Though perhaps she should apologize for having a child with you. That might be a sin worthy of condemnation."

"Says the woman who birthed a giant barbarian baby."

"The last order of business," Alaric said, cutting over them, "is that I would like to give special thanks to Sanctuary's in-house sorceress both for her continued efforts and her bravery of a year ago..." And he turned to the slip of a half-elf halfway around the table, "...thank you, Shirri."

"It seems unlikely any will forget you now, Shirri Gadden," Alixa said, and the Administrator of Emerald was suffused with great amusement. "They'll be speaking your name in tones of whispered awe a thousand years hence."

For her part the Sorceress simply blushed. "It's just nice to be counted among your number," Shirri said. "Really."

"Of course it is," Vaste said, beating out Terian's similar sentiment by only a second. "Naturally."

"I could have guessed it from her," Pamyra said, her own eyes glinting with pride. "After all...she does not come from cowardly stock. At least not on my father's side."

"And on that note," Alaric said, rising, "we are adjourned." He nodded to his wife, reached her, took her hand...and together they walked out of the Council Chambers.

"Give our best to Aemma," Cyrus called after Vaste. The troll waved, but he was already out the door. Cyrus could scarcely blame him; he had, after all, tended to a pregnant wife himself until just a couple months ago.

"She's not doing terribly," Merrish said, his face a bit pinched. "I stopped in to check in on her yesterday when I got back from Termina. A bit peaked – green, almost – but pregnancy seems to be suiting her."

"She's not actually green, then?" Cyrus asked.

"Hardly," Merrish said, and gave Cyrus a nod. "Though she did express her concern with what the baby would be called."

"Every mother struggles with that," Vara said, barely concealing a yawn.

"That's not what I meant," Merrish said, grinning. "I meant as a race. See, Vaste wishes to call such a human/troll hybrid 'Tromans,' but she favors, 'Trumans.'"

"I suppose 'holls' is right out," Vara quipped. "Though given it is Vaste's spawn, it would be entirely fitting."

Merrish flashed them a grin. "Indeed. I am on my way back to Termina. When will the Shelas'akur and the great General of Sanctuary be coming for a visit? Our people would adore seeing you and that little bundle of joy of yours. I can bring word to have your manors prepared any time..."

Cyrus exchanged a look with his weary wife. "Soon, I think," Cyrus said, and got a nod of acknowledgment from her. "Perhaps just a bit longer. The wee one is...taxing."

"They all are at that age," Merrish said with a chuckle. "Say the word. Termina would love to host you." And with that and a nod, he was gone.

"Termina's not the only one, you know." Terian sauntered over, smirking in a way that felt very much like the Terian of old. "Saekaj and Sovar wouldn't mind seeing the first couple of Arkaria – assuming you wouldn't mind deigning to come scrabble in the dirt with us."

"I thought you were slowly expanding back to the surface now?" Cyrus asked, suppressing a yawn of his own.

"We are," Aisling said, sliding in behind Terian. She looked good in her leather armor. Strong. "But still...a thousand years, more or less, in the dark...people are acclimating to the surface again. And it's not for everyone."

Cyrus glanced at the balcony. He felt a pull toward it, and answered it, stepping out into the light of day–

And there, sprawling before him, across the wide plains...

...Was the city of Sanctuary.

The buildings were not large thus far, but the hints of a permanent presence were there in the street grid that was starting to expand outward from the keep. Far beyond that, and the wall of trees that once more composed the idle, resting, Waking Woods, Cyrus could see the southernmost dark elven settlement. The tunnels extended all the way to the gates of Sanctuary, though when Terian and Aisling traveled here, they generally did so by portal.

"We'll find a time," Vara said. "Trust me."

"Oh, I do," Terian said, strolling away, "I'd just like to see you a little more often. Parade you to my people. Remind them I once strove with giants who saved us all – you know. Propaganda."

"I never deny that I know you, Terian," Cyrus said. "But I do wish you'd stop telling stories about me visiting whorehouses in northern Luukessia."

"Oh, I know you do," Terian said, almost laughing, "but if I'm going to tell those stories – and I do have to – I'll be damned if I'm going to own up to it being me that visited them. What would the people say?" And he laughed his way out the door.

"They all know it's him," Aisling said, following behind. "Don't worry about your reputation. It's safe."

"As is yours, Aisling," Vara said – and again, perhaps startling to Cyrus, if it were not so ordinary these days – there was no malice in it at all. It sounded like a compliment, in fact.

"Excuse me." Ryin popped out, stepping over the edge of the balcony, a spell already upon him. "I have to catch an airship; got some trees to round up." He disappeared over the side, but his head bobbed back into sight a moment later as he descended, running a spiral around the tower and reminding Cyrus of the first time he'd come up over the hill in the distance and seen this place standing here...

"And I need to start having some stone brought up from the tunnels," Baynvyn said, doing just the same as he started to pass between Cyrus and Vara. He paused at the edge. "Stepmother," he said, inclining his head respectfully to Vara.

"Son," Vara said, with a tired smile. "Do come visit your little brother soon, will you? We would all enjoy it."

Baynvyn paused, just for a beat. "Then it shall be done. This very day, if I can arrange it. Dinner?"

"We'll see you then," Cyrus said, feeling oddly choked up, though it passed in a moment, as Baynvyn swept over the balcony, disappearing into a run below. Cyrus leaned over and saw him spiraling down, following Ryin's path.

"It's quite the life you've carved out here." Isabelle spoke as they walked back inside, separate, yet together. She was lurking by the door, as if waiting for them in the empty Council Chamber as the wind whistled through.

"Are you talking about in Sanctuary?" Vara asked. "Or in Arkaria?"

"Both," Isabelle said, and hints of the impish smile she once had tugged at her aged cheeks. "And also, perhaps, simply between yourselves."

Cyrus exchanged a look with his wife. "Oh, yes...we are really living, aren't we, wife?"

"I feel as though I am dying, in fact," Vara announced. "But perhaps I'm just a bit tired from the middle of the night feedings and wakings and tendings."

"I believe that is how it is meant to be," Isabelle said, parting from them at the stairs; she moved to go down, the two of them started up. "At least at this phase of life." She was forced to move, however, when an armored figure nearly ran her over at the top of the stairs. "Longwell?" she asked, looking askance at the blued-armored figure with the spear.

"Sorry I'm late," Longwell said, fairly gasping for breath. He looked good; tanned, solid, straight of back and bright of eye. Cyrus might not have recognized him if he'd had naught to compare him to but the bearded skeleton that had stood next to Vara in the dark of the tent outside Pharesia a year earlier. "Did I miss it?"

"Sorry," Vara said, "but yes."

"Damn," Longwell said. "Transport's a bit unreliable from Reikonos, you know. Though we are working on it."

"How's it going up there, Samwen?" Cyrus asked.

The dragoon brightened. "Things are taking root, Cyrus, and life is returning to those old ruins. It is not near what it used to be, but the day will come, you mark my words, when it will be the foremost human city in Arkaria once more." He glanced through the open doors to the Council Chamber, and the balcony beyond. "No offense to your effort here. But we have a port."

"A sea port," Cyrus scoffed. "Who travels by sea anymore when the air is there for the taking?"

"A surprising number of merchant consortiums," Longwell said with a gleam in his eye. "In any case – since I appear to have missed the meeting, I will return next week. Perhaps stay over the night before, if room might be found for me."

"Room can always be found for you, Samwen," Vara said.

He clinked his spear and looked at Isabelle. "May I escort you down, my lady?"

She gazed at him cannily, wisdom beyond her years – but not her appearance – showing clear. "You want me to cast Falcon's Essence upon you so that we can take the shortcut down to the bottom, don't you?"

Longwell did not even blush. "Yes."

Cyrus turned away from that, perfectly content, to find Vara already walking up the stairs. They made it silently up to the officer's quarters – an expanded floor if ever there was one. Cyrus chortled. "Room enough indeed." The hall seemed to go on forever.

"Hm?" Vara turned to look at him; she seemed marginally more alive now, a little glimmer in her eyes.

"I thought you were going to nod off while Merrish was talking," Cyrus said.

"I nearly did," she said, yawning while covering her mouth with an exceptionally small hand. "That offspring of yours woke me what seemed like hourly last night, and drank me to exhaustion." The lids of her eyes fluttered.

"You want a nap?" Cyrus asked as they climbed the last set of stairs to the quarters atop the guildhall. Alaric had been generous and let them keep them even though he had resumed his post. "You have a bit more need for the space than I do," he'd said.

"Oddly...no," Vara said, pushing open the door, which now opened directly into the guildmaster's tower. Another clever rearrangement by Sanctuary now that there was danger of a certain someone falling down stairs. The balconies had tightly woven railings, too small for even a little head to fit between them, and high enough that they would keep any danger of fall at bay.

"We're back," Cyrus announced to the two figures upon the couch at the center of the room. One was but a child, small, and nestled in swaddling clothes. The other was quite the opposite...

"The little angel slept the entire time you were gone," Birissa said through those immense teeth. Her appearance had scarcely changed since the first time Cyrus had seen her, and yet there was a quality about her now that he knew he should have recognized even then. "I expect he's going to be sleeping for a while longer, too, if you're of a mind to take some time for yourselves."

"Thank you, Sanctuary," Vara said. She stared at the baby clutched in the troll woman's arms. "I think, perhaps..." And here she looked to Cyrus, "...yes. I would like to get away, just for a bit."

Cyrus nodded, sparing only a look for the softly snoozing child – his son – in the safest arms he could imagine. "Where would you like to go?"

They rode their horses out to the place that had once born gates and walls that girdled the place known as Sanctuary; Vara on a fine destrier, and Cyrus on a white horse that whinnied when he called its familiar name. He glanced at the memorial standing where it had stood all those years, taking particular note of that most recent addition to it, right at the top...

NIAMH

They rode through the streets with surprising energy to the hilltop where the old portal stood, still, now with houses and buildings all around....and then rode past it. Another hilltop, then another, they navigated out of the grid of streets and onto the green plains, reseeded by the efforts of Ryin and now coming into bloom with new life. A few trees were scattered here and there, and he wondered if they were watching. Almost certainly, he decided, though they reserved judgment on the activities of the blond paladin he chased over the hills until she finally pulled up the reins of her horse on a summit, and turned it so she could see the tower looming so far behind them.

He brought Windrider up short and received a whinny – a lovely sound, and one he'd missed. "What is it?" he asked, coming alongside his wife. Watching her golden hair dance in the wind, all trace of tiredness gone from her being, he felt a glowing admiration. Her breastplate gleamed silver in the sun, and her blue eyes were as lively as he'd seen them in some time. Certainly, at least, since the news of that second little bundle of joy on its way had come to them...

"I was just thinking how much things have changed," she said, holding tight to the reins as she admired the shining tower in the distance. "I never would have thought you'd make it a thousand years...let alone that we would, and that we'd be having, well..."

"Sex?"

She shook her head at his human immaturity, though he knew in his heart that it amused her. Else there wouldn't still be the sex. "You know what I mean. That life goes on here, on Arkaria, and life goes on for us, in spite of all we've lost."

"It goes on," Cyrus said, letting go of the reins and letting the mystic horse steadily bring him alongside, "because of all we've lost – and all we fought for."

"Of course you're right." She stared at the shining city on the horizon. "I just..." And she sighed, full and lustily. "...I don't want to leave again."

"We won't," he said, taking her hand in his, so warm, so small. "You heard Alaric. Ghosts fade. Heroes stay."

She nodded. "Very well. Are you ready to go home?"

He thought about those words, and the meaning they'd once held, a thousand years ago, when he thought he'd lost her. And then after, when he'd come back in her company, and thought he'd lost this land. "Yes...for now," he answered, and they set the horses to running back the way they'd come – to home, and to family. "After all...we have so much to do."

AFTERWORD

efender was the first book I ever wrote. It came out in June 2011. I knew I had an eight book storyline before me then, with a possible four more to follow it up, but I don't think I could have envisioned then where I'd be sitting now, almost twelve years later.

Twelve main-line books. Two half-series volumes (Thy Father's Shadow, Fated in Darkness). A short story collection (Sanctuary Tales). And a three book spinoff series (Ashes of Luukessia). Rage of the Ancients was the 98th book I've written.

Now...we've reached the end of this tale. Or at least the end for now.

I experimented with putting those two words at the conclusion of the epilogue: THE END. Simple. Definitive.

But they don't feel quite right. Because it's not really the end of Cyrus's story; whether I eventually write Volumes 13 through 16, or he shows up in some other epic fantasy tale that takes place in the same world, these characters are not gone. They're still doing their thing, living their lives, much as they did during the interregnum between the final chapter of this book and the epilogue one year later.

It's just...I don't really think I can write their stories any more *at present.*

I hope you liked this book, truly I do. I have done everything in my power to make it a worthy end for Cyrus and company, should I not return directly to these characters and their tales, their lives. But as I ask myself, with the cold eye of a disinterested party (tough to do with my own books, but still I try), "Was this ending a better, fuller, more fitting end than the one I managed at the finish of Volume 8?"

The answer comes back...maybe? In some ways, perhaps. In others perhaps not. And if I pushed things further, started writing books 13 through 16 TOMORROW...

...Would the finish of book 16 be better than this as an end? Or better than book 8?

At present, I conclude...no. I feel I've pushed these characters, in their own tale, as far as I can currently push them; a break is in order, in which I can explore new lands in the same world, write other things. It's been nearing a decade since I've started a new series, and with the conclusion of this as well as the forthcoming end of my Southern Watch series, I'll finally have time to dig into other story worlds I've been desiring to explore for years now. Perhaps you'll be interested in some of them. Perhaps you won't. Either is fine. I mean, I'd prefer if you were, but I understand if you aren't.

But none of this precludes the future return of Cyrus and company, either in other stories in the same world (likely) or volume 13-16, and maybe even 17-20, at some point in the future (we shall see).

I guess we'll just have to wait and see if I am drawn back this way again - to these people, to these lands, to their stories - as perhaps I could be...

...In the fullness of time.

Either way, thanks for reading.

Robert J. Crane
May 4, 2023

AUTHOR'S NOTE

*T*hanks for reading! If you want to know immediately when future books become available, take sixty seconds and sign up for my NEW RELEASE EMAIL ALERTS by CLICKING HERE. I don't sell your information and I only send out emails when I have a new book out. The reason you should sign up for this is because I don't always set release dates, and even if you're following me on Facebook (robertJcrane (Author)) or Twitter (@robertJcrane), or part of my Facebook fan page (Team RJC), it's easy to miss my book announcements because ... well, because social media is an imprecise thing.

Find listings for all my books plus some more behind-the-scenes info on my website: http://www.robertjcrane.com!

Cheers,
Robert J. Crane

Other Works by Robert J. Crane

The Girl in the Box
(and Out of the Box)
Contemporary Urban Fantasy

World of Sanctuary
Epic Fantasy
(in best reading order)
(Series Complete)

1. Defender (Volume 1)
2. Avenger (Volume 2)
3. Champion (Volume 3)
4. Crusader (Volume 4)
5. Sanctuary Tales (Volume 4.25)
6. Thy Father's Shadow (Volume 4.5)
7. Master (Volume 5)
8. Fated in Darkness (Volume 5.5)
9. Warlord (Volume 6)
10. Heretic (Volume 7)
11. Legend (Volume 8)
12. Ghosts of Sanctuary (Volume 9)
13. Call of the Hero (Volume 10)
14. The Scourge of Despair (Volume 11)
15. Rage of the Ancients (Volume 12)

Ashes of Luukessia
A Sanctuary Trilogy
(with Michael Winstone)
(Trilogy Complete)

1. A Haven in Ash (Ashes of Luukessia #1)
2. A Respite From Storms (Ashes of Luukessia #2)
3. A Home in the Hills (Ashes of Luukessia #3)

Liars and Vampires
YA Urban Fantasy

(with Lauren Harper)

1. No One Will Believe You
2. Someone Should Save Her
3. You Can't Go Home Again
4. Lies in the Dark
5. Her Lying Days Are Done
6. Heir of the Dog
7. Hit You Where You Live
8. Her Endless Night
9. Burned Me*
10. Something In That Vein*

Southern Watch
Dark Contemporary Fantasy/Horror

1. Called
2. Depths
3. Corrupted
4. Unearthed
5. Legion
6. Starling
7. Forsaken
8. Hallowed* (Coming in 2024!)

The Mira Brand Adventures
YA Modern Fantasy
(Series Complete)

1. The World Beneath
2. The Tide of Ages
3. The City of Lies
4. The King of the Skies

*Forthcoming, title subject to change

ACKNOWLEDGMENTS

Thanks to Lewis Moore for the edits, Jeff Bryan, for the proofing, and Lillie of https://lilliesls.wordpress.com for her work proofing and compiling my series bible.

Thanks as always to the great Karri Klawiter of artbykarri.com for the cover.

Thanks, too, to my family for making this all possible.

Also, to you fans who stuck with this series from beginning to (maybe) end. It wouldn't have been possible without you, either.